Sinclair

Tales of Tooley Street Vol. 1

Julia Herdman

The Fontaine Press

Published by The Fontaine Press, 2017

ISBN 978 0952 817819

Copyright © Julia Herdman, 2017
The moral right of the author has been asserted

A CIP catalogue record for this book is available from the British
Library

Typeset and designed by
Russell Wallis
RJW|Creative Design
www.rjwcreativedesign.co.uk

Table of Contents

Acknowledgements

I would like to say thank you to some of the people who have made this book possible. Firstly, my thanks go to my husband Martin for his patience, to Sue for her encouragement and endless positivity, and to Caroline Boucher and her book group friends for giving 'Sinclair' its first read through, and finally my thanks go to my editor.

The cover image is Portrait of '*Sir John Henderson of Fordell (1752–1817)*' by Gavin Hamilton, and is reproduced by kind permission of the Real Academia de Bellas Artes de San Fernado.

1
Lies and Ambition

'Gravesend, 1 January 1786'
It was dark when James Sinclair left the Anchor Inn and headed
for the docks. As he walked across the cobbles towards the
'Sherwell', the bitter easterly wind flecked his coat with icy
grains of snow. Moonlight broke intermittently through the
clouds, illuminating the mighty ship standing before him. He
paused at the foot of the gang plank and looked up. Yellow
lantern lights dotted through the rigging punctured the blackness
of the winter night, and the sails were reefed tight against the
restless blustery squalls. His stomach tightened. He was glad to be
on his way. He was sick of England; sick of money and
connections being the chief means of advancement, and sick of
never having enough of either.

He had spent his last day in England writing letters. One was to his sister Morag in Edinburgh, sending her a forwarding address in London; one was to his lawyer Henry Bowman in Cheapside, which he sent with a signed copy of his last will and testament; and one was to Iona McNeal, the woman he loved, telling her that he did not intend to return to Scotland, which was true, and indicating that she meant nothing to him, which was a lie. With these letters dispatched, and feeling confident that his affairs were in order, he pulled down his hat and boarded the 'Sherwell', a 758-ton East Indiaman bound for Madras.

Preparation for this journey had started earlier in the year when he attended a selection process at the London headquarters of the East India Company. It was a building he had passed many times: a neo-classical masterpiece, the mercantile heart of the City of London and the centre of the greatest enterprise on earth. Its wealth flowed through the banks and merchant houses of the City like the water of the Thames, washing them with silt of pure shining gold and, in the opinion of men of principle, corrupting everything it touched.

Although Sinclair was aware of the company's less than wholesome reputation, he knew that for men of ability like him it was still the goose that laid the plumpest and the most golden of eggs and he, despite his political misgivings and the pricks from his Presbyterian conscience, was very much hoping to find himself in possession of one soon.

With five other hopefuls, he underwent two examinations. The first tested his knowledge of anatomy, physic, surgery and midwifery, the second his knowledge of botany, chemistry, materia medica and the creation of healing medicines and remedies. Then he was interviewed in the Directors' Court, a room so vast in scale and decoration that if he had not been well prepared he might have been overwhelmed.

His interviewer, an elderly naval surgeon with a scrawny neck and trembling hands, fumbled through his papers looking for questions and then checking Sinclair's answers against his handwritten script. As far as Sinclair was concerned, the questions were mundane and easily answered. When the old man had asked him why he had applied for the position, he had replied that he wanted to seek out new treatments for tropical diseases using the flora of the sub-continent. He knew the answer he gave so precisely chimed with the political requirements of the company, it was no surprise to him when a few weeks later he heard that the post was his.

At the end of November, he was called to Leadenhall Street to complete the formalities and to be briefed on the company's new Indian Medical Service. There he was greeted by a keen, fresh-faced officer called Lovell, who looked no more than eighteen and was dressed in a uniform straight out of Hawkes. With a smile as bright as his brand new epaulettes, the young man said, "You will start your journey to India at the end of the year." Sinclair thought the boy's mother must be proud of her son's new position, and was sad that his father would not feel the same about his.

"That's the middle of winter," he replied, unsure about starting a journey when the sea was at its most treacherous.

"Yes, sir;" the young man beamed. "It's to catch the winds from the Cape in the spring. It's the quickest way to India."

"Aye, I see," Sinclair mused, trying to disguise his unease.

Sensing the doctor's reluctance, the young man set about reassuring him. "I can see you're not completely comfortable with the idea, sir. Your ship is the newly refitted 'Sherwell', one of the company's largest, under the captaincy of Mr Richards. Captain Richards is one of our most experienced men. He has already sailed the 'Sherwell' to Madras and China on several occasions, all without incident."

Sinclair nodded, accepting the young man's reassurance and allowing him to continue with the rest of his well-rehearsed lines.

"Your journey will start at Gravesend, and take you to Madeira, Gorée and the Cape of Good Hope. From there you'll sail across the Indian Ocean, landing in Madras at the end of March. Then a local ship will take you to Calcutta."

"Aye. That's more or less what I expected."

Lovell handed him a contract. Uninterested in the details, Sinclair scanned the contents, took a deep breath and wrote his name on the paper. He had learned his trade from the very best surgeons and anatomists in the world and now he was ready to take advantage of his investment.

Standing on the great ship, he felt his old and unhappy life was behind him, and the weight of years of disappointment and his father's disapproval seemed to lift from his shoulders.

"You'll find your accommodation on the lower deck, sir," said the boatswain. "You're with the ship's senior officers: Lieutenants Merrick and Allsop; the ship's surgeon, Mr Hodge; and a Captain Greenwood of the Bengal Army."

"Aye, thank you," Sinclair said, raising his hat to the short burly man and feeling the icy fingers of the wind running through his thick, sandy hair.

"Your accommodation is directly under that of the female passengers. The women are located on the first deck. There you'll also find the ship's saloon, the passengers' dining and recreation room. To find your cabin, all you have to do is look for the captain's quarters here," the boatswain pointed to the door directly under the poop, "and go down a couple of flights of steps."

Sinclair thanked the man again, and descended into the quiet golden belly of the ship.

When he had imagined himself on board, he had pictured himself in a cosy wooden cabin with a glass window and a comfortable cot. His cabin when he found it was a makeshift affair, constructed from canvas sheets stretched and nailed onto rough, wooden frames. His heart sank as he opened the door onto what was to be his world for the next three months. The cabin was dark and damp; there was a narrow wooden cot with a thin mean blanket. The belongings he had sent from London were there: a small writing desk, a basin and mirror for washing and shaving, a small armchair for reading, and his sea chest, containing everything he had accumulated in life so far including his medical books and equipment. Where the window should have been there was a leaky wooden hatch covering an unglazed porthole. It was battened shut, but the freezing wind was wheedling its way in with an icy chill.

He slumped into his armchair, feeling the fizz of his enthusiasm disappear. He had not expected to travel in luxury, but could not help registering the difference between his accommodation on the ship and the luxuries of the company offices in Leadenhall Street. Above, he could hear the giggles and shrieks of excited young girls, and he started to wonder if he had made a terrible mistake. Then his chair slipped backwards, and he realised the ship was being pulled away from the quay into the estuary. He was on his way, whether he liked it or not.

Knowing there was no going back, he made himself comfortable. He lit his lamp, took out a battered copy of 'Candide', his favourite book, and checked the hour with his treasured pocket watch. Like the book, it was French, and the most beautiful thing he had ever owned. He cradled it in his palm. The warmth of its golden body reminded him of the smoothness of a woman's skin; its pearly white face was elegantly marked with Roman numerals; and the back, the part that he loved most of all, was made of cobalt blue enamel and shimmered like the silk of Iona McNeal's ballgown the night they had danced at the Edinburgh Assembly Rooms. He turned it in his hand and kissed it then he put it back in his waistcoat pocket and started to read.

He chose the scene where Candide, the hero of the story, and his professor friend, Dr Pangloss, are nearly drowned in Lisbon harbour along with a sailor called Jacques. Candide and Pangloss survive, but Jacques dies attempting to save a fellow sailor. To explain how this is all part of God's harmonious plan, Pangloss says that Lisbon harbour was created specifically so that Jacques could drown there and fulfil God's divine plan for him. This was an idea so preposterous, like so many in the book, that it made Sinclair laugh out loud.

At eight, he joined the other passengers in the ship's saloon. It was a simple, lime-washed room with a low ceiling and skylights onto the quarterdeck. In the centre, there was a long refectory table with space for sixteen people to dine comfortably. Sinclair pushed his way into the throng milling around in the space between the table and the low wall-mounted lockers that doubled as seats when the room was used for recreation.

Captain Richards greeted him with a firm handshake. He was a man Scots would describe as 'braw', and was in his late forties by Sinclair's reckoning. "May I offer you a glass of Madeira, Dr Sinclair?"

"Aye, thank you," the doctor replied with a nod, acknowledging the equality of their ranks.

"Between you and our surgeon Mr Hodge we shall be in good hands on this voyage," Richards said.

"I pray my interventions will not be needed, Captain," Sinclair replied, making the older man smile.

"Experience tells me that on voyages like this anything can happen, Dr Sinclair."

"In which case, I am at your disposal."

The captain put his hand on Sinclair's shoulder. "I'm glad to hear it, sir." Then he pushed past him, to speak to the scarlet-coated army captain.

One of the ship's officers approached, introducing himself as Lieutenant Merrick. He explained that their purpose was to resupply Fort St George in Madras with fresh soldiers, their numbers having been much depleted during the last war. The lieutenant assured Sinclair that the men of the lower orders were to be confined to the ship's hold, but their captain, Mr Greenwood, would join the passengers and fellow officers for meals and recreation. Merrick rested his hand on his sword. "You won't be short of work in Madras, Dr Sinclair. It's a regular bloodbath. If it's not the natives, it's the bloody French! My cousin was with Colonel Kelly in '83; thousands dead or wounded, supplies of everything scarce, it's a miracle he survived. Who knows how long Prime Minister Pitt's peace with France will last, or what this new-fangled India Act will turn up."

"Indeed," replied Sinclair, "but I'm bound for Calcutta and the company's hospital there."

Merrick slapped him on the back by way of a farewell and whispered, "Much the same there, but very rich pickings. A man can make a mint of money with the right connections. Plenty of ladies too," he winked. "If you're interested, Mr Allsop and I have some private trade there, despite what Mr Pitt and the new governor say."

"Thank you. I'll bear it in mind if I may; but in the meantime I'm not interested. I hope you're not offended."

"Not at all, Dr Sinclair. We all have to find our own way." And with that Merrick was gone, leaving Mr Hodge, the barrel-chested ship's surgeon, to introduce himself. Sinclair could see immediately that Hodge had an eye for the ladies. "Lovely, aren't they?" the ship's surgeon said, looking at the captain with his daughters and stroking the plume of thick, grey hair that crescendoed to a single curl on top of his head. "Completely mercenary though, all of them," he continued, casting his lecherous eye around the room. "All they want is a rich husband, so watch yourself, laddie."

"I will thank you; but I'm not rich so I'm in very little danger," replied Sinclair, taking another glass of Madeira.

"Well, there's nothing to say you can't try your luck, it's a long journey; but take my advice, if you're not sincere in your intentions stay away from the captain's daughters. I'd hate to see you keelhauled."

"Oh aye; very funny, Mr Hodge. Trust me, I'm no imbecile," said Sinclair.

"I'm sure you're not, laddie," the surgeon laughed loudly, shaking his vast barrel of a chest. "I've got my eye on that filly over there." He pointed at a woman with dark hair. "She's a recent widow, by all accounts. I shall enjoy offering her a bit of comfort." Hodge licked his lips with bawdy anticipation. "Remember, I saw her first," he smirked, and headed off in her direction.

With Hodge gone, Sinclair took a turn around the room, introducing himself to the captain's young daughters, a middle-aged woman named Mrs Campbell and the elegant widow the ship's surgeon had his eye on. Her daughters were a little younger than the captain's.

As they sat down to eat, Sinclair found himself next to Miss Morris, the captain's niece. His eyes were immediately drawn to her handsome bosom. He could see that Captain Greenwood, across the table, had noticed her too. She smiled at him, then pulled her shawl around her shoulders, obscuring his view.

"What are your plans when you get to India, Dr Sinclair?" she enquired without any of the usual formalities, a social transgression that unsettled him immediately. He looked at her, and felt the painful awkwardness he had felt all his adult life when encountering attractive women.

"Good evening, madam," he replied, smoothing his napkin with fake assurance.

"That remains to be seen, doesn't it?" she flirted, doing the same.

"Indeed it does. Let us hope that neither of us is disappointed," he quipped in return. "To answer your question, madam, I shall work with the Surgeon General of the company's new Indian Medical Service. I'll be responsible for the organisation of the medical care for the company's thousands of military and civilian servants on the sub-continent."

"You're Scottish, Dr Sinclair. I've never met anyone from Scotland before. Pray tell me, sir, what is Scotland like?"

Taken aback by her complete indifference to his position in the company, he replied, "Well, that's a very difficult question because it's a country of many parts, most of which I have never visited."

She directed her gaze at him. "I am willing to be satisfied with the parts you know, Dr Sinclair."

"Madam." He paused to quell his consternation. How dare she show no appreciation of his rank, or his intellectual prowess? How dare she make him feel so uncomfortable with her beautiful breasts? He hated her already, and he had only just met her. "Well," he said, "I hail from Sterling myself. Now, what can I tell you about Sterling? Aye, it's a place with a big stone castle that has a little grey town attached to it."

Miss Morris sipped her Madeira and cast her eyes across the table to the scarlet-coated Captain Greenwood. "So, you didn't like living there, Dr Sinclair?" she smiled, but not at him.

Sinclair looked at Greenwood, who was returning his dining companion's interest, and replied with rising pique. "Stirling was not my favourite abode."

Unperturbed, or perhaps encouraged by her companion's mounting discomfort, she continued, "I'm sure Sterling has something to recommend it, Dr Sinclair?"

He thought for a moment, then replied, "Unfortunately, I missed its most exciting episode."

"What was that?" she said, taking one of the tureens and carefully dishing a portion of steaming hot broth into his bowl as if she were his servant.

"Well," he declared with increasing irritation, "it was when that young scallywag Bonnie Prince Charlie tried to take the place."

"Oh, it's not good to make light of enemies of the Crown, Dr Sinclair," she smiled, picking up her spoon.

"It was a jest, madam. I assure you I'm loyal to the Crown. I have no time for the Bonnie Prince and his Highland thugs. I am Scottish and I am British; my allegiance is to the King. If I may return to your question, the place I was happiest was Leiden. I studied at the University there. It's a beautiful town with elegant

14

buildings and a multitude of canals that freeze in the winter, when there is great entertainment to be had in skating."

Hoping he had satisfied her curiosity, he started on his soup. As he ate, he saw the dashing Captain Greenwood calmly watching him from the corner of his eye. Why couldn't he be more like him, he thought. Why did he always end up making a fool of himself as soon as he saw a pretty face?

With the first course finished, Sinclair took another glass of wine. "I'd like to know more about Scotland, sir. It sounds a fascinating place," his torturer purred by his side.

He braced himself again. "Indeed it is. My father is a minister of the kirk there."

"How interesting. My own dear father is dead, but when he was with us he was not of a religious persuasion."

"Neither am I," Sinclair replied with some relief, but then could not resist boasting. "My Father is a very popular preacher in Edinburgh." Her shawl slipped from her shoulders, allowing him a view of her breasts again. "He has a very successful formula for filling his pews on Sundays," he continued, distracted by the frisson of excitement in his groin.

"Pray tell me, sir, what is that?"

"Whatever the subject of his sermon he always ends it on the perils of licentiousness, madam." As the words left his mouth, his heart began to sink.

"Licentiousness is a very dangerous thing, Dr Sinclair," his companion smiled, turning his cheeks scarlet. "I am firmly of the opinion that men do not regulate their actions by anything the Church has to say. In my experience a man's conscience is entirely determined by his class."

He was astounded by the turn the conversation had taken. "Indeed, I believe that is an interesting and true observation, madam."

"For my part I have only ever known Deptford," she continued, "so I am in no position to contradict your opinion of Scotland or your father, but I suspect you are mocking a man who cares passionately about the welfare of his congregation."

"Indeed he does, madam, but unlike my father my passion does not necessitate abhorring human nature and making people unhappy."

"How interesting, Dr Sinclair. Pray, what is your passion?"

With great relief he proclaimed, "Medicine, Miss Morris; the curing of the sick."

"Then it is a passion every bit as worthy as your father's," she smiled. "You're perhaps more alike than you care to admit."

"I can assure you that my father and I have nothing in common, madam," Sinclair retorted, taking the platter of beef and potatoes that had arrived in front of him and slapping a portion on his plate. Then, deliberately ignoring the rules of polite dining which seemed to no longer hold, he pushed it towards her. Unembarrassed, she took the platter and served herself saying, "Deptford is a very dreary place. Ordinarily, there are two choices for women like me there: the drudgery of being a poor man's wife or the drudgery of being in the service of a rich one. That is why I am so grateful to my uncle for offering to take me to Bengal. You see, there are no castles or princes in Deptford, Dr Sinclair. Poor men work all the hours of the day and the rich drink and whore all the hours of the night. Tankards of ale and bottles of gin fuel passions there, not noble ideals and religious zeal. It's a very different place to Scotland, sir."

Chided and deflated, Sinclair bowed his head as he stabbed at the gristly pieces of meat on his plate, swallowing each in turn with a gulp of self-induced fury. When his plate was clean, he turned to Mr Hodge, who was sitting to his left, and introduced Miss Morris. Hodge, with instant and undisguised lechery in his eye, was delighted by the introduction. The ship's surgeon quickly appraised himself of her finer assets, saying that he would be happy to assist her with any complaint and that she was welcome to come to his sick bay at any time, day or night. Recognising Hodge's temperament immediately, Miss Morris thanked him for his concern, with the assurance that she was in robust good health and intended to remain so for the duration of the voyage – an assurance that disappointed him greatly.

At the first opportunity, Sinclair left the saloon for the rudimentary privacy of his canvas cabin. He was frustrated with himself. The evening that had started with so much promise had ended with him feeling deflated and humiliated. To console himself he smoked a pipe. As he sucked in the mellow tobacco he listened to the chatter of the other passengers making their way to bed. The rocking motion of the ship was vaguely soporific, but he could not settle; his mind was still in a state of agitation. He covered himself with his greatcoat and closed his eyes. Usually on New Year's Day he would have no problem sleeping: he would still be drunk from the celebration the night before. Indeed, after dancing with Iona at the Assembly Rooms the previous year he had immersed himself in the demon for two days to assuage the feelings of desire she had aroused in him.

Drinking to excess was a habit he had acquired as a student; it was a habit his father and sister abhorred and one that had got him into trouble with his professors. But despite their disapproval, he often found himself craving the temporary oblivion that only

17

its over-indulgence could supply. However, he thought tonight was not one of those occasions; and his mind turned to Iona again, wondering whom she had danced with and if by some chance she was lying in her bed thinking about him.

Despite their obvious delight in each other's company, he knew Iona was out of his reach. Her father was Britain's foremost medical educator, the son of the founder of Edinburgh's medical school; a man of the kirk like his father and of the university's governing body; a man with a reputation to foster and protect. His only daughter would marry a man of his choosing, a man whose work would advance the reputation of the great McNeal dynasty; not a man like James Sinclair, a man McNeal considered a godless, lazy drunk.

Then he thought about his encounter with Miss Morris. He was glad she was not interested in him; as it would save him the embarrassment of rejecting her. He concluded they were alike in many ways. They were clever, poor and gauche; she lacked the education and manners to make a good match in polite society, while he lacked the position and reputation to marry the woman of his choice. They were both unwilling to accept what fate had assigned them. Like him she was taking the journey hoping for fortune and success, and he had to admire her for that.

2
A Funeral in Yorkshire

As the *Sherwell* headed into the night, a long-cased pendulum clock struck midnight in a comfortable Yorkshire farmhouse. The house was a substantial brick-built property with an immense Dutch gable trimmed in whitewashed plaster that bore the initials R.R.L. and the year 1740.

The clock ticked on. Fourteen-year-old John poked at the yule log in the inglenook fireplace, making it splutter and spit. The glow of the fading fire radiated around the wood panelled room burnishing the rows of pewter plates and tankards on the dresser with its orange light. Apart from the fire, the only other light in the room was a candle in a pewter candlestick standing on his father's coffin.

The mantelshelf was swathed in sprigs of red-berried holly and white-berried ivy, but Christmas seemed a lifetime away. Above the inglenook hung a pair of crossed claymores, looted by his grandfather from the Culloden battlefield in 1746. His grandfather had joined the Prince of Wales Regiment to fight the Scots because he was for Parliament and a protestant king. John knew the Leadams were brave and loyal Englishmen, and he knew that his father would expect him to uphold that tradition at his funeral in the morning.

In the space of a week, his world had turned upside down. Before Boxing Day, he had been a happy young man on the verge of a career in medicine, but now as he sat staring into the fire he had no idea what his future would be. He jabbed at it with the long iron poker, sending showers of red sparks up the chimney, and as he watched the little specks of light fade and die, he asked himself why God had taken his father.

His father was a good man, he reasoned: a surgeon at Guy's Hospital; a man who helped the poor in their time of need but he was also a man who dissected their bodies to find out what had killed them and to understand better how the human body worked. Was that wicked? Was that why God had taken him? And what of his father's soul and the day of judgement?

The clock struck one. John poked at the fire again and decided that his father would pass any test God could set for him. If death were truly an opening into another world, to a heaven without pain or suffering, what the ancients called the Elysian Fields, then his father's soul would already be there. He stood and looked at his father's coffin. In the morning he would bury his father's body, a body his immortal soul no longer required because it had departed with his last breath on earth. He did not know where his father's soul had gone, but he was sure that it had departed, and that there was nothing for him or his father to fear. He put the poker down and took himself off to bed.

Christopher Leadam's coffin was lifted onto the hearse his brother had hired for the occasion from Beverley. Robert Leadam took his nephew's hand and set off along the lane to All Hallows' church in the village of Walkington, with John's mother Charlotte, his aunt Mariah and his cousin Lucy following behind.

When they arrived at the small square-towered church, the grass was covered in thick white frost and the lichen-covered headstones sparkled with rime in the low winter sunshine. John had to admit that it was a more tranquil final resting place for his father than St Olave's in Southwark, but the thought of going back to London without him stabbed at his raw and broken heart.

When the service was over, and John had shaken the hands of what seemed like a hundred strangers, his uncle led his father's friends to the Fawsitt Arms, where he had purchased a cask of ale and meat pies by way of a wake. John and the women rode back to the farm on the back of the hearse.

The warmth of the farmhouse was welcome after they had been out in the cold for so long. Aunt Mariah poured sherry into small pewter cups and handed out sweet biscuits. "Hell fire, it's freezing out there," she muttered. "Now, Charlotte lass, get that down you, duck. It'll do you good. It's been right hard on you, lass." She picked up the poker to jab at what was left of the fire. "Come on, you bugger, burn."

"Mother, there's no need to swear," chided Lucy.

"I'll swear if I want to, thank you very much. We've had the luck of Job round here these past years, and we sure as 'ell don't want no more. This yule log will burn until Twelfth Night if it kills me. Fetch some more wood and get some life into this fire, child."

"I'll go," John volunteered. "You stay in the warm, Lucy."

Mariah sank back in her chair and heaved a weary sigh. "You got the best of the two of them, you know. I have to admit I hankered after Christopher myself at one time."

"Mother, for goodness' sake," Lucy squirmed. "Aunt Charlotte doesn't want to hear all this."

"Shush, child; I'm just saying what's true," retorted her mother. "Christopher turned the heads of lots of girls about these parts, but he were ambitious and he knew he could do better for himself in London. Besides, my father wouldn't countenance a marriage without land, so I ended up with Robert and this damn place."

"Mother, how can you say that? This is our home."

"Well, just look at it. Nothing's changed since the day it were built. We've no china to speak of, no wallpaper and no decent furniture. How can I invite the ladies of Walkington here, let alone anyone from Beverley, without being the object of sympathy or derision? You're old enough to know that your father spends his money on horse racing and whores."

"Mother, Aunt Charlotte doesn't want to know our problems."

"Shush, child, when I'm speaking," Mariah scolded.

"I'm not a child; I'll be twenty next year."

"Two bastardy bonds he has to his name – two!" Mariah declared, spitting with anger. "It may be Christmas, but we've no need of mistletoe round here. Robert doesn't need any encouragement to go kissing the maids, and more. You don't get bairns by a bit of kissing, do you?" The women nodded their heads in agreement. "And if he sees a nag with long odds at

22

Beverley or York you can be sure he'll have money on it. It's no wonder I'm ashamed to venture into the town. You may not have had him for long, Charlotte, but Christopher was a good husband to you, I know he was." And she started to cry.

John returned with the logs and soon the fire was roaring again. They sat drinking sherry and talking until it was dark. His aunt was concerned about Lucy losing her bloom, but as far as he could see she was very pretty, and he could not understand what the women were worried about.

* * *

On the 'Sherwell' that evening Sinclair's dining companion was the elegant widow from Maidstone. As they ate and chatted, he wondered whether she would succumb to the overtures of Mr Hodge. He knew that in the coming weeks he would pursue her not because he had feelings for her but because she was untainted by the horrors of venereal disease.

Across the table, Miss Morris was deep in conversation with Captain Greenwood. She was wearing the same sky-blue dress she had worn the night before. It suited her well, and in his opinion was a good investment for her cause. He had no doubt that some young buck with a bob or two would snap her up as soon as she got to one of the big garrison towns; if the handsome Captain Greenwood did not get there first. He seemed to have formed quite an attachment to her already. He retired early, slept soundly and woke the next morning to the sickening smell of bilge accompanied by the rhythmic sound of pumping from the hold. To his dismay the sunshine of the day before was gone, and the sky was a blanket of thick grey cloud. The sails were heavy with ice and salt, and the grey of the sea merged with the sky in all directions. They were stationary, snow fell all day, and the pumping continued.

At supper, Sinclair fell into conversation with Captain Greenwood, a young man like himself who was intent on forging a successful career in the East. He was a retired British Army officer who, like so many others, had been let go after the defeat in America. Sinclair could see that both the men and the women on board admired Greenwood, much to his chagrin. His good looks and easy temperament seemed to smooth all his social interactions: he was gracious, charming and good company. He spoke eloquently of his experience in the American War, saying that he had had a mainly diplomatic role and had not seen much in the way of fighting. Sinclair was jealous of this man of easy conversation and conscience. Greenwood seemed to have no moral quandaries to wrestle with and was content to accept the world as he found it.

The ship was moving at speed when Sinclair made his way on deck the next day. This was the first time he had really needed his sea legs.

"Bracing, isn't it?" said Hodge, holding onto his hat.

"Aye, you could say that," replied Sinclair. "It's a wee bit rough for my liking."

"Ah, this is nothing, laddie. Wait till we get to the Cape. You'll know what a rough sea is then."

By lunchtime, the wind had become a gale. Sitting in the saloon with the other passengers Sinclair felt a knot of fear tightening in his belly. Like the women, he was trying to distract himself with a book, but even Voltaire could not make him laugh in these circumstances.

Captain Greenwood was with his men. They were young and inexperienced, boys from farms and small towns unaccustomed to the confines of a ship and life at sea. The ship was pitching wildly as it rode the mountainous waves. Coupled with the disgusting odour of the bilge, the motion of the ship and the airlessness of the hold, the atmosphere was one of putrefaction and terror. The younger recruits were calling for their mothers and puking in their hammocks, while the more experienced cursed and fought. Anything not tied down slewed across the stinking slime of the deck, rattling backwards and forwards through the rolling puddles of vomit and piss. As the afternoon drifted into evening the atmosphere on board became as tight as a drum skin. Suddenly, the tension broke as the ship lurched to starboard with a mighty crack. In the saloon, the women screamed as the floor slipped away from them, and Sinclair was flung against the cabin wall with them. The table stayed in place but the chairs slewed across the room, ending up on top of them.

He pushed a chair away and watched as the women steadied themselves, their faces dazed and white. The chandelier was hanging at forty-five degrees and above them waves were crashing into the deck.

As they silently wondered what would happen next, the ship righted itself with an elastic thwack that sent them and all the furniture hurtling back to the other side of the room, and blowing out the candles in the chandelier. Sinclair found a candle on the floor and lit it on a red-hot coal. In the gloom he moved from passenger to passenger, attending to each in turn and asking them about their injuries. Much to his surprise, the women seemed to accept his ministrations and reassurances, and once he was sure they were calm he went to find out what had happened.

As he opened the door onto the deck, a blast of snow-laden wind smacked him in the face. Merrick saw him and commanded him to go back inside. Reluctantly he obeyed. In the saloon he took out his pocket watch, and turned it in his hand before flipping open its gold case. It was six o'clock. The wind was screaming like a demonic choir but the ship was steady again.

Mrs Campbell gathered the women around her and started to pray. Sinclair's thoughts turned to Voltaire once more. He understood the women's need for comfort, but to him the act of prayer was one of self-delusion. How could the words of man alter the course of nature? He felt alone. The wind picked up again and the ship pitched hypnotically, sending him into a trance-like state. He was not sure how much time had passed before the ship rolled again, sending him and the women and all the furniture flying like gaming counters against the cabin walls.

The saloon was as black as pitch once more. He fumbled around in the pile of furniture and frocks for a candle, eventually finding one and lighting it. The women were sprawled across the lockers with their petticoats and stockings on full display. Sinclair lit more candles while they waited for the ship to right itself, as it had before.

Suddenly there was an ear-splitting crack followed by a thunderous crash. Sinclair's heart leapt and he let out a low groan. Surely this was it: the ship was breaking up and he would soon be on his way to a watery grave. The ship shuddered from bow to stern, then in one swift motion it righted itself, tossing him and the women back to where they had started.

Merrick opened the saloon door. "Dr Sinclair, come with me. Mr Hodge needs you." As soon as the door closed behind them, Merrick said, "The mast's gone; we have five men overboard and seven injured." He led Sinclair through the forest of stinking hammocks in the hold, past Captain Greenwood towards the front of the ship, where they found Hodge stroking his plume of grey hair.

"Ah, Dr Sinclair, we'll deal with this one first," he said, pointing at an unconscious man on the floor. Sinclair held up a lantern to get a better look. The lower part of the man's left leg was a bloody pulp of crushed skin and bone, oozing clouds of scarlet blood.

"Aye, Mr Hodge. I agree."

"Right. You do the tourniquet and I'll whip the leg off. It'll give the poor sod a chance."

In the lamplight the two men worked with speed and efficiency. Sinclair tightened the ligature around the man's thigh to close the arteries that were spewing out blood, then Hodge cut away the man's clothes and sliced cleanly through the flesh with a large, flat blade. Sinclair handed him the saw, and with a few short strokes the crushed and broken limb was on the floor. He poured vinegar over the wound and gathered the flap of skin together, securing it in place with five large stitches. Hodge finished by binding the stump with clean linen as Sinclair released the tourniquet, and the man was taken away.

Their next patient was conscious and terrified. Sinclair found a packet of opium and stirred it into a cup of brandy. He cradled the man's head in his arms and pressed the cup to his quivering lips. "Drink this; it'll settle your nerves," he soothed, nodding to the orderlies that it was time to lash the man's writhing body to the table. He slipped a cylinder of wood into the man's mouth and cradled his head while Hodge completed the amputation, removing the mangled foot with speed and precision. He was astonished at Hodge's skill, even thinking that he could give the great McNeal a run for his money. With his foot gone the man began to convulse, a symptom of major body trauma that Sinclair had seen many times before. The man was taken away, and two patients who had splinters the size of kindling embedded in their thighs were brought in. The two surgeons took it in turns to hold the lantern while the other gently eased the shards of wood away from the flesh, then doused the wounds with vinegar before stitching up the holes. Next they set a fractured radius, stitched a ripped ear back on and sewed up a wide gash across another man's face.

When they were done, Hodge congratulated Sinclair. "You did a good job. I had my doubts about you with all that book learning, but we made a good team tonight."

"Thank you," Sinclair replied, offering Hodge a cup of brandy. "You're a very accomplished surgeon yourself, sir. I know because I've seen the best. You were every bit as good as Alexander McNeal in Edinburgh and John Hunter in London."

"Thank you," Hodge chuckled, sipping his drink. "I'll tell the Captain that when I ask him for a pay rise. So you know them, do you?"

"Aye, I do. McNeal better than Hunter, but I've had dealings with them both."

"Well, what are you doing here? With connections like that you should be on the staff at one of those charity hospitals."

"Aye, well, that's a long story. Let's just say that it's my sister who has the family connections: she's McNeal's cousin by marriage, and McNeal and I, well, we don't see eye to eye."

"You mean you're not a Tory?"

" No, I'm a Whig if anything. McNeal was my professor in Edinburgh and he took against me then. He doesn't like men who drink, Mr Hodge," he said, taking a gulp of brandy from the bottle. But more importantly I can't be doing with all that kowtowing to lay governors and their wretched God that you have to do in those hospitals. I've worked in a few of them, the

Infirmary in Edinburgh and St George's in London, and to be frank with you I'm glad to get away from them."

"It's just as well you're off to India then, son; nobody gives a damn about that sort of thing there. A lot of men turn native, you know. They take up all manner of heathen ideas. It's the women you see – they're bloody stunning. A man would believe anything for one of them. There's nothing duplicitous about them; no paint, no corsets, no wigs. What you see is what you get, and you get to see a whole lot more than you do in England. You'll see what I mean when you get there. And when they dance, laddie, there's so much silk and hair and skin on show you feel like King bloody Herod watching Salome."

"That sounds very appealing. I'm glad there will be some compensation for the tribulations of this journey."

"Oh, there'll be plenty of compensations for the likes of you. The women, both English and the natives, will be throwing themselves at you. You'll be spoilt for choice. I'd stick to the natives. They'll do anything you want, you know, in the bedroom, and they keep the house nice. In fact I wouldn't mind settling down with one myself."

"Well, I wish you well with that, Mr Hodge," Sinclair said, taking out his pocket watch to check the hour. The wind had died down and the ship was rolling less menacingly. "I think it's time for me to try to get some sleep."

"Of course, doctor. Thank you for your help this evening. It was much easier working with a man who knows what he's doing than with a regular midshipman."

Sinclair walked back the way he had come. With the storm abating the young soldiers were sleeping, and there was no sound from the women's accommodation either, which was a good sign.

The only light on was Greenwood's, so he knocked on the door and waited to see if there was any reply.

"Come in," said Greenwood, raising his head from the pillow. "I can't sleep."

Sinclair looked at the handsome young man lying in the cot with a bottle in his hand. He looked worn out and his face was wet with tears. "Well, that's not surprising. It's been a terrible night," he said, leaning on the door frame to steady himself as the ship gently rolled.

"It was so dark when all the lights went out. I hate the dark, I always have. Those bloody ruffians gave me hell. I had to threaten to shoot two of them to keep them from killing each other. They went crazy, Sinclair. I don't know how I kept the bastards in order. I thought I was going to cop it."

"Would you like something to help you sleep?"

"If you have something that will work. I've nearly finished this bottle to no effect."

Sinclair fetched a small paper packet from his sea chest and mixed it with a little claret, then gave it to Greenwood.

"What is it?"

"It's a wee something to calm the nerves and help you sleep. Just get it down you and you'll be asleep in no time." That was all the assurance Greenwood needed. He drank the bitter, opium-laced wine in one gulp, and Sinclair closed the canvas door and headed for his own bed.

At midday, Sinclair stood silently on the blustery deck watching puffy white clouds skim across the blue of the sky with the assembled passengers and crew, as Captain Richards led a funeral service for the men who had lost their lives. Although he had no desire to confess the inadequacy of his soul or give thanks for deliverance from a god who dispensed random acts of destruction, he wanted to wish the injured men well and to offer his thanks to the brave and unlucky sailors who had died saving the ship. Despite his Presbyterian upbringing he did not believe that man was predestined in any way; Voltaire had shown him the insanity of that. He believed that all men were born equal and free to live according to their consciences. If there was a God, he believed he was the creator of the natural laws that governed the universe, and that he had given man a rational mind to understand them. Miss Morris had been right to say he was more like his father than he cared to accept. He had chosen to study natural philosophy and to practise medicine as his way of making the world a better place, and not religion as his father wished, and it had made them irreconcilable.

That afternoon Sinclair dozed peacefully in his cot for the first time since he had joined the ship. He had grown accustomed to the sound and smell of the bilge pumps. He woke in the dark to find the ship pitching and tossing in mountainous waves again; another storm had blown in as he slept. His stomach clenched and his mind was alive with fear again. He made for the saloon, where he found Mrs Campbell praying with the other women. He could taste the fear in the room, and not wishing to pray he took himself off to the sick bay to sit with Mr Hodge.

In the hold Greenwood felt lost in an eternity of darkness. Beneath him, he could hear the sound of water sloshing and barrels rolling, but the fetid stink of the bilges was gone. Now the cold sharp smell of the ocean was in his nostrils, and he knew that the ship was sinking.

When he had boarded the 'Sherwell' Frank Greenwood had considered himself a success, a gentleman and a competent officer, but now sitting in the darkness waiting to die he found himself questioning his abilities and his conduct. He longed to be home at Panton Hall again; he wanted to be clean, to lie in a bed that did not move, to sit by the window in the green drawing room with a cup of coffee in his hand. He thought about his mother, Lady Frances, and how she would weep when she heard the news of his death. He hated the idea of upsetting her. Then he thought about his father, Sir Bramwell, and how much he loved him and how he wanted him to be proud of his achievements. Finally he thought about Miss Morris, the most attractive woman he had ever met. She was lively and without the artificiality of so many women of his own class. He was not sure she was the sort of woman who would make a good wife for an ambitious officer, but he thought that if by some miracle they survived he would like to get to know her better.

His morbid contemplations were disturbed by the arrival of Lieutenant Allsop, who advised him of the ship's perilous situation. "We cannot turn the ship; the wind is too strong," he explained in a low voice, so that only Greenwood could hear. "We're heading straight for the rocks, and will hit them some time after midnight." Greenwood listened to the news of the impending disaster in silence. He did not know whether to be angry with God for the injustice of it all or simply to accept what had been decreed for him. "Wait below until the ship has grounded. Your men will be washed overboard if they venture onto the deck before that. When the ship has come to rest, it's every man for himself. Do you understand, Captain?" Greenwood nodded numbly. "Hold these bastards with that pistol if you have to so you can get off yourself; that's my advice. Good luck, Captain."

News of the impending disaster arrived in the sick bay with Allsop. Sinclair said goodbye to Hodge as he took a lantern. He caught Greenwood's eye as he passed through the hold, and although he waved he did not stop. Once inside his little canvas cabin he loosened his clothing so that he could dispose of it easily, then took his pocket watch and checked the hour; it was nearly midnight. He closed it and kissed the back, then took a clean neck-tie from his chest and secured three guineas in it in knots, and tied it around his waist. He reckoned that if he survived he would need money to get back to London. Then he lay in his cot and smoked a pipe. He was enjoying what he thought might be his last earthly pleasure when he became aware of Miss Morris standing by his door with an empty claret jug in her hand.

"Come in," he said. "What can I do for you?"

"I found these in a locker," she said, brandishing the jug in one hand and a bottle of brandy in the other. "Could you give me some of that power you gave to Frank the other night? I wouldn't normally ask but Mrs Campbell's praying is getting hysterical. We need something to calm us down."

He rose from his cot and put down his pipe. "I assume you're planning on staying on board when the ship grounds?" he said.

"None of us can swim so we have no choice."

"In that case, I see no problem with satisfying your request, Miss Morris." Sinclair lifted the lid of his sea chest and took out two packets of opium.

"Will you give it to us? I'm not sure Mrs Campbell will take it from me."

"If you think it'll help," he smiled, warming to her at last. He followed her up to the saloon and pushed open the door. "Good evening," he proclaimed, holding up the jug. "I've found us a little comfort on this tempestuous night." The women looked to Captain Richards for his response. Sinclair steadied himself and continued. "Miss Morris, would you fetch some cups?"

33

Mrs Campbell was first to her feet, complaining that she had no intention of meeting the Lord in a state of intoxication. Sinclair touched her arm gently to reassure her. "The Lord is infinitely merciful, Mrs Campbell, and will not begrudge you or anyone here a wee dram to keep away the chill tonight." Then he turned to Mrs Evans. "Would you like a wee dram of brandy to keep you warm?"

"Yes please, just a small one," she whispered nervously, clutching her shawl. Then she turned her gaze to her daughters. "Could the girls have one too?"

"Of course; there's plenty for everyone," Sinclair said, pouring the brandy into the collection of chipped cups that Miss Morris was fishing out of the lockers. Captain Richards beckoned to his daughters to go forward for theirs, and soon Mrs Campbell was waiting in line for hers. Miss Morris took her own cup and gulped down the bitter liquid, feeling it burn all the way into her stomach. Within minutes, the opium began to work its magic. Sinclair could see that the women were less alarmed.

He thought about the possibility of his own death, realising it was an event that in all likelihood would come much sooner than he had anticipated. Looking at the women, his mind turned to his sister. Morag had looked after him after their mother had died. He remembered the comfort of her embrace and the warmth of her smile. The memory of her was so powerful that he almost cried. He was six when she married Andrew Rankin and left him alone with his father.

His pocket watch gave out a single chime and he knew it was time to go. He said his goodbyes and left for his cabin. There was a volley of cannon fire from the deck announcing their imminent impalement on the rocks. In the companionway Allsop and Merrick were both stripped down to their shirts and breeches.

"We'll make landfall at any moment. Keep your lantern with you; you'll need it," advised Allsop. There was a sickening jolt, and they all found themselves on the floor.

"That's it. Every man for himself," announced Merrick, scrambling to his feet and heading for the steps, with Allsop scrambling along behind him.

Sinclair followed them onto the deck, but instead of pushing forward he sheltered under the poop. Flashes of silver lightning turned the snow-filled sky from black to white. Through the blizzard and the spume, he saw a trail of yellow dots moving along the deck as the crew scrambled for the rocks. He was already soaked and freezing, his teeth were chattering and his chest was tight. He stepped forward, holding up his lantern in an effort to see what was happening, and immediately felt the full blast of the ocean's fury. Retreating to the shelter of the poop again, he stood waiting for the right moment to make his move, not sure what that moment might be. Then an enormous wave lifted the ship out of the water and pounded her onto the rocks with an almighty thud, and he knew he had to leave. The line of lanterns that had been there only moments before had disappeared. He stepped out into the squalling wind and started to pick his way along the fractured deck. Out of nowhere a massive wave hit him broadside, knocking him off his feet. He landed on the deck with a heavy thud; he snatched a breath and blew out the pain. The next wave soaked him. His lantern was gone but he was still on the ship. In the darkness he wrestled off his wet coat and started to crawl along the broken deck. Another wave hit him and dumped him in the sea with the force of a prize fighter's punch. Not knowing which way to swim, he stopped and allowed his body to float, hoping that he would go up and not down. He felt the pull of the current sucking him down and he was running out of breath. Just as he was thinking his lungs would explode, the current released him, his face broke the surface and he gulped in a breath of icy air. He was upright for a moment, then another wave thundered over his head and dragged him under again. The spiny rocks were slicing into his flesh as the foaming water raged over his head. The current held him in its vice-like grip, drawing him deeper into the watery blackness. His arms and legs became weaker and the pain in his chest more and more intense; death seemed only moments away. For the first time in his life he really wanted to live. Then he felt the current release its grip and his head popped out into the air. He snatched a breath, panting out the pain in his chest. The water was calm and there was no wind or snow. He could hear the strange echoey sound of men's voices. I must be in a cave, he thought, and started to swim towards them. After a few strokes he bumped his head on a ledge, and as he grabbed it with both hands he called out to anyone who was there. To his great relief he heard Merrick telling him to get onto the ledge.

Exhausted, all he wanted was to lie down, to close his eyes and to sleep, but he knew that if he did he would most certainly die. Beyond the shelter of the cave, the storm crashed on. The wind roared, waves pounded the shore and lightning raked the sky. Through the din, Sinclair heard a familiar sound. His heart leapt: it was his pocket watch, and it was still working. The three small chimes told him it would be light in four hours' time. With his hope rekindled, Sinclair determined to stay awake and to live.

To keep himself awake he started to recall everything he knew about human anatomy, the name of every organ, every bone and every blood vessel. He even started to recite the passages from the Bible he had learned as a child. He thought about Iona and of their trip to Arthur's Seat. He pictured the wind in her hair;

he recalled the smile on her face as he swung her around in the dance at the Assembly Rooms, their conversation about Voltaire and Defoe. Occasionally he heard the sound of one of his companions falling into the water and he redoubled his efforts to stay awake, but eventually exhaustion overtook him and he closed his eyes.

He woke to the freezing grey light of dawn. Now he could see that the ledge was some ten feet above a pebbly beach, and just inside a cave. He looked down to see the bodies of his shipmates dotted along the beach and drifting out to sea. The ship was gone, smashed to pieces, and as the light grew stronger he counted the prostrate bodies in red army coats splayed out like starfish on the shore. There were hundreds of them, and he was sure he could see a woman's petticoat floating in the surf. He retched, and his mouth filled with hot, acidic vomit. He spat it out and wiped his lips. Looking around, Sinclair discovered he was alone. Where had everyone gone? His legs were cold and stiff, but he pushed himself to stand. As the blood started to flow back into his veins the pain was excruciating. He had no idea how long it took him to reach the open air, but when he finally raised his eyes to the sky he discovered he was at the bottom of a ninety foot cliff of jagged grey rock. Where were the men he had spent the night with? Where was Merrick? He was just about to panic when he saw a loop of thick rope moving in front of him. He reached out and grabbed it, and when he pulled on it he felt it jerk upwards. Hesitating briefly, the doctor placed it over his head so that it sat on his waist. He gave it a couple of jerks, and the rope tightened against his back, his body started to rise, and suddenly his world went black.

3
The Widow's Journey

Three days after his father's funeral, John Leadam and his mother Charlotte were packed into a pony cart by his uncle for the journey to York. They travelled in silence for many dull miles before his uncle spoke. "I'm sorry things turned out as they did, me lad. We had such plans, you know, your father and me. We fancied a day at the point to point."

"Father would have enjoyed that," said John.

"As far as I'm concerned there's nowt like the thrill of a race. I've spent a right few bob on horses in me time as I'm sure your aunt has told you. Lucy loves horses just like me. I'm of a mind to get me hands on one of them thoroughbred mares, but I'll have to go up north to Bedale or Masham to get one. There's plenty as wants a good racer or a good hunter in these parts."

"Would you breed racehorses then, Uncle Robert?"

"Oh, aye, I do already, but they ain't Arabians. I had great hopes for Blaze. He had a coat as shiny as a conker, but he fell in the first steeplechase I put him in and I had to shoot the poor bugger. Cost me near fifty guineas. Mariah were furious with me, but when have women known anything about having a bit a fun, eh, John?"

"I heard that, Robert Leadam," his mother retorted with feigned coolness. "And I'll ask you not to go corrupting your nephew with ideas about gambling and horses."

"Now I'm in trouble with your mother," his uncle chuckled. "I expect you're more like your dad, John. I bet you're a sensible boy who works hard at that grammar school you go to in London. It never appealed to me, all that Greek and Latin. What does a farmer need with it? Now, your dad were a different kettle of fish. If the old man hadn't insisted on educating me there would've been enough to send your dad to Oxford, or some such place."

John looked at his uncle. "I think he would have liked that." Then he noticed his mother staring out across the frost-covered fields, and said, "But then he wouldn't have met Mother and everything would have been different." His mother turned her head and smiled at her son. Robert rattled on, oblivious of the deep emotion that was passing between his passengers, and pushed the piebald ponies on with a swish of his whip.

"Aye, lad, fate's a funny thing. None of us knows what's in store for us or how the choices we make will turn out. We just have to make the best of what we've got, don't we?" Charlotte Leadam nodded her head and pressed her hand into her son's under the blanket, reassuring him of the unbreakable bond between them.

It took the whole day to travel the thirty-five miles from Walkington to York, and it had been dark for several hours when they reached the terminus of the London mail coach at the York Tavern.

At five o'clock the next morning John Leadam stood in the tavern yard watching flurries of soft fat snow dancing in the light from the inn. The London Flyer was in the yard ready to go. The snow fell thickly, swirling towards the ground then disappearing into muddy puddles in the gravel. The driver was checking tickets while his assistant, a skinny little man dressed in leather from head to foot, strapped the luggage to the roof. Inside, Charlotte Leadam was saying her last goodbyes. She thanked her brother-in-law, and said that she would write as soon as she got home to Southwark; then she crossed the gravel yard and joined her son.

"Well, look after your mother, John, that's what your father would want," said his uncle.

"I will, sir."

"That's a good lad. Now off you go, the pair of you, and remember, if you or your mother need any help, you've only to ask, John."

John allowed himself to feel the comfort of his uncle's embrace for one last time, then pulled himself away and joined his mother in the padded box on wheels that would take them back to London in less than forty-eight hours. The driver climbed into his seat, his leather-clad assistant picked up his blunderbuss and climbed up beside him, and the coach pulled slowly out of the yard. John pushed down the glass window and leaned out to wave goodbye.

The city streets were dark and silent, except for the sound of horses' hooves and the rumble of the carriage along the cobbles, as they headed south onto the Great North Road. Their companions were an elderly canon and his wife; a plump and excitable woman dressed in a brown coat and a soft felt hat decorated with a pair of enormous pheasant feathers. "My goodness, it's chilly. We're for Doncaster, Mrs...?" the woman said, letting her words hang in the gloom of the lamplight while she waited for his mother to reply. In an effort not to appear too eager to start a conversation, his mother allowed the pause to hang just a little longer than was polite. "It is Mrs Leadam, and this is my son Mr John Leadam. We are travelling to Southwark in London."

The coach slewed along the slippery cobbles as the driver let the horses pick up speed, and soon John was asleep. Memories of their journey north, less than a month before, flooded into his unconscious mind. He saw his mother and father sitting opposite him in the coach; they were smiling, their eyes full of excitement and happiness, unaware of the horrors to come. He was woken by a sudden jolt as the carriage flew over a bump, and almost landed in the canon's lap. The coach carried on, and as the day became lighter the driver drove the horses faster. With each twist and turn in the road, the passengers slipped and slid on the hard leather seats, and the constant up and down and rocking motion made them all feel sick. It was too cold to open the windows, so Mrs Jackson kindly offered her vial of hartshorn smelling salts to Mrs Leadam, who gladly accepted it.

After three hours they arrived at Selby, where the horses were changed. Gratefully, Charlotte and John climbed down, and crossed the inn yard to the dining room, where hot coffee with cream and candy sugar was being served at tuppence a cup. They sat silently by a window, glad to be still for a moment and watching the soft flurries of snow dancing in the wind. Another coach arrived, disgorging its passengers into the dining room, but

Charlotte and John sat in silence amongst the clatter of coffee cups and friendly conversation not having the heart to talk.

Soon they were back in the coach and on their way to Doncaster. The morning sky was smoke grey with pink-edged clouds a sure sign of more snow to come. John rested his head on his mother's arm and looked out of the window. The barren winter fields were dusted with snow and the hedgerows bristled with thick hairs of hoarfrost. The hardness of the ground allowed the fresh horses to make good progress along the old Roman Ridge as the driver pushed them further and further south. Occasionally, a large flake of snow settled on the carriage window and slid down to the bottom, but the threatened heavy snowfall did not arrive and they reached Doncaster shortly after noon. They bid the canon and his wife goodbye and the horses were changed again. An hour later they were on their way to Grantham. Charlotte Leadam rested her head on her son's shoulder and closed her eyes. John wondered what she was thinking. Was she reliving the awful events of Christmas the way he did every time he closed his eyes to sleep? Did she see his father's face as life slipped away from him? Was she reflecting on the moment when his father told her that he loved her, and that she should not mourn him when he was gone? John stared silently out of the window watching the frozen landscape go by. He realised that the few days he had spent with his parents in Yorkshire were the first time he could remember being alone with them. His father had worked six days a week, rising before seven each day to open the surgery and to supervise the work of his apprentices, before visiting his patients in their homes. At noon he had attended operations at Guy's and after lunch he had made his hospital rounds or taught. When all this was completed he attended hospital committees and functions in the evenings. Even on Sundays they were rarely alone. They either went to his grandparents' house in Wimpole Street, to his Aunt Emma's in Bread Street or to Mr Hoare's in Gracechurch Street, or their family and friends came to eat with them at Tooley Street — except for his grandmother, who made a point of never travelling south of the river. In fact, when John thought about it he had hardly spent any time alone with his father at all. His mother had taught him to read and write, even in Greek and Latin, and it was his father's apprentices who had helped him with his homework from the grammar school. Only after his father had died had his uncle told him stories about their childhood: his father had never done so. Robert had told him how he and Christopher had got into trouble with the local constable for being drunk when they were boys; that he had envied his father's cleverness when they were at school; and that his father had envied his brother's ability to attract the prettiest girls at the Beverley Fair, a boast that made his aunt cry. His uncle told him how much he had missed his brother when their father had sent him to York to become a surgeon, and that he was sad Christopher had not come home to Yorkshire more often.

The Leadam brothers looked alike in so many ways. They were both tall with thick blond hair and bright blue eyes, but there the similarity ended. His uncle was the older but not the wiser, in John's estimation: Robert was reckless with money, and made his wife and daughter sad, whereas his father had been an upright man, a pillar of the medical community in Southwark, a hard-working, industrious surgeon who was careful with his money; and theirs had been a happy family.

The snow that had threatened all day arrived south of Newark. The wind whipped up the river valley, funnelling the stinging motes of ice into the horses' eyes and the driver's face.

Although the blizzard spun in every direction the driver pressed on. The landscape became featureless and white, apart from the broad black streak of the river, and they were two hours late when they arrived in Grantham. The inn was full of people oblivious to the weather, eating and drinking and making merry. In the chimney a great golden fire roared, and on the sideboard stood a huge Twelfth Night cake covered in pink sugar paste. The weary travellers were invited to join the revellers but his mother elected to eat in their room, and they were both asleep long before the dancing began.

Before dawn they were back in the coach, the driver warning them that he would turn back if they encountered deep snowdrifts or fallen trees. They set off in trepidation, the driver holding the eager horses to a slow walking pace. The passengers exchanged the requisite morning greetings with Mrs Leadam and her son, then settled down to sleep off the excesses of the night before.

John leaned on his mother's arm and closed his eyes. His mind was still full of questions to which he had no answers. Resting on her arm, he realised that more than anything he wanted to be a boy again; he was not ready to be a man.

The weak winter sun raised its head above the horizon at about half past seven. As the light improved the driver's confidence grew, and he loosened the reins and eased off the brake. Four hours after they left Grantham they arrived at the Ram Jam Inn. When John asked about the peculiar name, a passenger told him that it was because some years ago a blackguard who could not pay his bill had offered to show the landlady a trick: he had claimed that he knew how to pull one pint of beer from two barrels at the same time, so the gullible landlady had followed him into the cellar. First he drilled a hole in one barrel, then to stop the beer pouring out asked the old woman to put her thumb in it. Then he did the same with the second, and when she was rammed and jammed, with both thumbs stuck in the leaking barrels, he made off without paying his bill. They all laughed at the man's story, and John noticed that even his mother smiled. They were on the road again less than half an hour after they arrived at the inn, with fresh horses and a renewed sense of purpose. The driver pushed the horses to a full canter, cracking the whip to make up for lost time.

They arrived at the ivy-covered White Horse Inn in Eaton Socon more or less on schedule. Once again, the horses were changed and new passengers joined them for the final fifty miles to London. It was past two o'clock when they finally got underway. The carriage was full for the first time and John found himself squeezed into the corner on the front-facing seat next to his mother. Two middle-aged sisters from Chelsea wearing large felt hats and carrying a little dog called Rolly took their seats opposite them, along with a dark suited young man carrying a violin case. The last person to join them was a muscular scarlet-coated dragoon returning to his regiment after Christmas leave. On top, riding post, there was a full complement of six passengers and a hotchpotch of bags and boxes.

The packed coach lumbered onto the London Road, its wheels sinking deep into the turnpike gravel and slowing it down. Inside, the tightly packed passengers rose and fell like waves on a beach with each bounce of the coach's long steel springs as it picked up speed. As the horses broke into a canter the little dog spewed up the contents of its fat belly all over the dragoon's shiny black boots. The dragoon thumped the roof, bringing the coach to a screeching halt and sending the passengers crashing into each other. The guard jumped down, blunderbuss in hand, and opened the door. The dragoon pointed to his boots and the guard flipped out the steps. The sisters scrambled out, holding the offending animal aloft and bowing apologetically to their fellow passengers.

"Oh, Rolly, you're such a naughty, naughty boy," the larger of the two chided.

"We're so sorry. Please forgive us," pleaded the other.

The dog was banished to the driver's bench, and completed the journey tucked up between the driver and the guard.

At six o'clock they passed through the Highgate Archway five miles from the centre of London. John looked out of the window at the sea of lights in the valley below. The driver applied the brake and the heavily laden coach began to edge its way slowly down the steep incline. For the first time they passed shops and ale-houses, saw people on the pavements and smelt the sharp whiff of coal smoke, earthy ale and the aroma of hot food as it drifted on the cold night air.

The road levelled out into the broad Thames valley and the horses picked up speed again. They dashed through Kentish Town and Camden, then along the Euston Road and into Tottenham Court Road, before finally arriving at the Black Swan in Holborn just after seven. John's uncle, Henry Bowman, was waiting to meet them.

Henry bundled his in-laws into a hired cab and in less than half an hour they were at the elegant, five storeyed, townhouse of his grandparents, the physician Dr Charles Martin and his wife Eliza, in Wimpole Street.

"Now, let Millie take your coats my dears," his grandmother directed as she led them into the large and comfortably appointed drawing room. "John, you sit next to the fire with your grandfather and Charlotte, dearest, you sit next to me. Henry," she said, turning to her son-in-law, "will you be staying?"

"No, Mrs Martin, I must be away. Emma will be waiting for me."

"Give her my love, Henry," Charlotte called to her brother-in-law as he made to leave.

"You can give it to her yourself. She'll be here at ten o'clock tomorrow," he said, as he bowed to his father-in-law and waved them adieu.

Mrs Martin turned to her daughter. "Your father and I were so distressed to hear your news from Yorkshire, Charlotte dearest. Christopher was so young. Who could have possibly imagined that he would die? Oh, it's so tragic. It must have been terrible for you to have been among strangers when it happened."

Dr Martin put his hand up to correct his wife. "Eliza, they were not among strangers; they were with Christopher's family. I am sure our daughter could not have been in a better place."

Dr Martin was more than ten years older than his elegant and domineering wife, and was one of London's leading physicians. Taking a long, slow draught on his pipe he said, "We shall all miss Christopher sorely; he was not only a good son-in-law but my friend. I am sorry that your mother and I were not able to attend his funeral. We would have liked to have paid our respects. I hope that Guy's will hold a memorial service for him."

His wife concurred, dabbing the corner of her eye with her handkerchief. "Your father is right: we shall miss him." She turned to John, ignoring her daughter. "John, my dear, you have been so very brave."

"Thank you, Grandmamma," he replied, thinking that the atmosphere in Wimpole Street was very different from the farmhouse in Yorkshire. At Wimpole Street the rooms were decorated with fine wallpaper and paintings. Mirrors hung on the walls, reflecting the light of the candelabras on the mantelshelf, and there were Kidderminster carpets on the floor. In the huge white marble fireplace the most expensive sea coal burned, blasting out much more heat than the wood fire in the farmhouse inglenook; but for all its physical warmth there was an air of coldness and hostility in the room.

The maid arrived with dishes of hot milky tea and plates of bread and butter, which John and his mother ate while his grandfather smoked and his grandmother fidgeted with her handkerchief.

"Your father has a new patient, Charlotte," John's grandmother said. "His name is Sir Hubert Husselbee, a baronet from Burton-on-Trent. Rumour has it that he has ten thousand pounds a year! Can you believe it? They say he gets his money from coal mines."

Dr Martin looked up. "Well, we burn enough of it to make any man rich, my dear. I don't know what delights your mother more, Charlotte, the fact that he is a knight of the realm or that he is rich."

"Your father jests because he thinks I despise these men of new money," Mrs Martin protested, looking to Charlotte for support that did not come, "which of course I do not."

"But, Mother, you do. That's why you didn't like Christopher: he was only the son of a farmer, not a gentleman with a country estate."

The old man flashed a warning glance at his wife.

"Nonsense, child; I admired him greatly. I just wished..." she murmured, unsure she should say what she was thinking.

"What did you wish, Mother?" demanded Charlotte, with a sliver of ice in her voice.

"Well, my dear, I rather wished that you had lived this side of the river. I never liked the fact that you lived in Southwark. It's not respectable. There, I've said it and I'm not ashamed of it."

John looked at his grandmother in disbelief. He knew that she never visited them in Southwark but he had not realised that she despised their home. It was his father's house and he loved it.

"Now you two, this is no time to quarrel," interjected Dr Martin, waving his pipe at his wife. "John, take no heed of this female nonsense."

"I won't, Grandpapa. My father was the best of fathers, even if he did live in Southwark."

"That's right, my boy. Did you hear that, Grandmamma?"

"Yes, Charles, I did. John, dearest, you know I'm not heartless. I loved your father and I'm very sorry he's gone." Tears welled up in her enormous blue eyes, leaving John wondering whom the tears were for. He glanced at his mother, who was silently fuming beside her, and decided that the best course of action was to console his grandmother before she caused even more upset. "I know you loved my father, Grandmamma," he said, looking at his mother for reassurance. "We're all fatigued from our journey and should get some rest."

"What a very sensible idea, John," said Dr Martin. "Your father would be proud of you; you're such a sensible young fellow. You have looked after your mother well but now it is our turn to look after you. Grandmamma has rooms ready. I suggest that you take yourselves off to get some rest. We can talk in the morning."

Relieved to be out of the claustrophobic and hostile atmosphere of the sitting room, and anticipating the prospect of some privacy after three days of being on the road, Charlotte and John climbed the marble staircase with alacrity. When they reached the spacious landing, Mrs Martin said, "I thought you'd like your old room, Charlotte." Then she gave John a candlestick and directed him to the room at the back of the house.

As Charlotte entered her childhood room it wrapped its comfort around her like the embrace of an old friend. Her old bed was still there with its green damask cover; so too was the washstand, and the mirror where she used to admire herself before she blew out the candle and dreamed her carefree dreams about the man she would marry. The only difference was the addition of a copper bathtub filled with water next to the fire.

"You and John will stay here with us now that Christopher has gone," her mother said, in a tone that indicated it was not a matter for discussion.

"That's very kind of you and Father, but Christopher has not gone, as you put it. He died; my husband is dead. I am a widow, not an abandoned child."

"We know that, dearest. Your father and I comprehend your situation all too clearly," her mother replied, handing her daughter a fresh towel and a bar of soap. "You're a woman without a husband and without an income. You cannot simply go back to your old life Charlotte; it no longer exists. Your father and I have discussed the matter, and we have decided that it is best that you and John stay here where we can provide for you. That is, until you marry again."

The flame of ire burning in Charlotte's chest was rekindled and refuelled. Whilst she could not dispute her mother's analysis of her situation, she was nonetheless livid with her for expressing it so clearly. She bit down on her lip, and breathed the long slow breaths that Christopher had taught her to use in such situations. Experience told her that this was not the time or the place to have an argument with her mother. Losing her temper never worked;

she had to be more cunning than that. As calmly as she could she said, "Mother, I have no plans to remarry."

"I'm not saying that you have to forget Christopher. I'm not that cruel and insensitive." Her mother pointed to the bath. "Your father took this in lieu of payment from a whore in St James's. The poor woman could not pay her rent either, so your father took the bath before the landlord did. My friend Mrs Peacock says that bathing is a great benefit for the nerves, so I thought you might like to try it. I shall not be doing so, of course: I'm too old to change the habits of a lifetime. Besides, they cost a fortune in hot water – which is all very well for Mrs Peacock: her husband is a banker. And I can't use poor Millie like this again; she is exhausted with carrying the pails from the kitchen."

When her mother had gone Charlotte launched herself face down onto the bed and let out a long, low scream of frustration. How dare her mother decide what she was going to do with her life without even talking to her about it? And why had she told her about the whore? Was she trying to warn her about what happens to women who are left on their own?

Furious, she stood up, unfastened her dress and let it drop to the floor. She kicked it away, then picked it up and threw it at the door, followed by her petticoats and corset. Standing only in her stockings, she untied the garters and let the knitted tubes slide down her calves; then she stepped out of them and into the gleaming tub of golden water.

Charlotte sat in the warm water and stared into the fire. Her hands were chapped and her feet were chilblained but the rest of her body was smooth and pale; even so it seemed alien and ancient. She dipped the bar of lavender-scented soap into the water, and as she rolled the sweet-smelling soap in her hands a piercing pain rose from the pit of her stomach. It travelled into her chest and exited from her mouth in a deep mournful wail. Like a lanced blister it throbbed and flared, venting her anguish in a series of body-jerking sobs. She wanted her husband back. She wanted to feel the warmth of his body next to hers, to be wrapped in his affection and his reassuring embrace. She wanted someone to ease her pain and to calm the fears that were welling up inside her. She wanted someone to protect her, but she didn't want it to be her mother.

Wrapped in the clean white towel, she sat next to the fire, overwhelmed by the enormity of what had happened and of what lay ahead. Charlotte looked around her girlhood room. Memories flooded back. She had planned to be a wife and a mother, and to be happy for the rest of her life. In her girlhood dreams she had never imagined herself as a widow. The man she had married was not supposed to die; she was not supposed to be on her own.

Perhaps her mother had a point, she thought. It would be easier to stay with her parents in their comfortable house rather than return to her own home in Tooley Street. If she stayed in Wimpole Street her father would take care of John's education and ensure he had a profession, but this was not the life she had chosen when she married Christopher Leadam. Even though she had gone against her mother's advice, she had been happy. She had loved her husband. Working in the apothecary shop with him had given her a sense of purpose and independence. She did not want to give up the shop for a life of idleness and subservience, no matter how comfortable it might be.

The following morning, Charlotte found her sister Emma drinking coffee by the fire with her father. Her younger sister had always been her mother's favourite. Charlotte put this down to the fact that Emma was prettier than she was and more easily manipulated: Emma usually did exactly what her mother wanted, often without even being asked; and, of course, she had done the sensible thing and married a man her mother approved of, the lawyer Henry Bowman.

Henry had never achieved his goal of practising as a barrister, but working as an attorney in Cheapside was lucrative enough. He spent his days acting for litigants in the Court of Chancery, drawing up commercial contracts, property deeds and wills, and occasionally acting for clients in the common law courts at a hundred guineas a time. Their house was north of the river with two live-in maids and fashionable furniture, and Emma was always dressed respectably à la mode, unlike her dowdy elder sister.

"How are you feeling, my dear?" her father enquired as she sat down on the couch.

Her father had always been her champion, and she was so immensely grateful that he was there to help her. "I am as well as can be expected, Papa."

Emma rose from her chair and embraced her sister warmly. "Oh, Charlotte, my poor darling. Mother has told me what has happened. I'm so sorry we could not be there to help you. Henry will do everything he can to be a good brother to you. He is Christopher's executor and will find a buyer for your house as soon as he can."

"What do you mean, Emma? I have no intention of selling my house, and as far as I know Christopher left no instructions to that effect!"

Emma's face flushed. "I'm sorry if I've spoken out of turn, but you can't seriously think that you and John are going to return to Tooley Street?" She turned to her father, "Besides, there are others to consider now, Papa." Dr Martin waited for his younger daughter to explain her train of thought. Emma nervously smoothed the folds of her dress. "Papa, please do not take offence. I know that you think you're indestructible, but you're not. Both you and mother are getting old now and…"

Her father raised his hand to interrupt her. "In my profession I am acutely aware of a man's mortality, my dear. I am the very last person to think that I'm indestructible."

"Nevertheless," Emma continued, "you and mother are not getting any younger, and Charlotte is now ideally placed to fulfil her duty and care for you in your old age."

Charlotte looked at her father aghast as her sister continued to explain her plan. "Henry's business has never been more demanding, and he needs me to support him in it. I know that Christopher worked very hard, but that is no longer relevant, is it? Mother has told me that you have no plans to remarry, and indeed it would be a brave man who took you on. You're an independent spirit, and no man wants an unruly wife"

Charlotte watched her father in stunned silence, waiting for his reply. He took off his spectacles and rubbed the lenses with his handkerchief before speaking slowly and quietly. "I see you and your mother have everything in hand, my darling. It is so kind of you to have planned out our lives so efficiently, but it really isn't necessary; we are quite capable of organising ourselves, are we not, Charlotte?"

The anger Charlotte had been suppressing since her arrival at Wimpole Street erupted. "Emma, I can see that you and Mother are of one mind when it comes to organising my life, now that you think I have no husband to do it for me. Why you should think I need the likes of you to do that for me I cannot comprehend. Christopher was never one to organise me, or my life; our marriage, unlike yours, was a marriage of equals. It was not one where one partner sought to take advantage over the other – and I'm not unruly!"

Emma folded her arms and threw her head back. "Papa, stop her! She is being unspeakably horrid again. I never try to take advantage of Henry!"

The old man laughed softly. "Haven't I always told you not to start things that you can't finish? Pray continue, Charlotte: I want to hear what you have to say."

"Thank you, Father. It is true my husband is dead and that I'm a free woman, but it's a freedom I have never sought and shall never enjoy. I loved my husband and I shall miss him forever, but I'm not a child and I will live what is left of my life as I see fit."

"Well said!" cheered her father.

"Oh, you always take her side," Emma squealed indignantly, storming out of the room to cry.

4
Starting Again

Sinclair became aware of a soft pink light; he felt comfortable and weirdly light as if he had no body. Had he arrived in that unspecific place his father called "the world to come", he wondered. Should he be preparing a defence for when he came before the Almighty? He was determined he was not going to the other place without a fight. Lying in this state of comfortable bewilderment, he gradually became aware of the rise and fall of his chest. He was breathing and warm, and a wave of relief started somewhere in his brain and flooded through his body. As his consciousness grew, he became aware of the linen against his skin and the warmth of the mattress underneath him. He cautiously opened his eyes. The light was blinding, so he closed them again and listened to the sounds in the room. Close by he could hear the crackle and hiss of a fire, and he thought he could hear someone moving about next to him.

"Ah, Dr Sinclair, I'm glad to see you again," said a familiar voice.

With some discomfort he turned his head towards the voice. "Greenwood," he murmured hoarsely, looking at the dishevelled young man wearing a battered army uniform sitting on a stool next to his bed. "Where am I?"

Greenwood smiled at him, and took the pipe from his mouth. "We, my dear fellow, are in the delightful house of Mr and Mrs Farland in the village of Eastington in Dorset. Mr Farland is the quarryman who pulled us up from that ghastly cliff."

Sinclair nodded, but could remember nothing of a cliff or being brought to a cottage.

"I ended up in the drink for a while, but I wasn't in it as long as you so I didn't get the drubbing you got from the sea. If truth be told we thought you were dead. You were so cold, Sinclair: you were that close to the angels."

"How long have I been here?" the doctor rasped.

"This is your third day. My God, you can snore. I think the local quack gave you some of that magic powder you gave to me the other night."

"I think he did more than that," said Sinclair, feeling the rawness in his backside.

"Oh, yes he did, now you mention it. He stuck a pipe up your arse with a pair of bellows attached to it, and buggered you with tobacco smoke. He said it would warm you up from the inside."

"That accounts for the pain," Sinclair groaned, raising himself onto his elbows. "Do you think I could have some water?"

"Oh, of course, how thoughtless of me," said Greenwood, putting down his pipe and holding the cup to Sinclair's lips.

With his thirst sated, Sinclair asked, "How many of us are there?"

"You mean survivors?"

"Aye." Sinclair ran his bruised and scratched hand through his hair.

"Well, the muster of men alive at Eastington Farm was seventy-four on Saturday, including you and me. Merrick was there, but he's gone to London to make a full report at Company headquarters."

"You mean only seventy-four out of the two hundred and forty who set sail with us?"

"Yes," replied Greenwood neutrally. "I'm told on good authority that eighty-eight people were rescued but fourteen have since died, leaving the likes of you and me and Merrick to tell the tale."

"Sweet Jesus," gasped Sinclair. "Did any of the women survive?" he asked, remembering the petticoat in the surf.

"No," Greenwood replied curtly, pursing his lips and swallowing his pain.

"I'm so sorry, Greenwood."

"Oh, call me Frank: all my friends do," said Greenwood, visibly fighting back his tears.

"Miss Morris was a beautiful and kind young woman, and I know you had formed a special attachment to her," Sinclair said. "I'm sorry."

"Oh, God," Greenwood wailed. "I should have done more for her. I should have saved her. I let her down!"

"You shouldn't blame yourself. When I saw her she was content with her decision to stay on board. From what I learned in the short time I knew her, she would not want you to rebuke yourself on her account."

"Nevertheless, I feel the less for it," bleated Greenwood. "I'm not the man of honour that I wished to be."

"Honour is a rare commodity in difficult circumstances, Frank." Sinclair put his hand on Greenwood's." Don't judge yourself too harshly. Miss Morris made her own decision, and as far as I'm concerned it was the right one for her. She could not swim."

"Thank you, Sinclair: that is very noble of you, but I fear it will be to no avail. I have failed the woman I loved. I thought only of my duty and my own survival. I have dishonoured myself and my family, and that is something I will have to live with for the rest of my life."

Sinclair patted Greenwood's arm in a gesture of reassurance.

"Thank you," Greenwood smiled. "By the way, your pocket watch and three guineas are in the drawer over there. The Farlands are good honest people; we should organise a reward for them. Many of the poor wretches living along this coast would have robbed us and left us to die."

"I agree, but when we get back to London," Sinclair groaned, already exhausted with the effort of speaking.

"I couldn't borrow one of those guineas, could I, to get a ticket to London on the Dorchester Post?" asked Greenwood.

"Only if you get me one at the same time," replied Sinclair, falling back onto his pillow.

"It's done." Greenwood jumped to his feet and made for the drawer. "My father has a house in Westminster. We should head there first, but I think you should take it steady for a few more days."

"Where are my clothes?" said Sinclair, looking around the room.

"Ah, well, there wasn't much left of them after the sea had finished with you, except that neck tie tied around your waist with your treasure." Greenwood held up Sinclair's pocket watch and the three gold guineas. "I'm sure I can find you something to wear if you're not too fussy about where it comes from. Look what the sea turned up for me," he said, lifting his arms above his head and giving a spin. "This is a private's uniform and the boots are two inches too long, but they're better than the ones I took off."

"I'm not fussy as long as they're clean," replied Sinclair gratefully. "Just get me something that will get me to London."

They remained in the care of Mr and Mrs Farland for ten more days. As Sinclair became stronger they walked the cliff tops and Greenwood searched the horizon for any sign of survivors. At night Sinclair heard Greenwood crying in his sleep, and he felt sorry for him. When he slept himself, it was fitful. He woke frequently, not knowing whether he was under the waves or under sheets, and each morning Mrs Farland commented that his bed looked as if he had been fighting in it. The nightmares were terrifying, but every time he woke he told himself that he was dreaming and that there was nothing to fear, and that calmed him. If there was a God, Sinclair decided He had given him a second chance at life and an opportunity to do things differently. The experience of nearly drowning had left him overwhelmingly glad to be alive, but the happy carefree man who had boarded the ship on the first of January called Captain Greenwood was gone.

A fortnight after their rescue, they said their farewells and boarded the mail coach for London. The two men tumbled onto the Holborn Road two days later and headed for a chop house in the Strand to spend what was left of Sinclair's guineas. Sinclair's secondhand boots pinched his frozen feet and the coat Greenwood had procured for him was too tight under the arms and across his chest, making him feel like an overstuffed scarecrow. Greenwood's clothes, on the other hand, were too big for him, and his boots made a soft squelching sound like bellows as he walked. Like Sinclair, Greenwood had lost his heavy greatcoat and hat, and the pair shivered as they made their way through the crowds of Londoners spilling out of the theatres into carriages and taverns under the golden orbs of the city's lights.

At the corner of every street and emerging from the darkest alleyways were girls, little more than children, and cold white-bosomed women with scarlet lips, who blew them kisses and beckoned them towards their lairs with blanched, spidery fingers. There were white-faced men and boys too, wriggling their arses provocatively, showing off their wares.

"Don't think about it, it's not worth it," murmured Sinclair as he caught hold of Greenwood's arm and pushed him on along the crowded pavement. "It's a moment of pleasure for a lifetime of pain."

"I thought that you were all for pleasure, Dr Sinclair. Didn't you say that you despised your father for being against it?"

"Aye, I did, but it's more complicated than that, Frank. I know what a dose of the clap does to a man, and believe me you don't want it, no matter how much pleasure there is in acquiring it. And as you're asking," he said, guiding his friend across the busy road, "I believe it's a man's moral duty to strive for happiness, not just pleasure, and what is more I intend to spend the rest of my life doing so."

"Happiness? How can that be a moral duty? Most of what makes me happy my mother considers immoral," Greenwood laughed.

"That's probably because it is," replied Sinclair, with a knowing but friendly smile. They continued along the thoroughfare arm in arm, Greenwood's boots squelching and Sinclair's pinching. "You see, Frank, the pursuit of happiness is different from the pursuit of pleasure. True happiness cannot be found in the material indulgence of our passions, or by denying them."

"How the blazes do you get it then?" demanded Frank.

"Well, that's the tricky bit. It seems to me that at times a man's life is a constant battle between his passion and his reason, but I believe that if there is a God, which on many a day I doubt, then He should help us to balance these two forces within us so that we may be happy. Happiness as far as I am concerned, my dear fellow, is about having good friends like you; having enough money to live comfortably with a wife and children; and, of course, being in good health. That is one of the reasons I chose medicine over the Church as my career."

"I don't think you'd have made a good vicar, Jamie. My brother is a vicar, and you're much more fun than him."

"You're right: I would have been a terrible vicar. I struggle to believe in any god most days, and as for the Church, well, my father's view of it at any rate is abhorrent to me. A man cannot live by denying his nature or by abandoning his reason for a belief in a supernatural being that dispenses random acts of benevolence and punishment. If a man is to be happy he must learn to live with and control his passions, enjoy what is good in life and abhor what is evil."

"My God, did you think of all this yourself?"

"No, Frank, I got it all from books. I could lend them to you if they weren't at the bottom of the sea with everything else I possessed."

"That would be absolutely no use," retorted Frank.

"Why?"

"Because I wouldn't read them," Greenwood replied, making them both roar with laughter.

When they found the chop house they ordered beef steaks and ale for sixpence. As the waiter cleared their plates Sinclair took out his pocket watch and checked the hour. It was past nine o'clock. He flipped the case closed and rolled it slowly with his fingers, then he kissed the back and replaced it in the pocket of his coat.

"Why do you do that?" asked Greenwood.

"Do what?" retorted Sinclair, irritated that his friend had noticed the little ritual.

"Roll your watch between your fingers, then kiss it before you put it back in your pocket."

"It's a habit, that's all. It reminds me of someone."

"A woman?" said Frank, tilting his head to the side.

"When you were growing up, did your brothers tell you it wasn't polite to ask questions?"

"Of course they did, but it's advice I've always chosen to ignore. I find that people rarely volunteer interesting or important information. I suppose my position is born of being the youngest in the family, and always being the last person to be told anything."

"Well, being the older and wiser of the two of us, I say we get to your father's house in Westminster before we're robbed and left for dead in the street," said Sinclair, rising to leave.

"Absolutely, old man; we should get going. We don't want to upset Ma and Pa by arriving too late, do we?"

They made their way out into the cold night again, Sinclair in the lead. The Strand was still busy with carriages and night-time revellers as they struck out towards Westminster. Being short of cash they decided to walk; as well as saving them money it would do them good. They had been cooped up for too long, first in that ill-fated ship, then in the cottage in Wiltshire and finally in the coach from Dorchester. They strolled toward the Charing Cross and turned into Parliament Street, then made their way past the Abbey and on into Tothill Street. It was past ten o'clock, and heavy rain was falling as they meandered through the warren of unlit streets leading to Great Peter Street and the Greenwoods' house at Good Acre Court.

"I think about her, you know," said Greenwood, wiping the rain from his face with his sleeve.

"You mean Miss Morris," replied Sinclair.

"Yes, I dream about her every night, and it's not a pleasant dream. I see her in the ship's saloon in that lovely blue dress and she's calling for me. She reaches out, but I can't reach her. Then I see her floating in the water like a marionette. Her face is angry and she hates me."

Sinclair put his arm around his companion. "It's only a dream; it's not real. You know, I often wake in a sweat not knowing where I am and struggling for breath. But I remind myself it's just a dream and that I'm all right. You should do the same."

"Is that your advice, as a doctor?"

"Aye, it is. I know you feel you should have done more to help her, but you must understand there was nothing that could have been done to save her. Trust me, Frank, when I saw her before I left the ship she was content; you have it on my honour."

"Thank you. I know you're doing your best to help me, but I'm a disgrace and I know it."

"No; believe me you're not. These bad dreams will pass."

They arrived at Good Acre Court soaked and shivering. Frank rapped on the door, but there was no reply. When he rapped the knocker again a footman, a boy in his teens wearing a crimson coat over his bed shirt, opened the door a crack and peered at the two bedraggled men.

"The master's not here. Come back tomorrow," the boy complained, slamming the door shut.

Frank thumped the door and shouted, "It's Mr Frank Greenwood: let me in. We'll catch our deaths out here."

The boy opened the door a crack again, and this time Frank charged at it before he could slam it shut, sending the lad tumbling. A light appeared at the top of the stairs and a man dressed in a nightshirt and nightcap shouted, "Who goes there?"

"It's Mr Frank Greenwood, sir; son of Sir Bramwell."

"He's dead, you vile scoundrel. Now get out of this house before I fetch a pistol."

"Sir, if you would only look at me you would see that I'm not dead. I sent my father a letter from Dorchester a week ago to let him know that I had survived the wreck of the *Sherwell* and was on my way to London."

The man in the nightcap slowly inched his way down the stairs. "A letter from Dorchester addressed to Sir Bramwell?"

"Yes."

"We did receive such a letter, but we sent it on to Panton Hall as Sir Bramwell was not at home." The man came closer and held

65

the candle to Greenwood's face. "But that does not negate the fact that I do not know you gentlemen."

Exasperated with the man, Frank let out a sigh. "My father is the Member of Parliament for Staffordshire, my mother is Lady Frances and I have three brothers who are all older than me: Bramwell, Sandon and Tobias. I am the youngest and named after my mother. The reason you do not recognise me, sir, is that I am dressed in the clothes of an ordinary soldier. By that I mean my friend and I are dressed in clothes retrieved from the wreck."

The man in the nightshirt still looked sceptical.

"Now listen to me," Frank jabbed the manservant's head with his forefinger, "I know you must be new around here, whatever your name is, but my friend Dr Sinclair and I have had a very long day and we wish to go to bed. I command you to summon the household that fires be lit and that clean linen is put on our beds. If you do not do as I say immediately my father will hear about it, do you understand, you numskull?"

"Very well, sir," the man conceded, visibly shaken by the force of Frank's rebuke. Then he shouted, "It's Master Frank with a friend. Raise the household and make up the beds."

* * *

It was ten o'clock when Charlotte Leadam climbed the narrow, twisting staircase to the third floor of 124 Cheapside, where Henry Bowman kept a small and untidy office. She found the door with the brass plate bearing his name and thumped it once with her gloved fist before walking in. Her brother-in-law leapt out of his chair, sending his wig flying towards her. She caught it on the edge of the desk and handed it back to him, then seated herself in the visitor's chair in front of his cluttered desk.

66

"Charlotte, sister, welcome. Emma told me that you would call today," he squirmed as he sorted through the papers in front of him.

"I have no doubt she did, Henry." Charlotte replied, sucking in her anger.

"You are here to hear the contents of Christopher's will," he said, rummaging again in the pile of papers on his desk.

"Yes, I am. I understand there are things that I have to do to set his affairs in order."

Henry rummaged some more. "Ah, here it is. I had it to hand as I knew you were coming." He handed her a roll of parchment covered in smooth cursive writing without gaps or punctuation. She looked down at the closely written text, not knowing where to start.

"The gist of it is that Christopher left everything to you; the house, his practice for what it's worth, and all his goods and chattels. You are now a woman of property, dear sister, but not much income. I'm not sure how much cash there is in the bank. I will have to write to ask them to assign the funds to you. I will, of course, do that today."

"Thank you, Henry. I would expect nothing less," she replied, finding a space for the parchment on the table.

"As to other matters," he paused before speaking with a note of resignation in his voice. "I'm very sorry about what happened on Saturday. Emma had no right to say what she did."

"Thank you. My sister has a good husband, although she does not appreciate it. She's far too easily led by our mother; you have my sympathy."

As much as he loved Emma, Henry knew that his independent minded sister-in-law was right. His wife was her mother's poodle when it came to matters of family. He watched as Charlotte stood up and moved towards the small fireplace in the corner of the depressing little room. He marvelled at her courage and strength. She removed her gloves and warmed her hands by the fire as she peered out of the grubby third-floor window onto Cheapside, watching men and women the size of mice scuttling about and a stream of carriages and wagons ploughing up and down the road.

"You will have to place an advertisement for a creditors' meeting in the *London Gazette*," Henry continued. "You set a time and place for people who are owed money from Christopher's estate to present their accounts. He was good with money so there should not be any problems. I'm sure you will find his outstanding bills in his office."

"Yes, I know where they are," Charlotte replied, still looking out of the window and thinking how odd it was to be speaking of death in the midst of such life.

"Good. If you wish I can join you for the creditors' meeting."

"I would like that very much, Henry," she replied, grateful for her brother-in-law's kindness. "When could you let me know how much cash is available?" she enquired smoothly having regained her composure.

"I should have a reply by the end of the week. In the meantime, should you need to borrow some money..." he said uncomfortably.

"No, that will not be necessary; but thank you for your offer." She put on her gloves to leave.

"Charlotte?"

"Yes, Henry."

"How are you going to manage without Christopher's income?"

"I don't know yet. I have to think about it," she said, opening the door.

"Oh, and you must write to the people who rent his properties in Yorkshire to let them know that you're their new landlord."

Charlotte was surprised. "I didn't know he had any property in Yorkshire."

"Oh, it's not much, just a few acres of pasture and a couple of houses in Hull. I think he inherited them from his father," said Henry, recalling his conversation with Christopher when he had commissioned the will.

While Charlotte was in Henry's office, John was making his way to Tooley Street with the help of a barrow boy, whom his mother had hired to transport their luggage on the final leg of their journey home. Following the scruffy urchin, he crossed onto London Bridge and joined the column of people making their way to Southwark and Bermondsey. The urchin pushed his way through the crowds, eager to get back to the City to find his next job and his next sixpence.

On the bridge John paused for a moment to look over the parapet at the water rushing through the starlings. Then he turned his gaze to the City, with its rows of fine yellow-brick warehouses and the magisterial dome of St Paul's rising behind them. The City was the respectable side of London: the place where the merchants and bankers lived, the side of town his grandmother approved of. Beyond them were the neoclassical columns of the new government offices at Somerset House, where the revenue men inspected and taxed goods arriving from all over the world; where the Navy Offices were and the galleries of the Royal Academy. Below him the watermen were plying their trade from shore to shore, carrying people and goods in small rowing boats across the rushing sludge-grey water. London was the greatest port and the greatest metropolis in the world and John loved it, with all its contrasts and quirks; its filth and its wealth. To him it was the best place in the entire world. It was the place where vessels from Jamaica brought sweet candy-cones of crystal sugar, barrels of fiery rum and gallons of sticky black molasses; where the East India Company landed lead-lined chests of tea and spices, Kashmiri shawls, Chinese silks, Arab horses, precious stones, fine painted porcelains, and beautifully printed calicoes and muslins. It was the place where sumptuous Arctic furs and timber came ashore from the snowy wastes of Russia; where the Hudson's Bay Company traded thousands of beaver pelts; where Chesapeake and Virginian tobacco was landed from America; and where the wine and brandy from Europe started its journey to the dining tables of England.

The south bank was completely different, with its hotchpotch of clapperboard sheds, jetties and wooden wharfs. The warehouses there fed the metropolis, and it was the place where the city's sick and its poor came to be treated at its great teaching hospitals – St Thomas', St Bartholomew's and Guy's. It was the great city's dark underbelly, the place where the less fortunate ended up in its debtors' prisons and where men came to protest against Parliament on Potter's Field.

John looked along the bridge, but the barrow boy was already out of sight. He pushed through the throng of people into Duke Street, where he saw the urchin heading into the Borough High Street. Chasing the ragged little nipper, he finally caught up with him as he turned into Tooley Street. He followed him past the limestone facade of St Olave's Church with its round arched windows and high square tower; past his old school with its red brick Elizabethan gatehouse; past the steaming clapperboard brewery and the weatherboarded warehouses of Chamberlain's and Topping's Wharf; then across the busy street filled with lines of carts piled high with baskets and sacks; and to a terrace of substantial four-storey timber and brick houses with steeply pitched roofs and dormer windows. The boy was standing at the last but one house in the terrace, with a golden pestle and mortar sign over the door, between the house of the corn merchant Mr Naylor at number sixty-seven and the physician Dr Collingwood at number sixty-three. John joined the boy outside number sixty-five and read the familiar sign: 'C.R. LEADAM, SURGEON & APOTHECARY'. He pushed the front door open as the barrow boy deposited their bags on the pavement. At the same moment their housekeeper Mrs Dredge came crashing through the scullery door at such a speed John was sure she would fall over. He put his arms out to steady the elderly woman, but she grasped him tightly and hugged him.

"Oh, Master John, I've been that worried about you," she sobbed. "Where's the mistress?"

"She's at Uncle Henry's sorting things out," John replied, happy to be in the comfort of her arms.

"Master William is with Mr Hoares on his rounds. They'll be back for lunch. Oh, I'm so glad to 'ave you back and so sad about Mr Christopher. I just can't believe he's not coming home no more."

"Neither can we, Mrs Dredge. We'll have to manage without him now."

"I know, lad, but it's not going to be easy. It's never easy for a woman on her own."

* * *

71

Although the house seemed the same as it always had, everything about it was different now there was no resident surgeon. William Whitfield, his father's sixteen-year-old apprentice, and his old friend Mr Hoares had kept the apothecary shop and surgery open, but now his father's absence was permanent there was no morning or evening surgery, and anyone who called for treatment was told to go elsewhere.

With no school to go to, John found himself mooning around the house looking for distractions. He sat with Mrs Dredge in the scullery for hours, recounting the awful events in Yorkshire, talking about his father as he nursed Queenie their tortoiseshell tabby on his lap and drank cups of tea. He did not want to go out and he had no interest in books; he was at a loss as to what to do with himself. It seemed that his world had come to a juddering halt and he had no idea if it would ever start up again. He was worried too: worried about his mother because she was so sad and exhausted; and because he did not know how they would live when his father's money ran out.

Charlotte took the tea things down to Mrs Dredge in the scullery. "Everything all right, duck?" enquired the old woman, who had been her housekeeper since she was married but was now her helpmate and her second, kinder, mother.

"Everything's all right, thank you. I'll need some more tea when Mr Hoares arrives. In the meantime I'm going to go through Christopher's things."

"No you're not, young lady. You go and have a lie down. I'll make sure there's tea ready when Mr Hoares arrives. He'll talk to the boys first so I'll have plenty of time."

Charlotte was so exhausted that she was happy to obey the old woman. Upstairs in the front bedroom she lay on the bed she had shared with her husband, thinking about her life and the

72

house. The bed was old and unfashionable, like all her furniture and the house for that matter, but it was the place she had made her life, where she had made the transition from innocent young girl to wife and from wife to mother. The bed held so many happy memories for her. She was glad that Christopher had not died in it, for she was not sure how she would feel about sleeping there if he had.

The winter sun was fading, leaving the warm red glow from the coal fire to light the room. Through the window, Charlotte watched as the pattern of roofs and chimneys on the other side of the road turned into sharp, angular silhouettes.

Eventually she lit a candle and watched the circle of dull yellow light flicker on the low uneven ceiling that was as familiar to her as her own skin. She brushed away the morbid and frightening thoughts that were drifting uninvited into her mind and thought instead about the house she loved.

Over the years she had made it her own, choosing the paint and paper for the walls, the drapes for the casement windows and the linen for the table and the beds. The house had its faults, the least of which, as far as Charlotte was concerned, being its location south of the river. There was a smell from the paint factory across the road and a constant rattle of carts and wagons along the cobbled street. The old house had irritating uneven treads on the stairs, rippled planking on the landings, wavy plaster and wavy walls, and cracked and uneven ceilings, but despite all these imperfections, or perhaps because of them, she had grown to love the place, and she did not want to give it up.

Since their return from Yorkshire, she had succeeded in keeping the apothecary shop open with Mr Hoares' help; but she knew that the patterns she had lived by for the past fifteen years had broken irrevocably with her husband's death, and that she had to find a new way to live as a widow. She just wasn't sure how she was going to do it, and if she was honest she was too tired to think about it.

Downstairs in the shop John idled away the afternoon pretending to read Mr Sharpe's A 'Treatise on the Operations of Surgery' while he watched his father's apprentice, William, gazing out of the window. Tooley Street was a narrow and winding thoroughfare running east to west parallel to the river. It was always busy, but William was not watching the carts and drays piled high with goods from the warehouses but a line of pretty girls from Mrs Tucker's Day School, who were making their way towards St Olave's Church.

William was a clever but shy young man from Dover, whose aim was to become a ship's surgeon like his father. He had lived with the Leadams for two years, and in that time his once clear complexion had mutated into a landscape of angry pimples and downy whiskers, and his once luxurious dark brown hair now clung to his head like an iron helmet. The effect of this ugly transition was acute self-consciousness.

"You should be working, William; Mr Hoares will be here soon," rebuked John from behind his book.

"I am. I was just looking out of the window for a moment," William replied, as the gaggle of girls passed in their pretty bonnets and swishing skirts.

"You were looking at those stupid girls from Mrs Tucker's," challenged John.

"No, I wasn't," William lied, flushing red and resenting being told what to do by the younger boy.

"You know what my father said about girls?" John continued, sensing his advantage.

"Yes, of course I do. Beware beautiful women; Hermes gave them deceptive hearts and lying tongues."

"So stop looking out of the window and get on with your work," John snapped, unable to see why the girls were of any interest to William at all.

When Mr Hoares arrived later that afternoon he was tired after a long day of visiting not only his own patients but also those of his former business partner. Between them Mr Hoares and Mr Leadam had a large client book of chronically sick and incurable patients in the City. The elderly man started by checking off the list of tasks he had given the boys that morning. John had delivered all of the day's medicines and completed his prescribed reading, whilst William, being the older of the two apprentices, had attended and dressed the wounds of their patients at Guy's and written up the patient records, in case their cases were called for discussion at the hospital committee on Friday.

"William, how many patients do we have left at Guy's?" asked Mr Hoares.

"Mr Leadam has three patients, sir, and you have four."

"What is the prognosis for Mr Leadam's three?

"The patient with scrofula has the typical abscess on the neck and is suffering from a persistent fever together with the usual weight loss. The man has already had surgery to remove the abscess, but it has returned with increased vigour and size. I'm proceeding with Mr Leadam's prescriptions for the man's comfort. I believe he has less than a week to live."

"Good work, William. And the others?"

"There is a woman with an abscess in her gum. The rotten tooth was removed and the wound drained at St Thomas' but the infection persisted, so she was moved to Guy's and assigned to Mr Leadam just after Christmas. She has a persistent fever and has been bled twice by you since then. The inflammation seems to have progressed to her brain, and she is unlikely to live to the end of the week."

"That will be an interesting case for post mortem. Make sure you're there if they open her up."

William nodded respectfully and continued with his report. "And the final case sir is a young boy, aged twelve, who was run over by a carriage on Christmas Eve. He had his left leg and arm amputated at St Thomas' but has since developed gangrene in the leg wound. He was bled yesterday and is comfortable on a prescription of Peruvian bark and opium. The sepsis will most likely take its course over the next twenty-four hours."

"Yes, I remember it well. Poor boy. I am glad his anguish will be over soon," Mr Hoares said, wiping his glasses and adjusting his short grey wig. "Have you made up the medicine supplies and bills for tomorrow's patients?"

"Yes, sir. John has made up the pills and I have made up the powders and liquid medicines, which Mrs Leadam has checked ready for delivery tomorrow morning."

"Good work, boys. I'll see Mrs Leadam now. Off you go."

Upstairs, Charlotte poured tea for herself and Mr Hoares, offering him a slice of Madeira cake. He declined, saying that he would prefer to smoke instead. She sensed that he had something on his mind and that their meeting was to be confined strictly to business matters. Lighting his pipe, he stood by the fire. Charlotte had known him for nearly half her life and he was her senior by at least twenty years, but he was a friend. He sucked in the mellow tobacco smoke and blew it out slowly and thoughtfully. "Charlotte, you know that as well as being Christopher's former partner he was my friend."

"Yes, Frederick, I know that," she replied, sipping her tea.

"You know also that when I think about him, I think of him as a father would think of his son, especially since Marie and I lost our own son in the American War. You and John are very dear to us, and I will do everything in my power to help you."

"I'm so very grateful to you."

With a sigh of weary resignation, Mr Hoares continued. "I'm an old man and I feel the burden of my years. I would love to be able to take on Christopher's patients, but as you know with Marie being so unwell I cannot. Christopher's practice at the hospital is naturally running down and I have started to recommend his private patients to other practitioners in the district. What I am saying is that I think I can clear what is left of Christopher's practice fairly quickly, and that I should press ahead and do so."

Charlotte raised her tired eyes to him. "Dearest friend, I'm aware of your position, and it vexes me greatly that I have used you so very poorly in these weeks since my return from Yorkshire. I know that our arrangement was to be temporary, and I'm very grateful to you for all you've done for me since Christopher passed."

"Charlotte," the old man protested; but she would not let him continue.

"I'm most grateful to you and Marie; we could not have wanted for better friends in this time of trouble. It has taken me some time to think about the future. As a woman I obviously have no profession, and although I am as good as any man as an apothecary I'm not able to earn a living from it."

He shook his head. "That, it seems, is the way our society is organised, and as much as I would like it to be different I can do nothing to change it."

77

"That is why I have decided to take your advice: to close the practice and to take in paying boarders. Of course our circumstances will be much reduced, but it will enable me to maintain this house and ensure that John is apprenticed to a good master."

"I think that is a very wise decision, my dear. What arrangements will you make for Mr Whitfield?"

"I shall have to return his fees to his father. I shall miss the boy; he's become like a son to me these last two years."

"I'm so sorry it's come to this, Charlotte, I truly am. With respect to Mr Whitfield I may be able to find him a place with another master."

"I think his mother and father would appreciate that. I'll write to his mother and ask for her permission, as his father is still in Canada. Frederick, would you do me one last favour?"

"Of course, my dear. What is it that you would like me to do?"

"Could you help me find a master surgeon for John to study with?"

"It would be an honour. I shall make enquiries with my colleagues immediately."

"Thank you, dear friend." Then she thought about the creditors meeting. "I've placed an advertisement in the 'London Gazette' giving notice of a creditors' meeting at the Red Lion on the twenty-eighth, to wind up Christopher's affairs. It would be helpful if you would let me have an account of what I owe you before then."

"As you wish," he replied, "but there's no hurry on my part. I'm glad to be of service."

5

The Man in the Beaver Hat

The door to Henry Bowman's office was open when Sinclair arrived. Henry was at his desk engrossed in a document, and did not notice him waiting at the door. Eventually, Sinclair spoke. "Good morning, Mr Bowman. I'm glad to see that some foolish knave has provided you with work."

The attorney sat bolt upright, startled to see a man in the room. "My God, Dr Sinclair, I thought I'd never hear your weaselly Scottish voice again. I was convinced you were dead."

"Well, I very nearly was," Sinclair smiled.

"My goodness, this is a turn-up. I was just about to write to your sister in Edinburgh with the bad news."

"Well, luckily for me at least, that won't be necessary. But I fear it will be unfortunate for you, as there will be no estate to mine."

"Now, now, Dr Sinclair, that is unjust, very unjust. An executor must make a living too," chided the attorney, standing up and walking around to the front of his desk.

"Aye, I suppose you're right. You lawyers can't help it if people think you're self-serving cheats."

"The reputation of my profession is held in no less esteem than that of your own. No one submits himself to a quack unless he has to. At least I can say that the clients of the law are usually alive when we've finished with them, unlike so many of yours." They laughed and the two men embraced. "Oh, it's so good to see you, Sinclair. I thought you were a goner."

"Well, by some miracle I survived, but I'm in desperate straits, Henry. Everything I own is at the bottom of the sea."

"I can see that by the look of you. What's this?" Bowman said, pulling at Sinclair's beard.

"That's not the worst of it. Look at this." Sinclair pushed up his sleeves to reveal lacerations and bruises.

"My God, and what are these awful clothes, my friend?" Bowman said, pulling at the lapels of Sinclair's tight-fitting coat. "And that beard has definitely got to go," he said, tugging at it again. "You look even more like a Scottish weasel than you did before you left."

"I'm not joking, Henry. I only have what I'm standing up in and a few coins in my pocket."

Bowman began to pack up his papers and put on his coat. "Come; let's to Garraway's. We can get coffee, and the place is much more convivial than this dreary little office," he said, ushering Sinclair out of the door.

"Only if you're paying. I'm broke."

"I'll lend you some cash, then you can pay me back," sighed Bowman, with a twinkle in his eye.

"I thought I was the parsimonious Scot."

"You are, but you're not very good at it."

"Aye, well, I shall have to take lessons from a blood-sucking Englishmen like you, I suppose." Sinclair laughed, and gave his friend a fraternal slap on the back.

Over several dishes of hot, treacly coffee, Sinclair recounted what had happened on the '*Sherwell*'. The coffee house fell silent as the customers strained to hear every detail of Sinclair's first-hand account of the tragedy, which had been the subject of every paper and magazine in town. Henry was transfixed. "My God, you survived all that? It's a miracle. What are you going to do now?"

"I'll have to decide if I still want to go to India, and what I'll do if I decide not to. That position with the East India Company solved a lot of problems for me."

"All families are tricky, Sinclair, I can vouch for that. Think of all the trouble I have with Emma's mother and the rest of my in-laws. Surely you don't have to go all the way to India to get away from yours? Wouldn't London be far enough?"

"You don't know my father. And I'm broke. I need a job that pays well, and there are few that are attractive to me. I don't want to be an anatomist. I'm not a showman. I went into medicine to make people well, not to carve them up in public and present their innards in glass jars."

"I'm sure we'll have you back at St George's."

"Thanks, Henry, but I don't have twenty-five pounds to pay for the privilege or any books or equipment. No, I have to give my future some serious consideration."

After leaving the coffee house they went to a bank in Cornhill, where Henry vouched for Sinclair so that he could access the small pot of money he had set aside for emergencies. He withdrew ten guineas and went straight to a bootmaker in the Strand, and then to an inexpensive tailor behind Covent Garden to be fitted for a new coat and breeches. On the way back to Westminster he stopped at a stationer's shop, and bought paper and ink to write to his sister.

Sinclair thought long and hard about his future as he sat in his room at Green Acre Court. He consulted with his employers at the East India Company Offices and found that the position he had applied for was still available to him. The problem was that if he wanted it he would have to take the next ship to India, which left in a fortnight. He thought about the tiny cabin on the *'Sherwell'* and his fight to stay alive; then he wrote:

Dearest Morag,
You may already know of the terrible disaster
that befell the Sherwell, the ship I took to India
on New Year's Day. The story is in every
newspaper and magazine so I'm sure that the
news is also widespread in Scotland. By now,
you will realise that I am writing to you as one
of the lucky survivors of that ill-fated ship. I not
only survived but I was uninjured, and I am
tremendously grateful for that as so many good
souls were lost that day.
The position I intended to take in Bengal is still
available to me, but I have decided that I shall
not put myself forward for it again. In truth, I
cannot face the prospect of life on board a ship

so soon after this calamitous experience. I shall
stay in London and seek a position here.
I know that you and Andrew will want me to
return to Edinburgh, but you will understand
that apart from you I have no attachment to the
city; in fact there are many reasons for my
antithesis towards it, including most obviously
our father. When you speak to him on this
subject, as I know you must, please assure him
that I am still resolute in the opinions he finds
abhorrent, despite this close encounter with
death. Consequently, we must remain estranged.
I send you my most loving regards,
Jamie.

Then he wrote to the East India Company, declining their offer of the post of Assistant to the Chief Medical Officer in Calcutta, and gave both letters to a manservant to post.

"That's two of us out of work then," said Greenwood, shovelling down his beef and dumplings at supper. "I've resigned my commission too. I'm never getting on a ship again, Sinclair. It's terra firma for me from now on."

"So a glass or two of wine by way of consolation would be in order," said Sinclair.

"Father has plenty of claret in his cellar," his friend replied, pouring two glasses and handing one to Sinclair.

"Have you any idea what you will do?"

"Absolutely none whatsoever, old man; I'm not sure what I can do now I'm no longer a soldier. I suppose I could always take myself off to the plantation in Jamaica but I don't fancy that. As I said I'm not getting on another bloody ship."

"I'll have to look for a position at one of the voluntary hospitals. I was hoping that I'd never have to go into one of those sanctimonious places again. It's not the patients that get me down, they can't help being sick or poor, it's all the praying and grovelling. Those hospitals are full of the most unpleasant people, Frank – pompous and incompetent men, self-satisfied arrivistes and simpering clergymen."

"Oh, life's full of grovelling and doing what somebody else wants, in my experience. Just try being in the Army."

"I know it has to be done from time to time, but I'm not good at it. Those poor patients have to pray for their souls and give thanks to their benefactors at least three times a day no matter how sick they are. A lot of them are at death's door, but they still have to get on their knees and give thanks to God and their wealthy benefactors."

"But it's better than being left to die alone and without any care, isn't it?" said Greenwood.

"Aye, I suppose when you put it like that it's a small price to pay for a warm bed, medicine and a bowl of broth, but it sticks in my craw. Why should these people be grateful for so little when the undeserving seem to have so much? Besides, this so-called charity work is false. It's the very thing that enables surgeons like Hunter to build their reputations and make fortunes in the City."

"So why can't you be like them, Jamie?"

"Because staff appointments aren't made on merit, they're made through connection and patronage, and I won't prostitute myself for these corrupt men of money. I put my principles aside to join the East India Company. I thought I could make myself happy by getting rich in the colonies, but thankfully I was saved from that folly. I now realise a man must be happy with his conscience if he's to be happy at all."

"That's the trouble with principles; they're very expensive for a poor man. Most of my father's friends, who are rich of course, claim to have principles, but somehow they make sure that they never have any that stop them making money or for which they cannot get others to pay."

"I think you're an even greater cynic than me, Frank."

"Oh, that's quite possible. My whole life has been spent in the company of politicians: I don't need the newspapers to know how they think. Have you seen the 'Recorder'?"

"No I haven't. What are they saying?"

"Terrible things, Jamie," said Greenwood, downing his third glass of claret. "They say that the men who survived the 'Sherwell', that's you and me and most of the ship's crew, were inattentive to their duties, and spent their time lying in their hammocks when they should have been manning the pumps as the captain had instructed."

"That's outrageous! Five of them died when the mast was cut down, and I personally operated on seven men with Mr Hodge."

"I know, and it was only when the ship crashed into the rocks that the pumping stopped. The 'Gentleman's Magazine' has questioned the story's validity but the 'Recorder' is sticking to its version. And you won't believe this," Greenwood continued, downing another glass of wine. "They said that the officers failed to stop their men going on deck when the ship ran aground, and that's why so many of them were washed away. That's me they're libelling Jamie!"

"How dare they! You're a guid cheil, tak na heed of 'em," said Sinclair breaking into Scots to express his outrage.

"Thank you, whatever it was you said. I was the last to leave that stinking hold even though I wanted to be the first. In fact, Allsop told me to hold the men back and get myself off, but I didn't in the end: I thought it dishonourable. I told my men they'd be washed overboard if they went on deck, but they couldn't wait to get off that stinking ship. How could I stop them? And what difference would it have made if I had? The ship was smashed to smithereens."

"You did your best, Frank," Sinclair consoled his friend. "We all ended up being washed overboard in the end. It was only the lucky ones like you and me who could swim who stood any chance of surviving."

"I know, but nobody will believe our side of the story after they've read this wretched stuff, will they? Merrick and Allsop have damned everyone except themselves and the captain, and they were the very people responsible for the ship!"

"The bastards," seethed Sinclair. "It seems to me that they're making the captain into a hero to distract everyone's attention away from their own responsibility."

"You're right. By the way, his body has turned up in Christ Church."

"Whose body?" demanded Sinclair, smacking his lips with anger as he downed another glass of Sir Bramwell's best claret.

"Captain Richards, of course; they're planning to give him a fancy funeral. The 'Gentleman's Magazine' has already printed a eulogy to him for his courage and self-sacrifice."

"What sacrifice?"

"Well, it seems that he's to be made a hero because he stayed with his family when he could have saved himself," said Greenwood, feeling that this was not his idea of a hero. "I think he was a good man, but it seems unfair to focus on him when so many others perished that night."

"Aye, it does."

"And it's not as if he were doing it all for King and Country. He told me that he fully expected to make ten thousand pounds on the voyage with his own personal trade; and of course he planned to marry his daughters and his niece off to some wealthy gent when he got to Madras into the bargain."

"I think everyone except you and me were on the make on that ship," said Sinclair.

Greenwood agreed.

"And I don't suppose they mentioned the fact that the ship was leaking like a sieve by the third day of our journey?"

"No mention of it at all," Greenwood slurred, opening another bottle of wine.

"I'm sure that must have had something to do with why the ship was so difficult to manoeuvre that night. We should have had a straight run into Studland Bay but they couldn't control the ship, could they?" said Sinclair, shaking his head. "I'm sure the captain was under pressure not to turn back. If he'd done so when we first got into trouble, the story would have been entirely different. Everyone who died would still be alive and we'd be on our way to Bengal."

"You're right, Jamie. I'm going to get my father onto this when he returns to Parliament."

"Aye, that's a good idea. We need to know the truth."

"To the truth," said Greenwood, raising his glass with a slur.

"To the truth," echoed Sinclair, quaffing his third glass of wine.

* * *

Charlotte was in the Red Lion Inn with Henry, waiting for her husband's creditors to present their accounts. She felt confident that none of the outstanding bills would be large, but had put ten pounds in the little cash box to be sure she could cover all eventualities.

For the first time she was wearing her new mourning clothes; a respectable but uncomplicated widow's cap and a full-length black cloak, both in black bombazine silk. The silk was not shiny like taffeta, but had a sombre matte finish that drained the colour from her face, making her look more tired and wan than she was. The clothes were a sign to the world that she was respecting her husband's memory, but they also told the world that she was lonely and vulnerable.

They sat in the crowded public bar on a high-backed settle with a long polished table in front of them and waited for the creditors to arrive. The Red Lion was a rambling old place that backed onto the river. The landlord, Mr Jelly, ran a respectable house with a clientele of local merchants and dealers, and the surgeons from the nearby hospitals at Guy's and St Thomas'. On Saturday afternoons workers from the nearby warren of warehouses and factories joined the usual clientele, spending their hard-earned cash on flagons of white-topped ale and plump hot pies.

At two o'clock, Mr Jones from the tobacconists in Tooley Street was the first to present his bill for ten ounces of pipe tobacco, followed by Mr White from the chemists in Pall Mall half a hour later with a bill for a small order of mercury, and at three o'clock Mr Hall of Hall's Coffee House in the Borough presented Charlotte with a bill for coffee totalling five shillings and sixpence. Thinking that their business was soon to be concluded, Bowman fetched himself a tankard of ale from the bar. "Well, everything seems to be going according to plan, Charlotte," he said. "I didn't think we'd see many people today.

When this is all over you will have more than a hundred and twenty pounds in the bank, which will see you through this year nicely."

"I must say I'm very relieved to get this done with. When can we leave?"

"We must stay until four o'clock as advertised in the 'London Gazette'," Henry said, looking at his time piece: it was two minutes to four. Just as he was putting his watch in his pocket, he spotted a tall man in a dark overcoat wearing a smart brown beaver hat. The man's expensive attire made him stand out against the crowds of black coated medical men and warehouse workers.

The man in the beaver hat approached them. "Sir, are you the gentleman handling the estate of the late Mr Christopher Leadam of Tooley Street, Southwark?"

"Yes, I am," Bowman replied, doing his best to hide the astonishment he was feeling. He had never seen the man before, and from the look on his sister-in-law's face neither had she. The stranger took a large scroll of paper from under his coat and presented it to him. "I've come from Lloyd's Insurance Company to present a bill in respect of the underwriters of the East India Company ship the 'Sherwell', the ship that recently foundered in Dorset. In particular I represent the interests of the ship's owners Lord Baunstone and Mr Monsell who were its 'husbands' and the people who chartered it for their consortia."

"I know of it, sir, but pray what has it to do with my dear departed brother-in-law, Christopher Leadam?"

"Your brother-in-law was part of the Halls' Coffee House Syndicate, which underwrote the ship to the value of ten thousand pounds."

Henry turned to his sister-in-law. Her face was white: ten thousand pounds was an unimaginable sum of money. Charlotte felt time freeze, her body swayed and the room began to spin. She opened her mouth to speak but no words came out. She felt Henry's hand on her arm, but she was not reassured.

"Ten thousand pounds you say, sir," said Henry, as he opened the scroll and looked down the list of names.

"'Tis but a fraction of its worth, sir; the wreck represents a loss to the company of sixty thousand pounds."

Charlotte looked over her brother-in-law's shoulder, running her panic-stricken eyes up and down the list. Then she spotted it and gasped. Christopher's name was about halfway down with his signature beside it.

Henry raised his head slowly. "How much does my brother-in-law owe, sir?"

The man pulled out another document and passed it to Henry. "Five hundred pounds, sir, and I should be grateful if I could take it today."

Charlotte found her voice. "This cannot be true, Henry," she said. "I knew nothing of it."

Henry took her shaking hands in his and looked directly into her terrified eyes. "I'll look into this, Charlotte. Now go home and I'll see you after I've spoken to this gentleman in private." He turned to the man. "I am my late brother-in-law's executor and attorney, and as such I will speak for my client, who is Mr Leadam's widow." The man in the beaver hat nodded his agreement, and Henry indicated to Charlotte again that she should leave.

Somehow she got home. Once she was through the front door she ran upstairs to the parlour, then she screamed, "What have you done, Christopher Leadam? What have you done? How could you leave me like this?" She pulled off her widow's bonnet and threw it to the floor, then she stamped on it. Next she ripped off her new black cloak and threw it at the wall. Then she kicked Christopher's chair, sending it skidding across the room. "Five hundred pounds! How could you? God damn you, Christopher Leadam. I hate you, I hate you!" She thumped her prized green velvet couch with her fists and the tears rolled down her face. "You've betrayed me, Christopher Leadam, you've betrayed us all," she wailed. "I thought you were the sensible one. Even Robert couldn't lose five hundred pounds with all his horse racing and womanising."

When Bowman arrived half an hour later he found his sister-in-law sitting on the rug in front of the unmade fire with her head in her hands, her eyes red and her voice hoarse. He sat down on the couch and she sat next to him. She liked Henry; everyone did. Poor kind Henry, who was loved and appreciated by everyone except his wife, her own sister. He was a good man, but there was nothing he could do to save her from this calamity.

"It's useless," she said, as he held her hands in his. "I'll end up in the Marshalsea. I haven't got five hundred pounds. I'll never have five hundred pounds. I'm utterly ruined, Henry."

"It may not come to that: we have some time to find the money. A writ won't be moved in the High Court until at least the end of February, so there's time for us to find the money."

"Henry," she said, "I don't have that sort of money."

He looked at her earnestly. "You have to think. Is there anywhere Christopher might have put the money to pay this debt?"

"I don't know. I didn't think he had secrets, but it seems I was wrong."

* * *

Alexander McNeal had made his name in the world of medicine as an anatomist and as a teacher. Although his academic career had begun with a degree in mathematics, he had followed his father into the Edinburgh University Medical School as an assistant anatomist and had qualified in medicine some years later. His primary work concerned the description of the human nervous system, although he also lectured in general surgery and comparative physiology, having most recently written a well-received book on the similarities between the physiology of fishes, other animals and men. He was a widower of mature years with three grown-up sons, all of whom were established doctors in the city; but his youngest child, Iona, still lived at home and kept his house.

He returned from his early morning inspection of the day's supply of cadavers at the university's Anatomy Theatre to find his daughter at the breakfast table reading a copy of the *Scots Magazine*. Iona looked up and smiled at her father. "You will be interested in this. It's an article about the natives of North America. Do you remember the controversy about North American natives and beards?"

"Aye," McNeal replied, taking his usual place at the table and picking up the newspaper. "It is an interesting case of physiology and race."

"Well," Iona explained, "a British army surgeon called McCausland says that contrary to popular belief and judging from his observations of the Six Nations in Niagara, these natives are the same as any other men. They only appear beardless because they pluck out the hairs on their faces. He says that Mohawks and Delawares who live with white men often shave with a razor!"

Professor McNeal buttered the piece of bread he had toasted at the fire and stuffed it into his mouth, dropping a shower of crumbs down his black frock coat. "So," he said, still munching on the toast, "there is no difference between these North American natives and the males of other races in their physiology?"

"No father."

He helped himself to eggs from the chafing dish. "Aye, that is interesting. I'll read it later. It will be a good topic for discussion with Dr Rankin when he comes to dinner next week." He poured himself a cup of tea.

"The evidence proves that all men are the same, does it not?" declared Iona, hoping to goad her father into one of his pompous rebukes. She was annoyed with him: how dare he take her interesting conversation piece and talk to Andrew Rankin about it and not to her. On this occasion, as in all others, she was not disappointed.

Her father took a long slurp of tea before replying. "I think that statement stretches the premise beyond its limits, my dear. It seems that it may be safe to say that all men have beards, but we certainly could not conclude that all men are the same."

"They are to me, Father," she said, flaunting the magazine in front of him to annoy him further.

"That is because, thankfully, you know so little about them, my dear," McNeal replied, taking the magazine out of her hand. That's what you think, Iona thought to herself. "Now run along to your cousin Morag's. She's expecting you to help with the girls. I'm away to the Infirmary and will be back at six. Tell Mrs Baxter to have supper ready for seven, and don't be late."

Iona was furious; once again, her father had refused to talk to her about anything other than housekeeping. Why was that, she wondered: she could read as well as any man, she was good at mathematics, she read Latin and spoke passable French, she could even produce a reasonable tune on the piano. She was interested in the world, she read books and magazines, she liked algebra and astronomy, she had things to say; but as far as she could see no one was listening.

She arrived at her cousin's house in George Street just as Dr Rankin was leaving for the University. As well as being University chaplain he was Professor of Rhetoric, and was required to give lectures on subjects such as the classical and modern theories of language for which he had a growing international reputation. It was Andrew who was her relation; he was her father's cousin, and had married Morag Sinclair a couple of years after his first wife, Una, had died. That was when he had been a young Minister of the Kirk in Sterling.

After her marriage, Morag had taken on the care of Andrew's two sons by his first wife, Blair and Charles; and some years later she had three children of her own: Ailsa, Fiona and Rhona.

When Iona got to her cousin's house in Edinburgh's New Town, she found Morag with her father, the Reverend Dr Malcolm Sinclair. She was holding a letter in her hand, and she looked as if she had been crying.

"Hello, Iona. This is my father Dr Sinclair," she said.

Iona made a polite curtsy and greeted the elderly cleric with a cheery "Good morning, sir."

Indeed it is a fine morning," the minister replied sardonically. "I have just found out that the Lord in His wisdom has spared my son from a watery grave. Why I do not know, when so many good souls were taken," he muttered, with his hands outstretched to emphasise his disbelief. "But we must accept that He works in ways that we mortals cannot comprehend."

Morag looked at Iona and shrugged her shoulders with a mixture of despair and resignation. The old man continued, wagging his finger vigorously in Morag's direction. "For my part I have never understood why the good Lord took his darling mother Margaret and my little Malcolm and left me with him. He's lazy and godless, and he drinks too much."

"Do you mean Dr James Sinclair, sir?" Iona said, as her heart made a small leap in her chest.

"Aye lassie, I do," the old man glowered. "And he's decided to stay in that pit of iniquity called London, which is hardly surprising. It's where he whores and drinks behind my back instead of coming home to his family where he belongs."

"Father, I'm sure that he does not whore, as you put it, although I agree he may drink too much."

"The boy is a drunkard, Morag. He should be here with me so that he can mend his ways."

"Oh, Father, is it any surprise that he decides to stay away when you're so cruel and unjust? Jamie's not a bad person, Papa; you were always too hard on him," protested Morag.

"I am not hard, I am truthful," he said. "And you are too soft on him; you always were. However, the fault does not lie solely with him. I am his father and I have let him down. I should have beaten the devil out of him when I had the chance. If he had followed me into the Kirk as I wished, none of this trouble would have occurred. He would be here with his family, and I would not have to worry about his soul."

Morag's face was hot with barely suppressed anger as she walked over to the ornate bureau under the large square-paned window and placed the folded letter on it. Iona could see her distress, so to save her from further embarrassment she offered to get the girls started with their arithmetic in the school room.

"That would be lovely, Iona, thank you," Morag replied, relieved that Iona would hear no more of her father's slanders.

As she walked to the school room at the back of the house, the thought that Jamie Sinclair was still alive gave Iona a warm feeling. She liked Jamie; he was good company and she knew that he liked her too. That was why he had sent the letter: it was his way of breaking off any attachment she might have thought had formed between them.

She had read the accounts of the disastrous voyage of the '*Sherwell*', but until now had not known if Jamie was one of the survivors. Now she knew he was alive a green leaf of hope sprang in her heart, the power of which took her quite by surprise.

She set each of the girls a piece of algebra suitable for their age and understanding, and took her usual place on the window seat. Her warm feelings lasted until the middle of the morning, when she suddenly realised that the antagonism between Jamie and his father meant he would never come back to Scotland. Jamie had been right to let her go. Their romance was like a bud that would never open; their families would make sure of that.

After her father had departed, Morag Rankin wrote.

> *Dearest Jamie,*
> *I thank God for his mercy and for your safety. I*
> *have spoken to Father to let him know that you*
> *are well and that you intend to stay in London.*
> *News of your ordeal has not mellowed him, but*
> *I am sure that he has affection for you in his*
> *own way even if we do not understand it.*
> *Blair is busy with examinations, but sends his*
> *regards and hopes to see you when he goes up*
> *to Cambridge at Michaelmas. Charles is still at*

Aberdeen and is making good progress with his Master of Divinity studies. If he does well, Andrew has a position lined up for him at St. Giles.

I know that you wrote to Iona McNeal before you embarked for India. (Rest assured, I know this because Iona told me not because I pry.) So you may be interested to know that she is helping the girls with their arithmetic, which is a great relief to me as I am not good with numbers. I think she is quite a mathematician. I often find her deep in conversation with Blair when he is at home. They can talk about Monsieur Laplace's Celestial Mechanics for hours, which is very unusual for a girl of her age in my opinion. Jamie, she is a lovely girl, and I was under the impression that you had formed an attachment to her. Please, if you cannot come home for Father or for me please come home for Iona. I know I should not say such things but I cannot help it; I think she would make an excellent wife for you. I am sure something could be worked out for you both. You need someone to look after you and to love you, and Iona needs a husband. I worry about you being on your own and I worry about you living in London. How will you live without money, and without your family and friends? Please come home, Jamie, I miss you terribly. Your loving sister, Morag

6

The Shadow of the Marshalsea

Charlotte and John were in the surgery at the back of the house in Tooley Street. The room was small, but it had a large window onto the yard through which the sun streamed in the morning. The furniture was functional: there was a small table for writing, a couple of chairs, one more comfortable than the other, a low table for examinations and treatments, and a glass-fronted secretaire for books and equipment with cupboards underneath. Charlotte put on her apron and called out, "Mrs Dredge, I need you to help me turn out all the cupboards in the surgery."

The old woman put her head around the door. "What on earth do you want to do that for? I'm in the middle of the laundry. I've got enough to do without more mischief."

"The laundry can wait, Elsie. This is more important," Charlotte commanded. "We'll start here and then we'll work through the rest of the house. John you get a stool from the apothecary and start with those top shelves."

"What are we looking for?" asked the old woman, with her hands fixed firmly in her pockets.

"Five hundred pounds, or something worth five hundred pounds," Charlotte replied.

"Five hundred pounds! I've never seen more than five."

"Well it must be here somewhere. I cannot believe Mr Leadam would leave us to pay a debt of that size without having made provision for it."

"A debt?" stumbled John.

"Yes, John. Your father was part of the insurance syndicate that underwrote the ship that sank off Dorset, and now we have to find the money to cover his part."

Stunned, John looked at the housekeeper and then at his mother.

"Come on," his mother commanded. "There's no time to waste."

Still reeling from the shock, John and Elsie started to turn out all the books on the shelves. They went through each cupboard, rummaging through stacks of old copies of the 'Gentleman's Magazine', but all to no avail. Then they moved onto the apothecary shop, where they churned through each of the duck-egg blue drawers and the medicine cabinets, only to find nothing that was not supposed to be there. Upstairs they looked under the beds, under the mattresses, in the chests of drawers and wardrobes, but there was no sign of a cache of money anywhere, not even under the loose floorboards in the master bedroom. As they worked through the rooms the little optimism Charlotte had of finding the money gradually drained away, until they got to the attic where it completely vanished, and she fell on her knees in despair.

John put his arms around his mother. "It'll turn up," he said, doing his best to console her. "Father wouldn't leave us like this."

"I know he didn't mean to," his mother wept. "But he didn't know he was going to die, did he? He thought he was coming home to carry on his work. Your father could have borrowed the money from the bank, but I can't. We're ruined John, ruined."

"It'll turn up, Mother, I know it will," her son consoled.

"You don't understand. People like us go bankrupt every day," his mother wailed.

* * *

In Yorkshire Lucy Leadam was assessing her life as she collected the meagre crop of eggs from the hen coop. Their empty little nests reminded her of her own lack of progress in life. It was early February, and she would be twenty years old the week after Easter. In those twenty years she had never once been courted or received a proposal of marriage. She was lonely and bored. She had been to school in Beverley when she was younger and had a few friends there, but most of the girls she had known were either married or engaged, and she felt left behind.

Lucy's life consisted of the farm, riding her horse and the occasional trip to Beverley or Hull, where she visited her mother's family at Rowley Hall. The highlight of her year was the annual trip to Beverley Fair in June, where she helped her father sell their yearlings and choose new bloodstock for the farm. The love of horses was the passion she shared with him. She was as good a judge of equine flesh as any son would have been and her father knew it. But the Beverley Fair was where, with the regularity of the arrival of swallows at the start of summer, her mother and father fell out. She knew that her father was reckless with money. She had seen him spending money he didn't have or paying over the odds for a horse he took a fancy to: he was too optimistic to be a good businessman. What was more, with a few jugs of beer inside him his wandering eye soon led him into some buxom barmaid's arms, and then to her bed. That was how he had ended up with two bastardy orders for Rosie Featherstone's bairns.

It was not that her parents did not care about her happiness; they did. Her father had offered to take her into the paddock at Beverley races and to the Risby Hunt, both excellent places to meet a prospective husband, but her mother objected on the grounds that she would be stared at by the wives and daughters of the county's squires on account of her father's misdemeanours. Her mother gave the same reason for not attending the dances at the Assembly Rooms too.

So, as Lucy foraged for the little white eggs she wondered how she was going to attract the attentions of a man she could love; a man of property, prudence and propriety. She was normally not one to fall into despair, but today she felt doleful and cursed.

She returned to the farmhouse to find her mother pummelling a huge pile of bread dough with her fists while Tilly, the young girl from the village who was their live-in maid, washed vegetables in the sink. The heavy kitchen table rattled on the stone flags as her mother picked up the dough and thwacked it this way and that, slapping it against the edge of the table. "Take that, ya bastard," she said, as she stretched it and pulled it, "and that. Tilly, put that down and get some more wood for the oven: it won't get hot enough with a couple of twigs, girl!" Tilly, who was no more than thirteen, scuttled off immediately to obey her mistress's instructions.

"Mother," Lucy interrupted, stopping her mother mid-thwack, "I think Tilly's terrified of you. You really shouldn't give her such a hard time."

"That's as maybe. It's never too early for a girl like her to learn that life is tough. The sooner she gets used to it the better. There was a time when I had my bread made for me, when I didn't have to dig up my own potatoes, but those days are long gone thanks to your father and his gallivanting. If this bloody farm is going to make any money we've got to make economies."

Lucy's heart sank as she watched her mother vent her frustrations equally on the bread dough and the maid. Perhaps now wasn't the right time to make her suggestion, but when would her mother be in a better mood? She was always angry. So Lucy held onto her resolve, plucked up her courage and said, "Do you think I could go to London to stay with Aunt Charlotte?"

"London! Good God, child, what do you want to go there for? I mean, I like your aunt and all but we've only just seen her." She slapped down the dough and wiped back some loose strands of hair with the back of her floury hand.

"I thought I could meet some new people there," Lucy ventured tentatively, waiting for an avalanche of objections to come her way. But her mother looked thoughtful for a moment as though she were concocting a plan. "New people. Now that would be very nice – no sneers or stares. Yes, I like that idea very much."

The fact that her mother had not instantly rejected her idea filled her with hope. "I've never been to London," Lucy said, as though it would make a difference if she had.

"You've never been as far as York, lass, never mind London!" her mother laughed. "Neither have I, for that matter, but I s'pose there's a first time for everything, eh? But there's the expense. How would we afford a trip to London?"

"I have money, Mother; I have my savings," Lucy offered.

"Yes, but they're not going to stretch very far for the two of us," her mother sighed, rubbing her hands on her apron.

"What do you mean, the two of us?" said Lucy, as Tilly crept back into the kitchen with an armful of wood and started to feed the huge bread oven at the end of the room.

"You can't go on your own, can you? You'll need a chaperone." Her mother was pleased with the idea that she would be forced to leave the drudgery of the kitchen to accompany her daughter.

"Oh, where are you off to?" said Tilly.

"It's none of your business, girl. Get on with what you're doing and be fast about it." Tilly turned back to the ovens resentfully and stuck out her tongue in silent protest.

"Do you think we could go to London if Aunt Charlotte would put us up?"

"Well, there's no harm in asking, is there?" her mother said, with a surprising hint of optimism in her voice. Then she raised the ball of bread dough she was punishing and gave it another thundering thwack.

"Are you sure we can afford it?"

"Your dad owes me a deal of money for what he's put me through these past years. This time he can put 'is 'and in 'is pocket and pay. You write to your aunt and ask her if we can come down to London in the summer. I'll sort the money out with your father."

"Oh, Mother, you've made me so happy."

"Well, don't count your chickens before they're hatched. Your aunt hasn't said yes yet."

* * *

Henry Bowman and his family were at St Andrew's by the Wardrobe next to St Paul's Cathedral, and the vicar was preaching a sermon on the presentation of Christ in the temple; but he was not listening and neither was Emma. Their boys were fidgeting with their prayer books, so he leant over and tapped them gently to bring them back into line. Then he tried to focus his mind by letting his eye follow the curve of Wren's great arched window in front of him. It was so simple and so beautiful, the perfect solution to the problem of maximising the light coming into the church, but there was no perfect solution to his sister-in-law's problem. What had Christopher been thinking when he signed his name to that insurance contract? He could only assume that his otherwise clever brother-in-law had not understood what he was getting himself into. In his head Henry ran the calculations over and over again, but whichever way he added up the sums he could see no way of keeping his sister-in-law out of the Marshalsea unless she sold everything she owned.

Emma's mind too was alive with fears for the future. She had always been afraid that her sister's eccentricity would land her in trouble, but she had never imagined that she might end up in a debtors' gaol. She could not help thinking about what would happen if Henry could not raise the money. Would she be shunned by her respectable friends, she wondered? Would her mother and father be disgraced? Would her father lose his patients and position at St George's Hospital? And what would happen to Henry's business? How would they live if the people they knew turned away from them? Emma felt as if she had landed in fires of purgatory, and the torment of not knowing when the torture would end was unbearable.

In Tooley Street Charlotte and John attended what they thought could be their last service at St Olave's. In their parlour afterwards Charlotte sat with her son and explained what his Uncle Henry was doing to help them. John listened with a heart full of anger and fear. His mother looked like a stranger to him: her beautiful face was grey with fatigue and her eyes red rimmed from crying. "John," she explained, "you've been very brave but you may have to be braver still. If Uncle Henry cannot raise all the money I may have to go to prison, and you will have to live with Grandmamma in Wimpole Street."

John felt that the worst thing that could ever happen to him had already taken place – his father had died – but now he felt that his life was about to fall apart again. The thought of living with his grandmother filled him with dread, but the thought of his mother in the Marshalsea was unbearable. If his mother went to prison, how would he ever get her out? Five hundred pounds was such a huge sum of money to raise. He was angry with his father. In fact, if he had not already been dead, John felt that he would have had to kill him for leaving them in such a mess.

* * *

As they walked back from Sunday Eucharist, Greenwood confided to Sinclair that he despised political lunches. Sinclair said that he thought that there might be some sport to be had as he was good at stirring up the indignation of self-righteous men.

"Oh, please don't do that. It would upset Mother."

"In that case I promise to behave myself," said Sinclair. He knew Frank had resigned his commission without discussing it with his parents and he suspected that they were secretly disappointed in their son.

"Thank you, Jamie. I'm not a scholar as you know. My idea of happiness is hunting: I love chasing anything that can be shot. I'm not a man of commerce or politics. I honestly couldn't give a fig what the government is doing. I had a commission in the British Army and my parents thought their work was done, but as you know I was let go at the end of the American War so they bought me a commission in the Bengal Army. Then I was shipwrecked and now I have no profession. So what are they to do with me, Jamie? I can't face the sea again, so I can't go to India or to my father's plantation in Jamaica."

"I see," said Sinclair. "I'm sure you'll think of something, my friend."

"I hope you're right," Greenwood replied, not feeling at all optimistic.

The Husselbees were the first of Sir Bramwell's lunch guests to arrive in their smart lightweight curricle. The contrast between the vehicle and its occupants could not have been starker in Sinclair's opinion. Sir Hubert had the girth of an ancient oak. His vast square head appeared out of his body without the necessity of a neck. The fine silk clothes he was wearing accentuated his size, clinging to his limbs with all the panache of sausage skin. His enormous powder puff of a wife equalled him in size but not in height. She was dressed in youthful pink with swags and rosettes around her ample middle-aged waist, while her tightly curled hair was piled on top of her head and powdered as chalky-white as her face, with the exception of her ruby red lips. Sir Hubert like so many of the men Sinclair attended in his medical practice, had pulled himself up from obscurity by his own efforts.

The Chilcrafts were altogether different. They were a young and elegant couple who arrived in a sporty phaeton. Sinclair watched Greenwood admiring the phaeton and Chilcraft's slim dark-haired wife, dressed in the most exquisite gold brocade, who swished past him with a sultry smile.

Sir Bramwell's table was a cornucopia of delights laden with boiled meats, batter puddings and small roasted ducks with cabbage and potatoes, as well as tarts and blancmange. Frank sat next to his mother while Sinclair was placed close to Sir Bramwell, and as Frank had predicted the conversation soon came around to money and politics.

"I see the Prince of Wales is petitioning Parliament to write off his debts," complained the neckless Husselbee, stuffing a thick slice of ox tongue into his mouth. "I don't know why he thinks we taxpayers should pay off his debts. He wouldn't give me a penny towards mine."

"Mr Fox is the same," agreed Mr Chilcraft, waving his wine glass excitedly. "He's a man of immoral excesses who runs up thousands in gambling debts, and what is more he's a wanton womaniser. The King considers him unprincipled and a bad influence on the Prince of Wales, and he's right. The man is an out and out scoundrel. I understand that he and the Prince share a dissolute nature, but his decision to enter into a political alliance with the drunken spendthrift is beyond me."

Greenwood sat silently studying Mrs Chilcraft as she plucked morsels of duck from a carcass and placed them in her mouth. He wondered what she looked like naked with an enjoyable quiver of excitement. He looked at her husband, the dashing young Member of Parliament and successful industrialist. Chilcraft was smart, rich and confident, and he had eaten of the delicious fruit that was sitting opposite him. Frank felt despondent. The conversation moved on, without anyone noticing his lack of participation. He looked at the men in the room with envy: his father was a landowner, Sir Hubert a rich mine owner, Chilcraft a wealthy arms supplier, Sinclair a well-qualified doctor; while he, Frank Greenwood, was nothing.

"But Fox is our man," droned on Sir Bramwell, playing the party loyalist. "He and Burke are pressing the King on the subject of India. Are we not the party that believes all men should have liberty under the law?"

"Absolutely, sir, and we must support our friend Mr Sheridan and his Society of Friends for the Liberty of the Press," said Chilcraft. "How can we tackle this rampant corruption in our nation without an unfettered press? We do not want to become what Burke describes in India; a land where there is no law except the law of profit and exploitation. Gentlemen, we know what happened in North America when good men were denied proper representation and were treated unfairly by a greedy state."

"I fear you're right as far as Fox is concerned, Mr Chilcraft," said Sinclair, to a general murmur of agreement. "Now that Fox has allied himself to the Prince of Wales the King will be obstinate when it comes to reforming the East India Company."

"Aye, Sinclair, you're right there," crowed Husselbee. "Mr Pitt is the King's man and he has a great advantage over Fox: he favours pragmatism over principle. Mr Burke's attempt to impeach Governor Hastings will inevitably fail, no matter how much mud Burke throws at him."

"I agree," said Lady Frances, much to the surprise of her guests. "The problem is that no one outside Westminster is interested in Mr Hastings, and so his like will be free to corrupt the body politic with impunity. As much as I would like to see the man cast asunder I am sure he will not be. On that less than optimistic note, gentlemen, may I suggest that we ladies leave you to right the problems of the world."

The women departed, and a selection of Sir Bramwell's best wines was brought to the table. When it came to Greenwood's turn to propose a toast he poured himself a glass of port and mumbled, "To all those who perish at sea may God bless them," and the men thumped the table and repeated "God bless them."

Then Sinclair raised his glass. "To life, gentlemen. May it be long and profitable."

Sir Bramwell finished the round with a toast to wives, which was received with loud hurrahs.

After the toasts Husselbee turned his attention to Frank and Sinclair. "Now what are you two young men going to do now you are without employment? Your father is very disappointed with you, young Greenwood," he said, scratching his crotch. Frank snapped out of his melancholy trance and shot an alarmed glance in Sinclair's direction. What had his father said to this bloated coal merchant?

Seeing his friend's distress, Sinclair intervened. "Sir, may I ask you a personal question?" he said leaning in Husslebee's direction to give the impression of concern.

"Fire away! I have no secrets, lad." Husslebee gave his crotch another scratch.

"I noticed that you're scratching rather a lot, sir."

"Young man, I hope you're not implying what I think you are," Husselbee replied indignantly, removing his hand from between his legs.

Greenwood looked at his father with growing concern, wondering where Sinclair was taking the conversation.

"Certainly not, sir. I was just wondering if you were also suffering from an unusual thirst."

"Thirsty? I'm always bloody thirsty."

"I thought that might be the case," Sinclair replied in his most solicitous voice. "Sir, as a physician I can see that you are suffering from the early stages of what we quacks call Polydipsia."

Husselbee looked around the room, unsure what to say or do. "Poly what's it? Is it serious?"

Chilcraft and Sir Bramwell looked on with concern. Frank looked down at the tablecloth, not knowing if he should be terrified or laughing.

"No, sir, it's not serious if it's treated at an early stage, although if left it's often fatal," Sinclair replied.

"Fatal! Bloody hellfire! Please excuse my language, Sir Bramwell, Mr Chilcraft."

Sinclair continued, "If you'd be so kind as to allow me, I will call on you tomorrow with a remedy. I assure you, sir, that the remedy will allow you to make a full recovery, but in the meantime I would suggest that you take some bed rest and avoid further vexations."

Husselbee summoned his wife and beat a hasty retreat, followed by the Chilcrafts, who were concerned the disease might be contagious. When their guests had departed, the family assembled in the parlour to put their feet up and digest the events of the day. "What an odious woman," moaned Lady Frances, returning to the sitting room.

"Which one?" enquired Sir Bramwell.

"Oh, who do you think, Bram? Mrs Chilcraft is an angel, but that overdressed gorgon, all she could talk about was how much she'd paid for this and how much for that. Anyone would think she ran a shop. She had the cheek to tell me that our house wasn't as grand as she'd expected! She thought we'd have somewhere newer and more fashionable, like the house she's renting in Dover Street. Do you know how much they're paying for it?

"I'm sure she told you," laughed Sir Bramwell.

"Of course she did: a hundred pounds a month!"

"I think the world has gone mad, my dear," mused her husband, sucking on his pipe. "It's this new money. By God, I wish I had more of it."

"Bramwell, you're incorrigible. Please do not hurry to accept a return invitation: it will take me quite some time to work up to another encounter. We must thank Dr Sinclair for his intervention, without which our ordeal would have been much extended."

"I think you scared old Husselbee half to death," Sir Bramwell snorted, trying to hold back the mirth that was bubbling up inside him.

"Aye, well he's in a bad way if he's got what I think he has," said Sinclair seriously. "It'll most certainly kill him, but unfortunately it will take some time," and they all laughed.

* * *

In keeping with his promise, Sinclair arrived at the Husselbee residence in Dover Street shortly before ten o'clock. After some time he was shown into a well-appointed drawing room decorated with fashionable yellow wallpaper from France. Husselbee met him dressed in a luxurious red dressing gown. He squeezed his bulk into a fine gilded chair and beckoned Sinclair closer. "Dr Sinclair, what do you have for me?" he coughed, holding out a stubby fat hand.

"The remedy I promised, sir," said Sinclair with a reverential bow.

"Will it cure me?"Husselbee grumbled, taking the little bottle of medicine from him.

"Aye, sir, it will."

"It's not big, is it?" Husselbee said, holding the bottle up to the light and examining its contents. "How much of it should I take?"

"Three teaspoons per day sir, one after each meal. It's very powerful, but to achieve maximum potency you must follow the instructions I have written out for you." Sinclair handed him a scroll of paper.

"O, aye, and what's this all about?" Sir Hubert said, holding the document away from him like a contaminated rag.

"Sir, to restore your health you must follow the diet I have prescribed for you, and I would recommend that you go to Bath to take the waters when you're able. If you do not do as I say then I fear you will be dead in less than two years."

"Well, you call a spade a spade and there's no mistaking. Two years you say. Hellfire, I'd better get the wife onto this." Then he turned to Sinclair. "How much do I owe you?"

Much as it galled him to say it he replied, "There is no charge, sir. You are a friend of Sir Bramwell Greenwood and he has been very good to me since my adventure on the '*Sherwell*'. As a favour to him I offer you my services on this occasion gratis."

"Grat what?" enquired Husselbee, screwing up his fat face.

"Gratis, sir; free of charge."

"Oh," he smiled. "I can see you're a canny bugger. You Scots give nothing away if you can help it. I expect you want to play me for the fool, but I warn you, Mr Clever Clogs, if this stuff doesn't

112

work you'll be hearing from me. I don't take kindly to being humiliated in public."

"I assure you the remedy will make you feel better, and if you follow the diet I have prescribed you'll no longer feel thirsty all the time, you won't need to urinate so often, the itching around your crotch will be reduced and your health will improve. Of course, if you choose to persist in your present ways I can assure you that you'll be meeting your maker much sooner than you need to. The choice is yours, sir."

"Aye, you're right there, lad, but as it 'appens I'll give it a go."

"I should advise you that if you choose to employ me as your physician in future I will charge you my usual fee of one guinea per consultation, plus the cost of the medicine prescribed."

"You say you were on the '*Sherwell*'. My God, that must have been dreadful," Husselbee said, with true emotion in his voice.

"It was, sir. Frank Greenwood and I were lucky to survive."

"Aye, I'm not surprised about that. From what me and Issy have read in the papers it was a terrible ordeal."

"It has been a pleasure to be of service to you, sir," Sinclair replied with a bow, hoping to make his escape.

"Aye, good day, Dr Sinclair. Will you come to see me again?" Husselbee asked, like a child saying goodbye to his mother.

"Not unless you need me, sir, in which case you may contact me through my attorney's office. The address is on the parchment."

"Well, I'm much obliged. Mason will show you out."

Sinclair headed for Westminster feeling pleased with himself. What had started out as the solution to a momentary social crisis

113

was turning into a wholly worthwhile connection. He knew that Husselbee would use the medicine he had given him in a matter of days, and would send for him to get some more.

7

The Apothecary Shop Inventory

In the apothecary shop, Charlotte Leadam ran her fingers along the long oak table that ran the length of the room, then along the wooden counters that lined its walls, enjoying their smoothness and familiarity. She had worked in the shop for seven years and she loved it. She loved the connection to the world it gave her, not only through her customers and patients but also through the collection of minerals and exotic roots from the far corners of the world that she used. It had become an integral part of her life, and she knew she would feel hollow without it.

Learning about the contents of its pretty blue and white jars, the potency of the powders in the racks of stiff wooden drawers and the effects of the fluids in the shiny glass bottles had provided the outlet for her energy and intellect she had needed when her only child went to school. Gradually, through hard work and study, she had filled the hole in her life that was her unborn children. The work she had done had given her a satisfying sense of belonging, and a bond to her husband and his business that few women enjoyed. In times past it had been the place where she could forget her troubles, but those times had gone.

She took a sheet of paper and a fine goose quill and wrote "Apothecary Shop Inventory, February 1786" at the top of the page. She decided to start with the books, taking the last one that Christopher had bought before they went to Yorkshire. It was called 'Account of the Foxglove' and the author was named Withering. She had read Christopher's books before, but always after him. This time she was the first. As she flicked through the stiff white pages she found herself being drawn deeper and deeper into the text. It gave details of how to prescribe extract of foxglove, or more correctly digitalis, in the treatment of dropsy, an uncomfortable swelling of the feet and ankles that was a common problem especially for elderly patients. It also suggested it could be beneficial in cases of vexations of the heart. When she had read enough to satisfy her curiosity, she wrote its name on the paper. Then she turned to the rest of the books. There were books on midwifery by Chamberlain and Smellie; two volumes of 'Drake's Anatomy'; McNeal's 'Observations on the 'Structure and Functions of the Nervous System'; a book by Hamilton on Fevers, one by Hillary on smallpox, Mr Harvey's *Exercitatio anatomica de motu cordis et sanguinis in animalibus*', which concerned the movement of the heart and the blood in animals; Mr Cheney's 'Diseases of the Body & Mind'; Hoffman's 'Endemical Diseases'; a book by Turner on syphilis; two volumes of 'Shaw's Chemistry'; Mr Pitcairn's 'Elements of Physics'; and volumes on surgery by Ellesmere, Cooper, Sharp and Turner.

Finally, she added Mr Culpeper's 'Complete Herbal' followed by two volumes on dispensing, one by Pemberton and the other by a man called Quincey, to her list.

She was in the process of deciding where to begin with the rest of the stock when William appeared. She put down her pen and said, "I have written to your mother to let her know that Mr Hoares is seeking a new Master for you at Guy's or St Thomas'."

"Thank you, Mrs Leadam, I'm most obliged," he replied.

"May I ask what you're doing?"

"I'm making an inventory, William. I'd appreciate your help."

"What would you like me to do?"

"I thought we might start with the ledger. We could go through it and see how much of everything we have left, then we could give it a value. I'm sure there's at least a hundred pounds' worth of stock here. It's important I get the right value for everything. I can't afford to be sold short on anything."

Together they worked their way through the row of handsome blue and white delftware jars each with its own cartouche surrounding the Latin inscription describing its contents. Then they turned to the drawers, tackling the contents in alphabetical order. They started with the Aloe; a simple laxative extracted from plants grown in the West Indies, gradually moving through to Raw Peruvian bark, the casing of the cinchona tree, also called Jesuit bark because it was exported to Europe by them. It was their most commonly prescribed remedy for fever in adults. Then they turned their attention to the opiates and metals. They counted the packets of dried herbs that Charlotte turned into therapeutic teas; the alcohol, the vinegar and the glycerine she used to make up tinctures and syrups; the packets of pills and lozenges they sold for colds and chills; the jars of beeswax and almond oil she used to make ointments and rubs; the rolls of clean cotton for bandages and the trusses for hernias. When they were done, Charlotte totted up the long column of figures and found that the value of the stock amounted to £96 12s 6d.

William looked around the room. "We haven't counted the equipment, Mrs Leadam."

Charlotte could see that William was right. They had not examined the boxes of syringes and pipes or their collection of braces and splints. Neither had they counted the sets of sharp scalpels; the hook shaped needles they used to sew flesh back together; the pliers they used for extracting teeth. Mr Leadam's set of amputating knives and bleeding bowls were sitting on the counter and Charlotte realised that she had not included the forceps, an aid to childbirth and their most expensive item of equipment. Neither had she considered the brass scales and weights, the mortars and pestles for grinding roots and minerals into powders; and then there were the sieves, the pill and lozenge moulds, the glass bottles and the stoppers, the corks and the glass phials.

"You're right. All these things must have a value, and so must the cupboards and benches. I'll look at Mr Leadam's papers and see what I can find out. Thank you. You've been a great help, William."

The willowy young man turned to her. "I don't want to leave you, Mrs Leadam. I like it here, and I'll do everything I can to stay. I've heard stories, horrible stories, from boys at the Apothecary's Hall. They say some of them sleep in rooms next to piles of stinking cadavers and that their masters treat them like slaves."

Charlotte placed her hand on the boy's shoulder. "I don't want to have to send you away, but you must understand that everything has changed with Mr Leadam's passing." The boy nodded his head. "Mr Hoares will find you a good and kind master I'm sure, and you'll always be welcome wherever we are; be assured of that."

"If the worst does happen and you have to go to the Marshalsea, I'll visit you. I won't turn my back on you and pretend that I never knew you."

"Oh, William, I hope we can avoid that; but if we can't I shall be glad to have you as my friend. In the meantime, try not to worry."

Charlotte looked at her lists. Everything she owned would have to be sold, and for the best price, if she were to avoid the horrors of the Marshalsea. When she thought about what might happen she shuddered. Why had Christopher risked everything they had worked so hard for on that wretched ship? It was so unlike him; his brother was the gambler. But perhaps her husband had been more like his brother than she knew. Perhaps he had been tempted to take a risk because he was bored with his life, or bored with her. Perhaps she had simply failed to see his faults because she loved him and trusted him too much. Whatever the reason, she knew that within a few weeks, if she were lucky, she would be living with her mother and father in Wimpole Street and her life as a surgeon's wife would be over. Charlotte recoiled at the thought of her mother's gloating when she turned up penniless on her doorstep. It was a torment she would have to bear until the day her mother died, but it was preferable to prison.

* * *

In his office, Henry Bowman opened his copy of the 'Public Advertiser' and quickly ran his eye down the columns of print until he saw "For Sale By Auction, Apothecary Shop, House and Contents, 65,Tooley Street, Saturday 11th March, 11am." He put the paper with the others on his untidy desk, and hung his coat on the peg on the back of the door. His office was cold and he felt unusually depressed. He sat down, stared at the piles of unfinished work and sighed, then decided to call the boy from down the hall to make up his fire. When he opened the door he found not the coal boy but a beaming Jamie Sinclair in front of him. "My God, Sinclair, you shouldn't frighten a man like that," Henry said, ushering him into his office.

Unaware of his friend's melancholy mood, Sinclair announced, "I'm here to take advantage of your good nature and your purse, Bowman. We need to go to Garraway's to celebrate."

"To celebrate what?" said Bowman, looking at the pile of documents on his desk.

"I'll tell you all about it when you've bought the coffee. Come on, get your coat: there's no time to waste."

Without a word of protest Bowman followed his friend. The coffee house was full of smoke and steam and the hurried talk of business, but they managed to find a place near the window and sat down to two dishes of their favourite syrupy coffee.

"So, what do you have to tell me, Sinclair?" enquired Bowman as he found a sixpence for their drinks.

"I have my first patient in London, Henry!"

"My God, you've dragged me all the way here and robbed me of sixpence just to tell me that?" complained Bowman.

"Well, you have to ask me who my patient is. Be a little more inquisitive," teased Sinclair.

"Well, I know you're good, but I don't think you've landed the King, so who is this illustrious figure who's going to help you make a fortune in this city of crooks and whores?"

"With that view of the world anyone would think you were a Presbyterian," Sinclair spluttered. "My patient, as you're so keen to know, is Sir Hubert Husselbee."

"And who the blazes is he?"

"He's no one of importance except to himself, as so many of these men of money are. The important thing is he's worth at least ten thousand a year and he's as sick as a dog. I call that a coup worth spending your sixpence on, Bowman."

"You've developed an admirable mercenary streak since you got off that boat. You'd make an excellent lawyer."

"Thank you, Bowman. That is true praise from a man like you."

"So why am I paying for the coffee? How much has he paid you?"

"Nothing yet: it's early days."

Bowman's shoulders started to move up and down, and with a deep and hearty laugh he sprayed his friend with hot sweet coffee.

"No, don't laugh; it's not funny. I'm drawing him in. You know that in business you can't land a big fish like him with just one worm."

"Sounds as if you're a little premature with your celebrations," Bowman continued.

"Possibly," Sinclair said, looking down at his coffee-splattered coat, "but I'm confident I've got him, and with him others will come."

"I'm sure you're right," said Bowman, wiping his friend down with his handkerchief and apologising. "I'd get a bill in quick, though, in case your fish is attracted to some other worm."

"All in good time, all in good time. My next task is to find a job and a place to live. I have written to the administrators at

Guy's and St Thomas'. I'm sorry, I don't fancy coming back to St. George's; it's too small and Hunter's on his way out. He's going to concentrate on what really earns him money, the anatomy school and his private clients. I'm sure he'll be resigning soon. Today, I intend to visit St Bartholomew's and The London to see what's happening there."

"Couldn't you get some work at one of the anatomy theatres?" asked Bowman, casually knowing that Sinclair was not fond of the idea.

"I could try, but I don't like carving up stinking corpses, as you know. The occasional autopsy is all right but I really don't want to be doing it day after day. Getting a position as a house doctor at one of the hospitals is probably the best way to build up my reputation and client book, but it will cost me. Henry," he said cautiously, "would you write to Mr Lovell at the East India Company demanding some recompense for my losses on the 'Sherwell'? They'll have insured themselves, and when I added up the value of everything I lost it came to well over a hundred pounds."

"Of course. I don't know why I didn't think of it myself," Bowman replied. "Well I do, actually," he continued thoughtfully. "I've been preoccupied with the affairs of my sister-in-law. She's recently widowed, and has found herself in financial difficulties because her husband held a part share in the insurance contract for the 'Sherwell'; so, yes, they were definitely insured."

"My goodness, what a strange and unfortunate coincidence," replied Sinclair, draining his cup. "Henry, I can't take advantage of the Greenwoods' generosity for much longer; that's why I gave him your office address for correspondence."

"Gave who my address?" enquired Bowman, lost in thoughts about Charlotte again.

"Husselbee. I expect Husselbee to be in touch early next week."

"So I'm to be your post box too."

"I'm sure you'll add it to your bill."

"Absolutely, old man; and talking of finding somewhere to live, my sister-in-law will be selling a property that might be of interest to you."

"I'm a long way off buying somewhere, Henry. I'll be lucky if I can scrape the rent together over the next six months."

"Well, I thought it was worth mentioning to you as it has an apothecary shop with it."

"Thank you, but I'll be looking for rooms."

* * *

Frank Greenwood stood silently in his father's study, "This is not the behaviour we have come to expect from you," his father said, standing with his hands pressing down into his pockets. "What has happened to you, son? You never used to drink like this."

Greenwood sensed that the rebuke was as difficult for his father to give as it was for him to receive. "I'm sorry, Father; I haven't been myself since the incident on the '*Sherwell*'."

"That is what I don't understand. You survived. You should be grateful, not melancholy and drinking yourself into oblivion every night."

Greenwood continued to stare at the floor, not knowing how to explain the sense of failure that haunted him.

"I don't understand you, Frank," his father railed. "Your mother and I care about you; we want you to succeed, but you're throwing your life away. Your mother is very upset, and if she's upset I'm upset. Do you understand me?"

"Yes, sir," Greenwood replied, feeling the weight of his self-loathing pressing into his chest.

"We need to know what you're going to do now that you have resigned your commission."

"I know, Father," he whispered, still with his eyes fixed dejectedly on the beautifully patterned carpet. "I'm sorry to be such a disappointment to you, but I don't know the answer to your question. I'm not sure what I can do."

"Well, I do," replied his father with rising exasperation. "I've arranged a job for you at the Navy Board with my old friend Lord Wroxeter; it should keep you out of trouble and in funds until you decide what you're going to do with the rest of your life. You start tomorrow, so you'd better pull yourself together."

"Yes, Father," Greenwood stumbled, still staring at the carpet. "Father, they're writing terrible things in the press about men like me. They say that the officers on the 'Sherwell' were remiss in their duties. It's not true. I'd like you to ask a question in Parliament about why the ship sank. It was taking on too much water long before the fateful storm, but the captain didn't return to port to make repairs. Sinclair and I feel that if he had turned around earlier the ship and everyone on it would have been saved."

"I have no doubt you did your duty, Frank, and your friend may well be right about the ship, but believe me there's no appetite for an investigation. The East India Company's only interest is money. You must understand that its influence has seeped into every crevice of public life. Its men have colonised every part of the state. Look at the difficulty Mr Burke is having in trying to get charges of corruption to stick to that prince of nabobs Warren Hastings. That man has robbed the shareholders blind and sucked the peasants of Bengal dry, all for his own aggrandisement, but he has powerful friends and I can't see him being convicted. President Dundas will collect the insurance money on the '*Sherwell*' and that is that. He's not interested in an enquiry. I'll ask around in private but I won't make enquiries in public. The company has its men everywhere and I can't be seen to be undermining it: the directors and Mr Dundas will not tolerate it."

"But more than a hundred and sixty people died, Father; surely that is worth asking about? Do you not support the efforts of Mr Burke to reform the company?"

"I'm sorry about the people who lost their lives, truly I am, but I can't do anything for them. I can't be seen to attack the company personally; it must be Parliament that takes a stand. Individuals can't hope to go up against a body as powerful as the East India Company and expect to win. Who knows what they would do to me. Do you want your father to be a laughing stock? Do you want to see me thrown out of Brooks's and your mother socially disgraced?"

"No, Father."

"Good. Besides, the Government wants to make a hero out of Captain Richards and the men from the quarry who saved you. Did you know that this shipwreck is the first where those who survived were not robbed and left for dead by the wrecking men? You were very lucky, Frank, and you shouldn't forget it."

"Yes, sir," Greenwood muttered dolefully, casting his eyes to the floor again.

"Now get out of my sight. I don't want to have a conversation like this again, do you understand?"

"Yes, sir."

It was exactly half past eight when Greenwood arrived at Somerset House feeling tense and hung-over but determined not to let his father down. He reported to the duty office, where a young man about the same age as himself dressed in a naval uniform asked him to wait in an elegant room, the walls lined with paintings of famous sea battles. As he gazed at the pictures of the ships set in foaming white seas, the tension in his stomach ratcheted up another notch. His hands were wet with sweat when an elderly man dressed in a long black frock coat and pince-nez spectacles appeared.

"Your father has asked me to find you a temporary position at the Navy Board, and as an old friend I am more than happy to oblige him. We are in the final stages of moving our offices, by which I mean the Navy Victualling Offices, from Seething Lane behind the Tower of London to our new offices here at Somerset House. I need a man to organise the transport of our archives and furniture from there to here. You were an army captain, I believe."

Greenwood nodded. "Yes, sir. With Lord Dorchester in America and lately with the Bengal Army."

"So you can organise that for me?"

"Yes, sir."

"Good man. Finch, the man who showed you in, will take you to Seething Lane and show you what is to be done. You will have five men and five carts. I want the job done quickly and efficiently. If you are successful, Mr Greenwood, I will consider you for other work. Do you understand?"

"Yes, sir."

"You will be paid eight guineas upon completion of the task."

"Thank you, sir."

"You are dismissed," commanded the old man, pointing him towards the door.

Finch was waiting for him, and the pair made their way through a maze of long echoing corridors to the river frontage. "Magnificent isn't it, Mr Greenwood?" said the young man as he opened the door onto the first-floor terrace that afforded them a view of the river and the port of London.

"It's incredible," replied Greenwood open mouthed, as he looked down at the forest of masts anchored in the river.

"You can see the Tower from here," said Finch. "We could have moved everything from Seething Lane by naval barge if we had a mind to, but as you can see trade is so brisk these days we'd be hard pressed to get a barge in." Greenwood nodded in agreement, still taking in the view. Then Finch said, "I heard you were on the 'Sherwell', sir."

Greenwood took off his hat and rubbed his mat of blond curly hair. "I was one of the lucky survivors, Mr Finch. I'm not very keen on water at the moment," he smiled.

"That's understandable. Anyone who's gone through what you have would feel the same." Frank felt one of the knots in his stomach start to uncoil. "Many of my fellows believe that learning to swim is the harbinger of bad luck. I am not of that opinion and I have decided to take lessons."

"I think that's very wise in your profession," said Greenwood, "I learned to swim in our lake at Panton Hall. It stood me in good stead on that fateful night, but it was luck that saved me. The storm was a demon from hell; it chose who would live and who would die. The ship was compromised, you see: as well as losing two masts, the hull was full of water so it was too heavy for the captain to manoeuvre."

"Well, I can assure you there'll be no water involved in this job except perhaps a drop of rain. I'll show you the offices here and then take you to Seething Lane, where you'll find everything you need."

* * *

Sinclair received an invitation from Bowman for him and Greenwood to dine at his house in Bread Street on Friday. After a week of hauling rolls of parchment and ledger books from one end of London to the other, Greenwood was grateful to be in town with his friend. Bowman's house was the antithesis of his office. Where his office was small and untidy his home was spacious and comfortable. Sinclair could see that the Bowman home was his wife's domain and was a model of good taste, with elegant mahogany furniture, fine paper on the walls, and delicate porcelain plates and silver candlesticks on the table.

The men swiftly demolished Mrs Bowman's beef and oyster pie and two bottles of claret, and were settling back with their pipes when they heard a knock at the front door. "That's unusual. We don't normally get callers this late at night," said Bowman. He stood, then heard his wife answer it. As he sat down, a woman dressed in black burst into the room.

"Henry," she spluttered breathlessly, "I've found it!" And with a proud flourish she placed a black metal box on the table.

"Charlotte, what are you talking about?" demanded Mrs Bowman, who was standing in the doorway behind her.

The woman with the beautiful but flushed complexion tore off her black bonnet, revealing a head of luxurious auburn hair.

Sinclair looked at the women and immediately realised they were sisters. Emma Bowman was a slightly younger and paler version of her older sister; the widow Henry had told him about.

"It's in the box, Henry. Look in the box," the woman commanded.

Bowman opened the box and started to turn its contents out. From where he was sitting, Sinclair could see two silver cups and a pile of papers. Greenwood looked bemused, and said to no one in particular, "What's this all about?"

Without looking at Greenwood, the auburn-haired woman said, "It's the money, Henry. Christopher had it all along."

Sinclair reached out and picked up the two palm-sized silver cups. "These are Quaichs, Highland whisky cups," he said, holding them up for everyone to see. "They are very fine." He traced the engraved borders and the crests with his finger. "This one is Clan Ogilvy," he said, handing it to Henry, "and this one is Clan MacIver. Both clans were with Bonnie Prince Charlie at Culloden."

"There must be about ten ounces of silver in them," said Bowman, holding one in each hand. "I reckon that must make them worth at least twenty pounds."

"Oh at least," Sinclair agreed.

Along with the deeds to the house in Tooley Street there was a bundle of share certificates for the South Sea Company. Bowman counted them onto the table. "There's two hundred pounds' worth here."

"And there are these," said Emma, holding up a golden crucifix encrusted with blood-red rubies as long and as thick as her index finger, a golden snuff box and a ring with a sapphire as big as a man's thumbnail.

Sinclair looked at the crucifix and mumbled, "These are Jacobite relics."

"I don't care what they are. What are they worth?" the woman in black snapped.

"What my friend means, Charlotte, is that we cannot sell them on the open market. They are either Catholic items of devotion or the possessions of traitors. Christopher had them hidden away because he knew they'd be difficult to sell. There's still a deep suspicion attached to anything Jacobite even forty years after the rebellion. His father must have picked them up on the battlefield and brought them back to Yorkshire."

Emma held the crucifix up to the light, watching the light from the candles dance in the wine-coloured stones, "That is such a shame because this is so beautiful." Then she slipped the sapphire ring onto her middle finger, admiring its glassy brilliance.

"They are Catholic and seditious," said Sinclair with growing concern. "The Bonnie Prince is still alive and living in Italy. He's still a threat to the nation."

"I'm sure that even if you have to take these fine things to some back street chappie in the City you'll achieve a good price, madam," Greenwood interjected. "Loot of every description finds its way there. I believe there are men who make a good living extracting the value from objects whose provenance is either dubious or undesirable."

"I think this calls for drinks all round, Emma, don't you?" said Bowman, feeling much relieved. With harmony of a sort restored, his wife poured the Madeira and her sister started to cry. Bowman put his hand on his sister-in-law's shoulder. "You've done it, Charlotte: there's no need to cry. Where did you find it?"

"It was at the bank with the deeds to the house," she said, dabbing her tears with the handkerchief her brother-in-law had given her. "I went there this afternoon. The man at the bank gave me the box but I didn't open it until this evening. I was busy helping my neighbour, Mrs Naylor, with her hair. She'd dyed it using a preparation that was too strong, and now half her hair has broken off. The rest is as dry as straw and her scalp is red-raw. There wasn't a lot I could do, so I washed it with milk, applied some almond oil and cut off the most brittle clumps. I expect most of it will fall out." She paused again and dabbed her eyes. "The silly woman didn't want to bother me for the correct preparation because of Christopher's death, and now she looks like a witch."

Sinclair put his hand to his mouth to cover the smile that was breaking across his face as he imagined the hideous sight, but the woman in black caught him. "It's not funny, Mr whatever your name is," she snapped. "My friend is distraught."

"It's Sinclair," he said, but still smiling. "You did a good job."

"And what would you know about it?" Charlotte fired back.

Bowman played peacemaker again, explaining that his friend was a doctor and surgeon, and his sister-in-law was forced to apologise.

Sinclair finished his wine. "It's time for me and Greenwood to be heading back to Westminster, Henry. Thank you for a splendid evening."

They made their farewells and Emma Bowman showed them to the door, but she stopped before opening it. "Would you do me a favour, Mr Greenwood?" she ventured. "If I paid for a cab would you accompany Mrs Leadam to her house in Tooley Street? As you can see, my sister's in a state of agitation and I

131

don't feel it's safe for her to be alone on the street, especially with that box. I know it's out of your way but the journey won't take long in a carriage."

Greenwood looked at Sinclair, who shrugged his shoulders. "Of course, it would be our pleasure, Mrs Bowman, and don't worry about the fare: Dr Sinclair and I will sort it out. Dr Sinclair will fetch a cab and be back here in a trice, won't you?" Sinclair gave another shrug, and disappeared towards Cheapside to find the required transport.

"This is very kind of you," Emma cooed, holding her handsome captive's hand as they stood in the hallway waiting for Sinclair's return. "Mrs Leadam is not in her right mind at the moment: her husband died suddenly and since then she has been in some financial distress; but thanks to the contents of that little box I think her problems are over. Please accept our apologies for her behaviour. I will let her know that you have offered to take her home. My sister is very stubborn, and she likes to do things her own way. I know she'll be reluctant to accept an offer of assistance from me, but she'll find it harder to decline if it has come from a gentleman like you."

Greenwood smiled, enjoying the feeling of being needed and appreciated. Sinclair arrived at the house with the cab some moments later, and Greenwood helped Mrs Leadam in, then sat next to her with Sinclair opposite. Sinclair mirrored Mrs Leadam's icy glare as they confronted each other in the cramped cab. He was sure she didn't like him and he certainly did not like her, even though he thought she was extraordinarily beautiful for a woman of her age. The cab pulled away with a sudden jolt, propelling Sinclair into her lap.

"I'm so sorry, madam, please forgive me," he said, scrambling across Mrs Leadam's knees and back into his seat. His embarrassment was greeted with a look of such quivering fury he felt he should curl up and die. When they got to Tooley Street, Sinclair threw the door open and jumped down, allowing the source of his vexation to vacate the cab. He held out his hand to aid her down the steps, and she accepted it with another blood-curdling look. With her hand firmly in his, he walked her to her door. "Good night, madam," he said with exaggerated finality.

"Good night, sir," she replied. "Please thank Mr Greenwood for his generosity."

"I will, madam," Sinclair replied.

"My goodness, she's a bit of a handful, don't you think?" said Greenwood as Sinclair climbed back into the cab.

"She certainly is, Frank. Bowman told me his wife's family was difficult. Now I know what he means."

8

The Matchmakers's Plan

Eliza Martin was standing in the spring sunshine of an early
March afternoon, waiting for her daughters outside Kensington
Palace Gardens. "Good afternoon, my dear," she proclaimed as
Charlotte alighted from her cab.

"Good afternoon, Mother," Charlotte replied, taking in her
mother's immaculate sea-green dress and matching coat which
she had topped off with an extraordinarily large black felt hat,
trimmed with a green ribbon and a quivering white ostrich plume.
Charlotte looked at her own apparel with dismay; she hated the
drab black mourning cape and the ugly crepe bonnet, but was
determined to give her husband the respect he deserved: she was a
widow, and she would dress as such until she felt it was morally
right not to do so. Mrs Martin viewed her daughter with an

undisguised grimace. "That bonnet looks hideous. When your father passes I swear I shall never wear anything that ugly. I don't know if I care to be seen in public with you looking like that."

Charlotte composed herself, determined to maintain the little serenity she had. "I see you are well and on your usual good form, mother."

"Of course I'm well, I'm always well. I must be the only woman to be married to a physician who never has need of one, which is just as well as there is never one in the house, is there, dear?"

"Charlotte nodded, not wishing to contradict her mother and sympathising with her, for if she had not worked in the apothecary shop she would hardly ever have seen Christopher. That was the problem with being married to a doctor: the patients always came first.

"Your sister will be here shortly," said her mother, still interrogating her with her critical eye. "I thought it would be nice for us to spend a little time together now that everything is settled."

Charlotte, who was well used to her mother's euphemisms, allowed herself a little prod in retaliation. "You mean, now you know that I will not be sent to the Marshalsea?"

"Well, if you must put it like that, the answer is yes, dear," her mother huffed. "Respectable people take their walks here. You, of course, may not be allowed in looking like that!"

Smoothly and determinedly, Charlotte replied, "I am perfectly respectably dressed, Mother. I have both a hat and gloves. I am sure that a grieving widow will not be denied the solace of a walk in the Queen's gardens."

Another hired carriage pulled up, and her sister Emma alighted, dressed in a fabulous blue woollen coat with a dark-blue

135

felt hat trimmed with a complementing red ostrich-plume. Despite their difficult relationship, Charlotte admired her sister's good judgement when it came to clothes. The combination of bright colours complemented her pale skin and hair beautifully.

"Charlotte, that bonnet is truly awful," Emma said by way of greeting. "I'd have thought that you would have got yourself something more…" she paused, looking at her sister's mourning attire.

"Something more attractive, is that what you were thinking?" demanded Charlotte.

"Yes, that was exactly what I was thinking," she said, turning to her mother. "I'm sure Mother thinks the same."

"I've already told her I think it's hideous," her mother said, and turned to go through the gates into the park. The two sisters followed as their mother strode out along the gravel path towards the Round Pond. Experience of many such walks had taught the girls that their mother was a fast walker and that it was important not to get left behind. Although in many ways she agreed with her mother's and her sister's comments about her attire, Charlotte thought that she should not let the opportunity to defend herself go by. "I'm sure you'll understand," she said to her sister, "I'm not feeling in the least bit attractive at the moment. In fact, I feel quite wretched. I couldn't care less what I look like. Besides, now I don't have the money I used to have for hats and dresses."

"Keep up," called her mother. "I have said we will meet Mrs Peacock at three at the far side of the lake." Silently, the two sisters followed in their mother's footsteps past the drifts of spring daffodils dancing in the breeze and towards the Round Pond, which despite its diminutive name was a large ornamental lake dotted with clusters of snow-white swans, fat, brown geese, and all manner of brightly coloured ducks.

When they reached the edge of the lake Charlotte braced herself to speak again. Talking to anyone in her family was difficult at the best of times. "Emma," she ventured, "I want to thank you and Henry for all the help you've given me over the last few months."

Emma turned her beautifully coiffured head in her direction. "I should think so too. Henry has gone far beyond his duties as an executor."

Charlotte fought against the feeling of crushing futility that her mother and sister aroused in her. "I know that; he's been a true brother to me, and I want you to know that I'm truly grateful." Why she wondered, did the women in her family make it so hard to say even nice things? Why did they always have to be angry or spiteful?

As they walked, Charlotte thought that she would much rather have gone for a walk with her father, but he was at a meeting of the Medical Society of London; the place where he had first met Christopher Leadam as an ambitious young surgeon. Her father had always liked Christopher. He had invited him back to Wimpole Street and introduced the tall and handsome stranger with his curious Yorkshire accent to her family. Charlotte remembered with a powerful mixture of sadness and affection how her stomach had turned somersaults when Christopher had looked at her across her parents' dining room table, how her cheeks had flushed when he spoke to her and the disapproving looks her mother had given her. Their courtship was short. Her mother was against it, saying that she was too young to know her own mind, mainly because she wanted time to change it for her, and her father was all for it because he saw the great affection they shared. Luckily, despite all appearances to the contrary, her father held the upper hand when it came to matters of importance in the family and they were married on her seventeenth birthday at the church in Marylebone.

Now, as Charlotte chased her mother around the lake, that first meeting seemed a lifetime away. She looked down at her dowdy clothes and felt she had lived a thousand unhappy years, and yet she knew that it wasn't true. She had been happy just a few months ago, before Christopher had died and her world had collapsed.

"Well, I'm glad the whole affair is over with," said Emma as Mrs Peacock came into view. "I was seriously worried Henry would have to visit you in the Marshalsea, and that would not have been good for business."

To everyone else Christopher Leadam had been a handsome, educated, and clever man, but to her mother he was a rough farmer's son and no better than a blacksmith. Now that her less than desirable son-in-law was dead, Charlotte knew her mother saw an opportunity to marry her up a social rank to a man who better fitted with her aspirations; a man with a respectable profession and a house north of the river.

Emma pulled her hat down as the breeze turned into a squall and quickened her step to keep up. "Did you know that awful doctor friend of Henry's has stolen one of Papa's patients?" she said to Charlotte. "I think that's very low, don't you?"

"Yes, I do. I'm sure Christopher would never have done such a thing."

"Mother is furious, of course," Emma continued, ignoring the opportunity to praise her dead brother-in-law. "Sir Hubert Husselbee was worth more than ten thousand a year, and Father had yet to prescribe him a thing."

"I've rarely met with such ill manners and rudeness; that awful Scottish man is obviously a charlatan. I cannot think how he's a friend of Henry's."

Gratified by her sister's support on this vexatious matter, Emma continued. "I've told Henry to give him up, and that he's not welcome in my house again."

"And what does Henry have to say about that?" probed Charlotte, wondering if there was an opportunity to undermine her sister's ascendance in the Bowman household.

"Henry will do as he is bid. Of course, if he maintains his friendship outside the house that is entirely his affair, but I will not have Dr Sinclair in my house again.

* * *

John and William were on their way to Guy's to meet Mr Hoares. They headed along St Thomas's Street, then passed through the postern gate and headed for the entrance. It was not the first time John had been inside the hospital, as he had attended many services in the chapel with his mother and father, but today its grey Portland stone walls seemed particularly intimidating because it was the first time he was entering it on his own account, as a walking student with Mr Hoares.

Guy's was the largest and richest of London's seven charitable hospitals, with nearly 400 beds. Work at Guy's was highly sought after by aspiring surgeons, and his father had had no trouble getting apprentices because of it. Like all the charitable hospitals, it took its patients on the recommendation of the parish Poor Law officers but unlike its sister institution, St Thomas', located just a stone's throw away, Guy's was founded to treat patients who were deemed to be incurable.

These 'incurable' paupers received the best treatment that medicine had to offer, and in return became the training material for the students and doctors. The hospital setting allowed for detailed observation and the scientific monitoring of their diseases; and death, when it came, brought the opportunity for dissection and autopsy. The autopsies and the debates that followed in the weekly hospital committees were the most important and sought-after part of surgical training in England. Those apprentices lucky enough to access it were provided with a more complete picture of disease than could ever be acquired by attending the public anatomy demonstrations given by Mr Hunter or at any of the other private medical schools in the city, including the acquisition and dissection of one's own cadaver, which was a common practice for the more affluent students. Consequently, competition for places was intense and the price of entry was high. Today, Mr Hoares planned to introduce William to Mr Cooper, one of Guy's most celebrated surgeons, to see if he would take him on as an assistant, for a price.

As the boys crossed the courtyard, John looked up to the roof. "Do you know who they are, William?" he said pointing at the statues.

"They're Aesculapius, the Greek god of medicine, and his daughter Hygieia, the goddess of cleanliness," William replied.

"Ah, the son of the god Apollo," said John. "He killed his wife in a fit of pique because he thought she'd been unfaithful, but it turned out she hadn't and was pregnant with his child."

"That was unfortunate," said William.

"When he realised, he cut the child out of her womb, then gave him to be raised by a centaur called Chiron, who taught him the arts of medicine. He became so good at it that he was able to raise people from the dead."

"My God, is that why his statue's there? If you ask me it's a queer sort of story to have on top of a hospital that's meant for incurables."

"Does no one come out alive?" John asked, feeling nervous about going onto the wards.

"Oh yes. Guy's is supposed to be for incurables, but the demand for beds at St Thomas' is so high that Guy's takes surgical and medical patients now," said William. "The patients come here when they can't be cared for at home or in the poor house. Some are nursed until they die; others are treated and go back where they came from. About half the people we see go home." John felt relieved and grateful he was not about to enter the antechamber to a charnel house.

"Good afternoon, gentlemen," said Mr Hoares as he met the boys on the steps. "Shall we go in?"

* * *

After their walk in Kensington Palace Gardens, the women retired to Mrs Peacock's in Golden Square to take tea. Never one to miss the opportunity to display her wealth to those who coveted it, Mrs Peacock led her guests into her green and cream drawing room with her little black dog at her heels. "My dears, I hope you like it. The paper was brought in from France only last month." Pointing to the drapes she continued, "I'm still waiting for the curtain material to arrive. Doesn't it look a ghastly mess?" Her guests made a range of appropriate and consoling comments, which she lapped up enthusiastically as she chased the yapping little monster between the finely turned chair legs and under the taffeta-covered sofas. Eventually, she scooped the dog up like a baby, scolding him with a jewel-encrusted finger and invited her guests to sit.

Like their mother, Mrs Peacock was immaculately attired. Her coiffure was powdered grey and decorated with a large ruby and pearl comb. Her dress was pea-green silk brocade, which she had adorned with a matching ruby pendant drop set on a string of seed pearls. With the errant dog under control, she rang a small silver bell with a flourish. The dog, which was sitting on her lap, snarled and dribbled, but within moments was distracted by the appearance of a woman dressed in a plain brown dress, not dissimilar to the one Charlotte was wearing, much to her mother's horror. The maid poured a kettle of hot water onto the tea in Mrs Peacock's beautiful Chinese teapot and a second maid brought in a tray laden with plates of bread and butter and generous slices of pound cake. As they drank their tea, Mrs Martin lamented the recent passing of her son-in-law, who as far as she was concerned had died tragically young and before he could achieve his full potential, as she was sure he was destined to be elected onto the staff at Guy's. Mrs Peacock listened attentively, stroking the dog and feeding it slices of bread and butter from her plate. Emma nodded her head from time to time to support her mother's version of events, while Charlotte buried hers in her tea dish, knowing that this was never to be Christopher's destiny. Men like Christopher Leadam rarely made it to the dizzy heights of being on the hospital staff.

"Oh my dear Charlotte, how terrible for you," the elderly woman said, patting her with a heavily ringed hand. "Had your husband been at St George's I am sure we could have put a word in for him, but we have no influence at Guy's. Nevertheless, you have no need to worry; your mother and I have a plan. With our help all your problems will be over within the year," she smiled,

142

smoothing her frock where the dog had been sitting. "Of course you must remain in mourning a little longer, my sweet. Six months is an acceptable time, don't you think, Eliza?"

Her mother agreed. "Oh, quite adequate, Vanda dearest."

"Good. That means all this mourning can be over with by the autumn, which will place you well for the season," said Mrs Peacock, tipping the dregs of her tea dish into the slop tray and pouring herself another cup. "Of course competition for a man with money is intense. There is always a ready stream of pretty little virgins up from the country to attract a man's fancy, and they do fancy them awful young these days if I may say so, Eliza."

"Oh, I agree, my dear; some of them are barely out of the nursery. Men have no shame when it comes to wanting, well, we all know what they want, don't we?"

"We are all women of the world, are we not?" Mrs Peacock tittered. "Your mother and I are certain that with your looks and the fact that you have only had one child, and can have no more, you will be an attractive prospect to a widower with children and means. A sensible man is prepared to exchange a little slackness for the benefit of a woman's experience in the nursery and the bedroom; especially when he has a sufficient brood already and is in the mood for rutting without the risk of more."

"Thank you, Mrs Peacock. I'm very grateful for your concern, but please don't make any special arrangements on my behalf," Charlotte mumbled into her cup, doing her best to stay calm.

"Nonsense, child, your mother and I are looking forward to it, aren't we, Eliza? I love a bit of match-making, don't you, Emma?" Mrs Martin smiled and Emma nodded her agreement, aware that her sister might explode at any moment.

143

Charlotte arrived home in a state of pique, not because of her mother's plan, she had expected that, but because she had enlisted the help of Mrs Peacock. God knows what sort of lecherous old man Mrs Peacock had in mind for her after her comments about slackness and rutting!

In the parlour, John, William and Mr Hoares were looking dejected.

"What's happened?" she said, taking off her bonnet and cape.

Mr Hoares stood up to speak. He cleared his throat, then announced that Mr Cooper would not take William as a dresser or as an apprentice, because he was taking on his nephew and would not have sufficient time to devote to the instruction of two young men.

"What utter nonsense!" Charlotte railed, throwing her hands in the air.

"I know. The man usually takes as many students as he can: last year he had four.

"Oh, William, I'm sorry," said Charlotte, visibly shrinking as her body deflated, weary with the struggle.

"Mr Hoares did his best; besides Cooper is very expensive," said William in Mr Hoares' defence. "He charges sixty-five pounds to work as his dresser. I'm sure something else will turn up."

"I hope so," muttered Charlotte.

John put his arm around her. "Mother," he said.

"What is it?"

Her son pulled himself up to his full height. He knew that with the death of his father his automatic access to hospital training had disappeared, and that his mother would have to find him a master if he was to become a surgeon. "Mr Hoares and I have also made enquiries at the hospital about becoming an apprentice there."

"Good. That is what I wanted you to do," she replied, sensing there was more bad news to come.

"It seems that to be apprenticed to anyone at the hospital it will cost at least two hundred pounds, plus other fees and expenses."

"Two hundred pounds! Good God, your father never charged that much," Charlotte shrieked. "Where am I going to find that sort of money for both of you?"

Mr Hoares sat down next to her and took her hand. "Try not to panic. I'm sure there are other options we can explore. I will ask at St Thomas' and at the London. I'm sure that something can be arranged."

"Oh, I do hope so, Mr Hoares, because I'm quite worn out with all this worry."

9
Mr Bowman's Suggestion

Frank Greenwood joined Sinclair and Bowman at the Sadler's Wells theatre, buoyed up by the eight guineas in his pocket he had earned from Lord Wroxeter. The atmosphere was vibrant and expectant as the fashionably dressed audience took their seats. A pair of red velvet curtains hung across the gilded proscenium, hiding the delights to come, and in the pit there were two enormous A frames supporting a slack line that ran front to back, high above the audience's heads, ready for a display of rope-walking.

"Goodness, I haven't been to the theatre for years," Greenwood gushed, taking his seat. "I've spent far too long in barracks or in the country chasing foxes. This is wonderful," he rejoiced, gazing at the tiers of ornately gilded boxes opposite and admiring the young women playing coyly with their fans.

"As a married man I have no interest in the ladies," said Bowman with happy resignation. "One woman is more than enough for me."

"But looking is permitted," said Sinclair, "and from what I can see is positively encouraged. I prefer it that way if I'm honest. I find that admiration from afar is often preferable to an actual encounter with the female of the species."

"In your situation, Sinclair, it would be wise to stay well out of Cupid's range. Wives have many delights and great benefits, but they're fearfully expensive creatures to keep and you, my dear friend, are broke." Bowman turned to Greenwood. "I blame Sinclair for my addiction to the theatre; he drags me out whenever he's in town."

"Aye," Sinclair chuckled. "I'm making up for all those years of misery in Scotland."

The drums rolled, and the Master of Ceremonies stepped in front of the curtain. "Tonight for your delight and delectation, ladies and gentlemen, we have a show featuring breathtaking rope-walking from Naples; death-defying tumbling, acrobats from China and the music of an angel, the virtuoso Madame de Chanson with her timeless songs of amour." The three men roared their approval with the rest of the audience, the red curtains opened and the show began.

The friends watched open mouthed as Signor Romeo and Adriani walked the rope at the same time as they juggled with batons and hoops. The act finished with Signor Romeo performing the splits above the heads of the audience, who thundered their applause. The Joseph Brothers somersaulted and rotated across the stage at amazing heights in their yellow and red costumes, and the Chinese acrobats made a tower of human flesh ten men high. Finally, Madam de Chanson, a buxom woman dressed in white with flowers in her hair, played a golden harp and sang French songs with an exquisite and lilting voice that moved the audience so much that even the hardest hearted of them were forced to wipe a tear from their eyes.

When the performances were over, the friends made their way to the lobby feeling happy and relaxed, enjoying the jostling crowd with its smell of perfume and powder and the opportunities for surreptitious bodily contact with the ladies and girls as they made their way out onto the crowded street. Bowman managed to attract the attention of a driver with an empty cab, and soon they were on their way to Bread Street. "I'm sorry I can't ask you in at the moment," he apologised. "It's just that Emma has banned Sinclair from the house for stealing one of her father's patients."

"What?" demanded Sinclair. "I've never met the man. How could I possibly steal one of his precious patients? I only have the one!"

"Precisely, and my father-in-law had his claws into him first, according to Emma."

"Well, how was I supposed to know he had a doctor?" protested Sinclair. "Husselbee said nothing to me, did he, Frank?"

"Er, no, he didn't," Greenwood agreed.

"Well, whatever happened, the result is you're banned, Sinclair."

"What about me," inquired Greenwood, fishing for a compliment?

"Oh, Emma thinks you're a true gentleman, unlike your colleague Dr Sinclair, who apparently fondled my sister-in-law's knees in the carriage the other night."

"Oh for goodness' sake," bleated Sinclair. "Women are a mystery to me. I had absolutely no desire to fondle her; it was just an unfortunate accident."

"That's women for you; they're always making something out of nothing. They're a mystery to all of us, old chap," replied Bowman, consoling Sinclair with a pat on the knee.

"Be careful, Henry," Sinclair retorted, with a weary smile on his face.

"I don't think women are a mystery," interjected Greenwood. "You just have to talk about the things they find interesting."

"Like what?" demanded Sinclair scornfully.

"Well, mainly themselves, I find," said Greenwood. "I usually admire their clothes or their hair, or both. I say something like you look lovely in that dress or you look heavenly in that hat."

"How do you do that? Doesn't it feel as if your nose is curling up with embarrassment?"

"As it happens I don't feel the least bit embarrassed. You only have to look around to see that most women put a great deal of effort into preparing an ensemble. And in my opinion if they make so much effort to be admired one shouldn't let them down."

"There you are, James: the end of your financial problems is in sight. All you have to do is go to Tooley Street and pay my sister-in-law some compliments and she'll be eating out of your hand. It would be worth a bit of nose-curling embarrassment if you could get your hands on that apothecary shop. I would, of course, have to charge you handsomely to draw up the contracts and protect my sister's interests."

"Steady on, Henry. I hardly know the woman and it seems that I'm already 'persona non grata'. What on earth could I say to persuade her that she should sell or lease her shop to me, even if I wanted it, and I'm not sure I do?"

"Oh, I don't know, James, you're a clever man," Bowman sighed. "I'm sure you can come up with something." He thumped the cab roof and opened the door. "I'm out here, gentlemen. Good night."

* * *

Charlotte placed a candle on her dressing table and read the letter she had received from Yorkshire for what seemed like the tenth time, trying to decide how to reply. She looked at herself in the looking glass; her hair hung limp and lifeless framing her sad and worn out face. Knowing she had no option but to disappoint Lucy, she picked up her pen and wrote:

> *Dearest Lucy,*
> *John and I love you and miss you all.*
> *Unfortunately, our situation is far from settled*
> *following Mr Leadam's passing, and*
> *consequently we are not in a position to*
> *entertain guests this summer. I know this will be*
> *disappointing to you, as it is to me, but I we*
> *hope we will be able to return the kindness and*
> *generosity you and your family showed to me*
> *and to John later in the year. In the meantime, I*
> *ask you not to worry. I promise to write with*
> *more news soon.*
> *Your loving aunt,*
> *Charlotte*

It was done; she had done the sensible thing and said no to her niece. She folded the paper, sealed it with a blob of scarlet wax and wrote the address on the front. Exhausted, she slipped into her side of the bed between the cold white sheets, with the empty space beside her that was her nightly reminder of her loss and loneliness, and went to sleep.

Charlotte woke to the sound of Mrs Dredge shuffling around the bedroom. "Here's a cup of warm milk for you, ducky. Now make sure you drink it all up. You need to keep your strength up, my love, and we can't afford to waste it, can we?"

"Thank you, Elsie," she yawned. "Could you ask John to take that letter to the mail office in Holborn?"

"Right you are," the old woman chirped, drawing back the curtains. "When you're ready there are a number of accounts to be settled. We owe the butcher, the dairy, the coal merchant..."

"All right, all right, that's enough. I get the picture," Charlotte snapped, immediately regretting it. She knew the old woman was doing her best to keep the household running on a shoestring. "I'll get dressed and see you in the kitchen shortly; we can sort the bills out then."

As her housekeeper closed the door, Charlotte threw her head back against the pillows in a silent scream of frustration. Money, she hated it! Why did everything come down to money? If the bills would just stop coming she knew she could get on her feet again. Lying back on the pillows, she realised that cancelling the sale of the house when she found Christopher's haul of Scottish treasure had been a mistake. Renting out rooms would not produce the income she needed to get her son started as a surgeon, so she would have to sell the house in the end.

Her mother was right: without a man to earn money for her, or a respectable way of earning money herself, she was doomed to poverty. The thought of having to swallow her pride and submit herself to Mrs Peacock's odious plan filled her with rage, and once again she found herself wondering how a man who had seemed to have everything in life under control could leave her in such a mess. She was so angry with Christopher that she turned to his side of the bed, and thumped the pillow where his head had rested for so many years with such force that she hurt her wrist.

Rubbing her injured hand, she slumped back onto the pillows and her mood turned from frustration to melancholy. She felt a deep longing not just for her dead husband but for the life they had lived together. She loathed the sense of powerlessness and vulnerability that had been thrust upon her by his death.

Throwing back the bedclothes, Charlotte silently acknowledged that the sense of independence she had enjoyed in her married days had been counterfeit. In truth, she had never been independent; her sense of worth had come from her husband's abilities and money, and not her own. She was learning the most painful lesson she had ever learned; it was more painful than her barrenness. She lived in a man's world, and they would not let her be independent.

* * *

At Good Acre Court Sinclair was pacing up and down in his room. The conversation with Bowman the night before had set a hare running in his brain. Could he face Charlotte Leadam again, he asked himself. If he did go to see her, what would he say? Greenwood's idea of compliments was all right over the dinner table, but he was hardly going to walk into an apothecary shop and tell its owner, a woman who already thought he had wronged her, that she looked lovely in whatever dress she was wearing, and expect her to enter into a business arrangement with him.

If he were to make this woman a proposition, what sort of proposition should it be? He had no idea; he had never been in business before. If she did agree to sell him the shop, or lease it to him, where would he get the money to buy it? Henry clearly wasn't thinking straight. He recalled the night's events again. Henry had not been drinking, in fact he was stone cold sober when he made the suggestion; so perhaps, he mused, there might be some possibility of success.

He took out his pocket watch, flipping the front case open to check the hour. Then he closed it and rolled it around in the palm of his hand before kissing it and putting it back in his pocket. It was half past ten, and with nothing better to do he decided to put himself out of his misery by walking down to Tooley Street to view the property.

He crossed London Bridge at around noon and entered Tooley Street a few minutes later, passing St Olave's Church and the old grammar school. Looking up, he saw a terrace of four-storey timber houses, one of which had the traditional apothecary's sign of a golden pestle and mortar hanging over the door. He read the brass plate on the door, "C.R. Leadam Apothecary & Surgeon", and he knew that he had found the right place.

The windows of the shop were small and square. Four large blue and white apothecary pots were displayed there. Peering into the shop he could see the walls were covered with what looked like a well-stocked range of duck-egg blue cabinets. There were counters for weighing and mixing medicines, and a large oak table ran down the centre of the room. In one of the panes close to the door there was a notice saying "CLOSED".

Having seen enough, he was about to leave when a distressed-looking woman with a baby in her arms approached and knocked on the door. There was no reply, so the woman knocked again. Eventually, a boy appeared. "We're closed, Mrs Middleton. You'll have to take Samuel to Mr Lloyd in the Borough High Street."

The woman thrust the child towards the boy. "I want Mrs Leadam to have a look at Sammy; he's not right, I know he's not right."

Sinclair watched from his position by the window as the woman insisted that the boy fetch his mother. He was about to offer his assistance when Charlotte Leadam appeared in the same brown dress she had worn the night of their first encounter. She gently pulled the blanket away from the baby's face and felt the child's forehead. "He's very hot, Mrs Middleton; in fact he's too hot. But I can't help you now that Mr Leadam is no longer here."

"But I don't trust that Mr Lloyd. Oh please give me something for him," the woman pleaded. "I know you can make him better."

"Excuse me, madam, may I be of assistance?" Sinclair offered from the pavement. Charlotte looked at him with astonishment and surprise.

"Mr, er, I'm sorry, we met at my brother-in-law's house," she stumbled. Looking at him in the light of day she noted that he was taller than she remembered; not as tall as Christopher had been, but his figure was handsome enough. Under his hat she could see that the colour of his hair was not brown, as she had remembered, but the colour of sand; and his hazel eyes were flecked with specks of green.

"Yes we did, Mrs Leadam. My name is Sinclair and I am a physician and surgeon." He turned to the woman with the child. "Madam, I would be very happy to look at Samuel if you would permit me."

The woman looked at Charlotte and then at Sinclair. "You'd better come in," she said, leading them into the shop. The boy who had opened the door trailed behind. Sinclair asked the child's mother to lay her baby on the long oak table while he took off his coat and hat. He looked at the layers of blankets and clothes and started to gently unwrap the little human parcel. "He's breathing, that's always a good sign, Mrs Middleton," he said in a soothing Scots brogue. The child's mother did not look impressed, and neither did Mrs Leadam. "Would you be so kind as to fetch me a large bowl of cold water?" Sinclair said.

"Of course," Charlotte replied, and left for the scullery, leaving the boy leaning against the counter to watch him suspiciously.

"Son?"

John looked up. "Me, sir?"

"Aye, you. Does your mother have any towels or cloths?"

"Yes, sir."

"Well, could you get somea couple for me?" said Sinclair, leaning over the baby and listening to its rasping breath. He put his ear to the child's chest and listened to its heart. "He's got a good little heart. I'm sure he's going to grow up to be a bonny laddie," he assured the child's sceptical and anxious mother.

The child's chubby legs lay still as he pressed his fingers into their flesh. "Good. No discolouration of the skin and no obvious rash." Then Sinclair took the child's head in his hands and looked at him; his left ear was bright red. "I think this is the problem, madam. Your son has a blockage in his ear. This is causing him

155

pain and making him unwell. We just need to reduce the fever and he'll soon be on the mend."

Charlotte returned with the bowl of cold water. "Now, Mrs Middleton, if you could undress wee Sammy we'll give him a nice cold bath.

"A cold bath? Do you want to kill him?" the woman screamed.

"Trust me, he won't die," the doctor soothed.

Charlotte put her hand on the woman's arm. "Perhaps we could start by cooling him with a wet cloth. Here, you take this," she said, dipping a towel into the water. "Put this on Sammy's head." The woman followed Charlotte's instructions and started to nurse her child.

"Do you have a tincture of meadowsweet or feverfew, Mrs Leadam?" asked Sinclair.

"I have both, and a tincture of willow bark."

"Which would you recommend?"

"I'd recommend the meadow sweet in the case of an infant, sir," she replied, heading towards the small bottles of tinctures on the shelves. Suddenly Mrs Middleton gave a scream. "Oh my God!" she wailed. "He's gone all stiff!" Sinclair looked at the child, who started to cry as if something terrifying was happening, and then, as suddenly as he had started, stopped. His little fists clenched. "He's having a fit!" his mother shrieked.

Sinclair looked at the child, who was now twitching violently on the table, his lips going blue. He picked the baby up and plunged him into the bowl of cold water. "Hold him while I pour the water," he commanded the white-faced woman. Gradually the twitching subsided and the child lapsed into unconsciousness, his eyes open and unfocused.

"I'm losing him!" the woman cried, clasping her child to her breast.

Sinclair looked on without concern. The child had turned a light shade of grey and his breathing was laboured. "Your son has had a convulsion because of the fever. They're extremely common, Mrs Middleton. Now he's a little cooler he'll pick up very quickly. Hold his head up so that Mrs Leadam can give Sammy some medicine. I'm sure he's through the worst now."

Charlotte pressed the child's lips with a spoon and poured in the bitter liquid. Sammy caught his breath, screwed up his face and tried to spit out the foul-tasting liquor. "There, that's a good sign," she said reassuringly.

A few minutes passed before John ventured forward to look at the baby, who was now moving his arms and legs normally and sucking on his mother's finger. "Shall I ask Mrs Dredge for some tea, Mother?"

"I think that would be a very good idea. Would you like tea, Dr Sinclair?"

"Aye, that would be grand. "Now, Mrs Middleton, keep wee Sammy comfortable but not too hot, give him one teaspoon of tincture every four hours and put an onion poultice on his left ear to draw out the humours that are causing the blockage. I'm sure he will be well in a couple of days but I'll call in tomorrow, if I may, to check on his progress."

"Thank you so much, Mrs Leadam, and thank you, Dr Sinclair. I knew this was the place to come. Thank you."

Upstairs in the parlour, Charlotte poured the tea and asked Sinclair where he had learned about seizures in babies. He noticed that although she was listening intently as he answered there was a weariness about her that he hadn't noticed a few weeks earlier. Her luxuriant auburn hair, the first thing he had noticed about her the night she had burst into Henry's parlour, was now limply tied up in a ponytail, and her fabulous blue eyes that had flashed like polished steel in the candlelight when they first met looked more like two icy pools of misery. "I was speaking to your brother-in-law yesterday," he ventured, "and he suggested that you might be looking to sell or lease the apothecary shop, so I decided to walk over and take a look. That's why I was outside when Mrs Middleton arrived with wee Sammy."

"Well, that was very presumptuous of my brother-in-law, but just as well for little Samuel. I think you saved his life."

"I'm sorry if I was misled about the property, but I think wee Sammy would have recovered on his own. I just made him more comfortable."

"Well, Mrs Middleton thinks you're his saviour, and if you are going to practise around here you picked the right baby to save. Her husband owns the grocery shop on the corner of Pickled Herring Street and she's the most notorious gossip. Everyone in the district will know how you saved little Samuel by the end of the week." Charlotte's smile only emphasised her fatigue. "As far as the property is concerned you weren't really misled, Dr Sinclair. My brother-in-law was just premature with the information. As things stand I have little option but to sell."

"I'm sorry to hear that."

"Thank you. I know that I'm battling against all the odds, but I'm reluctant to give up my son's birthright without a fight."

"That's very noble of you, Mrs Leadam." Sinclair admired her spirit and her sense of responsibility, but did not want to give her false hope. "If truth be told I'm in no position to buy at the moment; I was merely curious. You see, everything I owned is at the bottom of the sea, and I have no material assets to call on. It's true that I still have my qualifications and references, but I have only what I stand in, together with a few guineas in my pocket. However, if I were in a position to make you an offer I would. This practice is in a good position and is, from what I've just witnessed, well respected. It would be a good investment for any surgeon with means and ambition."

"Thank you, Dr Sinclair. Did I hear you say that everything you owned is at the bottom of the sea?"

"Aye. I was on the 'Sherwell' when it went down," he said cautiously, not knowing how she would react.

"Oh no, not that ship again. I've had my own problems with the 'Sherwell' but I'm sorry to hear that you had yours too. I had no idea." Charlotte lowered her gaze in a mixture of sadness and embarrassment. "It must have been a horrific experience."

"Aye, I still have nightmares about it. But no less horrific than the sudden loss of a much-loved spouse."

"Thank you, Dr Sinclair," she replied, with an audible crack of emotion in her voice. "Our positions are more similar than one might at first imagine," she said, wiping an unbidden tear from her eye. Perhaps my brother-in-law is more perceptive than we think."

Sinclair sat silently for a moment, deep in thought. That old rascal Henry Bowman was up to something. He had deliberately suggested that he should visit his sister-in-law. "I know this is an impolite question, but may I ask you how much money you need to raise?"

"I need to pay for my son's apprenticeship, for the remainder of my husband's apprentice William's training, and I need an income for myself."

"How much does an apprenticeship cost?"

"About two hundred pounds plus other expenses at Guy's; there are cheaper alternatives. I think Christopher charged a

159

hundred and forty pounds, so I owe William's parents that much at least, less if I can find a new master for him. You're a surgeon, Dr Sinclair. Do you not know these things?"

"I was never an apprentice, madam. I am Scottish, and as such I'm a university man. Our system of medical training is very different from the chaos in London. I've a medical degree and diplomas in surgery from Leiden and Paris. I've worked almost exclusively in hospitals, first at the Edinburgh Infirmary and when I returned from Europe at St George's here in London."

"Which is where you met Henry. He's their attorney; and my father is on the staff."

"Aye," nodded Sinclair. "Of course I had my own patients, but I treated them in their own homes in the same way a London-trained physician would do. I was on my way to India to take up the post of Assistant to the Surgeon General with the East India Company in Calcutta when I was shipwrecked."

Charlotte looked directly into Sinclair's handsome face and said, "Do you still plan to go to India or will you return to Scotland?"

"I intend to stay here, in London. I have no plans to return to Scotland."

"You have no family or friends to return to?" she enquired tentatively.

"None, madam," he lied, feeling a searing pang of guilt shoot through his veins.

Having established her ground, she ventured a little further. "Could you take on apprentices if you had a surgery?"

"I don't see why not, although I'd have to know the curriculum I was to teach them." He sensed he was being led down a path that he was unsure about travelling.

"Dr Sinclair." Charlotte paused to be sure of her words. "Would you be interested in some sort of quid pro quo arrangement with me? I have a surgery and an apothecary shop neither of which I'm allowed to use, and you're a surgeon in need of patients. Perhaps if we joined forces we could solve both of our problems."

He looked at her in astonishment: she had made him a proposition and not the other way round. He had to admit that Christopher Leadam had been a very lucky man; his wife was not only handsome, but she was spirited and clever too.

"What did you have in mind, Mrs Leadam?"

"I'm not sure, but you and Henry could work out the details; perhaps I could provide you with the premises in return for your taking on my apprentices. I'm sure we can come to a mutually acceptable agreement for accommodation costs and sharing the apothecary shop profits." She tilted her head towards him, pleading with her luscious eyes, which shone with a new and brighter intensity that he could only assume was hope.

"Em," he replied thoughtfully, feeling slightly flustered by her boldness and excited by the power of her gaze. "Aye, I would, thank you, Mrs Leadam."

Charlotte leapt to her feet with a strong desire to throw her arms around him, but instead she headed for the dresser and the last bottle of Madeira. "I think this calls for something stronger than tea," she smiled.

10
The Knight in the Attic

"John, go and knock on Dr Sinclair's door again and tell him to get up. There's a queue of people waiting to see him. Tell him that if he's not up in ten minutes I'll drag him out of bed myself. That should do the trick."

"He was out all night delivering Mrs Willis's baby in Gracechurch Street," John replied in Sinclair's defence.

"I know he was, but we have a business to run and no matter how tired he is he has to get up and see his patients. I'll get William started on the dentistry. Now off you go."

John ran up the three flights of stairs to the attic apartment. Sinclair heard the thud on his door. He rubbed his tired eyes and dragged himself away from its warmth and comfort of his crumpled bed. He stretched out his arms, touching the ceiling around the dormer window and taking in the yellow crack of dawn that was breaking through the grey November clouds. "Tell your mother I'm on my way," he mumbled irritably, just loud enough for John to hear, then he peered into the mirror at his unshaven face, straightened the clothes he had slept in all night and grumbled, "Good God, is there no peace to be had in Tooley Street?"

On his way downstairs, he ran his hands through his uncombed hair and rolled up his sleeves ready for the fresh crop of suffering humanity seeking his help. How many more for teeth?" he shouted from the bottom step. Two rough-looking men shot up their hands. "Mr Whitfield will see you shortly," he said, nodding in their direction. "Now, how many of you want home visits?" Four people, two footmen and two ladies' maids, put up their hands. "You see Mrs Leadam; she'll give you an appointment." Then he looked along the line to see who was left. There were two young women both with babies and a man with a young child in his arms. He pointed to the man carrying the young child and beckoned him over. "You all right with me seeing the child in the shop?"

"I don't care where you see him," said the man, who was dressed in the black of a lawyer's clerk.

Sinclair placed the child on the long table in the centre of the room and quickly diagnosed scarlet fever. "I'll give you a prescription to ease the fever but there's little to be done. If he gets worse make an appointment for a house call, and I'll bleed him to reduce the fever."

William appeared, having completed the morning's dentistry, and Sinclair showed the woman with a baby into the small room at the back of the house that was now his consulting room. He

163

offered her the more comfortable of the two chairs, then sat down himself. "What can I do for you today?"

"It's Mary, she's not right, doctor," the woman said. "She's my third, so I know there's summut up wi' her."

"Well, let's have a look at the wee lassie, shall we," said Sinclair, taking the child and placing her carefully on the examination table. "How old is Mary?"

"She's five weeks. She's always been a bit on the blue side. I thought she would pick up when she started feeding properly, but it ain't really happening."

"I can see that, Mrs…"

"It's Smith. Me husband has a stall at the Borough Market, sir."

Sinclair put his ear on the baby's chest and heard the sound he was dreading: a sort of swishing sound along with the sound of the regular heartbeat. As he straightened himself he said, "Would you mind if my apprentices took a look at Mary? There's something I want to teach them."

The woman nodded her consent, and Sinclair called for William and John. William was the first to arrive. "William, put your ear to wee Mary's chest and tell me what you hear."

William stepped forward and placed his ear to the child's chest. "I hear another sound in addition to the normal heartbeat, sir."

John arrived and did the same.

"Very good, gentlemen; I'll speak to you about this when Mrs Smith has gone. Now off you go." Sinclair ushered them out of the room and wrapped the baby in her blanket before gently placing her back in her mother's arms. The woman's face was resigned. "It's not good news is it, doctor?"

"No, Mrs Smith. I'm afraid it isn't," he said, returning to his seat. "Wee Mary has a problem with her heart. It doesn't work properly and it never will. All you can do is keep her comfortable until the angels come for her."

"When will that be?" the woman asked stoically.

"I think she'll live another few weeks, that's all. I'm very sorry there's nothing I can do to help her."

The woman shook his hand and thanked him.

"Tell Mrs Leadam I said there's no charge, Mrs Smith." And with that, Sinclair went outside to call the second woman in.

When the patients were gone, the household retired to the upstairs dining room at the back of the house, where Mrs Dredge had laid out breakfast. Charlotte gave Sinclair a list of patients who required home visits that morning, together with Monday's list of regular patients.

Sinclair discussed the case of the baby with the heart problem with his pupils, then gave them his instructions. He sent William to see his patients at St Thomas', where he was now working as a house surgeon, saying, "I want dry dressings for all my patients. I don't want those balsam-soaked ones or any of those milk and bread dressings that Mr Ellesmere insists on; they're no good at all. If you have any trouble getting what you need let me know, and I'll see the hospital apothecary this evening when I do my rounds. And don't forget to write up the case notes, William, in case we're called to present a case at the surgery committee on Friday."

"Yes, sir."

John, who had now completed the first six months of his training, was set to working on the prescriptions with his mother. "Get Mrs Leadam to check everything that goes out and make sure that everyone pays for their orders: we don't extend credit to anyone. If they can't pay they can't have it, do you understand?"

"Yes, sir."

"Mrs Leadam, would you make up the bills falling due tomorrow, so that they can be delivered when I make my house calls? And John, when you've got a moment I want some more ointment made up: the one made up of equal parts of wax, turpentine and hypericum."

"Yes, sir."

Having given his instructions, Sinclair went upstairs to his attic apartment. Although the ceilings were low and the windows were small it was his space. He had never been so busy or so tired, but he had never been happier either. Mrs Leadam and the old woman Dredge ran the house like clockwork. He never had to think about what he would eat, cleaning his room or his laundry. He did not even have to think about getting up in the morning: if he was not at work by seven someone would be sent to drag him out of bed. Sinclair was enjoying his work in the surgery far more than his work at the hospital. As he prepared for another day in Tooley Street, he knew he had made the right decision when he had agreed to go into partnership with Charlotte Leadam. This, he decided, was the life he had always wanted, although he had had no notion of it before.

It was almost a year since he had tried to leave England on the ill-fated 'Sherwell'. The nightmares about drowning he had suffered in the months following the wreck no longer dominated his nights, but he was still waiting to find out if he would receive any compensation from the East India Company for his losses. He was reluctant to ask Bowman to press them further as each letter added to his unpaid bill. And then there was the problem of Christmas. Morag would be writing to him soon, asking him to come back to Scotland for the holidays, and he really didn't want to go.

Downstairs in the apothecary John packed his father's old bag with fresh dressings, the made up prescriptions and the bills for Sinclair to take on his rounds, while his mother counted the morning's takings and wrote them up in the accounts.

Sinclair took out his pocket watch to check the hour. It was five to nine, and time he was on his way. He picked up his coat and hat, and wondered if he could afford to buy himself a replacement for the one he had lost in the wreck.

As he was about to leave, Mrs Leadam said, "Dr Sinclair, I have had word from my family in Yorkshire. They are coming to visit us at Christmas. I was wondering what plans you had for the holiday."

A pang of guilt shot through him, sending his mind into a momentary state of confusion.

"Aye, Christmas," he said, nodding. "Well, it's nothing special to me. I was planning to stay here and work if that's all right with you."

"Oh, that's perfectly all right. I just wanted to let you know that we will have company, and that you're welcome to join us for the celebrations if you wish."

"Thank you, Mrs Leadam; that's very kind of you. I must be away now. I'll see you at lunchtime."

As Sinclair went out, Connie Collingwood, Charlotte's friend from next door, came in. "Charlotte, dearest, would you be an angel and sit with Father this afternoon? I've picked up a couple of hours of music tuition for a family in Cannon Street. If it turns out to be a permanent arrangement I'll get a proper sitter, I promise."

"It's no trouble, Connie, honestly, but I do have one condition; well, two actually."

"That sounds ominous. What are they?"

"You have to help me plan some entertainment for Christopher's family when they come from Yorkshire, and you have to come to Mrs Peacock's supper party with me. It seems that Mrs Peacock and my mother have decided I've been in mourning long enough, and plan to parade me like a horse in the paddock at the Christmas Wife Stakes."

"Oh, is it that bad? Of course I'll help you with Christopher's family. It'll be a pleasure. And I'd be happy to go to Mrs Peacock's party with you. The only trouble is I don't have anything to wear."

"You don't need a new dress unless you're looking for a husband. Are you looking for a husband?"

"Well, no. I have Father to look after," said Connie.

"Neither am I. I've told my mother that I have no intention of remarrying. I shall make myself as unattractive and bad tempered as I can, and I shall wear my widow's weeds."

"You would undermine your mother like that?"

"It's the only way. She won't listen. Christopher hasn't been dead twelve months." Charlotte let the vexation she felt ride in the air. "I shall comply with my mother's wishes, but not quite in the manner she expects. In that way, we'll both get some of what we want."

* * *

In the parlour at Highfield Farm Lucy Leadam was leafing through a stack of old 'Le Cabinet des Modes ou les Modes

Nouvelles' magazines, feeling peeved and disgruntled. "Mother, haven't we got anything more up to date?"

"Your father picked them up at a sale in Beverley. He thought you might like them," Mariah replied from her chair by the inglenook.

"Well, I don't. They're useless," said Lucy, throwing the November 1786 edition back onto the pile. For the last hour, she had been looking at drawings of extraordinarily dressed women wearing enormous hats decorated with bows and feathers, trying to imagine what she might look like in one of the costumes; but now she was bored.

Ever since her aunt had written to say they were invited to London for Christmas she had thought of nothing else. Even when she was riding her horse Buckeye her mind was consumed with worries about dresses and shoes and dancing. She imagined herself dancing with handsome young men: sometimes she saw herself with a captain in a scarlet uniform, sometimes with a merchant in a dazzling waistcoat and sometimes with an attractive but soberly dressed doctor or lawyer; but increasingly she feared that men would look upon her and think her old and ugly. She was acutely aware that she was now twenty years old, and she knew that many men would consider her bloom to be on the wane. When she was feeling low, she worried that her only suitors would be the old lechers and the short, brutish men with terrible clothes and appalling breath that the younger, prettier girls rejected.

Neither was she sleeping. Each night she played with her hair, shaping it and curling it to see which style suited her best; she practised whipping out her fan with a dramatic flourish, then hiding coyly behind it the way the heroines in the magazine stories did. When she finally slipped between the sheets and closed her eyes, she imagined herself falling into the arms of a handsome stranger who kissed her passionately, and of walking down the aisle with her father at her wedding.

Sitting in the farmhouse waiting to go to London, Lucy realised how bored and frustrated she was. "I'm going to look a total fool in London," she moaned, looking out of the window across the bare winter fields. "Everyone wears the latest fashions in London. How can I be expected to go about in respectable society looking a year out of date?"

"Heavens, child, don't fuss so. Mrs Arkwright will see you more than adequately dressed. She could dress the Queen of Sheba from that little shop if she had a mind to. You're not the first of her customers to go to London, you know."

"She says she has customers in London, but I bet they go no further than Hull," Lucy pouted, taking a turn around the room.

"If they're good enough for the showiest people in Hull or York, then Mrs Arkwright's dresses will be good enough for us."

"What about hats? We'll need hats and gloves and shoes. I can't go dancing in these boots," Lucy said, pulling up her skirts and brandishing her foot.

"There's no end to your wanting, is there?" her mother chided. "Everything that needs to be done will be. I have it on your father's word, for what that's worth. Now settle down and read your magazines."

"They're French, and I can't read French!"

"Well, look at the pictures or read summut else. You're getting on me nerves, Lucy."

"Can we go to Beverley on Saturday to pick out the fabric? I want something in red. You don't think red is too brash, do you?"

"Stop fretting. Mrs Arkwright knows what's in fashion. Now be patient and have a little faith, child."

***

It was the morning of the second Saturday in November. Sinclair and Greenwood were walking along the Strand towards Garraway's Coffee House to meet Henry Bowman. They found him waiting for them outside with two envelopes in his hand. "Good morning, gentlemen. I'm the bearer of glad tidings. Come inside and find out all about it."

Bowman opened the door, letting the warm coffee house vapours float over them as he ushered his friends inside. They made themselves comfortable at a long table by the window with the Saturday morning clientele. Henry ordered three dishes of their usual hot, syrupy coffee and handed out the envelopes. Sinclair took his and examined it carefully. It was made of the finest quality vellum and embossed with the coat of arms of the East India Company, a shield bearing the image of three ships supported by two lions with the motto "AUSPICIO REGIS ET SENATUS ANGLIÆ", which Sinclair translated as "By right of the King and Senate of England".

Frank ripped his envelope open without ceremony and started to read.

> *Sir,*
> *The Court of Directors has met and considered*
> *your claim for compensation following the loss*
> *of the Company's ship the Sherwell on January*
> *6th in the year of Our Lord 1786.*
> *The ship was wrecked owing to an*
> *unforeseeable natural phenomenon, for which*
> *no human agency could have been responsible*

*and which it was not possible for the Company
to guard against. Nor could the disaster have
been prevented by any more foresight, planning,
or care than was already taken by the Company,
and as such the Directors are under no
obligation to you. However, the Directors are
willing to make an ex gratia payment of £33 18s
9d in respect of unpaid salary, and to
recompense you for the distress you suffered.*

"So," Greenwood said, "they're paying me the wages I'm owed plus an extra month to compensate me for the distress I suffered. They could have returned my commission fees. Don't they know that they've ruined my life? And all because the timber on their ship was too dry when it went to sea. That's the only reason anyone at the Navy Office can think of that explains why a newly refitted ship would take on as much water as the 'Sherwell' did. In short, gentlemen, the '*Sherwell*' was sent to sea too soon, and these directors are saying they had nothing to do with her leaking like a sieve. What nonsense! What about you, Sinclair, what have they offered you?"

Sinclair read his letter again. He was being offered £120 in compensation for his books, and equipment plus six months' salary at £25 per month, making a total of £270. "Oh, nothing spectacular," he fibbed, not wanting to hurt Greenwood's feelings more than he had to. "They've covered my losses and given me a couple of months' salary in compensation."

"Well, it could have been worse, gentlemen," said Bowman. "They could have offered you nothing; that's what they usually do. I think it's only because your father is an MP that they gave you anything, Frank. Remember that the rest of the survivors had

172

to walk back to London, and as far as I know they have received no compensation. The quarrymen who rescued you were given a reward of fifty guineas when the King went to see them, and that's it. Let's face it, Frank: they could have charged you with dereliction of duty for not accompanying what was left of your men to London. They could have charged you the cost of your musket, but they didn't. I think you've both done well."

"When you put it like that it doesn't seem quite so bad," Greenwood conceded. "I'll try to be more grateful," he muttered resentfully.

In an effort to brighten the mood, Bowman asked, "How's life with the widow?"

"It's going well, Henry. Her in-laws are coming down from Yorkshire at Christmas, so I may need some distraction."

"I won't be here, old chap. I have to visit my parents in Kent, and then in the New Year Emma and her mother have me fully booked up." Bowman wiped his brow, mocking the exertion of it all. "I'm surprised Charlotte hasn't mentioned her in-laws to Emma. I expect we'll have to meet them."

"I think she only found out this week. I'm not party to the plans."

"I'd steer clear if I were you," his friend replied, with a look of foreboding. "What are you up to for Christmas, Frank?"

"Oh, I have a contract at the Navy Board until the twenty-second so I'll be forced to stay in London. I'll go home to Panton Hall in the New Year, and stay there for a couple of weeks for the hunting."

"Would you like to spend Christmas Day with me at Tooley Street?"

"Thank you, Jamie. I should like that very much."

Later the trio sauntered off to the Haymarket, where they bought tickets for the matinee performance of the opera 'Gli Schiavi per Amore', The Slaves of Love, at the King's Theatre. Greenwood wasn't keen on this, but when Sinclair told him that there were three beautiful female dancers in it he was convinced. With their entertainment secured, they dawdled off to Wright's Chop House for a lunch of rib eye and potatoes washed down with a couple of pints of ale.

Full to bursting, they settled into their box just before curtain up. "This is the life," Sinclair declared. "What more could a man want out of life than a belly full of beef and the prospect of delightful entertainment?"

"Well, I can think of a few things," replied Greenwood, staring across the cavernous theatre at the women sitting opposite. "By God, there are some beauties here, Sinclair. Look at that girl in the red dress," he said. Sinclair spotted a raven-haired woman in a red dress. "My God," he said, "the old lecher!"

"Who?" demanded Greenwood.

"It's our old friend Mr Husselbee; he's following the diet I gave him," laughed Sinclair. "He must have lost pounds. Look at him: he has a neck!"

"My God, you're right! Do you think she's his niece?" Greenwood asked hopefully.

"Mistress more like," replied Bowman, dampening his friend's ardour.

"We could introduce ourselves during the interval," suggested Sinclair mischievously.

"Why not?" chuckled Bowman. "It can only add to our entertainment."

The music master tapped his baton and the overture began. The curtains opened revealing a man, a woman and a beautiful and defiant young heroine, playing cards and talking of love and marriage. The heroine was determined to consult only her own feelings in the matter of love, but her uncle had other plans, saying she must marry a man of his choosing. As the drama unfolded, it became clear, even though most of the singing was in Italian, that all of the characters were in love with the wrong people.

Sinclair was the first out of his seat when the curtains closed for the interval. With Bowman by his side, he made his way to the other side of the auditorium to seek out Husselbee and the mystery woman in red, leaving Greenwood sitting alone, deep in contemplation. That was the problem with love, he thought. It didn't matter who he fell in love with; the chances were the girl's father wouldn't approve of him.

Greenwood knew he needed a profession, but what business might he apply himself to? It seemed to him that every profession and indeed every trade required time to acquire it, and what was worse money for training as well. Nothing, it seemed, could be wrought from nothing. Every man who was in need of money was entirely excluded from all means of acquiring it. Consequently, he had nothing to offer a woman of his class except his adoration, and he knew adoration was not a currency a good father was likely to deal in.

The more Greenwood thought about his future the more his thoughts returned to Susan Morris and the '*Sherwell*'. Miss Morris would have made him a good wife, he thought: she had been beautiful and clever, and prepared to accept him as a captain on captain's wages. Now, he thought gloomily, he couldn't even make that.

On the other side of the theatre, Sinclair was shaking hands with Mr Husselbee. "My goodness, you're looking well," he said proudly. "I see you've been following my instructions."

"Aye, I took your advice and it worked. Never felt better in me life!

"Thank you, sir," Sinclair replied. "Who, may I ask, is your delightful companion?"

"My niece, sir, down from Burton."

Sinclair proffered his hand to the woman in red. She was certainly young enough to be Husselbee's niece, but he was sure she was not: there was absolutely no family resemblance. The Husselbees were short and stocky and this beauty was as slender as a willow twig.

"Good day, Dr Sinclair," the woman replied, without a northern note in her voice.

"I hope you're enjoying your time in London, Miss…"

"It's Miss Husselbee to you."

"Of course it is. Pray excuse me," replied Sinclair coolly. "I hope you're enjoying your stay in London, Miss Husselbee."

"I am, thank you," she replied, dipping into a shallow curtsy and opening her fan in front of her face in a coquettish peek-a-boo manner, confirming everything the two men wanted to know.

"Henry was right," said Sinclair as he returned to his seat. "Husselbee's got himself a mistress."

"Have you got a remedy that could do the same for me?" groaned Greenwood.

"Oh, Frank, don't be like that. The ladies love you. All you have to do is look at them and they're swooning, you lucky dog."

But Greenwood did not feel lucky; he felt cursed.

* * *

It was Saturday afternoon and the first part of Lucy's dream was coming true. She was in Mrs Arkwright's shop in Beverley. Arkwright's Emporium was in the market square, and its walls were lined with racks containing bolts of the world's finest silks, muslins and lace. In addition to her sumptuous range of fabrics, Mrs Arkwright also possessed a formidable haberdashery of ribbons, feathers, buttons, buckles and beads. Lucy watched her mother trying on the biggest hat she had ever seen, and ran her fingers across a bolt of damson damask, enjoying its sumptuous silky smoothness.

"Now, Mrs Leadam," Mrs Arkwright said, "I would suggest the light-green felt for a woman of your age and complexion. It's quite the thing in London this year." She showed her client the back of the hat with a hand-held mirror. Satisfied the hat was right, the little woman produced a drawing of a travelling habit. "A double-breasted coat with these large flat buttons, in this lovely grey and green stripe, would complement the hat perfectly, madam. It's very flattering for the more mature woman."

"Aye, happen it is, Mrs Arkwright. What's it going to set me back?"

"What is money when your daughter's happiness is at stake, Mrs Leadam?" Mrs Arkwright soothed, expecting her client to agree; but she was disappointed.

"It's still money and it's not to be spent wantonly. I'll have what's needed and no more. I'd rather spend the money on Lucy."

Lucy protested from the other side of the shop. "You must have something nice for yourself. You deserve it."

"That's enough," Mariah replied. "Now, what would you suggest for Lucy?"

The little woman with grey powdered hair cast her eyes along the bolts of cloth and beckoned the girl over. "I like the red, Mrs Arkwright," Lucy ventured.

"Red!" she cried, throwing her hands in the air. "We don't want you looking like a tart, my dear!"

"My Lucy could never look like a tart, madam," Mariah bellowed in her defence.

"I will ensure that, madam," Mrs Arkwright replied, pulling her tiny body up to its full height. "I can assure you that I have all my customers' best interests at heart; you may read my book of testimonials if you wish."

"That won't be necessary," Mariah conceded.

"So, ladies, if I may continue," Mrs Arkwright huffed. "Women of refinement wear their clothes on the pale side," she said, standing next to the bolts of lighter coloured silks. "I would suggest ivory, sand, light blue, blue-grey, silver or pink for Miss Lucy if you intend to land a big fish in London. I'm afraid you'll look like a shopkeeper's daughter at best or a rich man's harlot at worst if you wear anything bright."

"In that case, we should skip the red," said Mariah.

"I suppose so," said Lucy, letting her fingers trail along the smooth damson silk one last time.

It was dark when they got back to Highfield. In the stables Lucy could tell Buckeye was as glad to see her as she was to see him. She hung up the lantern and refilled his hay net, giving him an affectionate stroke. In return, the horse nuzzled her, seeming to know intuitively that she needed his love. "You should see the dresses I've ordered, Buckeye. Mother and I are going to look so good when we go to London. You'll be really proud of us. I promise I'll bring us back a handsome beau so we don't have to be alone any more."

After they had said their goodbyes and Greenwood had gone on his way, Bowman produced another letter and handed it to Sinclair. "It arrived yesterday," he said.

Sinclair looked at the handwriting and recognised it as his sister's. "I've been expecting this."

"Are you all right, Jamie?"

"Aye, I'm fine. I'm just sad. Our families are supposed to love us and take care of us through difficult times. But my family's not like that: my father hates me."

"Surely not," said his friend. "Any right-thinking man must love his son. I love mine."

"That's because you're a good man. My father rejected me the day I was born. All my life he's blamed me for the death of my mother and my brother; which according to Morag were caused by scarlet fever and had nothing to do with me. He hates the fact that I'm alive and they're not. He hates the way I live my life, what I think and what I do. He probably wishes I'd drowned on the 'Sherwell', although Morag would never tell me so."

"When you put it like that I'm not surprised you wanted to go to India," said Bowman.

"If I'd gone to India the question of returning to Edinburgh would have been closed. As it is I'm four days away by coach, so the requests to go home will keep coming."

"Your father makes Emma's mother seem like an angel, which she's not; she's a gorgon. She's hatching plans to marry Charlotte off to some rich banker her friend Mrs Peacock knows."

Bowman's words shot through Sinclair like a musket ball. Charlotte married? It hadn't occurred to him that she might remarry and upset the life he was making for himself in Tooley Street.

"I can't see it myself," Bowman continued, unaware of Sinclair's consternation. "Not now she's got you slaving in her apothecary shop and working all the hours God sends, like her poor dead husband."

"I hope she doesn't," mumbled Sinclair. "Well, not yet. I don't mean I hope she doesn't ever. You know what I mean, don't you?"

"I do," Bowman conceded. "A bit of stability would be good for everyone in my opinion. My sister-in-law is a sensible woman and the last person to get pushed around by her mother, so there's probably no need to worry about getting another job just yet."

11

A Letter from Edinburgh

Arriving at the house in Tooley Street, Sinclair found a hired cab waiting outside the front door. He put his key into the lock and let himself in. He started up the stairs, but stopped when he heard footsteps on the landing above him. Charlotte and Connie Collingwood were coming down at a canter. "Good evening, ladies," he called as they reached the foot of the stairs.

"Good evening, Dr Sinclair. Is our cab still there?" they asked in unison.

"Aye."

"Thank God for that; we're late," moaned Charlotte.

"Will your mother be furious?" enquired Connie as they went out of the front door.

"She's always furious," Charlotte replied, climbing into the cab.

Upstairs in his attic apartment Sinclair stoked the fire, lit a pipe and settled down to read his letter from Morag.

Dearest Jamie,

I trust that you are well as I have not heard anything to the contrary. Please write more often, Jamie. I want to hear your news. You will not be surprised to learn that in Edinburgh life goes on much the same as usual.

Did you read about the meteor? It came down at about half past eight in the evening on 17th September. It was a marvellous and frightening event. I was in my chamber and could see the ball of fire in the sky. It crashed to earth east of the city with such an explosion that the sky was opaque for hours. Thankfully, no one was hurt so the spectacle is one that can be enjoyed without guilt. Father has called it a warning from God of course, but we are of the opinion it is a natural phenomenon and Iona's interest in astronomy has become even more intense. She is reading everything she can on the subject, including books Andrew borrows from the University library.

Sadly, there have been riots in Glasgow. The people are so poor it saddens me, and the press gangs have been about in Leith stealing foolish boys and errant husbands, causing misery everywhere they go.

On the lighter note we have a new sensation in town, a poet called Robert Burns. Andrew and I attended a reading of his poems with Charles and the McNeals at the Caledonian Hunt. Jamie, you would have loved it. I have ordered you a copy of his book and will send it as soon as it arrives. Mr Burns, who was a farmer until his recent success, is a man of dark secrets. Father has condemned the man from his pulpit, based on rumours he has children by two women, neither of whom he is married to. Speaking of Father, he has been ill with his chest but has made a good recovery, and he is back to preaching twice a day and three times on Sunday.

Charles is back from Aberdeen and is preaching at St Giles' and Blair is still in Cambridge. I was wondering if I could ask you to do me a favour, as I know without asking you that you will not be coming home for Christmas. Would you invite Blair to spend the holiday with you? I hate to think of him alone in Cambridge while we are all enjoying ourselves.

I miss you very much.
Your loving sister,
Morag

Sinclair poured himself a glass of wine and smiled. His father was the same as ever, but life for Morag was not too bad. He had no objection to inviting Blair to spend Christmas with him, except that he had told Mrs Leadam he had no family. How was he to explain this volte-face without undermining his credibility? He took his pocket watch and turned it slowly in his hand picturing Iona's face, and the way her nose wrinkled when she smiled. Before he knew it he was imagining his hands around her waist and her vibrant red hair flying in the wind at the top of Salisbury Crags. It was the picture that had sustained him the night of the wreck. Iona was his fantasy, but since he had been in London he had thought about her rarely. Despite their frosty start, he had grown to be comfortable with Charlotte Leadam. She was not the woman of his dreams but he liked her, and he liked the life he was living with her; and Bowman's news about the possibility of her remarrying had unsettled him more than he thought possible.

Was Henry right about Charlotte's reluctance to remarry? He hoped so. Anyway, Sinclair thought, what sort of man would take her on? She was handsome enough, but he was sure she was not the sort of woman who would settle easily for routine domesticity: she liked being involved in the business too much, and many men would find that unacceptable. Thinking about it, her interest in the world of medicine was one of the things he admired about her. Well, that was apart from her body, and particularly her breasts. He had a fondness for breasts and hers, he had to admit, were particularly fine. The more he thought about Charlotte Leadam allowing another man near them the more resentful he became. Why should he be overlooked as a possible husband? If she cared to look, she would see in him a man of intellect and accomplishment, indeed a most attractive marriage prospect. Like all men, he knew he had his shortcomings, but she wasn't in a position to be choosy. After all, she was a widow and past her prime. She was older than him, although admittedly not by much, and she could never give him the children he might

184

desire. Henry was right: he was in no immediate danger of having to find another job any time soon. In fact, Charlotte Leadam was the sort of woman who should be grateful to receive consideration from a man like him. He was sure it would be a while before any realistic suitors appeared on her horizon.

* * *

At her house in Golden Square Mrs Vanda Peacock greeted her friend Eliza Martin. "My dear, you look quite divine. Grey is absolutely the right colour for you. I could never wear it with such aplomb. It's a perfect match for your complexion Eliza."

"Vanda, you know my husband Charles, don't you?"

"Oh yes. Dr Martin, you're at St George's, aren't you?"

"I'm on the staff, madam."

"Yes, yes, I know you are. May I have a quiet word in your ear?"

Dr Martin looked at his wife with a resigned expression: another one of Eliza's cronies was wanting free advice from him. But he played his part as dutiful retainer perfectly, allowing Mrs Peacock to whisper in his ear. "I have a friend in need of your attention. If I were to give her name and address to Eliza, would you be a dear and visit her?"

"I should of course be very happy to do so, providing the lady in question has agreed to the consultation."

"Very good, Dr Martin. I'm sure I can prevail upon the lady in question to agree to your visit. I want her to see London's best, not the upstart whose treatments have so polluted her husband's mind that he now spends his days whoring in St James's instead of at home with his wife. Eliza will keep me abreast of developments. Now please excuse me; I must speak to Mr and Mrs Masterson."

Eliza checked the time, using one of the two watches swinging conspicuously from her waist on long gold chains, in the latest French style. "Where is our wretched girl?" she complained to her husband. Dr Martin ignored his wife as he always did on these occasions, and carried on holding forth on the events of the day to their host.

The minute hand on the ormolu clock on Mrs Peacock's mantelpiece was almost halfway round the dial and Eliza Martin was becoming increasingly anxious. "I am sure they will be here in a moment," she said, fanning herself in an agitated manner.

"I should jolly well hope so, Eliza. I have gone to a great deal of trouble tonight," her exasperated friend replied, rhythmically snapping her ivory fan shut with a crack, drawing it through her jewelled hand as if she were unsheathing a dagger and opening it again. "I have specially selected the most eligible families I know."

"And I'm very grateful, you know that, Vanda," Eliza soothed. "Your guests are truly of the highest calibre."

"Have you met Mr and Mrs Masterson, Eliza? Mr Masterson owns Masterson's Bank in the City. Let me introduce you," Mrs Peacock said, flashing her fan open again and commanding her companion to follow. "They are particular friends of mine and have a younger son who is a successful barrister, a King's Counsel. I think he could be a perfect match for Charlotte: he is a widower of thirty-six with two children. If she makes a favourable impression she will be on their dinner party list soon enough. Do remember, dear heart, to follow them into dinner with the Reverend Mr Walker, won't you."

186

While Eliza was being introduced to Mr Masterson and his wife, the footman announced the arrival of Mr Peregrine Podmore, another banker friend of the Peacocks from Birmingham, and Mr Joseph Marston, a gunmaker in the City.

Intentionally oblivious to his wife's distress, Dr Martin continued deep in conversation with Mr Peacock. "The sooner Lord Gordon is behind bars the better as far as I am concerned," he said. The man is a complete liability. It was only the offices of a good lawyer that saved him from the rope six years ago, and now the French ambassador is after him for defaming his Queen, Marie Antoinette."

"Well, if you ask me she's brought it on herself," Peacock replied. "Excess is her stock in trade. Is it any surprise that the woman has been associated with a fraud involving a two million pound diamond necklace? Who else but her or that wastrel of a husband could possibly have commissioned such a thing?"

"The necklace in question has disappeared, has it not, Mr Peacock?" said Mr Podmore, joining the conversation.

"Yes, I believe it has, but I've heard rumours that it has found its way to the City and is in the process of being broken up for sale," whispered Mr Peacock, providing his guests with the thrill of intrigue. "And as for Count Cagliostro," he declared, "he only has himself to blame for being held in the Bastille."

"I agree," replied Dr Martin. "The man is a lunatic. No man can make diamonds: it's beyond the laws of nature! No, Lord Gordon is stirring up trouble by defending him. Mr Pitt will have him behind bars soon enough."

"Hear, hear," agreed Mr Podmore and Mr Marston.

Then Dr Martin confided, "I have heard it on good authority that Gordon is now hiding in Birmingham dressed as a Jew!"

"My God, is he?" laughed Peacock. "I suppose a Jew knows a good diamond when he sees one! Perhaps he plans to deal in them himself and doesn't want Count Cagliostro's claims lowering the price!" This made his guests roar with laughter, much to Peacock's delight.

As the clock struck eight Dr Martin spotted Charlotte and Connie standing nervously by the door. "Ah, my daughter has arrived with her friend Miss Collingwood; please accept my apologies for their tardiness."

"It is a woman's prerogative to be late, is it not? All we need for our party to be complete is Mr Walker and our artist friend Mr Plinner."

Dr Martin went immediately to his daughter's side. "Now, my dear, I would steer clear of your mother for a while. She's on her best behaviour and giving a good impression of serenity, but we both know that she's silently frothing with rage."

Mrs Peacock had spotted them too. "Good evening, ladies," she glowered. "Dr Martin, I see that your daughter has at last deigned to grace our party." She pointed her fan, cocked pistol fashion, in Charlotte's direction. "I'm sure that your mother has something to say to you, young lady." The old woman stared down her stubby little nose and pursed her scarlet bee-sting lips.

"Good evening, Mrs Peacock," Charlotte replied, bowing her head in an act of overt contrition. Then she lifted her huge blue eyes slowly and deliberately, like a naughty child trying to charm her way out of trouble. "This is my friend Miss Collingwood. We are so sorry we're late."

Mrs Peacock and Miss Collingwood assessed each other in the bat of a critical eye. Connie immediately declared, "Quel merveilleux chambre vous avez, Madame Peacock. Je l'adore votre papier peint et les rideaux. They are French, are they not? I would love to be able to have a room like this, but sadly my funds will not run to it."

"Miss Collingwood," Mrs Peacock replied, taking her by the arm, "I could see immediately you were a woman of profoundly good taste and manners. Indeed, I had a dress almost the same as yours last year. I am sure that if you were not neighbours with Mrs Leadam you would hardly know her. Let me introduce you to our vicar friend, Mr Walker, I am sure you will have much in common with him, my dear. You are a music teacher, are you not?"

"Well done, Connie," Charlotte whispered, watching her friend being hauled off in the direction of a tall and handsome man in clerical dress.

"Well done, Charlotte, I say, for briefing her friend so well on our hostess," replied her father, taking her arm and leading her into the centre of the room. "I do like to see my girls in something pretty," he said, "so why are you wearing that awful grey sack?"

"Oh, Father, you know why. I have no intention of remarrying. You, dear Papa, have always been a fool for a pretty face and a few yards of silk."

"I know, my dear, and I've paid the price. How can your mother be friends with this woman?"

"They are two of a kind. She cannot recognise in others what she sees in her own looking glass each day; they are immune to each other."

"That's too strong, Charlotte. For all her faults, your mother has your best interests at heart. Nevertheless, I've found that giving your mother what she wants is the best formula for a happy home, so please be aware that she'd like it very much if you were nice to Mr Podmore and Mr and Mrs Masterson this evening. Mr Podmore has a bank in Birmingham and the Mastersons have one

189

in the City, so your mother is expecting you to make a good impression on at least one of them tonight."

Despite her father's willingness to acquiesce to her mother's demands, Charlotte was glad to have his protection, so she clung onto his arm for as long as she could. She knew that he wouldn't allow her mother or her odious snub-nosed friend to bully her into anything she didn't want to do.

It was after half past ten when Charlotte and Connie got into their hired cab and headed back to Tooley Street. They were both tired and more than a little tipsy.

"I don't know about you, Connie, but my corsets are killing me."

"Here, let me undo you a bit," offered Connie with a giggle as the cab slewed around a corner and away from Golden Square. "Mrs Peacock really is odious, isn't she?"

"You didn't believe me, did you? Charlotte laughed as her friend released the pressure on her stays. "Here, let me do yours." She turned to face her friend. "Her particular brand of vileness is so common among the rich. I hate people who equate their wealth, from whatever means it's gleaned, with their virtue."

"Absolutely," agreed Connie. "The woman wears her condescension as if it were a mark of rank. I can assure you we weren't the only ones to notice. Mr Walker for one understands her true nature."

"Oh yes; I couldn't help noticing how attentive Mr Walker was to you."

"He wasn't attentive. He's just a very agreeable fellow doing very well for himself."

"No wonder he's on Mrs Peacock's list of eligible bachelors and widowers," giggled Charlotte.

"Do you fancy being a clergyman's wife?" asked Connie.

"No, I don't think I could stand all that seriousness and praying, and I'd find having to be in close proximity to the Mrs Peacocks of this world more than unbearably irritating."

"How did you find Mr Podmore?"

Charlotte kicked off her shoes and wriggled her toes. "I took particular note of his circumstances so I could give a good report to my mother. He's a widower with five children, I can't remember how many are boys and how many are girls because quite frankly I wasn't the least bit interested. The man lives in Birmingham at a place called Dale End. It sounds like a rural idyll, doesn't it, but he said it was in the centre of the ironworking district which, if you ask me, sounds no better than Southwark. Believe it or not his father was a buttonmaker."

"Oh, your mother wouldn't like that," giggled Connie.

"No," laughed Charlotte, rubbing her tired feet. "She'd be horrified: being related to the son of a farmer was bad enough!"

"But what was he like?"

"Oh, Connie, he was a bore. These men of money are so dreary, which is a great shame because having money is something I really do desire. The trouble is that when I compare Mr Podmore's conversation to the lively chatter I have with Dr Sinclair I have to say I found him dull indeed."

"Oh, so you like Dr Sinclair?"

"Of course I do; but not like that. Don't make anything of that statement because there's absolutely nothing in it!"

"I wouldn't blame you if you did; he's so handsome. How could you not notice those gorgeous eyes and that delicious voice? I'm sure that half the women in Gracechurch Street feign illness just to be examined by him."

"Don't be ridiculous. No one would do a thing like that, would they?"

"Well, if I've thought about it I'm sure someone else has."

"Connie Collingwood, I don't believe you," Charlotte said, hardly able to speak with disbelief.

"Honestly, you're such an innocent. Not everyone is as pure in mind as you, you know."

* * *

When Sinclair came down for breakfast on Sunday morning, Charlotte was working at the dining room table, making lists of things to do and buy for when her relatives from Yorkshire came to stay.

"Ah, Dr Sinclair, I need to know how many we will be at Christmas. Will you have any guests?"

He took his seat at the table and started to spear a thick slice of bread onto the toasting fork. "Aye, as it happens I will; my friend Mr Greenwood from the Navy Board and my nephew Mr Blair Rankin from Cambridge."

Yes, she thought, Connie was right: he did have a delectable voice. "How long will they be staying?"

"They'll both be here from the twenty-second of December. Mr Greenwood will leave before the New Year and Mr Rankin will stay until the Lent term commences at Cambridge. I shall of course cover all their expenses."

She watched him toasting his bread at the fire, admiring his lean muscular arms and his strong athletic legs, then reluctantly drew herself back to the task in hand. "My family will be here from the evening of the fourteenth and will stay until Thursday the third of January so we shall be quite a company."

"Who will be coming from Yorkshire?" he asked, turning the bread on the fire.

"Oh, only my sister-in-law and my niece. My brother-in-law will stay in Yorkshire to look after the farm. I have to entertain them over the holidays and I know that Lucy will be expecting to go to balls and such like, but I haven't been to a ball since I was a girl. Have you any ideas where we might go?"

Sinclair pulled the piece of hot toast from the toasting fork and covered it liberally with butter and marmalade. "My friend Mr Greenwood has tickets for the Navy Board Ball at Somerset House and I have tickets for the ball at the Barber Surgeon's Hall, if you think they'd be suitable?"

"I do. Could you get tickets for both? I don't want to disappoint Lucy."

He watched Charlotte write everything down on her list. She was wearing her old brown dress, and instead of wearing her hair under a cotton bonnet she was wearing it loosely gathered with a ribbon at the nape of her neck. For a moment he imagined his hand pulling on the ribbon in the first act of undressing her. He imagined his hands around her waist and his lips on her mouth. Then she turned and looked at him, breaking the spell. "I was so worried that we would have nothing to do. Thank you, Dr Sinclair. I'll need tickets for my relatives, John, William and myself. Now all I have to do is decide where to put everyone. Will your guests be comfortable in your room? That is if I get some more blankets and mattresses?"

"Aye, that will be fine, Mrs Leadam," he said, relieved that she could not read his mind.

She stood to leave. "Will you be joining us at church this morning?"

"Maybe, I'm not that keen on it, as you know," he replied, hoping to be released from the obligation.

"You should. It's good for business. People like to see that their physician is on the side of the angels."

"Aye, I suppose you're right. I'll join you and the boys at eleven o'clock."

* * *

After church, Charlotte and John went off to Bread Street for lunch with the Bowmans, leaving Sinclair and William with the option of one of Mrs Dredge's cold pies or dining at a pub or chop house. Sinclair knocked on William's door and suggested they should eat together.

"Thank you, Dr Sinclair," said a grateful William, glad to be invited into the world of men.

"Aye, well we men have to look after ourselves sometimes. We can't always be relying on women to do everything for us," Sinclair said, savouring one of the few benefits of bachelorhood.

William, who was now seventeen, was his right-hand man in the surgery, and Sinclair liked him. He was a tall and willowy boy with a spotty complexion, but he was steady and reliable. "So, shall we try the Red Lion, or do you want to go into town?"

"The Red Lion's fine by me, sir."

"Good. The pies are excellent there."

A few minutes later they were elbowing their way through the crowded bar. It was warm and cosy after the brisk November air. "So, how am I doing, William?" Sinclair said, putting two tankards of ale on the table. "Are you learning enough? Do I match up to Mr Leadam?"

"You're doing fine, Dr Sinclair. I'm glad that you and Mrs Leadam came to an agreement because I didn't want to be sent elsewhere. I've spoken to other boys like me at the Apothecaries'

Hall. Many are forced to sleep on mattresses at the back of their master's shop, and they're not looked after by the family like Mrs Leadam and Mrs Dredge look after us. We're never left hungry and we don't have to do our own washing. Did you know that some boys have to sleep next to their master's stores of cadavers?"

"Yes I do, but I don't think it's right."

"I have to share a room with John, but that's luxury compared to some."

"When you put it like that I can see why you're content. I was never an apprentice. I went to university in Edinburgh when I was seventeen and I lived with my sister's family before I moved out into digs in the Old Town. The rooms were pretty rough but there were no dead bodies next door. That reminds me, I'll have to start your training in dissection soon. We'll start you off with animals. I'll ask Mrs Dredge to order some whole carcasses from the butcher for you and John to practise on. Once you've got the hang of that you can start to attend anatomy demonstrations."

A large-bosomed barmaid brought their pies to the table. "Here you are, my loves," she said, putting the steaming pies on the table and treating William to an eyeful of warm female flesh. "Do you need anything else, sir?" she said, standing back with her hands on her hips.

"No, thank you," Sinclair replied, watching William's dazed expression. When she was out of earshot, Sinclair laughed. "Mr Whitfield, if you could see your face. You looked as if you thought she was going to suffocate you with those diddies."

"Well, they were a bit much, sir," the boy replied, with a blood-red flush.

"I couldn't think of a better way to go," laughed Sinclair. "I think all men feel the same about bosoms: men like them and women know it." William felt a wave of relief as he realised that he wasn't alone in his fixation with breasts.

"You'll have to get used to that sort of thing if you're going to work in this trade," said Sinclair, wiping pie crumbs from his chin. "The trick is not to think about your patients like that: you have to treat them with respect."

"Yes, sir," the boy replied, with growing admiration for his new master. Mr Leadam had never talked to him like this, nor had he taken him to the pub and bought him a pie. He was sure that he'd have got a good telling off for his wandering eye if Mr Leadam had been there; he had been a morally upright man.

"Can you dance, Whitfield?" enquired Sinclair.

"No, sir. Why do you ask?"

"Because Mrs Leadam has asked me to get tickets for a couple of balls before Christmas."

William looked perturbed. He had never been required to dance before.

"Don't look so alarmed! Girls don't bite, well, not literally anyway and certainly not the respectable ones. I suppose they're just as nervous as us when it comes to this sort of thing. I always get my tongue tied when I meet a particularly attractive one, but the form at dances is quite straightforward. Girls are expecting you to ask them to dance and are willing to give you a try. I don't suppose John can dance either."

William felt overwhelmed. The idea of being able to meet, speak and dance with girls all at the same time seemed impossible. He thought about his appearance. What pretty girl would want to dance with him, he wondered?

As if Sinclair had read his mind he said, "Don't worry about the little madams saying no when you ask them to dance; the chances are that even if they hate you they'll say yes. If a woman

196

turns you down she has to turn down every other request she receives, if she's respectable that is; so there's nothing to worry about." Sinclair looked at the boy's spotty skin and adolescent whiskers. "Of course making the best of yourself will help. You could ask Mrs Leadam for something to wash your hair with, and I can give you a few tips on shaving if you like."

"I'd like that very much, sir, thank you."

"Good. Now finish your pie so that we can get our afternoon rounds at the hospital done, then we can relax for the rest of the day."

* * *

At the Bowmans' house in Bread Street, there was a gathering of the Martin family. Charlotte found herself sitting with John and her nephews Matthew and Henry junior at her brother-in-law's end of the table, while her parents were in pride of place at the head of the table with Emma. The maid brought in a large tureen of soup, a haunch of beef, batter puddings, potatoes and cabbage, and an apple pie. Her sister ladled out dishes of soup while Henry carved the joint.

It was unusual for her mother to venture into the City, and Charlotte knew that she had come for a report on her introductions at Mrs Peacock's; but instead of starting with that her mother chose to interrogate her on the impending visit of her husband's relatives from Yorkshire.

"So," her mother sighed, "why did I have to find out from Emma that your in-laws are paying you a visit from Yorkshire at Christmas? Shall we get the opportunity to meet them at last or are you ashamed of us, Charlotte?"

"Of course I'm not ashamed of you. For goodness' sake, Mother, it's not a secret. John and I only found out this week."

"Good. We don't like secrets, do we, Papa?" her mother replied, turning to her husband for support. Dr Martin nodded his agreement, allowing his wife to continue in the same hectoring vein. "When will they arrive? We would all like to meet them."

Charlotte's heart sank as she imagined the discordant clash of the two families coming together, but she knew she had no option but to comply with her mother's wishes; and she knew also that Mariah and Lucy would be equally offended if she did not introduce them to her family in London.

"They'll arrive on the fourteenth of December and stay until the New Year."

"Oh, how disappointing. So a Twelfth Night party is out of the question," her mother replied between spoonfuls of vegetable broth.

Emma agreed from the head of the table. "I'm sure they'd love Mother's Twelfth Night party. We shall be coming back from Kent for it." Henry nodded his agreement. "We shouldn't like to miss it. We had such a marvellous time last year."

"Well, I'm glad you were enjoying yourselves while John and I were in the snow on the way back from Yorkshire."

"It wasn't that we were insensitive to your loss, Charlotte; there was simply nothing we could do to help you until you came home," her mother rationalised. "Your father agreed we should have the party, didn't you, dear?"

"Oh, please don't drag Papa into this. Papa would say anything to keep the peace. If you had a party just days after Christopher's death, then that's what you did. You don't have to make excuses."

"Good," her mother retorted. "After all, I have absolutely nothing to make excuses about. I'm entirely satisfied with my conduct in this matter." An uncomfortable silence descended, lasting until Henry finally broke it by offering his guests more beef, and by the time everyone was ready for apple pie the conversation was moving along at a comfortable pace again.

As the meal came to a close Henry broached the subject of Charlotte's in-laws again, giving her the opportunity to explain her plans. Secretly he was as concerned as his sister-in-law about the meeting of the two families, so when he heard about Charlotte's plan to take her visitors to a Christmas ball he saw an opportunity. "A ball! What a splendid idea, Charlotte: we haven't been to a ball in years. The Navy Board Ball is such a grand affair that it would be the ideal place for us to make our first acquaintance with Christopher's family."

Mrs Martin looked aghast. "This is not how things are done. I have standards, Henry. Dr Martin and I should invite them to dine at Wimpole Street, but of course if their calendar is already full then meeting them at one of London's leading social events could be an acceptable alternative."

Emma, sensing her husband's determination on the subject, was quick to agree with him. "Yes, Mother, it would be most acceptable. Indeed, your good character and taste will be most appreciated there."

"Excellent. I'll get the tickets then," Henry said, before his mother-in-law had time to change her mind.

12
Lord Wroxeter's Errand Boy

Frank's new task at the Navy Board was to oversee the refit of a
ship called the Bethia. This was to sail to the island of Tahiti in
the South Pacific to pick up breadfruit plants and transport them
to British territories in the West Indies. The aim of the mission
was to provide a cheap source of food for slaves working on
British-owned plantations there. In effect, the ship was to become
a seagoing greenhouse.

Frank alighted from his riverboat at His Majesty's dockyard
at Deptford with a huge sigh of relief; he was still uncomfortable
on water. In the office, he met a West Countryman called
Lieutenant Bligh from the Merchant Service who was to lead the
voyage for the Crown. Greenwood introduced himself to the

brusque barrel-chested man, who promptly told him to get the lazy-arsed villains in the dockyard to do some work.

At 215 tons, the 'Bethia' was small fry compared to the *'Sherwell'*, but the work was still behind schedule. Making the ship ready for the transportation of a thousand breadfruit trees entailed making a completely false floor for the plant pots to stand in, and the deck and sides of the ship had to be fitted with large windows to let in the light and air necessary to maintain the plants. Considerably more than that given to men, thought Greenwood, remembering the darkness of the hold on the *'Sherwell'*.

As he went about his business, assessing the work still to be done, he thought about Miss Morris. Her father had worked in the dockyard when he was alive and he wondered what her life had been like when she had lived there. He could see that the men worked hard; their hands and faces bore the hallmarks of long hours and low pay. He thought about his own life with its privileges and pleasures, and he was glad that he was not one of them.

Later in the day, Greenwood took his report to the ship's surveyor, Mr Dowling, a harassed-looking man in his mid-thirties who looked much older. "We're so behind here I hardly go home these days. My wife complains that I'm a stranger and my children have forgotten who I am. Most nights I just kip down in the captain's quarters. Don't suppose he'll mind as long as we get his bloody ship done in time, eh?" he muttered, placing Greenwood's report on his cluttered desk.

"I wouldn't be so sure about that; Bligh seems a bit of a tartar to me. But your secret is safe," Greenwood sympathised.

The surveyor shook his head. "It's always the bloody same. The Admiralty never learns. You can't do this sort of work on the cheap or rush it," he grumbled.

* * *

The surgery in Tooley Street was busier than ever as winter coughs and colds turned into bronchitis and pneumonia; and the usual winter diseases, such as measles, whooping cough and putrid throat, cranked up the deaths. The practice was dealing with an increasing number of men presenting with symptoms of venereal disease. Those who could afford it were prescribed mercury, the most expensive and effective treatment in Sinclair's arsenal, and snail water if they could not. For those in the terminal stages of the disease, opium was the only remedy that he had to relieve their suffering, and he was liberal with it. He did not believe in making people suffer for their misfortune, unlike some in his profession who took the view that the disease was a punishment from God for indulging in the sins of the flesh. Sinclair was also developing a growing practice in midwifery, supervising the births of children in the wealthier households of the borough and across the river in the City.

At St Thomas' his work continued in the Cutting Ward with the staff surgeon, Mr Ellesmere. This was a dismal assignment. Each week he watched as Ellesmere botched hydrocele operations. In his view, the operation for watery rupture in both infants and adults had its complications, but Mr Ellesmere seemed to have a knack of making his patient's problems worse. From what Sinclair had read and from his own experience he knew it was best to let nature take its course whenever possible, but if the patient was in pain a simple incision to aspirate the liquid from the scrotal sac was enough to provide relief. Ellesmere, however, did not read the literature and he did not listen to his colleagues. The result was almost certain death for his unfortunate patients. In spite of this, the man had a glowing reputation, spending much of his time writing and lecturing, giving the world the benefit of his expertise. This had its advantages, as it left Sinclair to do much as he pleased with Ellesmere's routine casework and gave him plenty of time to teach his apprentices.

* * *

Charlotte was making a batch of her best-selling cough mixture in the apothecary shop when Connie called through the serving hatch. "I've had a letter from Mr Walker, asking me if I will play at his fund-raising concert. It's to support the rebuilding of his church's spire. Do you think I should do it?"

Charlotte lifted the hatch and let her friend in. "Do you want to?" she replied, returning to stir the pot over the stove.

"I could offer to sing two songs," Connie spluttered, breathing in the cloud of clove and liquorice fumes.

"That's not what I asked you. Do you want to do it? Do you want to see Mr Walker again?"

'I don't know. He seemed very amusing at Mrs Peacock's. He's very tall, which for me is a great attraction as I tower over most men I meet, and he seemed interested in me."

"Connie, he looked more than interested in you: he was enthralled. He couldn't take his eyes off you."

"We talked about music, that's all. He plays the piano, and our conversation was about the pieces we like to play."

"Well, I think he's smitten."

"I'm not so sure. He may only be interested in selling tickets. He told me that he only attended Mrs Peacock's party because she's rich."

"Well, it doesn't have to be one or the other," said Charlotte. "He could find you attractive and want some help with fund-raising too. I could add the event to our Christmas entertainment. I'm sure Mariah and Lucy would enjoy a concert."

* * *

Greenwood met Sinclair and Bowman as usual on Saturday morning at Charing Cross, and the trio took themselves off to a nearby coffee house to take their first refreshments of the day. Inside, the aromas of strong coffee, cocoa, sugar and Virginia tobacco mixed into a warm and comforting fug. Sinclair ordered the coffee, as it was his turn to pay and to choose the afternoon's entertainment. As they made themselves comfortable in the little booth they had chosen by the window, Bowman confessed to being the architect of the plan to bring together the Martins with Charlotte's relatives from Yorkshire at the Navy Ball.

"So the whole family will be there," said Greenwood. "My God, it's going to be as bad as the balls at Panton. There I'm lucky if I get one dance with anyone single or half-decent looking. Henry tells me the two families are unlikely to get on. I hope I haven't spent a guinea on a bare knuckle fight."

"I'm sure the violence will be purely verbal; and if we do our part and dance with all the women they won't have time to fight, will they?" said Bowman.

"You mean I have to dance with your landlady and your landlady's mother, Sinclair?" wailed Greenwood in mock disgust.

"If you would, old chap," Sinclair pleaded. "Apparently the old dragon's a gull for a compliment, and you're so good at them, Frank. It'll be easy for you."

Greenwood looked unconvinced, and muttered something blasphemous into his coffee.

"But there is a silver lining to this cloud," said Sinclair.

"What's that?" said Greenwood despondently.

"Cousin Lucy," Sinclair proclaimed triumphantly. "She's only twenty, and if she's anything like her female relations she'll be a looker, Frank."

Bowman smiled, happy that his friend admired his choice in women. Emma had her faults but she was beautiful and he adored her. Then he realised what Sinclair had just let slip: he was admitting that he admired his sister-in-law too. He looked at Sinclair, who was completely unaware of his confession, and wondered whether the appreciation was mutual.

"Well, I shall have at least two dances with her if she is," said Greenwood, coming round to the idea.

"Excellent," said Bowman. "Now that's all settled, where are we off to this afternoon, Sinclair?"

"I thought we might give the Theatre Royal in Drury Lane a go. We can get a box for five shillings. The doors open at two o'clock, so we can get something to eat before the performance begins."

* * *

In the weeks leading up to Christmas Sinclair was as good as his word, asking Mrs Dredge to order a variety of small animal carcasses from the butcher for William and John to dissect in the surgery. The boys took it in turns investigating a suckling pig, a rabbit and a capon, with the added bonus of a dead dog that had been run over in the stonemason's yard. Sinclair supervised as they removed each animal's digestive system from tongue to anus, examining each organ with a hand-held lens, then making drawings of what they had learned. "Use your eyes, gentleman. Draw what you see, not what you think you see, and don't look at the book," said Sinclair. "You must learn to gain your truth from experience and not from books, because as you will soon find out so many of them are wrong."

When they were dissecting the pig, Sinclair held up a trotter and showed them how the muscle contracted when he pulled on the tendon. "This simple motion, gentlemen, is one of the most contentious issues in medicine today. In Paris, I learned about an experiment conducted by an Italian called Galvani. Signore Galvani was in his kitchen watching his wife prepare frog soup, a disgusting idea I know," he said, with a grimace that made his students laugh. "Galvani noticed that each time his wife's metal knife touched the frog's leg the muscles moved. This gave him the idea for an experiment, and in his laboratory he applied an electrical current to a frog's leg and got the same result. This experiment has led men of science all over Europe to the following question. Is electricity the motivating life force within the body?" The boys looked at each other, and then at Sinclair.

"What do you think, sir?" asked John, when he had processed the idea that life might consist of a substance that could be created using a jar, a piece of tin and some water.

Sinclair thought for a moment. "I believe there is more to the 'life principle', as Mr Hunter calls it. Like Hunter I believe that life is complex, not simple." His pupils looked at him with puzzled faces. "I am sure there must be more to life than a simple twitch," he continued. "Each of us has a life force, what some in

206

the past called a soul, but it leaves the body at the moment of death. I don't know what this thing is or where it goes but it doesn't come back once it's gone, no matter how much we might desire it."

"I agree," said John, thinking about his father.

"Me too," said William, having seen so many depart on the hospital wards.

"Excellent, gentlemen. Now where was I? Oh aye," Sinclair said, putting down the trotter. "As you are beginning to realise, the body is made of many parts, and each has its own function and way of working or not working. I would say that some of our body's processes are purely mechanical, but like Hunter, I believe many of the body's functions are chemical, and it is within this chemistry that the life principle resides. I had the unfortunate experience of nearly drowning last year, and the experience of not having enough air was painful and debilitating. As I used up the air in my lungs, my mind became confused and my limbs became weaker. Indeed, lack of air proved fatal to one hundred and sixty of my fellow passengers, but as you know, boys, most people don't die from lack of air; they die because of what is happening to their organs. If we want to save lives, we have to understand the body, how it works and how it goes wrong. The task is a vast and fascinating one, and our job as surgeons is to constantly learn so that we can better care for our patients."

"Yes, sir," his students replied.

"Good. After Christmas we'll start to visit Mr Hunter's museum in Leicester Square so that you can see his collection of exhibitions and specimens. Now finish your sketches and annotate them correctly. Leave your work in the surgery and I will look at it after supper."

"We've got dancing lessons with Mrs Tucker at five," said William.

"Well," said Sinclair, taking out his pocket watch, "you'll just have to make sure you complete the task quickly, won't you. Come on, boys, there's no time to waste, and make sure you give Mrs Dredge what's left of the pig. I'm sure she'll be able to make something tasty out of it."

* * *

In Yorkshire, Robert Leadam rose before dawn, saddled his favourite mare and drove five of his best beasts to the December market in Beverley, accompanied by his yappy brown and white terrier, Pincer. Trade was brisk and he had sold the animals by ten o'clock. With twenty pounds in his pocket, he made his way to the tenements in the North Bar to see his mistress, Rosie Featherstone, where he spent a happy hour playing with his boys Robert and Edmun. Then he kissed them all goodbye, collected his dog and walked to the Assembly Rooms.

It was seven years since he had been inside its elegant cream interior. "We're glad to have you back, sir. You'll need to bring these with you," said the clerk, handing the farmer three consecutively numbered cards. "The benefits of membership have not changed since you were here last: one assembly a month with an extra one for the Whitsun races."

Robert thanked the man, and returned to the livery yard to collect his horse and look at the brood mares on offer. He knew there was money to be made breeding hunters for racing and for sport. Not only was there racing at Beverley; there were meetings in Redcar, Pontefract, York, Catterick, Ripon, Weatherby and Doncaster. The trick to success was to get your hands on a long-legged Arabian, a horse fifteen to seventeen hands high, a descendant of the Byerley Turk or the Darley Arabian, and breed from it.

As he rode the four miles home, he hoped that his wife's trip to London would mellow her, and that she would allow him to invest in his plan without too much complaining when she came back. Women, he thought, were the root of all his problems. He couldn't help wishing that he hadn't married Mariah; they were not well matched. She had never liked horses and had no appetite for sex. So he messed around with other women, tumbled into bed with bar maids and suchlike; but when he found Rosie Featherstone at the Black Horse all that changed. He couldn't live without Rosie. She liked sex and would do anything he wanted; climb on top of him and ride him like a jockey in a race; make love to him in a slow meander as if they were riding through a warm summer meadow. She enthralled him for hours. Whichever way they made love it made him feel young and gloriously alive. But as much as he loved her, he wished she were a better mother. When he thought about his boys in those filthy rooms, he hated Rosie for her slovenly ways.

Robert stabled his horse and walked the short distance to the farmhouse in the fading afternoon light, pushed open the front door and strode across the darkened hallway into the parlour, where he found Lucy and Mariah making new petticoats for their trip to London. With a flourish, he gave the tickets for the Assembly Rooms to Mariah, who burst into a happy dance, performing a little minuet in front of the inglenook. Lucy dropped her sewing and threw her arms around her father. "Oh, Dad, I love you. Thank you."

"Well, you'll be going in the pony cart, so don't get too excited," her father warned. "You'll have to wrap up warm and make sure your hair's not too fancy."

"Do you think you could make it sound any less inviting?" Mariah laughed. "We'll brave whatever the weather throws at us, won't we, Lucy, even if we have to travel under a tarpaulin."

The tarpaulin was unnecessary when Robert drove his wife and daughter into Beverley a week later. A waft of warm air and perfume floated over them as they entered the Assembly Rooms. In the ballroom they could see groups of young men in their evening clothes roaming about, securing dances from the girls who stood with their chaperones waiting to be asked, while their younger siblings ran around in an impromptu game of Tick.

Lucy's stomach tightened as she and her mother made her way to the dressing room. Suddenly she felt the vulnerability of her years of isolation. She had entered the world of family and social connection, and she was aware that she was deficient in both. She turned to her mother for reassurance but found none: Mariah's handsome face was rigid with anxiety.

When they had hung up their coats and put on their gloves, mother and daughter held hands and walked towards the ballroom. At the door, the Master of the Ceremonies read out their names, but to Mariah's relief no one was listening. They walked silently into the vast space, with their eyes firmly fixed on the floor, and found a place under one of the six giant chandeliers.

Lucy could feel the prickle of her mother's anxiety crackling through the air. In her youth, Mariah had danced at the Assembly Rooms many times, and with both of the handsome Leadam brothers, but now she knew that the women in the room, if they had noticed the announcement of her name, would pity her for her choice of husband. Mother and daughter stood together feeling like a small island surrounded by a hostile sea. "Smile, Lucy, but don't look too eager," her mother said, fixing her eyes vacantly into the middle distance. "I hope your father's not in the Black Horse."

"Why?" Lucy asked, realising as soon as the words came out of her mouth what her mother was referring to.

"Because if he's in there with that whore I'll bloody kill him when we get home." Mariah spotted a small woman making her way towards them. "Look, it's Mrs Arkwright."

The East Riding's most celebrated dressmaker was wearing the finest silver-grey silk. Around her sinewy neck hung a beautiful cut glass and pearl necklace, which danced and twinkled in the light of the chandeliers. "My dears, you both look delightful," she said, admiring her handiwork. "Now," the old woman said, taking Lucy by the arm, "let me introduce you to some people I know."

When Robert finally joined them, Lucy's dance card was full thanks to Mrs Arkwright's introductions. In his full-bottomed coat with its high velvet collar Lucy thought her father looked statesmanlike, but it pained her that although her parents made a handsome couple they did not get on.

Lucy stumbled through the first hour of minuets with partners who, like her, walked the steps rather than danced them. During the interval, she retired to the ladies' dressing room to remove the hoops from her skirt ready for the country dances in the second half.

"Hello, Lucy," said a girl about her own age who was dressed in ivory brocade.

"Margie Hardaker," smiled Lucy. "My goodness, you've changed."

211

"Aye. I used to be a fat little thing with buck teeth and blonde hair. I've still got the teeth but my hair got darker."

"I think you look lovely, Margie. Was your dress made by Mrs Arkwright?"

"Aye. She's got a monopoly round here. I think she dresses everyone who's anyone."

"That means we must both be someone then," said Lucy. "Should we go in and find our partners for the next dance?"

"Aye. We don't want to get a reputation for letting our partners down, do we?"

Before the girls could get to the dressing room door they were confronted by two gaudy peahens brandishing their fans like daggers.

"Hello, Margie, who's your friend?" demanded the tall woman with rose-coloured lips and a thick rope of chestnut hair, flicking her gold-trimmed fan open and snapping it shut again with as much menace as she could muster.

Margie sighed. "Hello, Cynthia, this is Lucy Leadam. Do you remember her from Mrs Clough's?"

Cynthia smiled a lizard smile. "Aye, I do. What's a fornicator's daughter doing here with respectable folk like you, Margie?"

Lucy's face flushed. Her mother was right; everyone knew about her father and his bastards. "Hey, don't you go losing your head over Mr Chapman, Miss Leadam," Cynthia warned, wielding her fan threateningly at Lucy's face. "He's taken, do you understand?"

"Aye," chipped in the shorter girl standing behind her. "Miss Sedgewick will be engaged to him shortly."

Margie took Lucy by the arm and curtsied. "Thank you for letting us know, Miss Higginbottom. We have to go, don't we, Lucy?"

"Yes," Lucy said, feeling sick as Margie dragged her away.

In the ballroom Margie said, "Just ignore her. Your father is one of my papa's best customers at the bank and, as far as I know, Mr Chapman knows nothing about getting engaged to Cynthia Sedgewick. Cynthia is a jealous bully full of jaundiced bluster. Marcus Chapman isn't the most eligible man in these parts, but he's the most attractive – and he's rich enough to choose whom he likes. So, Lucy Leadam, if he wants to dance with you he's not just being polite."

"Thank you, Margie," Lucy said, knowing his name was already on her card.

After supper the country dances began, and as the clock struck eleven Lucy found herself dancing with a tall raven-haired man with disconcertingly blue eyes.

"Who's that our Lucy's dancing with?" Mariah whispered to Mrs Arkwright.

"That's Mr Marcus Chapman; his father owns the North Bar tannery. He has a warehouse in Southwark as well."

"By 'eck, he's a handsome beggar," said Mariah.

"Isn't he just," Mrs Arkwright sighed. "I do hope she's arranging to meet him when she's in London."

"So do I, Mrs Arkwright, so do I."

13
Lucy Leadam Comes to London

The Yorkshire Flyer paused as usual at the top of Highgate Hill. The driver applied the brake and the coach slowly began its descent into the city.

"Mother, look at it. That's London!" cried Lucy, feeling she would burst with the excitement of it all.

"By 'eck! I've never seen the like," said Mariah, marvelling at the dots of light that were as numerous as the stars in the sky. Lucy looked on with wonder, thinking how much she would have to tell Margie Hardaker when she got back to Yorkshire. She was especially looking forward to making Cynthia Sedgewick and her snidey little friend, Mary Higginbottom, green with envy when she told them how wonderful London was.

The driver cracked the whip and the horses raced on through the dark streets towards Holborn. At seven o'clock the coach, festooned with bags and passengers on top, swung into the Black Swan's yard, where Charlotte and John were waiting. Moments later Lucy and Mariah stepped onto a London pavement for the first time, and Charlotte threw her arms around them, giving each a heartfelt kiss.

John bundled the women and their luggage into a hired cab, and soon they were on their way to Tooley Street. "Ooh, this is very nice," said Mariah. "It's much better than our old pony trap."

"Yes, the pony trap's a bit nippy this time of year," said Charlotte, remembering her own journey to York the year before.

"Mother, look at the street lights! Look at the people!" Lucy exclaimed, winding down the carriage window and craning her head out.

Mariah reached over and gave her daughter a rebuking tap. "For goodness' sake calm down, girl."

"There are lights all along the Strand," said John, enjoying his cousin's excitement.

"I don't think she'll sleep tonight, Charlotte. Look at her," chuckled Mariah.

The streetlights faded as they neared London Bridge and the traffic began to thin.

"We're crossing the river now. Our house is on the south bank," John explained to his aunt. "It's closer to the hospital where Father used to work."

William helped John haul their visitor's luggage upstairs, and as soon as the bedroom was closed Lucy threw herself onto the bed. "Oh my, Mother, I can't believe we're here. This is the best thing that has ever happened to me."

"I'm glad about that, because it's been a bugger of a job to get here," her mother replied. "Let's go down and meet everyone and see if your aunt's got a bit of sherry. I could do wi' a drop of summut after all we've been through."

In the parlour Mariah inspected her nephew. "You've grown, me lad. You're more like your dad than ever."

"Thank you, Aunt: that's a great compliment to me," said John.

Charlotte smiled, admiring her son. He had grown six inches since his father's death, outgrowing three pairs of boots and three pairs of breeches, and now he was an inch taller than William; but like William he was as thin as a hop pole.

Charlotte poured glasses of Madeira and led her guests to the dining room for a supper of mutton and dumplings.

"How have you been?" enquired her sister-in-law.

"I'm well, thank you. As you know, things were difficult after Christopher's death but thanks to Dr Sinclair we're straight now. You'll meet him tomorrow. He's attending a hospital committee meeting with William, the boy who took your bags when you arrived."

"We're looking forward to it, aren't we, Lucy?"

"Yes. We want to meet this knight in shining armour."

"Oh, he's no knight," said John. "He's a clever man down on his luck; Mother is helping him as much as he's helping us."

Her son's comment about Sinclair stuck in Charlotte's mind. Henry had let it slip that Sinclair did not get on with his family in Edinburgh, but coming from a family where relationships were always strained she had assumed he was content to live at a distance from them. She suddenly felt guilty: in all the time he had been living in her house, she had never considered if he was happy.

"I must tell you about the house," she said, refocusing her thoughts. Charlotte explained the weekly routine in great detail, so that her guests would understand what was going on with all the comings and goings.

"My word, you are busy bees. It makes running the farm seem like light work," said Mariah, helping herself to another glass of Madeira.

"Oh, and sometimes Dr Sinclair is called out during the night. If you hear a knock at the door in the small hours don't be alarmed; William or I will answer it," said John.

Lying in her bed that night, Charlotte found herself thinking about what had happened since Christopher's death. She had been on the edge of disaster twice, and had survived with the help of the strange and attractive man who now lived in her attic. As she considered Dr Sinclair, she realised he was a mystery to her. He was polite and hard working but he could be grumpy and bad tempered, even childish at times. They chatted about patients and about books, but he told her very little about his personal life. He seemed to have no particular interest in women preferring to spend his free time with Henry and his friend Mr Greenwood, which was surprising because, as Connie pointed out, women found him attractive. He had certainly attracted more female patients than her husband had. She wondered if Sinclair had been disappointed in love. There was a deep sadness in him that she did not understand. Was it the experience of the shipwreck, she wondered, or his family, or his lack of faith in God? Whatever it was, she felt a strong desire to lift the burden from him; to help him in the same way that he had helped her.

* * *

Greenwood made his last weekly report on the 'Bethia', now renamed HMS 'Bounty', to Lord Wroxeter.

"Good work," said his employer over his pince-nez. "Bligh has orders to have the ship at Spithead before Christmas. I want you to go down to Dover and make sure he gets everything he needs. Be warned, Greenwood, Dover is a den of thieves. In times of war the people there live by piracy and in peace they turn to smuggling. It is a hot-bed of fraud and pilfering. I will not tolerate poor quality or corruption on the part of contractors or officials. I want you to check the ship's manifest against the accounts. Bligh has lobbied for an increase in his rank and pay, which has not been granted. Disappointed men are always trouble."

"I agree, sir," said Greenwood.

"Take this letter. You're working for me, not Bligh. Do you understand?"

"Yes, my lord."

"Good. Report back when everything is done. Get Bligh to sign off the supplies personally. Mr Finch will provide you with funds for travel and accommodation."

Greenwood left Lord Wroxeter's office wondering how long he would have to stay in Dover, and whether he would make it to the Navy Ball.

He wandered off to find Finch. "Ah, Greenwood, good to see you. The 'Bounty' is expected in Dover on the nineteenth ready for departure from Spithead on Christmas Eve."

"Damn it! I've got tickets for the Ball on the seventeenth," said Greenwood.

"So have I. You can come back to town on the Wednesday by coach and return on Thursday, and still get the Captain to sign off the provisioning. After all, the supplies are his responsibility, not yours; you're just there to cover Wroxeter's back. I wouldn't worry about it, old chap. I'm afraid you'll have to pay for the extra journey yourself: I can't put more than one trip on the chit."

Greenwood's heart lifted a little. He didn't like abandoning his responsibilities even if they were not vitally important in the great scheme of things, but he was happy to know that he could make it to the ball. To be on the safe side, he asked, "Lord Wroxeter won't be at the ball, will he?"

"He's far too old for that sort of thing," Finch laughed, making light of the situation; but Greenwood was still uneasy.

* * *

It was still dark outside, but Lucy could hear the rumble of heavy carts moving along the road and the murmur of a small crowd of people outside the house. Her mother was snoring beside her, oblivious to the sounds outside, so Lucy slipped out of bed and dressed in the dark. She made her way to the dining room where they had eaten supper the night before, but Mrs Dredge had yet to lay the breakfast. Standing on the first-floor landing not knowing what to do with herself, she craned her head over the banisters to see what was happening downstairs.

She watched a tall and dishevelled man with thick sandy hair directing operations in the hallway before disappearing into the surgery. That must be Dr Sinclair, she thought. The doctor was younger than she had imagined, closer in age to her aunt than her uncle had been. His voice was smooth and rich, and from her vantage point she thought he looked more than passably attractive; but she decided she needed a clearer view before she made up her mind.

Lucy was watching the crowd of people in the hall when three breathless men carrying a young woman balanced precariously on a chair burst through the front door.

"My daughter needs the surgeon!" the oldest man called out. Lucy watched her aunt lift the serving hatch and approach the woman. Her aunt put her hand on the woman's swollen belly and asked how long she had been in labour.

"This is the second day," Lucy heard the youngest man reply. Then her aunt explained that the surgeon was busy, and that they would have to wait to be seen.

Inside the surgery, Sinclair could hear the commotion in the hall. He was examining a woman from the fishmonger's shop in the Borough High Street. The woman claimed to be forty but looked much older. "You said that you're becoming breathless?" said the doctor, feeling the tell-tale swelling of the lymph nodes in her armpit.

"Yes, sir," the woman replied. "I can't get up the stairs any more."

"Do you have a family?"

"Yes I do, sir."

Touching the woman's arm to reassure her, Sinclair said, "You'll have to ask them to help you from now on, because you must rest. I can give you something to help you with sleeping and to ease the pain in your chest, but I can't cure you."

The woman looked at him with sunken eyes. "Am I going to die, doctor?"

"You have a tumour in your breast which has spread to your lungs; that is why you're out of breath. I'm sorry, there's nothing I can do to help you."

The woman looked almost relieved. "I thought so," she said, with a crack of emotion in her voice.

Sinclair lent forward. "Mrs Leadam can arrange for me to visit you at home if that's what you'd like."

"I think I would," the woman replied. "Do I have long?"

"No, but I'll make you as comfortable as I can." Sinclair wrote a prescription and instructions for Charlotte, and showed his patient out.

From her seat at the top of the stairs, Lucy watched him say goodbye to his patient. She thought he looked tired, and she was sure he had slept in his shirt. She watched as he called the men forward and invited them into the surgery. The men carried the girl in, followed by her aunt and her cousin carrying a bundle of towels and what looked like a pair of farrier's tongs. My God, Lucy thought, are they going to pull the baby out with those? The surgery door shut, and Lucy was left to imagine what was happening behind it.

Inside the little room, the exhausted girl was placed on the examination table. "It's Kitty, isn't it?" said Charlotte, stroking the girl's face to reassure her. You're with the surgeon now. Everything is going to be all right."

Sinclair lifted the girl's sweat-stained nightdress, revealing her distended belly with its craze of red-veined stretch marks. He could see that the contractions were weak, coming and going without effect. John watched Sinclair as his hands moved around the hard ball of flesh that was the girl's belly feeling for the position of the baby, then the doctor put his head down and listened for the sound of the baby's heart. As he lifted his head, John could see Sinclair signalling to his mother that the child was dead.

"John, fetch William," said the doctor, looking at Charlotte at the other end of the table. In the half-light of the early winter morning, she looked wonderful even in her old brown dress.

Still perched on her ledge, Lucy watched John reappear, then return to the room with William by his side without saying a word to the waiting men. As John closed the surgery door Mrs Dredge appeared with a tray of breakfast things from the scullery.

"Would you like some help with that?" asked Lucy.

"If you wouldn't mind, ducky. The mistress or one of the boys usually helps, but they've got their hands full this morning."

Lucy flew down the stairs and took the tray. When she had laid out the crockery, she went downstairs, whispering a quiet "Good morning" to the men standing outside the surgery door as she went into the scullery. Mrs Dredge's domain consisted of two rooms looking out onto a paved yard at the back of the house. The first was a huge kitchen, not unlike the one at the farm, with an inglenook fireplace and a large wooden table. Behind it was the laundry, with a pump for fresh water and a drain. She placed the empty tray on the table. "Is it always like this here?"

"Busy, you mean?" replied the old woman.

"Yes. No," Lucy stumbled. "I mean, do people come here to have their babies?"

"Not usually, ducky: most of them have them at home. Dr Sinclair charges a lot of money for a forceps delivery. Most of his customers are the wives of rich men. I reckon this lot are stevedores who work on the wharves. It don't look good for that poor girl."

"Do you think she's going to die?" asked Lucy, feeling a sickening lump in her throat.

"She might. Still, Dr Sinclair and the mistress will do what they can, but they can't work miracles."

"I didn't think it would be like this, Mrs Dredge," Lucy said, noticing the weakness in her knees. "She looks younger than me."

"She probably is, ducky."

222

***

With John and William supporting the girl on either side of the table, Sinclair turned to Charlotte. "Right, let's save the mother, Mrs Leadam."

John looked to his mother and then to Sinclair.

Aware of the lad's inexperience, Sinclair said, "If you feel sick or faint let your mother take over."

John swallowed hard: his knees were shaking and his palms were sweating. "I'm all right, sir."

Sinclair took a small blade and made the incision necessary to insert the forceps. John felt a shiver of pain ripple through the girl's body, but she was too exhausted to scream.

"Hold her steady, boys." The doctor slid the forceps into position, then told John to put his hand on the girl's stomach and tell him when the next contraction arrived.

"Now," John said calmly as the girl's stomach set like stone. Sinclair pulled as hard as he could, and felt the child move.

"Tell me when the next one comes."

"Now," commanded John, with a new sense of confidence and authority. Sinclair pulled again. On the third contraction he had the child half out, and on the fourth he held it in his hands. William cut the cord separating the dead child from its mother, then gently closed the baby girl's eyes, so that she looked as if she were sleeping, and wrapped her little body in a towel.

John looked at the child as his mother placed it on the girl's chest and wrapped her arms around it. He was amazed; it looked so perfect. Her little body was warm; she had a mat of wet brown hair on her tiny head, long eyelashes, soft chubby cheeks and a small button nose. "Kitty, you had a daughter – but she died before she was born. Hold her for a few moments. I'll tell you when it's time to say goodbye," his mother said.

In the hallway, Kitty's family were waiting. With no crying coming from the surgery they already knew her child was dead, and from the look on their faces Sinclair realised they thought Kitty was dead too.

"Who is the father of the child?" Sinclair demanded.

The youngest man stepped forward, head bowed. "You had a daughter but she died before she was born. Your wife is alive, but she's weak. We'll keep her here until this evening to give her some time to recover, if that's all right with you."

"Thank you, sir," the stevedore said with a bow.

"My fee for saving your wife is a guinea; less than half the fee I usually charge for a home confinement. I know it's more than you can afford to pay me now, so you can pay in instalments. Mrs Leadam will set up an account when she's finished tending to your wife."

Sinclair didn't like charging the man, but he didn't want to encourage others to bring their pregnant wives to the surgery; he would rather treat them in their homes. He admired these men. They had done something extraordinary for their kinswoman. In most households, a girl like Kitty would have been left to die for want of money, embarrassment or both, but he didn't want every stevedore in London knocking at his door.

It was after ten o'clock when they sat down to breakfast. Sinclair was in the process of buttering a thick slice of toast when they heard a knock at the door.

"Oh, no," Sinclair moaned. "Can a man not get his breakfast in this house without being disturbed?"

Charlotte poured the doctor a cup of tea in readiness for what she thought was his imminent departure.

William put his head around the dining room door. "There's a Mr Chapman downstairs asking for Miss Lucy Leadam."

Lucy choked and Mariah gave out a shriek of excitement. "Mr Chapman's asking for our Lucy. By 'eavens, we've not been here a day and already she has a suitor at the door."

Sinclair shot Charlotte an irritated glance, then bit into his toast.

"You can use the parlour if you want to see him, Lucy," Charlotte smiled.

Mariah was already on her feet and making for the door.

"William, would you show the gentleman up, please?" said Charlotte.

"How do I look, Mother?" asked Lucy, patting her hair and checking her nails in a state of excited consternation.

"You look lovely. Doesn't she look lovely, Charlotte?" said her mother. Charlotte waved to her sister-in-law to return to her seat. "Give William a moment to show the man upstairs, then let him wait a while."

"Oh, aye, you're right. It's not good to look too keen, is it?" replied Mariah.

With a look of alarm, Lucy said, "How long should I keep him waiting?"

Sinclair and John looked at each other, sharing a silent smirk. Charlotte rolled her eyes. How could he go from being the hero of the hour one moment to acting like an embarrassing youth the next? "Honestly, you men have no idea how difficult this is," Charlotte sighed.

"I beg to differ," said Sinclair. "We know it's a woman's prerogative to keep a man waiting. Might I suggest you torture this man for a good five minutes before you relieve him of his agony, Miss Leadam."

Lucy looked to her mother.

"The doctor's joking, Lucy; pay no heed. Anyway, what's five minutes of agony compared to a lifetime?" she said sourly.

"Don't go spoiling it, Mother," Lucy wailed.

"I'm sorry," Mariah replied, sinking back in her chair, feeling ashamed of her public display of bitterness.

Sinclair stood. "So am I, Miss Leadam. I was wrong to make fun of you. Please forgive me. Any man should be glad to wait five minutes for an interview with a woman of such obvious beauty and charm as you." Lucy's face flushed and Charlotte swiped him with one of her withering looks. Feeling scorched, he made a polite bow in Lucy's direction and left for his room.

In the parlour, Marcus Chapman was confident he would be well received. He was, after all, a man of property and enterprise with businesses and houses in Yorkshire and London. Any good parent would be grateful to him for courting their daughter. Besides, Lucy Leadam was worth the wait. Miss Leadam would make him an ideal Yorkshire wife, unlike the brassy and demanding Cynthia Sedgewick.

Mariah took a deep breath and walked into the parlour with all the confidence she could muster, with Lucy following behind.

"I trust your family are well, Mrs Leadam," said Chapman with a deferential bow.

"We are hale and hearty, thank you very much."

"My mother and father send their regards. I have it upon their instruction to invite you to supper on Twelfth Night if you're at home."

Although she was thunderstruck by the invitation, Mariah was determined not to show it. "That is very kind of Mr and Mrs Chapman. We'd be right glad to accept."

"That's excellent," Chapman smiled, turning Lucy's face pink.

"Are you in London on business, Mr Chapman?" Mariah enquired.

"I am: I have a warehouse here in Southwark and a house in Harp Lane on the other side of the river. I have a few days free before I return to Yorkshire, and wondered if you might allow me the honour of showing you some of the sights of London."

"That is generous indeed, sir. What exactly did you have in mind?"

"I understand that the Tower is very popular with visitors, madam. I thought we might make a start there."

"When do you propose we make this trip?" asked Mariah.

"This afternoon. I can send a cab to collect you at two o'clock."

Lucy's eyes flashed between her mother and her suitor. After what seemed like an infinite pause, Lucy heard the words she longed for as her mother agreed to Mr Chapman's suggestion.

As the clock struck two, Charlotte watched her excited in-laws climb into a cab on their way to the Tower. As soon as the cab was out of sight, her thoughts turned to her patient sleeping in the surgery. She put her head around the door and looked in. The girl's hair was tangled and her nightdress was filthy. Charlotte decided she could not allow the young woman to be carried through the streets in such a state, so she went upstairs to find some old clothes and a hairbrush.

With Mrs Dredge, Charlotte got the girl up and washed her. When she was clean they shuffled her into the fresh nightdress, tied up her stockings and swaddled her tightly in one of Charlotte's old shawls. The bewildered girl sat in a chair next to the window as Charlotte brushed her long brown hair. "There will be more babies for you, Kitty," Charlotte said, trying to console the girl; but she knew that conceiving and giving birth to children was the greatest part of life's lottery for a woman, and you never knew who was going to draw the short straw.

14

The Navy Ball

HMS 'Bounty' was anchored off the Downs when Greenwood arrived at the Jacobean mansion that was the headquarters of the Navy in Dover. The letter from Lord Wroxeter granted immediate access. He climbed the ancient staircase with its ornately carved oak spindles and knocked on the door marked Master Victualler.

Wroxeter had sent him to see a man called Carter, who shouted for him to enter. The room was cold and bare, and Carter was dressed in the meanest clothes a gentleman could wear without looking like a beggar. He opened Wroxeter's letter.

"So, Lord Wroxeter doesn't trust me, eh?" he said, sitting back in his chair and placing the letter on his desk. "He's sent his dog to sniff around my arse, has he?"

Ignoring Carter's slanderous description of him, Greenwood said, "I think it's more a case of wanting to protect the Victualling Board from Bligh if things go wrong."

"Yes, well, men like Bligh, they all think they're something special, don't they? Think they should have more than they need, but they're wrong. Look at me; I'm happy to eat stale bread. It's still bread and every bit as nourishing as fresh, and yet men complain about it. I don't understand why a man needs a candle when he can sleep in the dark, do you, sir?" Greenwood remained silent. Carter continued, "If people were more like me and made the best of what they're given, the world would be a far better place, Mr Greenwood."

Greenwood was beginning to understand why Wroxeter had sent him to check up on this snarling old miser. "It seems that Bligh's mission is already mired in disagreements sir," he said. "He's complained about the ship, the size, the rank and experience of his crew, and he's made several unsuccessful representations to have his pay and his own rank increased. In short, sir, Bligh is an unhappy man, and with this being such a vital project for the Crown, his lordship is keen to make sure that this office is seen to do its very best to ensure its success."

"Does he now?" said Carter, sucking his broken, yellow teeth. "He's a cunning old fox, Wroxeter. You can tell your master that Bligh and his ship will be treated the same as all others when she puts into Granville Dock on the next tide."

"I will, sir."

"I've been in this job for ten years without complaint. The Crown relies on men like me to get it a good deal on everything it buys. It may surprise you, but there are men out there ready to rob the unwary customer. I'm never unwary, sir, never," Carter snarled, through a lace of fine white spittle that dangled from his upper lip. "As you know, the lowest bidder always wins as long as he can supply what we want, and we always make sure we want what's cheapest. Our own bakeries and brewhouses here in Dover have provided the hard tack and beer, and the salted pork and beef are already on board from the slaughterhouse at Deptford. So as far as I'm concerned the old bastard has nothing to complain about. But that's not how it works, is it, lad?" he leered.

Greenwood nodded his agreement. Carter leaned forward. "Now, as it happens, old Wroxeter is right about Bligh being difficult and demanding; he's specifically asked for barrels of this newfangled sour cabbage stuff, a continental concoction of fermented greens I believe the men will not like. He says it's better for their health, but I remain to be convinced and I suspect his men do too. "That aside, Lord Wroxeter can rest assured that Bligh will have the requisite amount of food stuffs."

"Thank you, sir. Could I see your lists, so that I can include everything you've said in my report to his lordship?"

"Have what you like, boy: I have nothing to hide. I hear Bligh's made his own arrangements concerning his food, which he's entitled to do – but it isn't ideal."

"I agree with you, sir."

"I can tell you if Bligh's commission ends up in Davy Jones's locker it won't be the fault of the Navy Victualling Office, Mr Greenwood."

* * *

At the end of the evening surgery Sinclair and William joined Charlotte and John in the apothecary shop. Sinclair sat on the long oak table with his sleeves rolled up and his feet dangling mid-air like a schoolboy.

"There's a lot of influenza about at the moment. We've seen three cases today. I know some in the medical profession still see influenza as an imbalance of the humours, but along with a growing body of men I'm of the opinion that we're dealing with an agent that is highly infectious," said Sinclair. "If I'm right there will be many more cases in the coming weeks, and I think we should build up our supplies of fever drugs and cold remedies."

Sinclair could see that the news of extra work did not sit well with Charlotte. She had hoped the surgery would be quieter as they approached Christmas, and that she would have more time to spend with her family and friends.

Upstairs in the dining room Mariah and Lucy were waiting for them. Exhausted by the events of the day, they made their way wearily up the stairs to supper.

"How was your trip to the Tower of London?" asked John, sitting down next to his cousin.

"It were wonderful," Lucy beamed. You're so lucky to live in this wonderful place, John. Mr Chapman was an excellent host, wasn't he, Mother?"

Mariah smiled and nodded her agreement, pouring herself what she considered to be a well-earned glass of sherry. "Mr Chapman were a true gentleman. We saw the Royal Crowns and Good King Henry's armour, didn't we? By 'eck that King Henry were a big fella!"

"Enormous," chimed in Lucy. "And we saw great big lions, an evil-looking black panther, two tigers from India and four golden leopards with spots like tiny eggs; it were magnificent. When we went up to the lions one of them roared at us, and I was

232

that frit I near jumped out of me skin, but Mr Chapman assured us that we were entirely safe and that they couldn't escape."

"Aye, and one of the dirty beggars cocked his leg and tried to widdle on us through the bars of the cage!" laughed Mariah.

"He missed us, thank the Lord," said Lucy, "or we'd be stripped off with everything in the wash."

"Well, it sounds like you've had a very good day, ladies," said Sinclair, looking at Charlotte and observing how tired she looked. "Do you have any plans for tomorrow?"

"Not so far, Dr Sinclair. Do you have anything you can recommend?" asked Mariah.

"I was wondering if you might like to help Mrs Leadam in the apothecary shop in the morning."

Charlotte shot Sinclair an angry look, letting him know that he had crossed into her territory.

"I'd love to," said Lucy enthusiastically. "What would you like me to do?"

"Aye, I'd be happy to do me bit too, Charlotte. You and Mrs Dredge don't 'ave to do everything: we're not royalty, you know."

"Thank you, Mariah. I'm not sure what Dr Sinclair had in mind." Charlotte seethed beneath her smile.

John and William were about to make their excuses and beat a hasty retreat when Sinclair said softly, "I was thinking that Mrs Leadam and Miss Leadam might like to help with preparing the influenza remedies we spoke about earlier. I'm sure you know all about making up cough syrups and barley water."

"Aye, we do. I swear by a bowl of sweated onions and sugar when it comes to colds," said Mariah.

"Excellent, ladies. With your help we'll be able to build up the stocks we'll need over the Christmas period. Now I'm going to see my surgical patients at the hospital. I look forward to seeing you in the morning. Until then adieu." Sinclair bowed, then turned to William, indicating to him that he should join him, and the pair departed, leaving the Leadams to their supper and to talk amongst themselves.

Mariah poured her sister-in-law a generous glass of Madeira. "Get that down you, girl, it'll do you a power of good," she said. "We had no idea you worked so hard, Charlotte; you must be worn out, love. If we'd known we wouldn't 'ave imposed ourselves on you like this."

"Oh it's no trouble, Aunt. We're so happy to have you here," said John. "We've been longing to see you both. Father would want you to be here."

"John's right," said his mother. "We were just busier than usual today, and then Dr Sinclair told me he thinks there'll be an epidemic of influenza."

"Well, we're very happy to help you and Mrs Dredge; there's no need to stand on ceremony. Just give us a pinny and we can do our part. Don't be cross with the doctor, Charlotte, he's just trying to help you."

Charlotte felt chastened by the older woman as she realised Sinclair was thinking about her.

After an uneventful morning surgery the next day, Charlotte gave Mariah the job of making throat lozenges in the apothecary shop while Lucy was set to making lemon and barley cordial in the scullery. While her in-laws were busy Charlotte started on the Christmas orders with Mrs Dredge. In addition to the beer and wine, she ordered a cheese, a ham and a turkey, and a goose for Christmas Day. She decided she would buy the oranges, chestnuts and gingerbread together with the holly and ivy for decorations closer to Christmas Day. Then she turned her attention to the apothecary shop, and started to make a batch of laudanum, their best-selling sedative and pain reliever. It was a two-stage process. When she had completed the first part, she left the mixture to macerate until the evening, when she would add the alcohol.

With the shelves restocked there was time for Charlotte and John to walk to St Paul's with Mariah and Lucy. For the first time since she had lost her husband, Charlotte put on the blue travelling habit she had last worn when she went to Yorkshire, together with her black widow's bonnet. The afternoon was grey but warm for the time of year. When they got to London Bridge John showed Lucy the starlings, and the rush of fast-flowing water that streamed between the parapets. He explained how the watermen rode the raging torrent like a slide with their passengers holding on for dear life.

"I don't fancy that," said Lucy.

"It's great fun. Father used to take me sometimes, but Mother didn't approve so we didn't tell her," he giggled.

"That's Leadam men for you," said Lucy, "always looking for a thrill. With Dad it's horses and women."

"That must be very difficult for you. I know he does wrong, but I like Uncle Robert; he's a good man."

"We all like him; we just don't like what 'e does sometimes," said Lucy with a sigh. "Oh, let's talk about summut else. Tell me about your family. We're meeting them tomorrow, aren't we?"

The thought of his relations made John's heart sink. He wanted to like them but they made it such hard work.

"Come on, they can't be that bad. Aunt Charlotte is lovely."

"Well," said John, trying to work out how to describe them. "My grandfather is one of London's leading physicians and my grandparents live in Wimpole Street, a place you and Aunt Mariah would describe as fashionable, but my grandparents aren't

235

rich by London standards. They have a very fine house with live-in servants, wallpaper and carpets. I say these things because women seem to think them important."

"They are, John: a good home is vitally important to a woman."

"Well, if that's the case my grandmother should be happy, but she isn't. Mother and Grandmother don't see eye to eye on much, and especially on what Mother should do now she's a widow. Grandmother wants her to remarry. She wants her to marry a rich man so she doesn't have to work and live in Southwark."

"What's wrong with Southwark?"

"Grandmother says it's not respectable. Besides, Mother doesn't want to get married, and she doesn't want to give up the apothecary shop. She says it's for me but I know that she loves it for herself too."

"I'm sure your mother can't be forced into anything she doesn't want to do. What does your grandfather have to say on the subject?"

"My grandfather is a kind man; he'll support Mother. He would have liked me to be a physician like him, but he understands I wish to follow my father – even if he thinks I've chosen the inferior profession."

They passed the Monument to the Great Fire of 1666 in Pudding Lane and started along Cannon Street. "It's amazing how complicated your lives are here in London," said Lucy, looking up at the myriad of shop signs. "What's the difference between a physician and a surgeon? They're both doctors to me.

"Physicians are gentlemen with a university education, whereas surgeons are not. Dr Sinclair, being Scottish trained, is an exception."

"What sort of exception?"

"He's both, because he has a medical degree and he's a surgeon. They do it like that in Scotland. He works like a physician sometimes, taking a patient's case history, but he also has an expert understanding of anatomy. It's the surgeons who hold the upper hand in the hospitals today, because understanding the body is the way forward in medicine."

"So you could be better off being a surgeon?"

"Yes."

"That sounds all right. I'm sure we shall all be very proud of you whatever you choose to be. How strange it is to have your whole life depend on what you know rather than what you own. If Dad died tomorrow Mother would still have the farm. I understand now why it was so difficult for Aunt Charlotte when Uncle Christopher died."

They turned into St Paul's yard and Lucy saw the cathedral for the first time.

"Oh my Lord," she said, gazing up in wonder. "It's magnificent!"

They could see their mothers ahead, so they ran galloping up the steps two at a time, arriving breathless at the top.

"There you are, you pair of chatterboxes," said Mariah.

"Shall we go in?" said Charlotte, opening the door.

* * *

Sinclair was right about the demand for lozenges and barley water. Their supplies were gone by the end of morning surgery, so Charlotte and Lucy took a large basket and walked to the Borough Market to buy more lemons and sugar.

"So, Lucy, what do you think of Mr Chapman? Are you looking forward to seeing him again?"

"He's very handsome, and attentive too, but he had very little to say for himself."

"Perhaps he was nervous. Men often find conversation with women difficult until they get to know them."

"Maybe," her niece replied. "Aunt Charlotte, would you say that a happy marriage and a good marriage are the same thing?"

"I'd always prefer a happy marriage, one that is based on love and mutual support; but many women make good marriages without being in love and are perfectly content."

"My concern is that if I married Mr Chapman it would be a good marriage rather than a happy one."

"I can see you're giving this man serious consideration, and that's a credit to you, but you barely know him. I'm sure you'll know whom you should marry instinctively. I did. I gave it no thought at all. I suppose my parents would have prevented me marrying your uncle if they had thought it was going to be a disaster. I commend you for your prudence."

"I'm very impressed with Dr Sinclair, Aunt Charlotte. He's a bit odd at times but I think that's because he gets nervous around women. When he's in his own sphere he's quite masterful."

"Well, he doesn't seem nervous around me; then I suppose I'm an old widow and not the sort of woman he would get nervous around," her aunt replied, paying for the lemons.

"Oh, but you're not old," protested Lucy.

"I'm older than Dr Sinclair. Besides, he's not interested in me; I believe his heart lies elsewhere, probably in Scotland, but he keeps his own counsel on that and I have no desire to embarrass him by prying. You'll meet his friend Mr Greenwood this evening; now he's a charming man, but he has no business and no fortune."

"How disappointing," Lucy sighed. "Is it true your mother wants you to remarry?"

"Who told you that? John?"

"I'm sorry if I've said something out of turn."

"Oh, it's no secret. My mother and her friend Mrs Peacock want to see me married by next summer, but I have no corresponding plan of my own so it's unlikely to happen. Now let's get on. We have a deal of work to do before we can get ready for the ball tonight. I want to wash and dress my hair."

"Would you let me dress it for you? I have a pair of clay pipe tongs: all you have to do is heat them in boiling water and wrap the hair around them. The effect is very good."

"That sounds perfect, Lucy."

As the women washed their hair and powdered their faces, John whiled away the afternoon in the apothecary shop, making up prescriptions and selling cough sweets and cordials to a steady stream of customers. At four o'clock, he closed the shop and put a notice in the window saying the surgery was closed and would open as usual in the morning. He had seen neither William nor Dr Sinclair all afternoon and was beginning to wonder what they were up to. At half past six, William bounced up the stairs and into the bedroom they shared sporting a new haircut. "We've been to the barber's: what do you think?" he said, proudly showing off his new short style.

"It looks really good, and it looks as if you've had a proper shave too."

"Yes, I have. Now I shall clean my teeth and put on a clean shirt; then I'm ready to dance."

"I'm not sure I am."

"Oh, you'll be fine; your family will be there."

"I know; that's the problem."

* * *

The hired cab pulled off The Strand into the great quadrangle of Somerset House just before seven. "I'm not sure about this," said Mariah, taking in the enormous limestone edifice. "I've never been anywhere so grand before."

"Neither have we," said John.

"Well, it can't be any more intimidating than the Edinburgh Assembly Rooms," said Sinclair. "We don't know most of the people and never will, so don't get too het up. Let's just enjoy ourselves: it's Christmas."

"Well said, Dr Sinclair. I intend to make the most of this occasion," said Mariah, taking his arm to steady herself down the steps. She was wearing sage-green brocade with a matching bow in her silver-grey hair. Charlotte was next to alight, wearing the same grey she had worn to Mrs Peacock's party, but this time she had embellished it with a pair of crystal drop earrings. Last was Lucy, looking radiant in turquoise.

"Shall we go in?" said Sinclair, taking Mariah's arm and leading her towards the door. John followed with his cousin on his arm, followed by Charlotte with the newly clipped William by her side.

The dressing room was crowded, but Charlotte head a voice she recognised at once. "Ah, there you are," said her mother, tapping her on the shoulder with her fan.

Charlotte turned to see her mother dressed in the palest of greys, with a collection of gold watches hanging from her elegant waist. "Good evening, Mother. May I present my sister-in-law, Mrs Mariah Leadam?"

The two women cast their critical eyes over one another; Mariah taking in Mrs Martin's collection of watches and wondering what they were for.

"How do you do, Mrs Leadam?" Mrs Martin said with her usual air of self-importance.

"I'm very well, thank you, Mrs Martin," Mariah replied, taking out her expensive fan, determined to give the pompous woman no quarter when it came to status.

"Mother, this is my niece, Miss Lucy Leadam."

"How do you do, Miss Leadam?" her mother simpered, following the rules of genteel civility to the letter.

"I am well, Mrs Martin, thank you. I am very happy to make your acquaintance at last."

Charlotte watched as a malicious smile spread across her mother's lips, and waited for the crushing verbal swipe that was about to be meted out.

"We shall never be acquaintances, my dear; we are family, Miss Leadam. We are not strangers who pass each other on the street."

Mariah's face flushed. "You're quite right, Mrs Martin. In that case may I suggest we join the family in the ballroom? We've come such a very long way and we should hate to miss a moment of it, shouldn't we, Lucy?"

Without waiting for her daughter to reply, Mariah turned and headed for the dressing room door. "Of course, Mrs Leadam, I comprehend your situation entirely," Mrs Martin crowed behind her. "Yorkshire is such a long way from the civilised life of the capital."

Mariah pushed through the crowd in the vestibule and joined the people waiting to be admitted to the ballroom. When they got to the front of the queue the Master of Ceremonies handed them dance cards and supper tickets and announced their names. No one in the impenetrable wall of people milling under the chandeliers was listening. On the other side of the door they could see a large number of naval officers in blue and gold uniforms, scarlet-coated army officers and clusters of gentlemen in evening clothes, all surrounded by women and girls in sumptuous gowns and sparkling jewels.

"How are we going to find anyone we know in here?" said Mariah, feeling overwhelmed by the heat and the ocean of people in front of her. Lucy clasped her mother's hand. "We'll be all right. Look, there's John."

John brought the news that William and Dr Sinclair were with Mr Greenwood and his friend Lieutenant Finch. He led them through the throng, and soon Charlotte, Mariah and Lucy were being introduced to Sinclair's friends.

Greenwood was quick to put Bowman's plan into operation, and asked Mariah Leadam for a dance. "Of course, Mr Greenwood," she replied, enjoying the unexpected feeling of delight she felt receiving the attention of such a handsome young man. Then Dr Sinclair asked her for a dance, and once again she found herself agreeing. Then she added dances with William and Lieutenant Finch to her card.

"Are you dancing, Charlotte?" Mariah asked over the din.

"No, I shall watch from the side. I'm still in mourning, and the anniversary of Christopher's passing is so close that I really don't have the heart for it. I shall keep my mother company: I'm sure she won't be dancing tonight."

Charlotte felt a tug on her arm: it was John, who had found the rest of her family. She made the required introductions. "I'm delighted to meet you at last," her father said to Mariah with genuine affection. "I must thank you for all you did to care for my daughter and my grandson last year."

"It were no more than any right-minded family would do in the circumstances, sir," her sister-in-law replied. "Christopher was my husband's brother and we all loved him dearly."

"Nevertheless, I'm deeply indebted to you and your husband, madam. Now, if you will please permit me, I would like to present to you my daughter Emma and her husband Mr Henry Bowman."

When the formalities were out of the way, their attention turned to the business of the evening.

"John, how many dances do you have?" Emma asked her nephew.

"None so far, Aunt Emma," he replied.

"In that case you may ask me to dance."

"Thank you, Aunt." He bowed his head, as he had been taught at Mrs Tucker's, and requested a dance. "It will be my pleasure," his aunt replied. "Now ask your mother and your Aunt Mariah if they would like to dance too, and your pretty cousin, but don't ask Grandmamma: she's not dancing tonight."

"Mother isn't dancing either Aunt Em; she says she'll keep Grandmamma company."

"What nonsense," intervened his grandfather. "Let me speak to her."

With their names on all the women's dance cards except Charlotte's and her mother's, Bowman, Sinclair and Greenwood were content their plan would work. "You were right about Cousin

Lucy," said Greenwood. "Do you think I could ask her for a second dance?"

"I don't see why not, but you should know that she already has a suitor; a man called Chapman from Yorkshire," replied Sinclair.

"Is he a rich man, by any chance?"

"I'm afraid so, but she does have 500 acres of Yorkshire to her name. It's worth a try, Frank."

"Honestly, you make it sound so mercenary. Where's your romantic soul, Jamie?"

"I haven't got one. I don't believe in love," he declared, looking at Charlotte and feeling a sliver of guilt pass through his heart. He took out his pocket watch and turned it in his hand. The blue enamel shimmered in the candlelight, reminding him of Iona. He looked over at Lucy with her honey-blonde hair and her pretty face, and concluded that she was no match for either of the women he loved.

"So you believe in happiness but not in love: you're a strange fellow, Sinclair."

"I've told you before, the happiness I believe in is not about desires."

"So you do have desires?"

"I'm as human as the next man, Frank, but a man should be careful about whom and what he desires," he said, with his eyes still on Charlotte.

"I know all that, but it's Christmas and time for some fun. Come on; Finch will introduce us to some more girls. Let's go."

"All right, Frank; let's see what other pretty fishes are swimming in this sea," said Sinclair.

"We should take William and John with us," said Greenwood, pushing through the crowd, "and Miss Leadam too."

"You're sounding more like your old self," smiled Sinclair.

"That must be because I'm always at my best when I'm surrounded by pretty girls," Greenwood laughed.

15
Butterflies

The dances started with minuets. Charlotte watched the proceedings from the promenade with her parents and Mr and Mrs Peacock, together with their friend Mr Masterson, the son of the banker she had met at Mrs Peacock's party.

"It's such a long time since I attended a public ball, Eliza," commented Mrs Peacock, scrutinising the dance floor and fanning herself frantically. "Now I remember why I gave them up."

"Yes, I'd forgotten what an awful brawl they were," agreed Eliza.

Mrs Peacock held her fan close to her face and whispered, "How are the Yorkshire folk?"

"Tolerable, Vanda, thank you for asking, darling," Eliza replied.

"Perhaps you won't have to tolerate them for much longer. Look at Mr Masterson with your daughter. He makes a thousand a year, you know, and he has shares in the bank. She could settle him down, I'm sure."

"It was a stroke of genius to invite him; I'm indebted to you. What do you mean, settle him down?"

"Well, he has a certain reputation. He needs a good woman to keep him on the right path. We mothers know what is best for our children. My Amelia would never have married Sir Roger if her father and I had not given her a good shove in the right direction. Now she's Lady Bedridge with five thousand a year, a manor in Hampshire and a house in Bloomsbury."

"So Mrs Masterson would be pleased to see him settled?"

"Oh yes, dearest. Scandal is the last thing you want if your family is running a bank."

"I remember Sir Roger was older than Amelia."

"Only by twenty years, Eliza. Frankly, I'm surprised he's still with us. I was sure the exertion of marriage would finish him off and Amelia would be a happy widow by now but instead she seems to have given him renewed vim. She has five children and is pregnant again, but she has the money and the title and that's what counts."

"I see," said Eliza. "Do you think Charlotte is sufficiently alluring to keep Mr Masterson out of mischief?"

"Indeed I do, and with no chance of more children he should be more than happy. Should he stray once she has his ring on her finger it will be of no consequence, and she may even prefer it if he pays for his pleasures. A man with a strong appetite can be a vexation to a wife."

"Indeed," Eliza replied.

Greenwood stood opposite Lucy ready for their first dance, feeling delighted he had made it back from Dover in time for the ball. In the despondent months following the shipwreck, his interest in women had been covetous and passive, but now, looking at Lucy Leadam, his heart felt light and open once more.

The orchestra master thumped the floor and the music began. Lucy curtsied and offered him her gloved hand. As they came together to start the promenade, Greenwood caught her eye, making her insides tighten with a delicious twinge of pleasure.

"Are you enjoying your stay in London, Miss Leadam?"

"Very much, thank you, Mr Greenwood," Lucy replied, with undisguised joy in her eyes.

"I hear we'll be spending our Christmas together at Tooley Street," he continued, trying to maintain his composure.

She looked at him and smiled, making his heart leap in his chest. "I'm looking forward to it, Mr Greenwood."

He wanted to gather her up into his arms and press his lips against hers, but kept to the rules of polite society and acceptable social discourse and said, "I shall go to Panton for the New Year."

"What's Panton, Mr Greenwood?"

"It's my parents' house in Staffordshire. I'll spend the rest of the holiday with my brothers.

"How delightful for you. I am an only child, and I would have liked to have had brothers and sisters."

"A family is indeed a great blessing, Miss Leadam. Perhaps you will marry and have lots of children," he said, looking deep into her eyes.

"I hope so, Mr Greenwood," she replied, suddenly feeling there was no air in the room. Their dance ended, and with it their enchanted moment. They parted and returned to the promenade, where Lucy heard her mother saying, "Thank you, Dr Sinclair: I really enjoyed that. You should try dancing, Mrs Martin: the years just melt away; it's like being a girl again."

"Oh, Mrs Leadam, none of us wants to feel like that," said Eliza. "Youth is entirely overrated, is it not, Mrs Peacock?"

"I for one would not have it again, Mrs Leadam," Mrs Peacock replied, pursing her bee-sting lips with prim distaste. "We women spend our young lives at the beck and call of our parents; as young women we concentrate on pleasing our suitors; and when we marry we must serve our husbands with little thanks or respect."

"That is so true, my dear Vanda," muttered Eliza. "Men have no idea of the sacrifices we make for them. Look at Charles: he has hardly said a word to me all evening."

"You have my sympathy, dearest. Now that I'm old no one tells me what to do, not even my husband, and I find that I care very little for the wants of others. It is an independence to be treasured. No, Mrs Leadam, I would not be young again."

"When you put it like that, Mrs Peacock," said Mariah, "I find myself in complete agreement with you; but I will be dancing again, so excuse me: I have to find Mr Bowman." She swished her skirt like a young girl in search of her beau.

When the minuets were over supper was announced. Greenwood made a beeline for Lucy, who had been dancing with John. "May I escort you into supper?" he said, offering her his arm. She took it gladly, and followed Mr and Mrs Martin with Henry and Emma.

The tables in the supper room were laid with savoury pastries, dainty cakes and small fruit jellies. The gentlemen took their seats on the right with the ladies on the left. William and Mariah were the next to join them, followed by Charlotte who was escorted by Mr Masterson and Mr and Mrs Peacock. Dr

249

Sinclair and John were the last to arrive, each with one of Lieutenant Finch's sisters in tow.

Sinclair noticed Charlotte watching him as he made polite conversation with the elder of the two sisters. Eleanor Finch was a pleasant enough girl with a mass of thick, brown hair woven into a mound of curls on the top of her head. However, her complexion was sallow and her chest flat, so she was of absolutely no interest to him. Nevertheless he lent forward, attentively feigning interest in every word she spoke, knowing that the English mistress of his heart was watching his every move. When he thought she wasn't looking he snatched a jealous glance in her direction. From what he could see, William Masterson was older than Charlotte. He wore the well-cut clothes of a prosperous man of business, making him an ideal suitor for a young widow. Sinclair instantly despised him.

As the group left the supper room to begin the county dances, Sinclair made his excuses to Miss Finch and joined Charlotte and her father.

"Good evening, Dr Martin," he said with a slight bow of his head.

"Ah, Dr Sinclair; we've missed you at St George's. I don't suppose there's any chance of you coming back? I know that your Uncle Donald would like that."

"Thank you, sir, but Donald McNeal is not my uncle: he's my sister's cousin by marriage."

"Nevertheless we do need men like you."

"Thank you, but I'm fully engaged at St Thomas' and with your daughter's apothecary shop."

"Yes, well in that case I shouldn't be trying to poach you away, should I?" he smiled, "but you can't blame me for trying."

"No, you shouldn't," scolded Charlotte. "Father, you're an incorrigible old man!"

"In that case," Dr Martin chuckled, "will you please ask my daughter for a dance, Dr Sinclair? I don't like to see her playing the wallflower."

Charlotte's face flushed. Sinclair wasn't sure if it was anger or embarrassment.

"Papa!" she exclaimed. "I'm not fifteen. I don't need you to find me a dance partner!"

"I know that, my child, but you do need some encouragement to enjoy yourself."

Sinclair decided to try his luck and proffered his hand. "Mrs Leadam, would you do me the honour?"

She flashed him a withering look, but said, "It would be my pleasure, Dr Sinclair. I am happy to dance with any gentleman my father approves of."

The Master of Ceremonies called out the dance, a reel, and the music began. The opposing lines of men and women joined hands and moved towards each other. As their bodies moved closer, Charlotte found Sinclair's hazel-green eyes locked with hers, and a butterfly in her stomach fluttered its wings. It was a feeling she recognised at once. It felt absolutely delicious and at the same time shockingly wrong. She looked away from him, knowing she was betraying her husband's memory. Then an awful thought struck her: could Sinclair tell she was attracted to him? Could he sense the effect he was having on her?

"Are you enjoying yourself, Mrs Leadam?"

"I'm rather out of practice when it comes to dancing, Dr Sinclair," she replied, a little out of breath.

"Ah, we're doing fine, Mrs Leadam. We're keeping up with the youngsters."

"You mean I'm doing well for an old lady?"

"Now, now, I never said that."

"Well, I shall certainly need to sit down when this dance is finished," she said as they chasséd between the lines of dancers to the top of the set.

* * *

Morning surgery began at seven. Charlotte watched Sinclair as he yawned his way down the stairs. He was unshaven, his hair was a mess and his crumpled breeches clung seductively to his handsome frame. The queue outside the door was as long as ever. William had already dealt with the morning's dentistry cases when Sinclair poked his head around the surgery door to see his protégé carefully stitching a deep gash in a matelot's head. As usual, there was a line of anxious parents with children and babies waiting for his attention and a clutch of maids and footmen waiting for appointments.

"Can I see any of these children in the shop?" he asked as he walked the length of the queue. A woman came forward with a screaming baby in her arms, "All right, in you come," he said, lifting the serving hatch and inviting the woman in.

"Let's have a look at this baby, shall we?" he said unenthusiastically.

The woman removed the child's blanket.

"Has she had a fall, Mrs Wilkins? Or did someone smack her a bit too hard?"

"No, them just come up. I don't understand it. We ain't touched her, honest we ain't."

He felt the child's brow, then gently pressed his hand on its little barrel of a stomach. Underneath the tight hot skin he could feel swollen organs. He covered the child and said, "Mrs Leadam, could you find Mrs Wilkins a seat until William has finished in the surgery?"

Sinclair ushered the next two patients in: both were children with influenza. He prescribed a tincture of willow bark and a rub of lavender oil for both. As soon as the surgery was free, he asked Mrs Wilkins to join him, and instructed William and John to come in as well. He asked the woman if his apprentices could have a look at her child, and the woman consented. When they had finished he asked them to leave so that he could complete the consultation. The boys closed the door behind them, knowing that Sinclair was going to tell the woman that her child was dying. All the excitement of their new life of balls, dancing and girls faded away into a weariness with the world.

"What's the matter with you two?" Charlotte said.

"Oh, nothing; we're just tired," said John.

"And sad," said William. "Dr Sinclair's telling that baby's mother her child is going to die. I don't know how he does it."

"I'm sure he'll be very gentle," she said, putting her arms around her boys. "Now up you go and get some breakfast. I'll see to everything down here."

When the woman had gone, Sinclair handed Charlotte his prescription for the child. "I've given her the best pain relief we have. It's expensive but she won't need much," he said, running his hand through his hair.

Charlotte took the piece of paper and touched him lightly on the arm. "Are you all right?"

"Aye, I'm just tired like everyone else. Did you know some young woman kept me up half the night with her dancing?" And they both laughed.

* * *

Greenwood made his last report to Lord Wroxeter the morning after the ball. "Greenwood, I'm impressed. You've turned your hand to everything I've demanded. You're diplomatic, loyal, sensible and hard working. These are admirable qualities in any man. If you need a job when you come back to London I will see if there's anything here for you. If you need a letter of recommendation let Finch know and it will be written."

"Thank you, sir. If you would let my father know you were happy with my service it would mean a great deal to me."

"Of course I will. I'll make a particular effort to speak to your father at Brooks's. Now off you go. Enjoy your leave; you've earned it."

Walking along the Strand, Greenwood felt pleased with himself for the first time in what seemed like an age. The year that had started so badly was coming to a close. He was free for the first time in months and he was looking forward to getting to know Miss Leadam. The London air was sharp and sooty. It really was ghastly stuff, he thought, and he looked forward to riding across his father's fields in the fresh country air.

His priority was to find a gift for Mrs Leadam to thank her for her hospitality. Then he would buy a coach ticket for his return to Panton. He had agreed with Sinclair that they would send a letter with a small gift of money to Mr and Mrs Farland in Dorset, to thank them again for their kindness.

With a happy heart, he sauntered along the Strand looking in the shop windows wondering what he should buy. There was nothing that took his fancy, so he headed off to Piccadilly. He purchased a new riding crop for his mother at Brigg & Sons, a tin of coffee for Mrs Leadam at Nobbs and Holland and a Stilton

254

cheese for his father from Paxton and Whitfield in Jermyn Street; then headed back to Good Acre Court to write his letter and to pack a few things for the holidays.

16
Mr Walker's Kiss

Connie Collingwood was fretting. Had she chosen the right music for Mr Walker's concert? How would she feel when she saw him again? Was it possible he found her attractive? She was well past her bloom and there were so many young women to beguile him.

Connie looked in the mirror, calmed herself and arranged her hair. Then she dressed for the evening. When she was ready she went to her father's bedroom, and found him sitting in his box bed, propped up on pillows and staring vacantly into space. "Papa," she said softly, not wishing to startle him, "I'm going out this evening, so Mavis will sit with you."

Her father said nothing, so she walked up to the bed and took his hand.

"Who are you?" he demanded, pushing her hand away. "Get out of my bedroom. I don't like strangers; leave me alone."

"Mavis will bring you some dinner later, Father. If you need anything, ring the bell and Mavis will attend to you; do you understand, Papa?"

"Yes, yes, ring the bell," he muttered with growing irritation, eager to be rid of her.

Connie wished him good night, and collected her hat and jacket from her room.

At five o'clock she joined Charlotte and her guests in their hired cab and headed north through the City to the West End. The streets were full of evening shoppers and theatregoers. The traffic was slow moving along the Strand and they were worried that they would be late, but just before half past five they pulled up outside St James's.

They entered through the south aisle door and were greeted by a nervous Mr Walker and Lady Carmichael, the wife of the chairman of the restoration committee. The organist played a largo by Handel softly in the background, and the warden took their tickets and showed them to their seats.

"Performers at the end of the rows if you please, madam; Mr Walker will call you when it's your turn to play." They took their seats and waited. Above them flower-like chandeliers festooned with candles blazed with light, casting the church's famous Corinthian columns and Grinling Gibbons's carvings into sharp relief. The piano that Connie and the other performers was to play sat in front of the altar so that everyone could see.

"Oh Lord, I didn't think there would be so many people, Charlotte, I feel quite sick," said Connie.

Mariah fished a bottle of hartshorn from her purse and passed it to Connie. "'Ave a sniff, it'll sort you out."

"You will be absolutely fine, Connie," Charlotte assured her friend, patting her arm. "Just close your eyes and play like you do at home. Trust me, everyone will love you."

Mr Walker strode past and took his place in front of the piano. Connie looked at him. He was undeniably handsome, even dressed in clerical black. She watched him with admiration, as he welcomed the Chairman of the Restoration Committee, Lord Carmichael and the other members of his board, including the banker Mr Peacock.

"Oh no, that means his wife is here too," whispered Connie. "Let's try to get out before we have to speak to her."

"I agree," whispered Charlotte.

When the introductions were over the first person to take the stage was none other than the odious woman herself. She was wearing the same green dress she had worn on the night of the dinner party with what looked like a diamond and ruby necklace, but tonight her heavily powdered white face was painted in scarlet and black to ensure a dramatic effect.

Mrs Peacock made herself ready to play. "Ladies and Gentlemen," she said coyly, and with what Charlotte considered to be a vast amount of false modesty, "I should like to play you two of my favourite pieces from Mr Purcell's opera 'Dido and Aeneas'. As you are all ladies and gentlemen of culture you will know this beautiful opera opens with Dido, Queen of Carthage lamenting the state of war between her own land and the land of Troy. She sings the song 'Peace and I Are Strangers Grown', and this is the first piece I shall play tonight. The second piece I have chosen is when the handsome Trojan Prince Aeneas enters the court. Dido behaves very coolly to him at first, but is persuaded to marry him for the sake of her father and for the peace of the kingdom. A worthy sacrifice, I am sure you will agree."

"She believes in marriage as a sacrifice," whispered Connie.

"Yes, I know," said Charlotte. "She married her own daughter off to a hideous old lecher called Bedridge for five thousand a year."

A slow ripple of applause spread through the nave, then Mrs Peacock began. She clonked the keys and screeched her way through the two pieces, but the audience was charitable and applauded her efforts with great enthusiasm, which obviously delighted her. Mrs Peacock gave the deepest of curtsies and returned to her seat with what Charlotte considered the attribute she least required: an enhanced sense of her own importance.

Mr Walker stood up again, and Connie's knees began to shake. "I would like to introduce a new friend of St James's," he said. "Miss Constance Collingwood. Miss Collingwood is an accomplished musician and a music teacher."

Connie took a deep breath and walked forward with her music as the audience applauded. Her legs were jelly and her hands were shaking as she took her place at the piano. "I too would like to play two pieces," she said. "The first is a favourite of mine and is perhaps a little melancholy for the season, but I hope you will enjoy it. I have tried to compensate for the sadness of the first piece with the joy of the second, 'While Shepherds Watched Their Flocks'. I hope you will all sing as I play."

Connie gazed up to the ceiling as if praying for inspiration, then she cleared her throat. Charlotte held her breath, hoping her friend's nerve would not fail her. Then Connie struck the first chord and started to sing. She began timidly, but with each note her voice grew stronger. Her voice soared up to the rafters with her lament for lost love, 'Plaisir d'amour ne dure qu'un moment, chagrin d'amour dure toute la vie'.

259

Anyone would think Connie had had her heart broken a thousand times, thought Lucy, as she listened to the pain and anguish in her voice. The audience loved the way she interspersed the lyric verses with her own improvisations, and as she sang the last note they burst into rapturous applause. With a flushed face Connie began her second piece, the familiar and well-loved carol with new music by Handel. By the second verse everyone was singing, filling the nave with a glorious sound, and again the audience roared approval with loud applause.

Mr Walker stepped up and took her by the hand. "Well done, Miss Collingwood. Connie felt her stomach fizz with the excitement of his touch. "Enjoy your applause; you've earned it." He let go of her hand and she returned to her seat. "Thank you, Miss Collingwood, that was truly sublime," he said as she found her place. "Now for the highlight of our evening, ladies and gentlemen. I am delighted to invite the celebrated German opera singer Miss Gertrude Mara and her accompanist, the composer and impresario Mr Stephen Storace, to entertain you this evening."

The audience gasped, then clapped and roared as the pair made their way to the piano. "Well done, Connie, they loved you," said John.

"My goodness, I'm on the same bill as Gertrude Mara and Stephen Storace," Connie exclaimed.

An hour later Connie and Mrs Peacock were being introduced to the great soprano by a contented Mr Walker, accompanied by his daughters Hannah and Harriet.

"Mr Walker, why didn't you tell me about Miss Mara and Mr Storace?" demanded Connie when they had gone.

"I didn't know they would come until the last minute, and I didn't want to put you off."

260

"I most certainly would have been put off," Connie replied, feeling slightly duped. "I had no idea the concert would be such a grand affair, but what I don't understand is how you could ask me to perform at an event like this when you'd never heard me sing."

"I had every confidence in you. I knew from the passion you expressed for music at Mrs Peacock's that you would be a good musician, but I must admit I prayed to the Lord; just by way of insurance, you understand, and He has not let me down. By way of recompense, would you do me the honour of joining me and my daughters for lunch after Christmas?"

Connie felt her heart swell and her nerves tingle. She was confused; she liked the man but she wasn't sure she really trusted him. He seemed to sail far too close to the wind for her liking. "I should be delighted, Mr Walker," she replied, willing to give him another chance.

He took her hand and kissed it, "Thank you, Miss Collingwood." Connie's stomach somersaulted with delight, and her pale face flushed with such violence that her head and neck turned scarlet.

"I saw how he kissed your hand," said Lucy in the cab on the way back to Tooley Street. "If you ask me he's interested in you. No man kisses a respectable woman in public without knowing how it will be interpreted."

"Aye; it looks as if you've clicked there, lass. He was definitely laying claim to you, my dear," smiled Mariah, making Connie scarlet again. To spare her further embarrassment Mariah decided to change the subject, and started to tell her companions about her conversation with a pair of furniture-makers she had met at the concert. "They're supplying chairs to the Prince Regent. I've never met anyone that close to the King before."

"I'm surprised the Prince is buying anything," said William. "He's bankrupt. He's asked Parliament to pay his debts because the King won't. He has a hundred and ten thousand a year and yet he can't manage. I'm sorry, but he disgusts me."

"You're one of them revolutionaries, are you, Mr Whitfield?" blurted Lucy. She had never heard anyone speak so disparagingly of royalty and the government before.

"No, Miss Leadam; I am not a revolutionary," William replied, wishing he had not opened his mouth. "I am simply at a loss to understand why the people who rule us fail to tackle our corrupt and moribund political institutions."

"You mean the Prince of Wales and the monarchy?" said Mariah.

"Yes, and Parliament too; it's full of men who serve their own interests and ignore the people."

"My goodness, William: I had no idea you were such an idealist," said Connie. "I'm inclined to agree with you, though. The Prince of Wales brings the monarchy into disrepute, and as for our politicians, they speak of reform at every election but do nothing to bring it about."

"And they have no regard for women," said Charlotte, much to John's surprise.

"Aye, we women want our freedoms too," chipped in Mariah. "We should like some rights over our property. We can't vote so we rely on men like you to stand up for us, William."

"Indeed, Mariah," Charlotte agreed. "I used to be content with our position when Christopher was alive, but in my present condition I understand how detrimental it is. It's impossible for a single woman, or a widow for that matter, to make enough money to live by respectable means. Men have barred us from every profession that will earn us proper money. If we could change the laws that govern us we wouldn't be so disadvantaged."

"Aye," said Mariah. "I don't know what these men of power are thinking when they make life so difficult for us common folk. They think we know nowt and think of nowt, but as far as I can see we could say the same about them. It's obvious that not all women have husbands, brothers or fathers that can provide for them. Besides, I'm not sure I want a man to speak for me. Every woman has a mind of her own, don't they?" she said, looking around the carriage for support. "Well I do; I don't know about you," she chuckled.

"My goodness," said John. "I had no idea I was living in such a nest of radicals."

* * *

It was the last Sunday in Advent, and Charlotte was sitting in her usual pew at St Olave's with John and William on one side of her and her family from Yorkshire on the other. Connie was sitting a few pews away with her brother Jonathan and his wife. Sinclair was with Greenwood, standing at the back with the latecomers as usual.

As she recited the words in her prayer book that were supposed to save her from sin, Charlotte thought about how often she had found herself silently wishing for Sinclair's caresses since the night of the ball. Images of him slipped unbidden into her mind. Her stomach tightened as she pictured him unshaven in his crumpled shirt and running his fingers through his hair; then she silently scolded herself for her foolishness, telling herself she had no right to feel as she did – and that her duty was to respect her husband's memory and to care for her son.

After the service, they walked to Mr and Mrs Hoares' in Gracechurch Street. The midday sunshine was low and bright, and a north wind chopped up the surface of the Thames.

"I feel sorry for William. He's all alone 'ere in London. Doesn't he go home to see his family?" asked Mariah.

"He's catching the mail coach to Dover on Tuesday evening after the barber surgeons' ball," Charlotte replied. "He'll stay with his mother and his sisters for Christmas; his father's still in Canada."

"Oh, I'm glad about that. He's a nice boy. Him and John seem to get on well with Dr Sinclair."

"Yes they do. It couldn't have worked out better. You know I took an instant dislike to him when I first met him."

"Who? Sinclair or William?"

"Sinclair, of course," Charlotte laughed nervously, feeling guilty about just how much she liked him now. "I thought he was rude but I think we just got off on the wrong foot. He can be awkward at times but he's very good with the patients. We wouldn't be doing this without him."

Mr Hoares welcomed his guests. "It's so good to be able to meet Christopher's family at last," he said, shaking Mariah and Lucy's hands enthusiastically. "We were partners, you know; we worked together at Guy's. Christopher was such a dear, dear friend. We miss him, don't we?" he said, turning to his wife sitting by the fire. His wife nodded her head and coughed into her handkerchief.

"Dr Sinclair, I'm so glad you could join us. You've taken a great weight off our minds. I know Charlotte and John are in safe hands now. Now, you two do as Dr Sinclair tells you and you'll do well. He's better qualified than either me or your father, although somewhat less experienced," the old man said, with a cheeky wink in the doctor's direction.

Sinclair bowed his head. "Thank you, Mr Hoares. I'll endeavour to live up to your expectations. May I present my friend Mr Frank Greenwood: we were on the '*Sherwell*' together."

"Oh my goodness, the '*Sherwell*'. Marie, did you hear that?"

"Yes, my dear; how perfectly dreadful for you both," his wife said, with another bout of coughing. Lucy looked at Sinclair and then at Greenwood. Like everyone else, she had read the story of the '*Sherwell*', and she was amazed to find herself in the same room as two men who had survived it. "Did you know that, John?" she whispered as they sat down for lunch.

"Of course; that's why he's working for Mother. He'd be in India running a hospital if the ship hadn't sunk."

* * *

At the other end of the kingdom Morag Rankin was recuperating from another rancorous Sunday lunch with her family by finalising her Christmas correspondence in the quiet of her Edinburgh sitting room. Letter writing was something she enjoyed, although her family were always tardy with their replies, especially her brother in London. With a sigh of resignation, she wrote out her brother's new address in Tooley Street on the letter she had written to him, placing it with her gift, a copy of Mr Burns's poems as she had promised. Would he ever come home, she wondered. Would she have to wait until her father was dead to see him again?

Christmas was always a busy time of year for Morag, but this year it was particularly so because she was preparing to launch

265

her eldest daughter, Ailsa, into Edinburgh society. At lunch, her father had made his opinion on the subject clear, accusing her of planning to dress his granddaughter like a strumpet and parade her like a whore around the ballrooms of the city. He had suggested instead that in place of his daughter's plan to prostitute the girl she should be taken to church every day, where she would meet God-fearing men.

Andrew, her husband, had done his best to temper her father's puritanical views, but her stepson Charles, who was now a minister of the Kirk himself, had added fuel to what was already a burning fire by agreeing with his puritanical grandfather. Charles had upset all the women in the house with his views on dancing, saying its erotic gestures and touching were lustful and sinful in equal measure and should not be encouraged, especially in his sisters. Ailsa, who had been looking forward to the Christmas ball, had left the table and taken to her room, and was now refusing to come out. The whole household was in a state of consternation, and Andrew Rankin was beginning to have some sympathy for his brother-in-law.

* * *

After lunch with Mr and Mrs Hoares, the Leadams and their guests sauntered home full of roast beef and claret. Sinclair took William to the hospital and everyone else crowded into the parlour for tea.

Lucy sat next to Mr Greenwood but he ignored her, choosing to speak to her mother on the subject of hunting instead. Mariah, who was no lover of horses, said, "My brother can be very silly, Mr Greenwood. Toby bought himself a mettlesome stallion, an evil beast that really required a better rider than him. But despite

266

his wife Pamela's objections, he was determined to ride the nag. Well, he'd barely been on the beast's back five minutes when it started prancing and capering and snorting. It didn't take to our Toby, but being a silly old beggar he thought he'd tame the beast with his whip, and he gev it a good thwack. Well, you can guess what happened next: the brute made off with him, and at speed. My nephew saw the whole thing. He rode up and grabbed the beast by the bridle, but the devil reared up on his hind legs. Toby kept his seat but not poor Matthew. The fiend knocked him off his mount."

"What misfortune," replied Greenwood. "I hope he didn't come to mischief."

"Broke his arm. The doctor had him in a splint for three months!"

"Hunting can be devilish tricky, Mrs Leadam, especially with a new horse."

"I'm glad to say that Pamela made him sell the evil nag. Mind you, he's been miserable with her ever since."

Spotting a lull in the conversation Lucy said, "Mr Greenwood, you were on the '*Sherwell*', weren't you?"

He looked at her but not as he had before; Lucy thought she saw a dark cloud drift across his face. His body stiffened. "Yes, I was, but I'd rather not talk about it."

"I'm sorry; I didn't mean to pry," Lucy said, feeling crestfallen and embarrassed. As soon as she was able, she excused herself and went to her room, where she lay on the bed thinking that she had read him all wrong. She had assumed his jovial and good-tempered persona was the sum of him, but the look on his face when she mentioned the shipwreck told her there was a deeper strand to him. There was another Frank Greenwood below the surface, and Lucy did not know whether she should try to uncover it.

* * *

It was the last Monday before Christmas. There was a queue of people outside the house, but for the first time since Sinclair had lived in Tooley Street Charlotte was not in the shop when he came downstairs. "Where's your mother?" he asked John, feeling slightly awkward that for the first time Charlotte wouldn't be there to help him.

"Mother says she's not feeling well," John replied blithely.

"Can you manage the shop on your own?"

"Yes, I'll be fine. Mother says it's nothing serious; just a cold."

When the last patient was gone, Sinclair knocked on Charlotte's bedroom door. "Mrs Leadam, it's Dr Sinclair. Are you all right?" There was no reply, so he opened the door a crack and looked into the darkened room. He took a candle from the candleholder in the hall to get a better view. In the centre of the room stood an empty four-poster bed with a coffer for clothes at its foot. Peering into the gloom, he spotted her, lying on the floor next to the bed. He knelt down and gently cradled her head in his arms. The heat of her body told him she had influenza. "Charlotte," he said, stroking her face. "Wake up, bonnie lass, wake up."

When she opened her eyes, he slid his hands under her slender frame and lifted her onto the bed, feeling the swell of her hips and her narrow waist through the soft cotton of her nightgown. "Don't move," he said. "I'll get Mariah."

But there was no need: she was already there watching him from the doorway. Mariah looked at her sister-in-law lying on the bed. "I know someone who won't be doin' any dancing tonight, doctor. Oh Charlotte, you poor thing, you have the luck of Job, don't you?" Then she turned to Sinclair. "I'll nurse her, if you get me a bowl of water."

"Thank you. I'll send one of the boys up. Mrs Leadam's going to be in bed for a while, but she should be up by Christmas Day."

John arrived at the top of the stairs to see his aunt comforting his mother.

"Don't be alarmed, John: your mother has influenza but she's going to be fine. Can you get a bowl of water for your aunt? She's volunteered herself as nurse."

"Of course," said John, feeling fear spike his heart. "Are you sure she'll be all right?" he mumbled, fighting back the overwhelming feeling of déjà vu. It was just like when his father was ill in Yorkshire.

Sinclair saw the fear in the boy's eyes. "I promise you your mother will be fine. She has a fever and she's fainted, that's all. Your mother's strong and we're going to take good care of her. There's nothing to fear."

Lucy took over the nursing duties at eleven o'clock when Mariah visited Mrs Dredge in the scullery. The two women shared a cup of tea, then got down to the business of finalising the arrangements for Christmas. "It sounds as if you've got everything under control, Mrs Dredge," concluded Mariah.

"It's what I'm paid for. I have a good place here and I want to keep it: I intend to put off the poor house as long as I'm able. Nell Pickering will come in as usual to lay the fires and clean the rooms and help with the washing and ironing. She'll need paying

269

before Christmas: her man's at sea and she's got kids depending on it."

"Right-oh, I'll make sure that's done," said Mariah. "Me and Lucy will go to the market to get the decorations."

As Mariah was leaving Mrs Dredge said, "I'd like to nurse her. I've always looked after her when she's ill."

"Aye, I think Charlotte'd like that."

Returning from his rounds at St Thomas', Sinclair felt the house was unusually subdued. The excitement of the past week was gone, and with Mrs Leadam in bed the shop was quieter too. He climbed the stairs and knocked on her bedroom door. Mrs Dredge opened it. "She still has a fever but she's sleeping," she whispered. "Mrs Mariah Leadam's resting ready for this evening. Who will stay with Charlotte tonight?"

"I'll stay," replied the doctor.

Lucy appeared on the landing. "Oh, you don't have to do that, Dr Sinclair."

"Yes I do. I insist that you and your mother go to the ball, and I want the boys to go too. I'm Mrs Leadam's physician and I'll look after her."

Sinclair returned to his attic room, tired and glad he wasn't going to the ball. He and Greenwood had talked long into the night about the '*Sherwell*'. The problem was that Parliament wasn't interested in improving the safety of ships or in curbing the power of the East India Company. Mr Burke was labouring in the Commons to convict Mr Hastings of corruption, without much support or success because the Members' only interest was in curbing the power of the company's officers to ensure that the shareholders, men like themselves, were able to take a greater share of the plunder. Sir Bramwell's advice was disappointing but good. No individual could take on a company like the East India

270

Company and expect to win. It was a leviathan that pursued its own interests ruthlessly, with no sense of social or moral responsibility, and it was pointless to try.

Sinclair lit a pipe, and his mind turned from the '*Sherwell*' to Charlotte. He recalled the smooth curve of her hips, her tiny waist and the sly glimpse of breast he had stolen as he laid her on the bed. Was he turning into Mr Hodge, he wondered. He was definitely developing a lustful eye for a widow. He took out his watch and checked the hour, then rolled its golden body through his fingers. Was he finally losing his interest in Iona McNeal? His fantasies, when he had them, were populated by another woman now: the one lying in the bedroom beneath him.

Iona had been his intellectual ideal of love: her mind was mercurial and bright, her body light and vivacious. When he had imagined the sex he might have with Iona it was always light-hearted and fun. His desire for Charlotte Leadam was altogether different: it was primitive and earthy. Her presence in his life was becoming a physical necessity, and he was beginning to feel a sense of ownership over her. He was relieved that she was ill; he didn't want her going to the ball or to one of her mother's dinner parties to find someone else to love and marry.

At four o'clock Sinclair went down to the dining room, where he found the family and William eating bread and butter and slices of fruit cake.

"I'll stay with Mrs Leadam this evening," he said, helping himself to a cup of tea.

Mariah protested, saying she should stay with Charlotte, but Sinclair explained that Lucy would have no chaperone if Mariah stayed at home, and that was untenable.

"You're right, doctor: Lucy cannot go to the ball in the company of young men, no matter how gallant they are," Mariah conceded.

"William and John will have to do the introductions for you, as Mr Greenwood will not know the people there. Many of the guests will have worked with your brother-in-law. Christopher was a well liked and a well-respected surgeon, and anyone who knew him will be delighted to be introduced to his family."

The Barber Surgeons' Hall was more like the Beverley Assembly Rooms in scale than the ballroom at Somerset House. As soon as they arrived, William began introducing Lucy and Mariah to the surgeons he knew, rotund men dressed like churchmen in black and white, accompanied by their colourfully attired wives and grown-up children. Lucy's dance card was full within half an hour, with Mr Greenwood claiming the second minuet and the first of the country dances.

As Lucy took to the dance floor, Greenwood watched her from his vantage point on the opposite side of the room. She looked even more beautiful than the night of the Navy Ball. Her pale pink dress flowed over her perfectly proportioned figure, cascading over the hoops and down to the ground, and emphasising the slightness of her waist. The material of the dress perfectly matched the pink silk of her shoes and the lace trim on her gloves. Her honey-coloured hair was softly curled and hung loosely in a chignon at the nape of her oh-so-kissable neck.

Frank's partner for the first dance was the granddaughter of one of London's most revered surgeons, Mr Parker. The girl's mousey brown hair was curled and dusted with powder, and the pale blue of her dress matched the pale blue of her eyes. From what Lucy could see, Miss Parker was cock-a-hoop with her handsome dancing partner. And as far as Lucy was concerned she had every right to be so, because to her eye Mr Greenwood bore all the hallmarks of his breeding and class: he looked like a man who rode well, shot straight, held his drink and was gallant with the ladies. In short, he had everything she desired, unlike so many of the pallid and bookish men in the room.

She returned her attention to her own partner, who was prattling on about his recent trip to Europe and the books he had read, none of which was of any interest to her. She smiled politely, allowing the young man to expatiate upon his intellectual interests until the end of the dance. Eventually, she curtsied politely, and was gratified to find Frank quick to claim his dance. Waiting for it to begin, an agonising silence developed between them. Lucy, who had not an ounce of guile in her body, felt forced to break it. "Have you had a good day, Mr Greenwood?"

"I have, thank you. I went to visit my brother Sandon and his wife in Bedford Row." The music began and they started to walk the dance. As they joined the couple opposite to make a star, their eyes locked on each other, and something inside Lucy's stomach started a dance of its own. Greenwood for once was struggling for words, his usually brilliant faculty for conversation overtaken by the speechlessness of desire.

"What does your brother do, Mr Greenwood?"

"He's a King's Counsellor."

"Like your friend Mr Bowman?"

"Yes, somewhat; but my brother is better connected and more successful."

There was another long silence, as Greenwood looked at the floor instead of his partner.

"And what of your other brothers?" Lucy ventured, trying to reignite their connection.

"My brother Bramwell will inherit my father's estate at Panton Hall. He'll have ten thousand acres and mines and a small plantation in Jamaica. My brother Tobias is a vicar with a clutch of parishes in Staffordshire." He knew he sounded pompous and overbearing, but he couldn't help himself.

Lucy felt he was letting her know that she did not match his rank. "And you're going to Panton Hall after Christmas?"

"Yes, I am."

"That'll be nice. Is it where you do your hunting?"

"It is. It's great hunting country, Miss Leadam. We have over fifty hounds and plenty of deer and fox to chase."

"I love to hunt but I don't get the opportunity these days," Lucy smiled, hoping that she had found some common ground; but then the music stopped and so did the conversation.

Feeling deflated, Greenwood escorted Lucy back to her mother, where William was waiting to claim his dance.

"Miss Leadam," said William with a slight bow, "would you do me the honour?" With his new haircut, William had grown in confidence before their eyes, the exact opposite effect to the biblical Samson. William was proving to be quite a success with the younger girls. The fact he was about to dance with one of the most desirable women in the room only added to his self-assurance.

"Are you enjoying yourself, William?" asked Lucy.

"I am, thank you. I can't say I'm a good dancer, but I don't think I've trodden on any feet and I haven't tripped anyone up, so my currency is still good."

"Well, I'm not fantastic myself, so we shan't disappoint each other," Lucy smiled. The music began, and as she danced she looked about the room for Greenwood. He was standing with her mother and John, chatting to a group of medical-looking men and their wives. He wasn't looking at her.

"Do you think you'll see Mr Chapman again?" asked William. "He seemed a very agreeable gentleman."

"I will. My family has been invited to his house for Twelfth Night."

"Then may I wish you success, if your parents think he's a suitable match."

"Thank you, William."

"There are many eligible young surgeons here tonight, Miss Leadam. Do you think you'd like to be a surgeon's wife?"

"Oh no; I don't have the stamina or the wits of my aunt. I'm more suited to be a farmer's wife, but the right man might persuade me to settle in town."

She was conscious of Greenwood watching her all through supper as she made small talk with Mr Ellesmere, but their second dance was barely better than their first, with Greenwood silent unless she prompted him to speak. When Lucy got home, she threw herself face down onto the bed and screamed into the pillow. How could he do this to her? How could he be so contrary? She had never felt such anger, not even at her father. If Frank Greenwood did not want her, Mr Chapman was showing every sign he did. She would show Frank she was good enough to be the wife of a man of substance. He might think himself superior because he had wealthy relatives, but she had a farm and Mr Chapman had warehouses and a tannery. As far as she knew Frank Greenwood had nothing; he had no right to look down on her, no right at all!

* * *

Sinclair was up early the next morning to check on Charlotte. As he put his hand on her forehead, she stirred and opened her eyes. "Go back to sleep," he whispered. "I'll take care of everything."

Passing the boys' bedroom door he gave it a hefty thump, taking his revenge for all the times they had banged on his door demanding he get up no matter how tired he was. Now they would know what it felt like to drag their tired bodies out of their nice warm beds only to go down to the draughty surgery to deal with the stream of suffering humanity waiting for them there. "Come on you two," he called. "Time to get up! There are patients to be seen."

Five minutes later William and John appeared, tucking their shirt tails in. "Good morning, gentlemen," Sinclair crowed, puffing out his chest and sticking his thumbs in his waistcoat pockets.

"All right, all right," they muttered resentfully. "We know we're late."

"Welcome to the world of medicine, gentlemen," the doctor said. "Now let's to business."

On his mattress in the attic, Greenwood was dreaming a new dream. He was swimming in a wild ocean trying to stay afloat, but the more he swam the deeper into the abyss he sank. Susan Morris was there, floating in her sky-blue dress, and as usual she was screaming at him. In this new dream, another woman was by her side, a woman in a pale pink dress. He felt powerless to rescue either of them. As he reached out they slipped further and further away. He woke disturbed and angry. Although he wanted a drink there was none to hand, so he dressed and waited for everyone to go to breakfast before slipping out to his favourite coffee house on the Strand.

Full of soberly dressed men of business checking their stock and the latest prices, the coffee house was warm and steamy. Greenwood purchased a large cup of hot, syrupy coffee and settled at a table by the window to read the newspaper. Perhaps, he thought, he should take a leaf out of their book; after all, his problems all seemed to be about money, or more precisely the lack of it. He perused the tight columns of text looking for something that would interest him. He flicked aimlessly through the pages until his eye fell upon an advertisement that read "State Lottery Scheme 1786". He looked down the column of prizes: there were two of twenty thousand pounds, six of ten thousand, eight of five thousand and 18,700 of fifteen.

As he gazed at the ticket prices he found his hand already in his pocket, counting the coins. The tickets were to be sold by the Lottery Office whole or in parts. A whole ticket was £12 18s 6d, but it was possible to buy a sixty-fourth share for as little as 4s 6d. There were twenty thousand prizes and sixty thousand tickets, making the odds of winning one in three. This was good, he thought, and he began to wonder how much he should spend.

He could afford a whole ticket with his last payment from the Navy Office, but he didn't want to gamble it. A quarter ticket at £3 5s 6d would be enough to flutter the heart strings but insufficient to cause penury, he assured himself. With his hope rekindled, he finished his coffee and went off to find the offices of the State Lottery Company in the Poultry near Cheapside.

17

In Sickness and In Health

In Tooley Street Sinclair ran his eye down the list of house calls that John had put together as he buttered himself a piece of toast.

"John, this appointment for Husselbee you've given me. Is it for Sir Hubert or Lady Isabelle?"

"It's for Lady Husselbee," said John apologetically.

"Thank you," Sinclair replied, taking a large gulp of tea. He turned to his apprentices and gave them their instructions between bites of buttery toast. "You check up on your mother, John: she looked all right when I looked in on her this morning. And William, you mind the shop." He said his goodbyes to Mariah and Lucy, who were planning to buy Christmas decorations at the market, and went to collect his bag.

He walked towards London Bridge, skilfully avoiding the puddles from overnight rain and the piles of steaming horse shit, and crossed into the City where he hailed a cab to Dover Street. On his arrival, he was shown into the same yellow drawing room where he had met Sir Hubert before. The baronet was now some four stone lighter, and although he was still a big man he looked more comfortable sitting on his elegant French furniture.

"Good day, sir. How can I be of assistance to you?" said Sinclair, knowing there must be something seriously wrong as Husselbee did not like him.

"It's Lady Isabelle; she's not well. Dr Martin of Wimpole Street has been treating her, but she seems to be getting worse."

"I see, sir. I presume you'd like me to take a look at her?"

"Aye, I would. You're not my favourite doctor, as you know, but you seem to be good at what you do, so I thought a second opinion might help."

"Do you wish to be present when I examine your wife?"

"Aye, I'll come and see what you're up to," the lumbering king of coal said, opening the door and inviting Sinclair to follow him up the stairs. "I'm not sure I entirely trust you."

Lady Husselbee's bedroom was large and spacious, decorated in soft greens and pinks with wallpaper and carpets in matching hues. Sinclair found his patient in her mahogany four-poster bed with its green damask curtains closed. From behind them he could hear the sound of a woman whimpering.

There was little in the way of ornament or paintings in the room besides a dressing table, a tall free-standing mirror and a table beside the bed, with a bottle of Calomel, mercury chloride for the treatment of venereal disease, on it.

A young woman dressed in a grey dress and white apron sat next to the bed, the lady's maid turned nurse, Sinclair presumed.

The bored girl sat silently staring out of the window, doing her best to block out the sound of her mistress's agony. Husselbee looked at the girl and pointed his finger to the door. "You out," he said. The girl curtsied and hurried away. When she was gone, Sir Hubert poked his head between the bed curtains. "Issy, Dr Sinclair's here. I want 'im to 'ave a look at you, love."

"Lady Husselbee, I need to examine you if I'm going to help you," said Sinclair in his most solicitous voice.

"No, Bert, I don't want anyone looking at me."

Sir Hubert put his head between the curtains, "Issy, he's only trying to 'elp."

"No, Bert. I can't be seen like this," his wife groaned.

"Issy, I've 'ad enough of this. Open the bloody curtains, Sinclair. I can't be doin' with any more of her nonsense."

The doctor pulled back the heavy damask drapes, and as the light flooded onto the bed the baronet gave out a gasp of horror. "My God, Issy. What the 'eck's 'appened to you?"

Sinclair looked at Lady Isabelle. She was a shadow of her former round and rosy self. In the months since he had first met her she had halved in size. Her plump pink skin and snow-white hair were gone. The woman he was looking at was old and thin; her limp grey hair hung like rats' tails around the sunken features of her face. The sallow skin of her face was ruptured by the painful suppurating sores of venereal disease, and he knew that if she had them on her face she had them on the most intimate parts of her body too. But what shocked him most were her eyeballs: they were the same colour as her fashionable wallpaper downstairs, a vivid shade of yellow.

Sinclair leaned forward to get a better look. The woman met his gaze. "Lady Husselbee, show me where it hurts," he

280

demanded. Sensing his genuine concern for her, Lady Husselbee put her hand on the top of her stomach.

"Can I have a look?"

"No," she moaned, shaking her head, screwing up her face in protest.

Sinclair understood the woman did not want the indignity of him seeing the most secret parts of her body, especially now they were now so disgusting, but without a proper examination he would not be able to assess her condition.

He looked across to her husband, who was pacing up and down in front of the windows, refusing to look at his wife. "Sir Hubert, I'd like permission to examine your wife."

"Do it," he commanded, turning his back to them. With her husband's permission given, Sinclair took the sheets out of Lady Husselbee's hands and turned the bedclothes down. He pushed away her protesting hands, then pulled her cotton nightdress up to below her breasts. She was shaking and thrashing her head against the pillow, but wasn't putting up a real fight. He worked his way up the soft skin of her abdomen, pressing his hands into her flesh until he felt the swollen lump. He pressed into it and she winced. "Thank you, Lady Husselbee. Now tell me, does your back hurt?"

Accepting defeat, she nodded that it did. He took her sallow hand and stroked it. "I don't suppose you feel like eating do you?" She brushed away her tears. "You're a very sick woman. I'll give you something to ease your pain, then I'll speak to your husband about your treatment and care."

Sinclair took a small bottle of laudanum from his bag and poured some into the glass on the bedside table, then mixed it with a little water. "This is going to taste a wee bit strange, but I want you to drink it all," he said. "It'll take the pain away and make you feel more comfortable. If you feel a wee bit sick at first, that's normal." He cradled her head and pressed the glass to her lips. "Very good, Lady Husselbee, now let's finish it, shall we?" he said, encouraging her as if she were a reluctant child. "I'll have your maid sent in to make you comfortable while I speak to your husband. You're in safe hands now." The woman closed her eyes and Sinclair pulled the drapes back together, restoring her privacy and what he hoped were some shreds of dignity.

Having tended to his patient, the doctor indicated to Sir Hubert they should speak elsewhere. Downstairs in the drawing room, Sinclair did not mince his words. "Your wife is dying, Sir Hubert. She has the venereal disease you gave her, but that's not what's killing her. She has a cancer in her stomach that's painful and untreatable. You must prepare yourself; she only has a short time to live."

Husselbee's broad and ruddy face turned pale with bewilderment and shock. He swallowed hard. "Why didn't Dr Martin find the cancer?"

"Dr Martin is an excellent physician, but no doubt he respected your wife's wish not to be examined. This type of tumour gives very unspecific symptoms, and your wife may have associated them with the venereal disease or the treatment Dr Martin gave her for it. Then I suspect she became frightened and decided not to say anything in the hope it would go away."

"I've not seen her for weeks," admitted Husselbee. "I assumed everything was all right, but when I came home I realised that she wasn't getting out of bed any more." The big man started to pace the room deep in thought before turning to Sinclair. "So, what's to be done then, Dr Clever Clogs?"

"My name is Sinclair, sir," the doctor replied, thinking to himself, "That's another guinea on your bill, you ignorant oaf."

"Aye, I know that," Husselbee spat back angrily. "But you are a clever clogs, aren't you? You think you can run rings round us that are less educated than you."

Sinclair made no reply, mentally adding another guinea to the bill.

Then Husselbee slumped into one of his elegant French chairs, and tears started to flow down the enormity of his face. He sat with his head in his big square hands and blubbered like a child. "Come on, man," he pleaded. "You're the clever one. Tell me what to do. My Issy is dying."

Sinclair bit his lip before replying. His blood was boiling, but he wouldn't let this oaf get the better of him. He hated him. The arrogant boor had selfishly infected his wife with the vilest of diseases, a result no doubt of his adulterous liaison with that expensive little whore he had seen him with at the theatre, or perhaps some other trollop he had paid for. He had neglected his wife for weeks while she endured the repulsive treatment for the disease; and now he was insulting her doctor for trying to help! How stupid could a man be, he wondered?

As slowly and deliberately as he could, Sinclair said, "I can give Lady Husselbee something to make her end less painful and distressing."

Husselbee scowled. "Do it, Sinclair. Give her whatever she needs."

"In that case, I would suggest the services of a proper nurse. Someone trained in looking after a woman in your wife's condition, someone who can bathe and dress her sores and make her feel more comfortable."

"Can you organise that for me?"

"Yes, I can; and I would suggest she's tended by her physician every day to make sure she has the right level of medication to control the pain."

"I thought you might say that," Husselbee snarled.

"I'll only come if you desire it, sir," retorted Sinclair, letting the man know he was prepared to walk away.

"I don't like you, but you're good at what you do," Husselbee conceded. "Do whatever you think is best. I don't want Issy to suffer more than she has to. I'm not all bad, despite what you think. I love my wife. But I'm warning you, Dr Clever Clogs, don't try to fleece me. I won't pay an inflated bill."

"Of course you're free to seek an alternative medical practitioner if you don't trust me. My fee for this consultation is three guineas. We could leave it at that if you wish."

The big man cupped his face with his hands again and sighed. "Three guineas. I suppose that's reasonable," he said. "I can't 'elp the 'abits of a lifetime. A man in business 'as to be careful wi' 'is money. Everyone who can will try to cheat you if you give them half a chance; especially clever buggers like you, Sinclair. It's not as easy 'aving money as folks wi'out it think. But you've bin honest and straight wi' me even if you've taken me for a fool. I can see that I need to spend a few guineas on Issy. I've got to do the right thing by 'er. I want a clear conscience when she goes."

"In that case, I'll set about finding you a nurse and get some more medicine over to you, and I'll add Lady Husselbee to my list of home visits."

Sinclair was feeling pleased with himself when he got back to Tooley Street. He had secured a lucrative piece of work that would ease Lady Husselbee's suffering and, after a brief reconnoitre of the Cutting Ward, he was sure he could discharge his remaining two patients there before Christmas so he would not

284

have to visit them over the holiday. This left him with the duty of attending the hospital in case of emergencies, as his staff surgeon Mr Ellesmere would be on leave.

He opened the door to the dining room, expecting to enjoy a calm lunch of soup or stew, but found the household in a state of consternation. Charlotte was sitting at the table in her dressing gown coughing and sneezing, and trying to comfort Mariah who was howling like a dog with its tail cut off. John and William were sitting with Lucy as she wept.

"What's happened?" Sinclair demanded, taking a seat next to Charlotte. John passed him a letter to read.

The Tannery, Beverley, Yorkshire

Dear Mrs Leadam and Miss Lucy,
I am sorry to be the bearer of bad news
especially as you are so far from home. I will
make this message short as I want to get it into
the post as soon as possible.
I have to inform you that Mr Robert Leadam has
been badly injured in a fire at one of our
tenement buildings close to the tannery. It is
said that he was injured trying to rescue a
woman and two children when the floor of the
building gave way and he fell through it. He
was pulled from the burning building by some of
the tenants and taken to the Black Horse public
house, where the surgeon set his broken leg and
removed his badly burned right hand. Mr
Leadam is in the care of Mr and Mrs

285

*Braithwaite at the Black Horse, who say they
are happy to keep him until you come home.
Your cowman is taking care of the animals in
Mr Leadam's absence. I will do everything I can
to ensure Mr Leadam is as comfortable as he
can be, and that the farm is well managed until
your return.*

*Until then, I am your servant,
Marcus Chapman Esquire*

"This is terrible news." said Sinclair.

Charlotte put her hand on his."But he's still alive. It's bad, but it's not the worst news they could have had."

"Aye, when you put it like that there's hope, but I don't think they're seeing it. What can we do to help?"

"I suppose we need to get them home as soon as we can, but there are no more Flying Coaches until after Christmas."

"They're stuck here, then," said Sinclair.

"It looks like it," Charlotte spluttered, sneezing into her handkerchief again.

There was a knock at the door, and Greenwood's head appeared. He took in the scene, and retreated. Sinclair jumped up and went to speak to his friend in the hall.

"There may be a solution," offered Greenwood. "It's not ideal, but if they want to get to Yorkshire as soon as possible it could work."

"What do you have in mind?"

"The last Flying Coach to Burton leaves at six o'clock tomorrow morning. We could take it if there are any tickets left. It takes a day to get to Panton Hall. We could stay there overnight, then I could drive the ladies to Yorkshire in my father's coach. I'd be very glad to do it, Jamie; you know I can't stand moping around."

"All right," said Sinclair. "You make the offer and we'll see what they have to say."

Much to Greenwood's relief his offer was quickly accepted, and Mariah and Lucy went to their room to pack.

"Well, that's settled. We might as well have something to eat," said Sinclair, helping himself and Greenwood to stew. "William, you're off this evening, aren't you?"

"Yes, sir."

"My goodness, it's all go around here, isn't it?" said Greenwood, feeling grateful that he was needed again.

"Aye, and my nephew arrives from Cambridge at seven," said Sinclair.

"I'll go and see if there are any tickets left for Burton," said Greenwood.

"I'll come with you," said John; and when Greenwood had finished eating they left, leaving Charlotte and Sinclair alone.

"Do you want me to ask Mrs Dredge to make some more tea?" said Charlotte.

"No thank you," Sinclair replied. He put down his spoon and stood up. "You'll go back to your bed this instant and get better." He took her arm and placed his around her waist. Much to his relief she didn't protest, and they walked up the stairs together, each secretly thrilling at the contact between them. They paused for a moment outside Charlotte's bedroom door, then the doctor opened it and whispered in her ear, "Now go back to bed, Mrs Leadam, and don't get out of it again until I say you can."

Charlotte smiled back weakly. "Of course, doctor," she said; then she closed the door, leaving Sinclair standing on the landing, pleased that the object of his desire had accepted his attentions.

* * *

At six o'clock, Sinclair was standing outside the Black Swan in Holborn waiting for his nephew to arrive from Cambridge. He hadn't seen Blair for nearly four years, and he wondered what he would be like. He knew that the lad had a prodigious talent for mathematics but little more. The weather was still surprisingly benign for the time of year and there were lots of people out on the street. When the Cambridge coach drew up, a red-haired young man in cream breeches and a heavy brown coat jumped down.

"Hello, Uncle James," the young man smiled.

"Hello, Blair. My goodness, you've changed since I saw you last. You're quite the man now."

"Aye, thank you, Uncle. It's been a while, hasn't it? Thank you for offering to put me up. I told Mother I had to stay in Cambridge, but I was really coming to London all along – so your offer of a place was perfect."

"Oh was it?" said Sinclair, taking hold of his nephew's bag. "And why did you feel you had to lie to your mother?"

"I didn't want her to get her hopes up on a scheme that may come to nothing, and I didn't want Father interfering with things."

"Interfering with what, may I ask?" Sinclair asked, as they moved away from the throng of the crowd.

"I'm parched. Let's find a tavern, Uncle James, and I'll tell you all about it."

They decided on the White Horse and Sinclair bought the beer. "I'm here to meet a publisher," Blair explained." I've been working on a project at Cambridge. We're trying to put together a new magazine, well, a new section for an existing one. If we pull it off, it'll be part of the 'European Magazine'. The 'European' already has sections on Literature, History, Politics and the Arts, and if we have our way it'll also feature news from Britain and the continent concerning scientific discoveries and the latest medical developments."

"That's a huge undertaking."

"I know, but it's exciting, isn't it?" his nephew smiled. "It'll give the magazine a real advantage with the scientific and medical community and make its rivals look positively parochial."

"I see," said Sinclair, taking a sip of his beer. "It all sounds very worthwhile, so why do you need to keep it from your parents?"

"I just prefer not to involve them. I'm meeting my friend and potential co-editor Miles Somner tomorrow. His father will introduce us to the owners of the *European*, Mr Perry and Mr Reed. Perry is my father's publisher too, but I wanted to do this on my own. I don't want Perry to think I'm looking for favours."

"Aye, I can understand that."

"The other reason is I don't want my brother Charles to hear about it until I know it's successful. I know he's a man of the Kirk but, believe me, he'd ridicule me mercilessly if he knew I'd failed at something, especially something like this. He has a surprisingly resentful streak for an eldest son."

"In that case my lips are sealed, Blair." Sinclair took out his pocket watch and checked the hour. "Come on, drink up. I need to get back. I promised to be back for the end of evening surgery and it's nearly that time now."

289

Back in Tooley Street Sinclair introduced his tall and bony nephew to the rest of the household and guests.

"I think this is where Mrs Leadam keeps it," said Sinclair, delving into the large oak cupboard for a bottle of Madeira, before looking around for the glasses.

"They're in 'ere," said Mariah.

"I don't know about you, but I could do with this," said Sinclair, pulling the cork out of the green bulbous bottle.

"Ee, you're not kidding, doctor. Is there any sherry? I'd prefer that if you've got it, but I'll have whatever's going."

Sinclair looked in the cupboard again, and extracted another bottle.

"Thank the Lord!" exclaimed Mariah.

Supper was a subdued affair. John and Lucy sat close to each for comfort while Mariah snivelled into her handkerchief. When the women departed Sinclair opened a second bottle, and Blair told them more about his 'European' project. At ten o'clock Sinclair suggested he should take William down to the Talbot Inn, ready to catch the night coach to Dover. We could have a drink while we're waiting," he said.

"Good idea," said Greenwood. "I can sleep in the coach tomorrow. There'll be nothing else to do."

Twenty minutes later they were crossing the greasy cobbles of the inn's huge courtyard. The Dover coach was standing in the yard and the inn was packed with travellers and drinkers. "Are you nervous, William?" John asked.

"A little, if I'm honest. I've never travelled at night before."

"Well, I think you're exceedingly brave, Mr Whitfield," said Blair. "I certainly would not. I prefer to travel in the daytime." The red-headed Scot wrung his hands nervously. "At night there are villains lurking everywhere, ready to make off with your possessions or worse!"

"Thank you, Mr Rankin," said John, watching fear traverse William's face and wondering how the man sitting next to him could be such an idiot. This thin-faced, carrot-head might be a mathematical genius, but he was a complete fool when it came to people. "Mr Greenwood made the journey from Dover to London last week and had no problems, so I'm sure everything will be fine."

William thanked his friend for his reassurance.

"Well, rather you than me," said Blair, crossing his long thin legs with an audible sigh.

Sinclair and Greenwood returned with foaming tankards of beer. "Come on lads, get it down you," said Sinclair. "There's a queue of passengers waiting to get on this coach in the coffee room, I've been told. If you want a front-facing seat you'll have to get in the queue, William.

"Oh, I'm not bothered about that. I won't be able to see anything, will I?"

"Good point," laughed Sinclair. "It's been a long day and I'm not thinking straight."

"You'll have to walk up Shooter's Hill if the coach is full; the driver makes all the men get out," said Greenwood. "So don't get too comfortable until you're past Greenwich. Then you can sleep until you get to Dover, if you can ignore the other passengers' farting and snoring," he chortled.

They finished their drinks and took William to the coach. Sinclair slipped him a florin and wished him and his family a Happy Christmas, then they waved him goodbye as the coach pulled out of the yard and headed south to Greenwich.

"Well, that's William on his way," said Sinclair. "It's you and the ladies tomorrow."

"Oh, don't bother to get up early, Jamie; I can sort everything out. I've hired a cab for five o'clock," said Greenwood as they strolled back to the house.

"I'll get up," said John. "I want to see them off."

"Of course you do," said Sinclair.

"I'll write to you when we get there to let you know how things stand with your uncle. It seems Mr Chapman has everything in hand, but if I can do anything to be of assistance to your family I'll be happy to do it."

"Thank you, Mr Greenwood: that's very generous of you."

"Oh, it's no problem. I like to be helpful; it's the only thing I do well," said Greenwood, with the familiar ring of sadness and self-pity in his voice again.

* * *

The snow that had fallen thickly on Christmas Day now lay in icy ruts, making their walk to Holborn to catch the first mail coach of the New Year to Edinburgh treacherous. It was early evening, but the moon was already high in the cloudless sky casting its cold, blue light on the rows of houses and crowded pubs they passed as they made their way towards the golden street lights in Gracechurch Street. The mail coach was due to leave at eight o'clock, and Sinclair had allowed plenty of time for him and Blair to get to the terminus, knowing the state of the roads from his daily visits to Mrs Husselbee in Dover Street.

They arrived in the busy thoroughfare to find the coach, a small affair made for four with a mailbox and a guard on the back, waiting by the curb. Sinclair handed his nephew's bags to

292

the guard. "Are you sure you'll be all right? I know you're not comfortable travelling at night."

"Well, needs must, Uncle James. I've got to be back in Edinburgh as soon as possible. Please thank Mrs Leadam for a lovely Christmas."

"Aye, I will."

"Mother will be relieved to know that you've found yourself such a good place."

"Aye, you're right. The Leadams are very good people. Please give my love to your mother and thank her for the book of poems. Tell her I love them and that I'll write to her soon."

"I will, sir," Blair replied, closing the door and winding down the window. "I'll be back in London with Iona in February."

"With Iona McNeal?" replied Sinclair, feeling the pavement move slightly beneath his feet.

"Aye. We can get married now I have the contract with the 'European'."

His nephew's announcement hit Sinclair like a lightning bolt thrown by some Olympian god from his chariot. His mind was reeling; he was dumbstruck. Surly Iona could not be marrying Blair! He was a boy. Her father would not allow it, he reasoned. As his spirits plummeted he realised he was wrong; it was precisely the sort of match her father sought. Blair Rankin was from one of Edinburgh's leading academic families, and with his new position at the 'European Magazine' he would be able to promote McNeal's work and the work of the university all over Britain and in the colonies. After what seemed like an age Sinclair finally said, "Well, I can't say I'm not shocked, but may I be the first to offer my congratulations?"

"Thank you, Uncle," his nephew smiled. "We'll be staying with Iona's Uncle Donald at his house in Hyde Park before we head off to Bologna and Paris, but I know Iona will want to see you before we leave."

"I look forward to it," Sinclair stumbled, still feeling his nephew's dirk twisting in his heart. The driver let off the brake and cracked the whip, Blair shouted a happy goodbye and the coach was on its way.

Sinclair stood on the pavement. His stomach ached and he was struggling for each breath. He turned to go back to Tooley Street, but remembered he had promised to check at the post office to see if there was any news from Yorkshire. He collected two letters, one addressed to John and one to himself, and started to walk home. He was not sure how long it took him to get there, because he spent a long time looking into the black waters of the Thames thinking about Iona and Blair. Despite abandoning her, he couldn't stop thinking he should have been the man to marry Iona. He couldn't believe his own nephew, a boy in his eyes, was marrying the woman he loved. He had felt nothing but guilt when he rejected her, because his rejection had been a lie; he had loved her. The thought of her had always been with him: on the ship, on the cliff, and in idle moments before he went to sleep at night. Iona was still a part of him. He loved her, but now she had turned the tables on him; she had discarded him the way he had her, and the pain was unbearable.

As Sinclair stood starring in the black eddies of water under the bridge, he wondered if Iona had returned his feelings. Had he misinterpreted her enthusiastic conversation for love? How was a man to know if a woman loved him when they were allowed to say so little to each other? Sinclair's thoughts turned to his feelings for Charlotte Leadam. Had he misread her friendship as interest in him as a potential lover and husband? Had the look she had given him when they danced at the Navy Ball and in the apothecary shop the morning afterwards, a look that made his guts feel as though they were turning inside out, been nothing more than inconsequential flirting?

Sinclair took his pocket watch and checked the hour. It was late, and he knew that whatever her feelings for him were Charlotte would be worrying about him. He turned for home. Whatever the situation between them was, right now she felt like a consolation prize and he felt like a fool.

He found John and his mother in the parlour. Charlotte was sitting by the fire in her grey widow's dress with a fringed silk shawl over her shoulders. She had recovered from the influenza, but she looked wan and frail. He knew that she was emotionally exhausted as well, following the anniversary of her husband's death and the tragic events that had overtaken her family in Yorkshire, and his instinct was to care for her.

"We were wondering where you'd got to," Charlotte said with a tired smile. Sinclair made up a lie about the coach being late, gave John his letter and passed on Blair's thanks, then excused himself and went to his attic room, where he slumped into his reading chair feeling miserable and confused. His was the coldest room in the house, and the little fire spluttering in the grate was making no impact on the frigid air. He kept his coat on, lit a pipe and poured himself a glass of claret from a half-empty bottle. When he was comfortable, he fished the letter he had collected from the post office out of his pocket, cracked the blob of scarlet wax and started to read:

Highfield Farm, Beverley
27 December 1786

Dear Jamie,

*We arrived in Beverley on Boxing Day, having
spent one night at Panton Hall and Christmas
night in Chesterfield. Miss L caught the
influenza from her aunt and was very sick for
the duration of the journey, but was determined
not to be left behind.*

*We found Mr L in very poor condition at the
Black Horse where Mr and Mrs Braithwaite are
caring for him. He cannot be moved and the
doctor is not optimistic concerning his
recovery; his injuries are very serious.
Tragically, the fire killed the people he was
trying to rescue; his mistress and her two
children. Consequently, his spirits are very low.
I return to Panton Hall tomorrow and will be
back in Town at the end of the month.*

*Your friend,
Frank*

18
Twelfth Night, 1787

"Sinclair, you've got to get up! I can't do it on my own," John moaned through the attic door.

"I'm on my way," Sinclair groaned. "I'll be with you in a couple of minutes. Don't open the front door until I get there."

The water in the pitcher had frozen overnight. Sinclair punched it with his fist and splashed the freezing water on his face. The shock jolted his sleepy head and stiff limbs into action and brought his mind into focus; he took a deep breath, straightened his coat and ran his hands through his hair, ready to deal with the morning's fresh crop of affliction.

John had lit the candles ready for work when Sinclair finally appeared. "Are you ready?"

"Yes, sir."

"Good lad. Let's see what we've got today, shall we?"

"Very good, sir. Shall I open the door?"

"Aye, laddie, let's get started. The sooner we've got this lot out of the way the sooner we can have a cup of tea and some breakfast."

John opened the door to the usual collection of ladies' maids and footmen, parents with their sick children in their arms, and frightened men and women waiting for the doctor's verdict on their mortality.

Sinclair removed a tooth from a woman whose face was swollen with an abscess, telling her to come back if it did not go down within a day or two so he could drain the infection again at no extra cost. This was a simple act that would save her life, so he was insistent she should return if the symptoms did not subside. His final patient was yet another young man with an advanced case of venereal disease. Sinclair hated the repugnant disease, with its pain and disfigurement. He hated that the cure was so expensive too. Like many of the young men he treated, the patient opted for snail broth, as the mercury treatment was too expensive, and the doctor knew that within a few short years this vital young man would be pushing his way through the pearly gates with thousands of others like him.

Charlotte was already in the dining room and helping herself to tea and toast when John and Sinclair entered. She was wearing a pale blue dressing gown, with a silk cord belt around her waist, over a white cotton nightdress, with an embroidered silk shawl wrapped around her shoulders. The whole ensemble emphasised her small frame, her tiny waist, the curve of her hips and the swell of her breasts: it was a look Sinclair liked very much. To add to his delight she was wearing her long auburn hair loose, allowing its thick, luscious curls to flow down her back. Even as a consolation prize, Charlotte Leadam had many attractive features.

"Ah, good morning, Dr Sinclair. Can I pour you some tea?" she said, taking in his crumpled appearance.

"Aye, that would be much appreciated," he replied, taking off his jacket nonchalantly and trying not to look too interested in her or the way she was looking at him. He took his seat at the table and speared a slice of bread onto the toasting fork. "You look much better today," he ventured, turning the bread at the fire.

"I am, thank you. John, pass the butter to Dr Sinclair please."

"Yes, Mother," replied her son, picking up the dish and handing it to his mentor, then helping himself to a cup of tea and slice of bread and jam.

"Dr Sinclair," Charlotte said, "John and I will be away this evening at my mother's Twelfth Night party, and we'll be staying the night at Wimpole Street. I'm sorry to leave you on your own, but it seems that with William away there's no alternative."

"Oh, please don't worry, Mrs Leadam."

"I'll put a notice in the shop window to say there will be no morning surgery tomorrow."

"Thank you."

"And we should look at the accounts when I get back," Charlotte continued in a business-like fashion.

"Of course. It'll be interesting to see how we're doing. We're commanding some good fees at the moment."

"Yes, we are," she agreed, brushing a stray curl back into place. "You're proving a great success with the ladies."

"Oh, I really hadn't noticed," Sinclair lied, trying not to think about the number of bosoms he had had to examine that had proved to be perfectly healthy. He felt uncomfortable about his popularity with female patients, because it was a popularity he had never achieved in social situations.

Sinclair was aware of Mrs Leadam's eyes scrutinising him again, so he kept his head down and focused on his piece of bread. As he loaded it with as much butter and marmalade as he could, the date started to penetrate its way into his brain. Charlotte had said it was Twelfth Night, so it was a year to the day since he had nearly died.

"My goodness, is it Twelfth Night already?" he said.

"Yes; and my mother will be holding one of her famous parties tonight. Half the physicians in London will be there. I exaggerate, of course, but it will certainly seem like it. I don't really want to go, if I'm honest. I'm tired, and with everything that's happened I'm in no mood for frivolity."

"So why don't you stay at home?" he said, feeling he would prefer her to be at home too.

"Ah, if it were only that simple. If I were to let my mother down, there would be a deal of trouble wouldn't there, John?"

"She's prone to hold grudges," her son admitted, looking a little uncomfortable, although he knew he was saying nothing Sinclair didn't already know. "Mother," he continued, "why doesn't Dr Sinclair come with us tonight? I'm sure Grandpapa would be delighted to see him, and there'll be plenty of people he knows there."

"Oh no, I couldn't do that, John, I haven't been invited," protested Sinclair.

Charlotte gazed directly at him as he chewed on an enormous piece of bread. "You haven't been invited by my mother, it's true, but you could be invited by me."

"I don't want to cause any trouble," he protested again. "I know how tricky families can be."

"Oh, the trouble will be all mine," Charlotte smiled. "It won't be the first time I've done what my mother wants, but not quite in the way she expects. What a brilliant idea, John."

"Thank you," her son replied, realising that with Sinclair by her side his grandmother would find it more difficult to press his mother into the company of the men she was lining up to replace his father.

"So, Dr Sinclair, would you please do me the honour of accompanying me to my mother's party this evening?"

"I'd be delighted to join you, if you're sure it won't upset your mother," he replied.

"That's settled then," said Charlotte, feeling pleased to be complying with her mother's demands whilst asserting her own. This balancing act was one she had practised all her adult life. Her first successes had come with Christopher's help, but now she was a skilled practitioner in her own right. She recognised her mother's feigned affection for what it was, and no longer felt guilty about not pleasing her. Her mother's obsession with appearances and social climbing were part of her self-fixation, and Charlotte no longer had any qualms about disappointing her as long as she was comfortable with her own behaviour.

Alone in the empty dining room, Sinclair considered the date. He had been alive a whole year longer than he had expected on that fateful night. He still had the occasional nightmare, but he was happier now than he could ever remember. His life had changed so much in the last twelve months, and the man who had boarded that doomed ship seemed a stranger to him now. A year ago he had been full of hubris and loneliness, spending his evenings alone and with the bottle. For the sake of his ambition, he had been prepared to exile himself in a foreign land and give up the woman he loved. He had been prepared to abandon all thoughts of love and family, assuming they were unattainable at best and irrelevant at worst. Twelve months ago, he had wanted to prove himself to the world and to escape the derision of his father, but those things no longer seemed important. He had not become a man of wealth or an innovator in medicine, but neither had he sunk into a life of hypocrisy working for the East India Company. Despite everything, and even knowing Iona was going to marry Blair, he could not be disappointed with what had happened to him since he had returned to London. He had survived. He had found a good friend in Frank Greenwood, grown closer to Henry Bowman, and had found himself a happy and fulfilling situation in Tooley Street and at St Thomas' despite Mr Ellesmere's butchery. Financially he was better off, and most importantly, sitting opposite him each morning was the most attractive and alluring woman he had ever met. No, he couldn't be disappointed. In a strange way, he was grateful to the 'Sherwell'.

* * *

The party in Wimpole Street was in full swing when they arrived. Charlotte was wearing her grey silk dress with the embroidered silk shawl she had been wearing that morning and a short string of seed pearls around her neck. The house was crowded with medical men and their wives, and the sound of music was coming from the front drawing room. The maid took their coats and they made their way into the supper room at the back of the house, greeting old friends and acquaintances as they passed. There they found Mrs Martin supervising the cutting of an enormous meat pie.

"Ah, Charlotte, my dear, there you are," she called. "John, darling, come and help yourself to pie." Seeing Sinclair, Mrs

Martin grimaced. "Oh, you're here too. I suppose one more doctor won't make much difference. Help yourself to pie, Dr Sinclair. I'm sure you will find it superior to that which is commonly served in Scotland."

"Thank you, madam. I shall give you my opinion as to its merit when I've tasted it."

Mrs Martin turned her attention to her daughter, taking her by the hand and leading her out of the supper room and towards the front parlour. "Don't you have anything else to wear? This is a party. You could have made an effort. Honestly, you look like a pauper. How am I to raise the interest of a suitable man if you look as if you've borrowed your clothes from the poor house? At your age looks aren't enough. One has to be seen to be a worthwhile investment socially. I'm disappointed, Charlotte, very disappointed indeed."

As Charlotte was taken away, Sinclair searched around the table for forks. "I suppose we might as well eat these before we go and rescue your mother."

John watched as his Uncle Henry and Aunt Emma made their way across the room. Henry put his finger to his lips mischievously and tapped his friend on his shoulder. "Who invited you?"

Sinclair turned around sharply. "Henry, I might have known it was you," he said with relief. "Good evening, Mrs Bowman." He bowed his head respectfully in Emma's direction.

"Good evening, Dr Sinclair. I trust you're here with my sister."

"Indeed we are," Sinclair replied, including John in order to make the arrangement more socially acceptable.

"Aunt Emma, Grandmamma has taken Mother off to the front parlour for some reason."

"Oh, that's because she wants to introduce her to that nice lawyer Mr Masterson again. I think she has plans, so don't go interrupting, will you?" grinned his aunt, purring like the cat that got the cream.

"Oh, we're content to stay here with the pie," said Sinclair, feeling nonetheless that he should be in the drawing room keeping an eye on Charlotte. "Do you think we could get a drink to go with it?"

"My mother is famous for her rum punch. Henry, would you do the honours?"

"Certainly, my dear, four glasses of rum punch coming up," said Henry, leaving Emma and Sinclair looking uncomfortably at each other until Sinclair spotted Sir Donald McNeal and waved him over.

"Mrs Bowman, may I introduce Sir Donald McNeal," he said, relieved to find some distraction.

"Sinclair, I had no idea you would be here tonight. How marvellous to see you. I heard from Charles that you are now at St Thomas'."

"Aye sir, I am, and doing very nicely, thank you," he replied, wondering what conversation was passing between Charlotte and Mr Masterson in the parlour.

"Mrs Bowman, how lovely to see you again," said McNeal, taking her hand and brushing his lips across it. "It's a tragedy we only meet once a year." he let her see the wicked twinkle in his eye. "You and Henry must come to supper one evening, and you too, Jamie, of course. We Celts need to stick together in this terrible town, don't we?" Then he turned his attention to John. "Who's this handsome young man, Sinclair?"

"This is Mr Leadam, my apprentice and Dr Martin's grandson."

"Pleased to meet you, laddie; you've landed a good teacher in Dr Sinclair, despite what his father says about him, eh, Jamie?"

"My father holds none of us men of science in any regard," retorted Sinclair.

"Aye, you're right there. If prayer were enough there'd be no need for the likes of us, hey, Sinclair?"

"Indeed, sir," Sinclair replied, grateful to see Henry with the drinks.

McNeal saw his opportunity to make his exit. "Ah, Bowman, I must get one of those myself. Please excuse me, Mrs Bowman. I will get my man to send you an invitation to supper." McNeal smiled devilishly at her again, winking his rakish eye at her and making his escape.

"Did I see Sir Donald wink at you, Emma?" demanded Henry.

"You did," his wife replied, smiling triumphantly. "You should expect such things to happen, Henry. I'm an attractive woman." Emma pressed her fan to her lips as if inviting her husband to kiss her.

"Emma! He's an old lecher, and I don't expect that sort of behaviour from you in public."

"Oh, Henry, it was nothing," she countered, putting her hand on his arm.

"I've never liked him or his brother," said Sinclair in a low and angry voice. "The McNeals are all the same: they think they own the world and everything in it."

"Henry, we should keep him sweet; he's a very important man for us," Emma chirped.

"I know, dear, but I don't like it when he makes open advances to my wife."

"Well, it's safer than in private!" Emma giggled.

"And you didn't hear any of this, young man," Henry said to his nephew.

"My lips are sealed, Uncle Henry. Can I go and find Mother?"

"I'm sure she'll be glad to see you if her evening has been anything like mine."

"Oh, Henry, most men would be glad to have a wife who's admired by other men, especially rich and influential men; sensible men use it to their advantage. If you'd let me flirt a little," Emma said, closing her fan and running the tip of it around her glass, "I'm sure we'd have a lot more clients."

"I think you should follow John and find your sister. We're doing very nicely without your flirting, thank you very much."

"Oh very well then, dear, but don't blame me if men find me attractive," Emma replied, as she followed her nephew out of the room.

"I don't know what's got into her, Jamie," moaned Bowman. "It must be all this talk of finding Charlotte a husband. All she talks about is eligible men, frocks and parties. The only person who has her head on straight is Charlotte."

"My sister-in-law is a very sensible woman, Henry. Perhaps we should go and find out what she's up to."

"We might as well keep up with developments. How about another drink? This pie is awfully dry." Fortified by another glass of punch, Bowman and Sinclair made their way to the parlour, where the carpets had been rolled away and the furniture now lined the walls. A string quartet was playing a minuet for eight couples, including Charlotte and Mr Masterson. They looked around, searching for Emma and John, but instead found Mr Martin admiring his daughter with Mr Peacock.

306

"They make a handsome couple, don't they?" said Peacock, as Bowman and Sinclair joined them.

"Aye, they do indeed," agreed Sinclair, watching Charlotte as she moved to the music.

He's doing very well in the King's Bench Division. Your daughter could do a lot worse than him, you know," said Peacock, looking at Sinclair.

"Have you seen Emma, Father," asked Bowman, keen to find out what his wife was up to.

"I'm sure she's here somewhere. I saw her come in with John a while ago."

"Well, at least if she's with John she won't be flirting," Bowman said to Sinclair.

The music stopped, and Mr Masterson escorted Charlotte back to her father. Introductions were made, and Sinclair offered Charlotte one of the glasses of punch he was holding.

"Thank you, Dr Sinclair, that's very kind of you. I think I need some food with this."

Seizing the opportunity she had provided for him to take her away, he said, "In that case may I escort you to the supper room, Mrs Leadam?" She took the offer of his arm and allowed him to steer her away from his rival. In the hallway he took her hand and led her through the crowd of chattering men and women to the room where the supper was laid. Charlotte looked flushed and excited, but also relieved.

"Here take this," he said, offering her a slice of pie and sitting down beside her. "Your mother certainly puts on a good show."

"I know. I used to love these parties when I could enjoy them with Christopher. We danced until the small hours, and it didn't matter if we got a little bit tipsy. Now I have to be on my best behaviour. I think my mother is more controlling than when I was a girl. I've told her that I have no desire to remarry. Look at me; I'm not even out of my mourning clothes. The trouble is she despised Christopher, although she never actually said it."

"I'm surprised to hear you say that. Everything I've heard about your late husband has been complimentary."

"Oh, he was a good doctor and a good man, but he was only a farmer's son. My mother always wanted me and Emma to marry gentlemen. I was my mother's greatest disappointment. Although Christopher was a good surgeon, she knew that he'd never get onto the staff at Guy's because he was neither sufficiently gifted nor sufficiently well connected; meaning, of course, he would never be rich."

"That's the fate of many good men, Mrs Leadam."

"Thank you. My mother also hated the fact we live in Southwark. She grew to tolerate Christopher, but she never got over our living south of the river. I'm a social disgrace in her eyes. Now she's determined I should make amends with a socially advantageous marriage."

"Your mother is a woman of strong opinions and determination, like my father. If I were to tell you that my father disapproves of me and hates me, would that shock you?"

"Yes, it would. How can a man hate his child? My mother doesn't hate me; she just wants to improve me so that I fit more comfortably into her world."

"My father hates the fact that I'm a doctor and not a Minister of the Kirk like him; and he hates the fact that I'm alive when my older brother and my mother are not."

"I don't think you would have made a very good vicar, Dr Sinclair, and as to your father hating you for something I presume you had no control over, it seems very unfair."

"Thank you. I can assure you I had nothing to do with my brother's or my mother's death. Why do you say I wouldn't make a good vicar?"

"Oh, because any man who reads the books you do is unlikely to be a friend of the Church. I've seen you reading Voltaire and Rousseau, and I'm sure William got those books on understanding, passions and morals by Mr Locke from you."

"Guilty as charged, madam," admitted Sinclair, glad she took an interest in what he was reading and thinking. "I've been replacing the volumes I lost on the 'Sherwell' each month."

"You're a man who prides knowledge over belief; you're too brave and logical to believe in supernatural things, like us lesser mortals who cleave to them for comfort. Besides which, you're always reluctant to go to church on Sundays."

"Am I that obvious? You make me sound very boring and predictable."

"I wouldn't say that. I think for you this world is so full of wonder there's no room for belief in another. Your father's attitude towards you wouldn't have endeared the Church to you either. Perhaps it was easier for him to blame you for the loss of his wife and son than to blame it on the God he so profoundly believes in. Perhaps it was the only way he could keep his faith."

"I'd never thought of it like that," Sinclair conceded, feeling that Solomon was right. Wisdom was not just like a woman; it was very definitely female.

"And you're not boring, Dr Sinclair. You're hardworking and enthusiastic, and you seem to pass that enthusiasm on to the boys when you teach them. I'm very grateful for that. It's important John has a good mentor now he's lost his father." Sinclair reached over and put his hand on her arm, sensing the emotion she was suppressing. "You see, I believe a boy needs to be set on the right road in life if he's not to fall into bad ways."

"Trust me, you've nothing to worry about on that score; both John and William are exemplary young men and will make excellent surgeons. I enjoy teaching them. I must admit I was reluctant to take on the task at first, but now I look forward to it."

"Oh, I'm so glad; I'd hate you to leave us. You're happy with your situation, aren't you?"

"I am; I have no plans to move on. It's precisely a year to the day since I was in a doomed ship in the storm from hell, waiting to die. I feel blessed to have been spared when so many good people were lost. I've been given a second chance at life and I intend to make the most of it. I'm very happy to stay if you're happy to have me."

"We are indeed happy, Dr Sinclair." Charlotte touched his arm to reassure him.

"Thank you. As to your present predicament, I don't think the authority of any parent, no matter how well meaning, can oblige you to marry in opposition to your inclinations."

"No; thank goodness." Charlotte smiled at him, gazing into his hazel-green eyes and convincing him of the connection between them. They sat for a moment, absorbed by each other and oblivious to the world, until Charlotte suddenly broke the enchantment. "This pie is awfully dry, isn't it? Would you get me another glass of punch, Dr Sinclair?"

As his watch struck twelve, Sinclair stood on the threshold of the Martins' house, holding Charlotte as she swayed drunkenly in the fresh night air.

"Oh, I don't feel very well," she wailed. "I think I've had too much to drink."

310

They were joined by John and Bowman. Sinclair asked John to find his mother's shawl.

Bowman sidled up to his sister-in-law and put his arm around her. "Oh, Charlotte," he chuckled, "you've had a few too many cups of your mother's punch, my dear."

"Oh shut up, Henry," Charlotte snapped, letting a stream of hiccups escape. "It's only once a year, for goodness' sake."

"True, dear sister. Now hold your breath and count to ten, or I shall have to ask Sinclair here to give you a fright."

The two men laughed, and Charlotte held her breath.

"It could be arranged," said Sinclair. "I have a record of frightening Mrs Leadam in carriages!"

"Now, Jamie; I'm trusting you with the care of my sister-in-law. On no account is there to be any fondling of knees."

"Absolutely not," Sinclair replied, with a mischievous grin.

"We'll make a gentleman out of you one day," Bowman giggled, giving his friend a fraternal slap.

Charlotte gasped for breath. "I can hear what you're saying. I'm not deaf."

John came back empty handed. "I can't find Mother's shawl anywhere."

"Here," said Sinclair, taking his coat off and putting it over Charlotte's shoulders. "Come on, let's get home, John. I don't know how long I can keep your mother upright, so let's be quick!"

"Honestly, I'm not that drunk. Don't exaggerate," Charlotte protested.

Sinclair opened the cab door and jumped in. With one tug from him and a push from John on the pavement, he caught Charlotte in his arms. His face brushed hers and he breathed in a deep draught of her perfume, enjoying the thrill of her skin

311

against his. She did not protest as he held her for a moment or two longer than was necessary before settling her into her seat.

"Open the window, John. If your mother looks as if she's going to be sick stick her head out of it, will you. I don't want vomit on my new coat."

John had never seen his mother so drunk. When she had come back from parties with his father she had always been a bit merry, but he was sure she had never been this inebriated. He was embarrassed for her, and was sure she would regret her behaviour in the morning.

Charlotte was asleep when they got home. "Jump out and open the front door and I'll deal with your mother," instructed Sinclair. John did as he was asked, and lit the candles in the hall. Sinclair lifted Charlotte out of the cab and carried her to her bedroom, where John watched him lay her on the bed. The doctor rolled her over and removed his coat. "You take your mother's shoes and stockings off, John, and I'll loosen her clothes to make her more comfortable."

A wave of embarrassment overwhelmed the boy. He watched transfixed with horror as Sinclair unlaced his mother's dress.

"Help me get your mother out of this, will you?" Sinclair said. Then he unlaced Charlotte's corset and slipped it off, leaving her to sleep in her petticoats. "There, she can sleep it off comfortably now. It's time for bed, laddie."

"Thank you, Dr Sinclair," John replied, with a mixture of anger and relief. For the first time in his life he was ashamed of his mother. Sinclair, on the other hand, was very happy, and took himself off to his attic with his coat pressed under his nose, savouring the traces of Charlotte's perfume on it.

* * *

Connie knocked on the door the following morning, despite the notice saying the surgery was closed, and asked if the doctor could visit her father. Sinclair was reluctant to get out of bed, but when Mrs Dredge told him it was Connie he dressed quickly and collected his bag from the surgery.

He found Connie with her father in the front bedroom. Dr Collingwood was propped up on pillows in his box bed. The old man's mouth was crooked and his face was frozen folds of saggy skin."I think he's had a stroke," Sinclair said. "There's nothing I can do."

"I thought as much," Connie replied with a sigh. "Is he in pain?"

"I don't think so. It's a bad one by the look of it. I'm sorry but I think he'll just quietly slip away."

"Will it take long?"

"I don't think so."

"Thank you. That's a great comfort to me, doctor. Would you ask Charlotte to sit with me? I would appreciate her support."

"Of course, but I have to warn you she's a little the worse for wear. She had too much of her mother's punch last night."

"Oh, not again; she's the same every year. She'll have a fearful headache."

Mrs Dredge was doing her best to get Charlotte up. "Come on ducky, time to get out of bed," the old woman said, opening the heavy velvet curtains to let a shaft of bright winter sunshine into the room.

Charlotte raised her head slowly from the pillow, then slumped back down again. "Oh for God's sake, Elsie, close those curtains: my head aches."

313

The old woman ignored her mistress and offered her a cup of tea. "Come on, drink this; it'll make you feel better," she said. "Sounds like you got yourself in a fair old pickle last night, girl. Who was it that undressed you?"

"What do you mean?" Charlotte retorted, then looked down to see that she was dressed in her undershift with no corsets or stockings. "Oh no, he didn't …" she blushed.

"Well, I don't suppose he'll be complaining, will he?"

"What are you insinuating, Elsie?" Charlotte said, sipping her tea.

"Only that he's got his eye on you, ducky, and who could blame him?"

"That's nonsense!"

"No it isn't. I've seen him looking at you these last months. He's practically undressing you with his eyes every morning, so getting his hands on you; well, I bet he thought it was his lucky day."

"Elsie Dredge, get out of here this minute. There's absolutely nothing between me and Dr Sinclair," Charlotte said, feeling a painful stab of guilt in her guts.

"Have it your own way, ducky, but I ain't blind. He's got his eye on you and I'm pretty sure you've got yours on him."

"I'm not going to argue with you now because my head hurts, but be assured that I still love Christopher."

"I know you do"; the old woman replied. "And I still love my Jack even if he's been dead these twenty years. That's the trouble when you're a widow. If you're going to love someone new you have to love two people; the one what's dead and the one what's living."

Charlotte let out a deep sigh, knowing that Elsie was right. It was true: she still loved Christopher and cherished his memory;

314

he had been a good husband, and when she looked at John she was reminded of just how handsome he had been. But now she found she was attracted to Sinclair in a way that she had never imagined. What shocked her most was that her desire for him was physical: she wasn't in love with him in the same way she had been when she married Christopher. Then she had been a girl full of innocent and girlish notions about love and marriage, but with Sinclair there was no innocence. She wanted to be loved by him; she wanted him in her bed. She felt ashamed because if she had truly loved him that sort of desire should have died with her husband.

"Do you really think he likes me, Elsie?" Charlotte said.

"He'd be a damn fool not to, ducky," the old woman smiled. "Oh, and by the way, Dr Collingwood has had a stroke and Miss Connie has asked if you'll go and sit with her."

"Oh, why didn't you say that when you came in instead of all this nonsense about Dr Sinclair? Help me get dressed; I must go to her."

* * *

In Beverley Dr Turnbull was getting ready to move Robert Leadam from his sick bed at the Black Horse. "I've changed his dressings and strapped the splint on his leg."

"Right-oh, doctor," replied an apprehensive Mariah.

"And I've given him opium to ease his pain. Your husband is as comfortable as he can be. Now are you ready?"

"Aye, the cart's outside. Let's get him home, Dr Turnbull. You're coming with us, aren't you?"

315

"Yes, I'll ride with you and check on Miss Leadam if I may once we have Mr Robert safely home. I trust she's fully recovered?"

"Aye, the influenza's gone; she's just lovelorn and miserable now."

"Poor girl. We've all been through that at some time. We're all condemned to love once, are we not, Mrs Leadam?"

"Aye, I suppose," said Mariah, feeling she had chosen entirely the wrong person to love.

The farmhands lifted Robert from his bed and onto a long pine board from the undertakers, then carried him to the waiting pony cart. As they laid him down Robert opened his eyes and looked up at the sky. The vision in his right eye was as clear as it had ever been, and he could see the blue of the sky with its puffy white clouds, but the vision in his left eye was milky, confirming what he had suspected as he lay in the semi-darkness of Ted Braithwaite's back room; he was blind in one eye. The shock of the January air made him shiver, and his teeth began to chatter.

"Take deep breaths, Mr Leadam," advised his doctor. "The laudanum will start to work soon."

Mariah tucked a thick blanket over her husband and ran her hand over what was left of his thick curly hair before she climbed onto the cart. "We'll 'ave you 'ome in no time, love," she soothed. Then they set off at a walking pace.

Lying on the plank, Robert felt grateful to be alive and glad to be going home. But his heart was broken too; Rosie was dead. When he thought about her and his boys he felt numb inside. Rosie had her faults, lots of them, but he had loved her.

Ted had told him his boys had perished in the fire with their mother, but there was something nagging at the back of his mind that told him Ted was wrong. When he closed his eyes he saw himself carrying his sons out of the burning room. The pony cart clattered out of town and onto the open road. The opium was making Robert feel sick, and he found his mind drifting in and out of consciousness as they bumped along the rough, potholed lane towards the farm.

When the cart came to a halt about forty minutes later, he knew that he was home. Mariah climbed down from her seat at the front, and moments later Lucy was on top of him, hugging and kissing him, "Oh, Dad, I've missed you so much." Pincer jumped up to join her, licking his face between excited barks.

"Get that bloody dog off him, will you?" shouted Mariah. "For God's sake, let's get him inside before he catches his death."

With her husband safely installed in his bed, Mariah said, "You lot can leave us now; I'll see to him. Lucy, you see Doctor Turnbull before he goes"

Lucy ushered everyone out of the room and closed the bedroom door behind her, leaving her mother and father alone with Pincer standing guard on the landing.

Mariah sat on the edge of the bed and pulled back the blanket, bracing herself for the horror she knew must lie beneath. She took a deep breath, then opened her eyes and looked at her husband. When she had left for London less than a month ago, her husband had been a fit, handsome man who drove her mad with his horse-racing and womanising; now he looked like a broken toy lying on the bed: a toy that had been smashed in a fit of pique and then badly glued back together. His injuries were all down his left side: his leg was broken below the knee and splinted, his hand and forearm were missing, his skin, what was left of it, was scarlet and raw.

"Oh, you daft old bugger," Mariah sobbed. "You're a bit of a mess, ain't you?"

Robert sighed, closing his eyes to block out the pain of his wife's distress and his own shame. He had let everyone down: he had lost Rosie and his boys, and now his wife and daughter were left with a useless invalid. "Aye, Mariah, I am," he said in a hoarse whisper. He turned his head slowly towards her. "Can you forgive me?"

She squeezed his right hand gently. "Course I bloody can." Mariah felt a ton of pain on her chest. "I could've been a widow like Charlotte. I could've lost you, Robert," she sobbed. "You haven't been a perfect husband, but you're not all bad. Me and Lucy love you; and by the sound of that scraping," she said, looking at the bedroom door, "that bloody dog loves you an' all."

He squeezed her hand in return, offering her what comfort he could. "I love you too," he whispered. "I love you all; you, Lucy and Pincer and this farm; but I loved Rosie Featherstone and my boys, Mariah. I'm sorry, but I can't deny it."

"I know you did, but you can't blame me for hating her, can you?"

"No, I can't."

"You know you were lucky." Mariah dabbed away her tears. "If Ted and his mates hadn't pulled you out when they did you'd be dead like poor Rosie and her bairns, and I'd be visiting you in that bloody graveyard with your brother."

Robert closed his eyes, exhausted from the journey and the effort of talking, but Mariah kept on. "Mr Chapman told me everything. The parish buried Rosie and the boys the day after the fire. It were all done before we got back from London. He's been right good to us, Mr Chapman has. He's got his eye on our Lucy and I'm hoping he's going to propose. With property in Beverley and in London he's a good catch. Lucy could be very happy with him."

318

"Aye, as long as she's happy," Robert said, lost in thoughts of Rosie. "You do what you think's best. I'm going to sleep now."

19
The Spark of Life

As Connie had predicted, her father left the entirety of his estate to her brother, leaving her with her piano, her music and her clothes.

"It seems so unfair," said Charlotte as they left St Olave's the Sunday after the funeral.

"My father was a conservative man, traditional in everything he said and did. The fact that I'm a woman and without a profession seems rather to have escaped him. I suppose he thought I should have married and become some other man's responsibility. When I chose to look after my mother and father I also chose to be responsible for myself. I know some, including my brother, consider that scandalous, and believe that in making such a choice I became my own worst enemy."

"Well I don't," replied her friend. "Who would have looked after your father if you hadn't?"

"I suppose my brother expected me to do both. When it comes to caring, we women are the ones who do it. The person I feel sorry for is Mavis. She's been such a loyal and generous servant, and now I have to let her go."

"Even so, your father should have left you something, and your brother should recognise that you cared for your father for years; you even paid the bills. I just can't believe he's left you without a penny."

"Well he has, and I'll have to manage as best I can. I have my piano, thanks to Jonathan; he didn't have to give it to me, as it was my father's. He's made sure I can still earn a living. There's no use crying about it, no use at all."

Charlotte turned to speak to John, who was walking behind them with William and Sinclair. "Connie must come and live with us when the house is sold, mustn't she?" John nodded his agreement. "There, John agrees. You can have the back bedroom and you can use the parlour to give music lessons."

"I couldn't possibly impose on you like that. I'll find rooms."

"You won't be imposing; we shall charge you rent. A small one, of course, and you can teach me to play the piano. You know I sing like a scalded cat, so there's no point in singing lessons."

"Oh, I wouldn't say that; it's far too harsh," said Sinclair.

"How would you know? You always stand at the back of the church with the latecomers. You've never had the unfortunate experience of hearing me," Charlotte said, striking him with one of her withering looks.

Taken aback by the ferocity of her rebuke, he said, "Aye, well, have it your own way. If you say you sound like a squealing cat, who am I to argue with you?" And he stalked off ahead, with William and John following him.

"Oh dear, I think I've upset him," said Charlotte, watching him stride up the street.

"Perhaps he doesn't like the idea of having someone else in the house," said Connie.

"I don't think it's that. I think he was trying to be nice to me and I've just thrown his compliment in his face."

"You did rather. You should make it up to him, if you want to stay on good terms."

"Oh, dear Connie," Charlotte said coyly, as her cheeks flushed a vivid shade of pink, "I do. I very much want to stay on good terms with him. I just don't seem to be able to control my tongue."

After lunch, when Sinclair and the boys were at the hospital, Charlotte sat in the parlour watching the last of the daylight fade over the chimney pots thinking about the house and how quiet it was. She was tired and feeling just a little melancholy. She had upset Sinclair and she regretted it. She couldn't help feeling that life with Christopher had been more straightforward: he had never taken her outbursts personally. She wondered if Sinclair's back-handed compliment had been the opening salvo in wooing her now she was no longer in mourning. If it had been, she had done a good job of rebuffing him. She let out a long slow sigh, thinking it was just as well, as she was sure Sinclair's eye would soon be fixed upon some pretty girl with a dowry and not a widow like her. No, she counselled herself, she wouldn't let him into her heart, as no matter how much she might wish it otherwise, she knew water did not flow up hills.

Sinclair was as good as his word, and as soon as William came back from Dover he started taking his apprentices to Mr

John Hunter's newly opened museum in Leicester Square on Wednesday afternoons, where he began to introduce them to the intricacies of human anatomy. The collection was Mr Hunter's personal research collection, and reflected his own interests. This was unlike the collections Sinclair had seen in Paris, where a more pedagogical approach to the selection of specimens was practised, enabling students to learn all the parts of the human body. Despite its shortcomings as a teaching tool, Hunter's collection was probably the largest in Europe, and many of the specimens were of an extraordinary quality.

Sinclair decided to start with lessons in general physiology rather than the thousands of "monsters"; the remains of deformed foetuses floating in pickling alcohol that were the mainstay of the museum's vast, sunlit galleries.

Like most medical students in London, John and William were keen to see Mr Hunter's most celebrated skeleton, that of the Irish Giant, Charles Byrne, a man who was eight feet tall when he died in 1783 at the age of twenty-two. Mr Byrne had promoted himself as a freak of nature and had appeared in shows and at country fairs all over Britain, charging spectators 2s 6d to see him. Now his skeleton was displayed in Mr Hunter's museum, where John found himself gazing at the man's enormous reconstructed frame and wondering what had killed him. "I'm sure he would have made for a more interesting study if he'd been alive. Do you know what killed him, Dr Sinclair?"

"It was despondency and drink, I think, but there was no autopsy so we'll never know for sure," said Sinclair. "The enormous size of the bones makes them easier to study, particularly the very small bones in the hands and feet, at the top of the spine and in the ears. Take a good look at them and draw what you see. You can label your drawings when you get back to Tooley Street."

By the end of January his students had drawn and labelled all the bones in the human body, and were learning their names and positions off by heart. In February they were ready to move on to learning the names and locations of the major arteries and veins.

In the apothecary, Charlotte had doubled the production of cough sweets and remedies, and was selling everything she could make. With the anniversary of her husband's death now past, she no longer wore deep mourning. Sinclair noticed that she seemed happier and was making more effort with her clothes and her hair. He also noticed that he wasn't the only one to discern her change of mood and appearance; their customers, local surgeons and physicians, had perceived it too, and were happily flirting with her over the serving hatch.

* * *

Marcus Chapman took Sunday tea with Lucy and Mariah. He was just as handsome and attentive as he had been in London, bringing them slices of his mother's Twelfth Night cake as they had missed the party and a bottle of brandy for Mr Leadam, delighting Mariah. Lucy tried hard to feel delighted too, but she could not. It was not that Mr Chapman wasn't handsome; he was. His hair was thick and the colour of ravens, his countenance was fine, his teeth even and he had an exceptionally fine figure; but he was not Frank Greenwood. When Chapman looked at her she didn't feel as though she would die from the pleasure of it; when he spoke to her, her heart did not sing; and when he offered to take her riding, although she accepted she wished it had been Frank who had asked her instead.

As far as Lucy was concerned, Frank Greenwood had proved he loved her when he had driven her and her mother home in his father's carriage. She had written to him at Panton Hall to express her thanks, but there was nothing she could do to bring him back to Yorkshire, and without him her world was tasteless, colourless.

Mariah, however, couldn't have been happier with Mr Chapman's attentions. She liked the man and thought him an excellent prospect for her daughter. Lucy would be well provided for: she would have a house in Beverley, a tannery business and a house in London. She would have all the things that Mariah thought a wife should have: wallpaper on her parlour walls, fancy curtains, soft furnishings and rugs, coal in the fireplace, china plates, cups and saucers, silk frocks and fancy shoes, hats galore, and to top it all a carriage. In fact, all the things Robert Leadam had denied her. How could Lucy not be happy with such things? She was sure that Mr Chapman planned to propose to her daughter; it was just a matter of time.

Knowing Robert would never be fit enough to run the farm again, Mariah had decided their future was a shop in Beverley or Hull. A saddler's or an ironmonger's shop that would keep Robert busy and provide them with an income. The only thing that remained was to devise a method to accomplish her scheme. To attempt to reason the case with Robert did not appear to be one of those methods, as she knew Robert was not subject to reason when it came to maintaining his birthright; but with Lucy safely married to Mr Chapman she was sure she could persuade him to sell the farm.

* * *

325

Connie moved into Charlotte's back bedroom at the end of January. Her brother had moved swiftly and advertised the house for sale in the 'London Advertiser' a week after their father's funeral. The house was to be sold by auction, and already there were several buyers asking to view the property. The furniture was to be sold on the same day, and Mrs Jonathan Collingwood had already been round to make an inventory for the auctioneer, making sure that she took the family's silver with her when she went back to Islington.

"I don't think you should be here when the sale takes place, Connie. It'll be too upsetting for you," said Sinclair over breakfast.

"I agree. We should go out that day," said Charlotte. "Should I ask my mother or my sister if we could call?"

"Thank you, but there's no need. Mr Walker and his daughters have offered to take me to Westminster Abbey for the very same reason."

"Oh, that's good, isn't it, Dr Sinclair?" said Charlotte.

"Aye," the doctor smiled, feeling deeply affectionate towards the two women. "I hope it goes well."

"Thank you; so do I. I remain hopeful that we'll become more than friends."

"I do hope so, Connie, and I hope the house is sold to people who will be good neighbours."

* * *

Their new neighbours moved in during February. Mr Jeffrey Prentice was a large and avuncular man with a ruddy face latticed with broken red and blue veins, which Sinclair felt was a sure sign of a man who drank to excess. He had a confident air and

326

was jovial and friendly when he greeted them. His wife, by contrast, was pale and diminutive, and dressed more like a country servant than a cosmopolitan wife. Mr Prentice informed them the house was to be his new shop and gallery, where he would sell his aquatints and books. The Prentices had four sloe-eyed girls all with shiny ebony locks, and when Mrs Prentice was taking tea with Charlotte and Connie one Saturday afternoon they could clearly see they had another child on the way.

"You must see Mr Prentice's work at the Royal Academy," Mrs Prentice said. "His engraving of the Vauxhall Gardens is on display there. The print has proved to be a great success for us. Everyone it seems wants an image of the Duchess of Devonshire and her sister Lady Duncannon on their walls. Indeed, the Duchess herself has purchased several copies for her friends."

Their conversation soon turned to children and schools. Connie recommended Mrs Tucker's, saying the girls would be able to continue with their studies in drawing, music, dancing and French there. "I'm not sure that will be necessary," replied Mrs Prentice. "My husband spent many years in Paris before our marriage, and the girls are already more than proficient in the language; and they can draw too. Mr Prentice has a drawing school in the Strand."

"And what of music?" asked Connie.

"We will need to find a new music teacher, Miss Collingwood, particularly for our two eldest girls, Alice and Jessica. If I was not mistaken, there was a notice in your window concerning music lessons."

"Indeed there is," said Charlotte. "Miss Collingwood is one of the best music teachers in London. Girls from all over the Borough and the City come to her for lessons." And by the time they had finished their tea Charlotte had both the Prentice girls enrolled for weekly lessons with her friend.

* * *

Lucy and Mariah arrived at Margie Hardaker's in Beverley a little later than they had intended. Entering the Hardakers' drawing room with its floor to ceiling windows and mirrors they found Cynthia Sedgewick, dressed in an ostentatious, low-cut gold and cream brocade ensemble, hanging on the arm of Marcus Chapman. Lucy looked at the pair: they seemed to her eye to be perfectly matched. Chapman was handsome with an arrogance that unnerved her, and he was wearing the equally arrogant Cynthia Sedgewick like a gaudy bauble on his arm. Chapman saw her, and made his excuses to Cynthia. "My dear Mrs Leadam and Miss Leadam, how is your father?" he enquired, in his most solicitous voice.

"As well as can be expected," Mariah replied, as she made her way towards the couch where Mrs Hardaker and Margie were dispensing cups of tea to their guests. He offered Lucy his arm, and after a moment's hesitation she took it. He led her towards the windows, leaving her mother to pay her respects to their hostess.

Lucy felt his powerful presence, his raw masculinity, and her body trembled with a mixture of terror and thrill. She was excited, but not in the same way that she was when she was with Frank: her nerves fizzed with fear and her stomach was tight with apprehension. Chapman made her feel uncomfortable whether he was riding by her side or taking tea in her mother's parlour. Was that love, she wondered? Cynthia had told her to keep her hands off him at the Assembly Rooms before she went to London, but

Margie had assured her that there was nothing between them. What she had witnessed today had sown doubt in her mind, though.

"I'm not surprised you're friends with Margie Hardaker, Miss Leadam," said Chapman. "All clever and beautiful women have a friend who enhances their brilliance."

"I'm sure I don't know what you mean, Mr Chapman; I'm not clever at all," said Lucy. "I've known Margie since we were at school together and she is a lovely girl."

"Even with her buck teeth and sallow complexion."

"Mr Chapman, there's no need to be cruel."

"I'm not being cruel, I'm being honest. I like beautiful women, Miss Leadam. You raise such turbulent passions in me; you're quite the opposite of plain Miss Hardaker and the gaudy Miss Sedgewick, and my family will love you too."

"My goodness, Mr Chapman, you overwhelm me," said Lucy, fanning herself to relieve the blush on her cheeks.

Chapman looked at her, pleased with the effect of his words. "You are all I desire, Miss Leadam. You have no need to be clever for you will fulfil all my needs. You should know that I intend to ask your father for your hand in marriage." Lucy felt her knees give slightly.

A proposal of marriage was the very thing she had longed for and dreamed of, but instead of feeling elated she felt nothing but horror. Chapman was attentive, handsome and rich, everything she had ever wanted in a husband, but there was something about him she didn't trust; she didn't know what it was but it was something she could not ignore.

"I am honoured, sir," she replied. He looked into her eyes and smiled at her, but something inside her told her that they were both being deceitful.

They watched Cynthia make a beeline for the recent widower Mr Carr, a man who owned draper's shops in Beverley, York and Hull. Carr couldn't believe his luck as the glittering bauble pressed her hand into his. Carr's eyes moved around the pale flesh of her décolleté with undisguised lechery. "How base," opined Chapman, looking in Cynthia's direction; "offering her body to be debauched by that old man for money. You would never do that, Miss Leadam. You're an honest country girl, full of kindness and felicity, and that is why I plan to make you my wife."

"I see," said Lucy, once again astounded by Chapman's arrogance. "All Mr Carr seems to care about is lust, from what I can see," she said contemptuously, "so they are well suited."

"Yes," said Chapman. "Cynthia will be satisfied when he hands over his purse and he will be satisfied when she hands him her virtue in exchange; if she still has it, of course."

"Mr Chapman, that was not very nice. I am sure Cynthia has nothing to reproach herself for when it comes to her conduct."

"You are so right to criticise me, my dear. What I said was unkind and untrue, I'm sure."

"Would you wait a while before you speak to my father?"

"Why, Miss Leadam?"

"Because I have asked you, sir. If you hold me in such high esteem, you'll be pleased to do as I ask."

Chapman looked at her with his piercing blue eyes, which seemed even more sinister now. "In that case," he said, "your wish is my command; but I will not wait long. I'm off to London next week and will return at the end of the month. I shall ask your father for your hand then."

* * *

In the drawing room of Mr Walker's rectory Connie was taking tea with Mrs Peacock and Mr Walker's daughters Harriet and Hannah. The residence was modest but spacious, pretty and pleasant, and still bore the hallmarks of a woman's touch despite Mrs Walker having been dead for more than three years.

The drawing room was divided by two great doors which remained permanently closed and behind which Mr Walker wrote his sermons, managed the church accounts and met the members of his steeple restoration committee. The front portion of the room was the parlour, where Connie and the girls were taking tea with Mrs Peacock and where the odious woman was delivering her opinions on everything from the impending departure of the Government's first fleet of ships that was taking convicted felons to Australia to the reduction of tariffs on goods from France.

Mrs Peacock inquired into Connie's domestic situation and family minutely, almost as though she were Mr Walker's mother, and gave Hannah and Harriet a great deal of advice as to the management of their father's household, advising that it should be regulated to achieve the economy and modesty most fitting for their station.

"Now girls," she said, "remember the wisdom of Proverbs Twenty-Two. A good name is to be chosen rather than great riches, and favour is better than silver or gold."

Indeed, Connie found nothing was beneath this great lady's attention. When Mrs Peacock considered she had imparted sufficient of her wisdom, she rose to depart, smoothing the rich, aquamarine silk of her dress with her jewelled fingers. Then she put on her sable-trimmed coat, turned and said, "Good day, Miss Collingwood. Please give my regards to Mrs Leadam and tell her I expect her to be at the Mastersons' on Saturday; and advise her that she should wear something for a party and not her widow's weeds."

As she closed the door behind her, Connie and the girls let out an audible sigh of relief; and a moment later Mr Walker put his head around the door. "Have I missed her?"

His girls began to laugh. "You know you have, Papa, you're incorrigible."

He slid his long lean body past the door with a warm smile and sat next to Connie on the couch. "I know I'm a milksop of a fellow but I really can't stand the woman," he said. "Can you forgive me for putting you through that awful experience, Miss Collingwood? I only did so because I need her wretched money for the steeple."

"Oh, Papa, you should not have inflicted Mrs Peacock on Miss Collingwood; we were quite prepared to be lectured for your sake," said Harriet.

"It was of no consequence, Mr Walker," replied Connie, feeling that once again he had charmingly commandeered her to his cause without being entirely honest with her.

"Thank you, Miss Collingwood." Then, turning to his daughters, he said, "Now that Mrs Peacock has gone would you like to show Miss Collingwood the house?"

His daughters leapt from their seats enthusiastically, as though they had a preconceived plan, and soon Connie was being shown the dining room with its large mahogany table; Mr Walker's study with its lines of dusty bookshelves; and the music room where the sight of the pianoforte in the middle of the room took her breath away. She walked up to the instrument and stroked its smooth oak body, letting her fingers linger over it.

"May I?" she asked.

"Of course," the girls replied, opening the lid.

"It's beautiful," said Connie, allowing her fingers to linger over the glassy ivory keys.

"It's German, made by Johann Stein in Augsburg. Papa bought it for our mother before she died."

"What a wonderful gift. Did your mother get the chance to play it much?"

"No, she was too ill, but Father plays it sometimes, as do we. But our mother was by far the best musician in the family. Would you like to try it?"

"I would; it's so superior to my own." Connie ran her fingers along the keys, then set about a series of rising and falling arpeggios, taking in the soft ethereal sound of each note as the leather-covered hammers hit the strings. "It's sublime, truly sublime. You're so lucky to have such a magnificent instrument."

"Thank you, Miss Collingwood," the girls replied, looking pleased with themselves. "We thought you'd like it. Would you like to see the rest of the house?"

Connie smiled back. "I'd like to stay here forever, but that wouldn't be good manners, so let's continue with the tour."

Upstairs they showed her their bedroom, which was wallpapered with cream-coloured paper with garlands of delicate pink flowers with a matching cream and pink rug on the floor. "This was our nursery," they said, as she looked into a bare lime-washed room, and "this is the lumber room, and that is father's room over there."

When they had finished upstairs they made their way down the elegantly curved staircase with its fine spindles and mahogany handrail, and went into the back of the house, through the kitchen where the housekeeper was working and into the large town garden where Mr Walker was waiting.

"Thank you, girls. Now off you go, and give me a few minutes alone with Miss Collingwood, would you?" The girls curtsied politely and said their goodbyes. Mr Walker took Connie's hand and started to lead her down the brick path towards the orchard at the bottom of the garden.

"Do you like the house, Miss Collingwood?"

"It's lovely. You have a beautiful garden too. I never imagined a house in town would have such a large garden."

He kept her hand in his, and she was content to let it remain so as they walked further down the garden, disturbing the blackbirds and sparrows. When they were standing on the damp grass under the fruit trees and her shoes were getting damp, Mr Walker took her other hand in his. He looked directly into her eyes and said, "Do you think you could be happy here, Miss Collingwood?"

She looked back at him, feeling her stomach lurch with a mixture of excitement and fear. Was he going to ask her to marry him or to be his girls' new governess?

She chose her words carefully, wishing to avoid any misunderstanding that might embarrass them both. "It's a beautiful house. Any woman would be happy to live in it."

"Good. And you like my daughters?"

Her heart sank. He was going to ask her to be their governess; to teach his girls how to play that magnificent piano in the music room and to improve their French. He had taken pity on her. She was his social equal, but they were both aware that as an older woman with no income other than what she made from teaching, she was on the slippery slope to poverty and he was offering her a way out. Again, she chose her words carefully. "Your daughters are a joy and a great credit to you, sir."

334

"In that case, Miss Collingwood," he said, gazing intently into her eyes, "to whom should I speak if I wish to ask for your hand in marriage?"

Connie's face flushed as tears welled in her eyes. "I have a brother, but to all intents and purposes I am alone in the world, Mr Walker, and I would rather that you asked me."

He smiled down at her and cupped her face gently in his hands, brushing away her tears. Connie gazed up at him, knowing that they were feeling the same overwhelming emotion. "Will you marry me, Connie Collingwood?"

"You take me aback, Mr Walker."

"My name's Daniel, Connie. Please call me Daniel." Then she felt his breath on her skin and he kissed her on the cheek. A wave of agonising delight left her breathless and giddy. He put his hand in his pocket and produced a ring.

"Do you like it?" he said hesitantly, slipping it on her finger. "I know it's old fashioned, but it's a token of my affection. I hold you in the highest esteem and love you dearly, Constance Collingwood."

She gazed at the square diamond in the middle surrounded by a circle of smaller stones on her finger. "It's the most beautiful thing I've ever been given."

He kissed her hand. "It was my mother's. It's a family heirloom."

"I would be honoured to be your wife, Daniel."

"Good," he said, kissing her again, this time on the lips. Her knees buckled but he held her tight. Then he grabbed her hand and started striding towards the house. "Come, Connie, I want to tell the girls; they'll be delighted."

20
Passion Defeats Reason

The stagecoach from Edinburgh pulled into Holborn at eight o'clock with Blair and Iona Rankin on board. It was Iona's first trip to the capital: she was overwhelmed by the noise and smell of the place, but excited too. This is what she had longed for; a life away from the confines of Edinburgh. Blair hailed a cab and told the driver to take them to Hyde Park Corner.

They arrived at Sir Donald McNeal's brick-built mansion next to the park gate about an hour later. They climbed out of the cab and knocked on the door as the driver disgorged their bags onto the pavement. A haughty footman opened the door and informed them that Sir Donald was indisposed with the shingles and would not be receiving visitors. The man extended Sir Donald's apologies and advised them they should seek accommodation at an inn until Sir Donald was recovered.

"I don't believe it," moaned Blair. "Has he forgotten how far Edinburgh is from London? Doesn't he know how long it's taken us to get here? It must be past nine o'clock and we haven't eaten since lunchtime!" Blair instructed the driver to put their bags back in the cab.

"I'm sorry, Blair, truly I am. It's thoughtless and selfish of Uncle Donald to leave us like this. Do you have any idea where we might sleep tonight?"

"We could try the Somners in Islington or my Uncle James in Southwark," said Blair angrily.

"Which is nearer?" asked Iona, aware of her husband's petulant nature.

"I suggest we try Uncle James first. I know his landlady has a spare room. It may be possible to stay there, and if not we can try to get a room at one of the coaching inns south of the river until we can get something else."

An hour later they were standing outside the apothecary shop in Tooley Street under the sign of the golden pestle and mortar. Blair rapped the door knocker and a boy's head appeared from an upstairs window.

"Do you need the surgeon?"

"It's Blair Rankin for Dr James Sinclair. Is he at home?"

"Ah, good evening, Blair, we weren't expecting you. I'll get him," said William, ducking back inside the house.

In the parlour Blair explained their predicament, while Sinclair stared at Iona and smoked his pipe. Iona looked as beautiful as he remembered; more beautiful in fact. He couldn't believe she was standing in the same room as him. He wanted to hate her for marrying Blair, but he couldn't: she was too lovely for that. He had rejected her first; she had every right to choose another.

Unlike Sinclair, Charlotte was delighted to see Blair and his new wife, telling them all about Connie's engagement and updating him on events in Yorkshire. She arranged for plates of cold meat with bread and wine to be fetched from the scullery, and this was served in the dining room while she and Connie arranged the beds, leaving Sinclair to talk with his relations.

"So Sir Donald has the shingles; that's painful for him," said Sinclair, feeling that there was some justice in the world. "We were to dine with him and with you next week, but I suppose that will be cancelled or postponed."

"I'll write to my uncle tomorrow," said Iona, "to find out what's happening. I think he should have made better arrangements for us as we've travelled so far. We are very grateful for your assistance tonight, Uncle James."

It was strange hearing her call him uncle; it made him feel old and he hated it.

"I suppose this is the sort of thing we'll have to get used to when we're travelling in Europe," said Blair, feeling less irritable now they had accommodation.

"Aye, and more," said Sinclair. "You'll find life very different in France. You won't find many feather-beds in the inns there. Their customs and manners are filthy to us but you get used to them."

"You make it sound so unattractive. One wonders why the French have such a reputation of taste and excellence," said Iona, tired and quite perplexed.

"If you're rich in France there's plenty of luxury to be had, Mrs Rankin, but most of the people are poor; poorer even than a Presbyterian church mouse," said Sinclair, taking a draft from his pipe. "Having said that, I enjoyed my time in Paris; I was much happier there than I ever was in Edinburgh, but you know that.

Besides, you will be made very welcome in their universities and scientific institutes. How long will you be in London?"

"We have a passage booked at the end of the month, so three weeks," said Blair. "We head for Paris first, where we will investigate current thinking on hygiene and diet, then go on to Bologna and Padua to enquire into the progress of the late Giovanni Morgagni's work concerning the investigation of the causes of diseases through autopsy. We shall then come back to Paris and Leiden."

"So you'll be away a year or so?" said Sinclair.

"We have a year to make our connections and to find our contributors, Uncle. Demand for medical knowledge is growing at an amazing pace. There are private schools in London, Edinburgh, Glasgow and Dublin as well as the charity hospitals. The Navy alone recruits over two hundred surgeons a year."

"Aye," agreed Sinclair, "and there are thousands of apprentices studying to become surgeons and apothecaries up and down the country."

"That's why we feel there's a ready market for this type of news. When everything is set up all the European news will be handled through my office in Edinburgh, where we will do all the translations, and my partner, Matthew Somner, will deal with the news from London, Birmingham and Manchester. Between the two of us we will be able to provide a monthly digest of news regarding developments in mathematics, medicine, astronomy and industrial processes. Iona and I will cover the mathematics and astronomy. Iona already writes stories for 'The Lady's Magazine' under the pseudonym 'Miss Sigma'. And her father, Professor McNeal will oversee the medical news."

"It sounds as though you have everything in hand, Blair. Your parents must be proud of you."

"Aye they are, sir" he beamed. "They send their love and felicitations, as does Professor McNeal."

"Yes, my father sends his regards," said Iona. "He wishes you well with your work here in London, and Morag asked me to say that she'd like you to go home to visit her and your father."

"Aye, well, I'll think about it, thank you."

Charlotte returned to say that the Rankins' room was ready, and Sinclair immediately took the opportunity to say his goodnights. "I'm sorry to be so unsociable but have to get up early in the morning. Mrs Leadam will show you what's what. I'm in the attic if you need me."

Upstairs, Sinclair kicked off his shoes and got into bed. In the darkness his mind wandered where he did not want it to go: to Iona's body and his skinny nephew making love to her. He was angry and jealous and he hated himself for it. Tiredness overcame him and he drifted into a shallow and fitful sleep. As he drifted in and out of consciousness he felt the bedclothes lift and someone slide in beside him.

"Don't be alarmed, it's me," Iona whispered, putting her finger to his lips. He opened his eyes and took her hand away.

"Good God, what are you doing here?" he gasped.

"I wanted to see you," she whispered seductively in the shell of his ear.

"You're a married woman, Iona. You should be with Blair!"

"Actually I'm surprised to find you alone, Jamie. I thought you'd be with the widow. She's very nice, isn't she? Do you normally sleep with her?"

"No I don't!"

"Why not? Surely there's nothing to stop you?"

"That's none of your business," Sinclair hissed through gritted teeth. "What do you want, Iona?"

340

"This," she said, putting her hand on his cock and giving it a gentle squeeze. A pulse of pleasure shot through his body and a soft gasp escaped from his mouth. "Blair can't, you see; it doesn't go hard for me," she said, with her hand still on him.

He could smell the sweet scent of her flesh and feel the heat of her body next to his. He wanted her. His stomach fizzed with excitement while his brain fought for restraint. He took a deep breath and composed himself. "Well, perhaps he has a problem," he said, taking her hand away and holding it in his. "I can see him in the morning. Sometimes a little cut is all that is needed to achieve the required performance."

"Oh it's not that, Jamie," she said, sliding her body on top of his. "Blair assures me he can get it up for Matthew Somner. Matthew can do it for his wife and Blair has tried to do it for me, but he can't."

He did not push her away. "My God, that explains a lot," he said, sliding his hands around her waist. "He was always with Matthew when he was here at Christmas. Sweet Jesus, Iona, why did you marry him?"

"Because I want a life," she replied flatly, stroking his face. "I was bored of being my father's housekeeper and Morag's free governess. You left me; you didn't care about me. I had no one to introduce me to men whom I might marry: my brothers are all too busy being doctors like you. Blair's my relation, he's kind and he offered me a way out. He offered to let me share his life."

"I'm sorry, Iona," Sinclair whispered, cupping his hands around her face and feeling genuinely remorseful about abandoning her, "but you can't do this. If the marriage is unconsummated you can get an annulment. This is wrong: what you're suggesting is adultery."

341

"But I don't want an annulment, Jamie, I like Blair: I'm happy to be married to him. I just want to feel what other women feel. I want to be loved like a woman."

She kissed him on the mouth. He wanted to kiss her back, but instead he pushed her away. "Iona, it's not that simple," he whispered, thinking she was so like the rest of her family; determined to get what she wanted regardless of the price others would have to pay.

"Yes it is. You like me," she whispered. "I know you do. I know you want me," she sighed, sliding her hand over his cock again. "I've spoken to Blair and he's happy with my choice."

"Blair is happy? Good God, what is this marriage you have?"

"It's one where Blair and I are free to have relationships with other people as long as we tell each other; we do not intend to lie. Blair has Matthew and a friend at the university in Edinburgh; I have you and other men of my choosing, as long as I'm discreet. It's an arrangement that suits us both."

Sinclair was speechless; mortified by her attitude and her palpable lack of morality. "What about children, Iona?"

"Well that's always a possibility isn't it? I'm no fool. I know what happens when men and women sleep together. As far as I'm concerned, a child would put an end to any suspicion about Blair and me; it would make us look like any other married couple. If I have a child, Blair will care for it as he cares for me; we will be good parents. I didn't marry Blair by mistake, Jamie. I knew what he was like. He's been honest with me and I intend to be honest with him. You see, I married him because he includes me. He treats me as an equal and he listens to what I have to say."

"But he can't make you happy."

"You're wrong," she whispered, sliding her body provocatively against his. "He can give me many of the things

342

that make me happy, far more so than many men who can manage an erection when they're in bed with a girl; but you're right, he can't give me the physical love my body craves. I need other men for that."

"Other men like me?" said Sinclair, wondering how she could be so callous in matters of the heart.

"Yes," she said, sliding her hand towards his groin. "Is it such a shock to find a woman can use men in the same way men use women?"

"You mean for their pleasure?"

"Aye, for pleasure," she said, finding his cock and gently squeezing it. His body shuddered, tingling with anticipation and desire. She kissed him on the lips. God, he wanted to be on top of her and between her thighs. "You're being very persuasive," he murmured, allowing the pleasure of her touch to flow through his body, then kissing her in return, pushing his tongue into her mouth and tasting its sweetness. Blood rushed to his groin, and what was left of his conscience gave up the fight. He rolled on top of her, pressing his body against hers, enjoying the physical power he had over her. He kissed her again, pulling and teasing her bottom lip gently with his teeth, then he pushed her long red hair away and caressed her neck with his mouth until she writhed with pleasure under him. He pushed her nightdress up to her waist and she felt his hand between her thighs. "If we do this there can be no annulment, Iona. It cannot be undone."

"I don't want an annulment," she gasped, gripping the smooth taut skin of his buttocks and running her fingers along the well-defined arc of each muscular cheek. He kissed her breasts, teasing her nipples with his teeth while his fingers caressed the luscious wet crease between her legs. She groaned as his fingers

343

followed the slippery seam up and down, and when she began to snatch for breath he said, "Do you want me?"

"Aye, Jamie," she moaned.

"Like this?" he whispered, pushing himself into her.

"Aye" she gasped as he pierced her.

Being inside her felt so good. His mouth moved down her throat, kissing her. In response her hips moved to meet his as he pushed deeper inside. With each rhythmic stroke, the pleasure in his groin increased until he let out a low groan and the tension in his thighs drained away, leaving him with a deep sense of satisfaction that began somewhere in his belly then spread to the rest of his body. Eventually he whispered, "Are you all right?"

Iona kissed his cheek, enjoying the strange roughness of the stubble on his face, "Aye, Jamie. It was good," she said, feeling the delicious ache in her stomach and him still inside her. Wrapping her legs around him, she drew him as close as she could. They lay like that for a while, two bodies locked together, until Sinclair rolled onto his back and Iona raised herself onto her elbows. As she lay her head on his chest he stroked her hair, wanting her more than ever. "Your heart's so loud; it's pounding like one of those steam pumps," Iona whispered.

"That's generally a good sign. If you couldn't hear anything I'd be dead," Sinclair laughed, quietly feeling wonderfully relaxed.

"I was at Morag's house when she received your letter about the 'Sherwell'. Jamie, I was so pleased you were alive."

He put his arms around her and pulled her towards him. "Did you think you might love me then?"

"I did for a while," Iona confessed, sending a wave of relief through his mind. She wasn't so callous after all; she did have feelings for him. Half of him wanted to fall in love with her and to melt into her body again and again, to love her with everything he had, but the other half of him, the cautious half, told him to keep its guard, knowing that he was her plaything and that she could discard him at any time.

"I thought about you, Iona," he said, kissing her neck and running his fingers through her hair. "I never stopped regretting the letter I sent to you. It was the thought of you that sustained me at my lowest hour when I was waiting to be rescued from that freezing cliff."

"I'm so pleased it was me you thought of," Iona said, kissing his mouth so tenderly that all thoughts of her callousness disappeared and he opened his heart to enjoy his moment of bliss. Then she ruined it."We're the same, you and I. We both think of ourselves first. If we truly loved each other we wouldn't do that."

Closing his heart again, he replied, "I suppose you're right. Nevertheless, I'm glad you have some feelings for me."

"Oh, for a time I was in love with you, but I'm glad you walked away."

"Why, Iona? How can you say that?"

"Because I might have been tempted to marry you, Jamie Sinclair, and that would have been a disaster."

"A disaster?" Sinclair demanded incredulously, feeling that he should eject her from his bed there and then.

"It would be a disaster because I have no desire to be a surgeon's wife. I hate the stench of the dissecting room that follows all you surgeons around. I hate the fact that your patients and your students always take precedence over your family and friends. No, Jamie, I'm happy with Blair. Being married to him means I never have to listen to talk about bodies and diseases, I get to travel and make new friends, and I get to work on something more meaningful than household accounts and school book algebra."

"Thank you, Iona. You've made it very clear to me that my use is limited solely to my body, which I freely give, but you can't blame a man for wanting to be loved for himself."

"Oh, of course I love you, especially this bit of you," she said, putting her hand on his cock again. "But I don't want to be married to you."

"I'm sorry you feel like that," he said, still smarting from her rejection.

"It's better to be honest about these things. As it turned out we've both made the right choices for ourselves," she said, sliding her body on top of his. "Please, Jamie, I want you to do it to me again. Make love to me. Make me happy again."

After they had made love for the third time they lay in each other's arms staring into the darkness, knowing that this would not be their last encounter. They were bound together by some invisible thread that meant whoever they were married to they would not be able to give each other up. Exhausted but content, Sinclair was just drifting off to sleep when the thud on his door told him a new day had begun.

* * *

"Robert, the bairns are dead. If I've told you once I've told you a thousand times. Now give over, will you?" Mariah seethed.

Her husband looked at her through the milky lens of his left eye, bringing her image into focus with his right, "But they were alive before I went back into the building to get Rosie," he bleated, scratching his head.

"Oh for God's sake, will you stop scratching? You'll mek it bleed, you will," his wife snapped.

"It itches," he whinged, feeling sorry for himself and irritated that Mariah wasn't taking him seriously.

"That's because it's getting better. Now leave it alone," she said, slapping his hand away. "You've no idea what's what, Robert Leadam. You've got straw for brains and what's not straw's been addled by opium. If I'd had my way that wicked slut would have been whipped on the cart tail and not paid handsomely for her crimes."

"I won't have you talk about Rosie like that," Robert protested, still scratching at the flaky bits of skin on his head. Mariah put her hand on his and stopped him mid-scratch.

"We don't even know if they were your bairns," she said, trying to reason with him. "Rosie probably slept with every tom in town. You'd not be the first man to be duped by a whore like Rosie Featherstone. Her and her kids should have been the responsibility of the parish. I'd have put the little bastards in a basket and laid them at the churchwarden's door; it's what we pay our rates for."

"You're a heartless bitch sometimes, Mariah."

"I know you think that, but sometimes it's better for such creatures as your bastards to die in a state of innocence."

"God, you're an unfeeling cow. My boys were beautiful."

Downstairs in the parlour Lucy was feeling melancholy. Since the fire her world had taken on a new complexity. Before Christmas she had acted like a carefree girl, even though she was a young woman of twenty, allowing herself to be carried away with trivial thoughts of dresses and balls and suitors. Now, faced with the responsibility of choosing the right husband, the enormity of making that decision weighed heavily on her mind, for it would not only change her life irrevocably; it would affect her family too. It was important not simply to marry but to marry well. A husband was a lifelong commitment and Lucy knew that she needed a man who would not only care for her but a man who would also care for her parents. In that respect, Mr Chapman with his hide business was the obvious choice; but in her heart she still wanted Frank Greenwood.

Sitting in the parlour looking out over the winter fields, Lucy scolded herself for her self-indulgence. Who, she thought, was going to plough the fields now that her father could no longer walk unaided? Who would bring in the harvest? Who was going to take the cattle and horses to market and sell them for the best price? How could she be so selfish as to think that she might marry someone without the means to support her and help her family? Frank Greenwood was a good man and she loved him with all her heart, but she knew he was in no position to make her an offer. Frank was too honourable; he was the type of man who would only propose marriage if he could support a wife. The farm would not wait; spring was coming. Marriage, Lucy realised, was not a frivolous thing about love and feelings: it was a matter of survival, not just hers but her family's too, and she had no business being sentimental about it. After all, she reasoned, look at where sentiment had landed her father: following his desires had led them to the brink of ruin. No, she would not be sentimental: she would be sensible and write to Mr Chapman, telling him she would be happy to be his wife. She would give herself to him for the sake of her family; she would keep his house, bear his children and give him what affection she could. Then her parents could sell the farm and buy a shop, and they would all be comfortable and provided for.

With the letter written, Lucy went to see her father. "Dad," she said, "I've got summut to tell you. Mr Chapman has asked me if he may ask you for my hand in marriage."

"Oh, has he now? Do you love him?"

"Oh, Dad, how do you know when you love someone? " Lucy cried. "Mr Chapman's a good man and he can offer me a good life. Most fathers would think that more than sufficient to say yes to such a request."

"Aye, they would; but I'm not most fathers. I'm your dad and I want you to be happy."

"Did you love Mother when you married her?" asked Lucy, blowing her nose on the handkerchief her father offered her.

"I did and I still do. We just don't get on in the bedroom, and that's very hard to know before you're wed."

"Mr Chapman is a handsome and considerate man, and I shall have a house and servants and money for dresses. I promise you I'll be happy."

"A good marriage is about more than money, my love."

"I know, Dad, but it's hard to be happy without, isn't it?"

"Aye, there's wisdom in your words, Lucy. If you're sure it's what you want, your mother and I will be very happy for you."

* * *

Greenwood was at his tailor's being measured for a new coat and breeches. When he had ordered everything he wanted he walked to Latimer's and ordered a case of Margoose claret, with instructions for it to be delivered to Tooley Street as a gift to celebrate Miss Collingwood's wedding. Then he took himself off to Garraway's for coffee.

349

With his lottery winnings in the bank he could afford to be a man of leisure, to spend time in town dining with friends, going to the theatre and strolling in the park. He could even afford to go to Almack's in St James's, the place where people of quality went on Wednesday evenings to see and be seen in the hope of finding a suitable marriage partner. Notwithstanding the additional expense, he would fit in well at Almack's, at least for a short time, while his purse matched his rank. There he could seek out a rich debutante and court her. He knew that many men of breeding and no fortune sought out girls with money and no looks, but when he thought about the prospect of marrying such a woman he was revolted by the idea. He wanted a wife he would be happy to look at; a country wife and a country house. He wanted to be surrounded by fields and hedges riding around in the crisp morning air on a good hunter chasing a fox or a deer. In short he wanted land; a farm or an estate where he could make a living, support a wife and bring up a family. That was his idea of happiness. Frank decided that everything he wanted in life was in Yorkshire, and her name was Lucy Leadam.

Connie's engagement and the arrival of Blair and Iona threw the household at Tooley Street into happy turmoil. The parlour became not only a music school, with a trail of young beauties arriving for music instruction to distract William each day, but also a sewing room as Charlotte and Connie set about making Connie's wedding dress.

Iona and Blair went out most days either to the offices of the 'European Magazine' or to meet potential correspondents working in London's charity hospitals. When William was not at the hospital with Sinclair he was in the apothecary on the look-out for the eldest daughter of their new neighbours, the slender, sloe-eyed beauty named Alice. He positioned himself close to the window as he wrote up each day's case notes in the hope of catching a glimpse of her.

Mr Walker had arranged for the bans to be read at St Olave's, and the wedding was due to take place on the first Wednesday in March. Connie wrote to her brother Jonathan in Islington inviting him and his family to the ceremony and to the wedding breakfast, which was to be held in the parlour in Tooley Street. "I should invite Mr and Mrs Peacock," said Connie, looking up from her letters. "It's thanks to Mrs Peacock, as much as we loathe her, that I met Mr Walker."

"As much as it grieves me to say so I agree with you," said Charlotte. "The odious woman must be invited."

Charlotte took herself off to the Mastersons' party as instructed, and wore a new dress. The guests were deep in conversation when she stepped into the refined air of their mansion in Berkeley Square. Mr Masterson senior was a goldsmith and banker of the first order, producing his own banknotes at their premises in Lombard Street. The house was large and elegant with footmen dressed in scarlet and gold. As she was announced, William Masterson stepped forward and took her by the hand.

"I am so glad that you could come, Mrs Leadam," he said with a deep and fawning bow.

"I'm delighted to be invited, sir. Are my mother and father here yet?"

"Yes, your parents and your sister and her husband are with my mother and Mrs Peacock."

"Oh..."

"We don't have to join them if you'd rather not," he replied, taking her hand again and placing it in his warm, damp, palm.

"That would be nice, but I think they'd be offended if I didn't say hello."

"In that case I'm happy to escort you, madam," replied her overly solicitous host in a way that set Charlotte's teeth on edge.

"Ah, Mr Masterson, Charlotte, let me introduce you to Sir Gerard DeVisme and his wife," said Mrs Peacock, casting her critical but approving eye over Charlotte's new lavender dress. "Sir Gerard is a prominent member of the British Factory in Lisbon. I'm sure he won't mind me saying that he has made a vast fortune trading diamonds from Brazil, which I'm glad to say has enabled him to give very generously to the building of the British Hospital in Lisbon."

"It's an honour to meet you, sir," said Charlotte, curtseying to the elderly man and his wife. "My late husband was a surgeon at Guy's; he believed strongly in the benefit of hospitals for the poor. I'm sure the people of Lisbon are grateful for your generosity, sir."

"Hear, hear," said Henry, who was standing by her side.

"One does one's best, doesn't one?" the old man mumbled with feigned modesty to his wife, who was fanning herself vigorously and nodding her assent. "Indeed we shall be holding a small fund-raising concert at our home in Grosvenor Square next month. Could we entreat you to lend us your support?"

Mr Masterson was quick to spot his opportunity. "If Mrs Leadam is agreeable I would be delighted to purchase a pair of tickets from you, sir," knowing that Charlotte would not be able to reject his offer in public. Sensing his sister-in-law's rising panic, Henry quickly chipped in with an offer to buy two tickets for himself and for Emma.

"I'm glad to see you have made more of an effort this evening, Charlotte," said Mrs Peacock from behind her fan.

"Lavender is a good choice; demure but pretty. Well done: you have clearly made a good impression. I received Miss Collingwood's wedding invitation yesterday. I hope I shall be receiving one from you shortly, my dear," the odious woman smiled. "You seem to have made a good impression on our friend Mr Masterson. He must make a thousand a year. If you keep your temper under control I'm sure you will have his ring on your finger in a very short while."

"You're too hasty, madam," Charlotte snarled.

"Well, nothing would happen if we left things to you," said her mother. "Luckily Vander and I are here to ensure your success, are we not?" Emma nodded her agreement. I believe Mr Masterson is smitten, and that is all to the good as you have very little by way of fortune to attract him," she added.

Charlotte was tempted to say that it was her experience in the bedroom and lack of child-bearing ability that was supposed to be the draw, but instead she changed the subject. "Shall we play cards?"

"Ah, yes, a hand of rummy before we join the men would be very agreeable. Shall I deal?" said Mrs Peacock, commandeering the cards. "Eliza, you pour the tea, dear."

When it was time to leave, William Masterson escorted Charlotte to her cab, and as she turned to say goodnight he caught her hand and removed her glove. She looked at him in amazement, then he put her hand to his lips and kissed her palm, and then he rubbed his thumb into it. Her stomach tightened with the sheer eroticism of the gesture. It was the first time a man had ever kissed her in that way.

"Mr Masterson!" she said, swooning from the shock.

"A small example of what I hope is to come," he smiled, flashing his dark, lecherous eyes at her. "I'm looking forward to our evening with Sir Gerard and Lady DeVisme."

* * *

Each night Iona arrived in Sinclair's bed after the household had retired, and they made love until dawn. The hours of daylight passed slowly for Sinclair as he waited for the pleasure that each night would bring. With Iona in his bed every night, Sinclair was exhausted when he started work each day. One morning he looked so washed out that Charlotte asked if he was ill. He was too tired and too wrapped up in his nocturnal escapades even to muster his usual jealousy when Charlotte went to the Mastersons' dinner party without him. He knew Iona did not love him, but he was enjoying the sex. What was more, the imp in him relished the illicit situation, and the tingle in his guts every time he stole a look at her. In the surgery, Charlotte seemed distracted too. Often he looked at her and wondered what she was thinking, but he was too afraid to ask. Work in the apothecary shop carried on as usual, with Charlotte making up medicines with John. Occasionally he had to call her in to help with female patients in the surgery, but they said little to each other. What he dreaded most was her finding out his nocturnal activities. Mrs Leadam would not take kindly to him committing adultery under her roof, so he was glad she was occupied with catering for their guests and arranging Connie's wedding.

Two days before Connie's wedding Iona and Blair took the coach to Dover. The night before their departure was a sad one for Sinclair. After he made love to Iona they lay together, knowing that it would be the last time they would be together until she returned from Europe. Putting his hand on the soft skin of her belly, he whispered, "Will you be all right?"

"Aye, Jamie." Sensing he was thinking about the possible results of their union, she said, "If I have your child, Blair and I will be very happy, but you shouldn't worry. It took Morag years to get pregnant, and most of the women I know were married a good six months before they were with child."

"I hope you're right," he said, suddenly feeling responsible for what he had done.

"Whatever happens there's nothing for you to worry about. If I have your child, I promise you I'll love it." Brushing her lips against his, she said, "You've been a good lover, Jamie Sinclair. I'm so glad you were the first; you made it so easy for me."

"You'll always have a part of my heart," he whispered, slipping his hands around her waist and kissing her throat."

"You'll always be in my heart too," she murmured, sliding her body on top of his. "Will you court the widow when I'm gone?"

"Aye, I might," he mused, stroking her buttocks, his hands sliding effortlessly over her silky skin.

"I've seen the way you look at her," she said, brushing her lips lightly against his.

"Oh, and how do I do that?" he said, giving her a gentle squeeze.

"Like a husband, Jamie: you look at her as if you want to own her." Iona raised herself up and rubbed her nose down the ridge of his. "You should marry her; she'll make you happy."

The first night without Iona in his bed was a painful one. Part of him longed for her but he knew she was right about Charlotte; he wanted her, but he didn't just want sex with her; he wanted a life with her. Charlotte Leadam understood him; they wanted the

355

same things in life. Charlotte Leadam was fiery, exciting, compassionate and sensible all at the same time, but above all she was a woman he could count on to make him the man he wanted to be. Although he knew it was hypocritical, he didn't want her loving anyone but him.

21
Self-Inflicted Wounds

Connie Collingwood looked radiant in her pale pink dress and matching bonnet as she walked down the aisle on the arm of her brother Jonathan, with her bridesmaids Hannah and Harriet behind her. Sinclair sat next to Charlotte with William in the third row of pews, behind the groom and his supporter in the first row and Mr and Mrs Peacock, Mr and Mrs Martin and John in the second. Charlotte sobbed quietly through the entire ceremony. To Sinclair's eye, she looked lovelier than ever in her lavender dress and straw hat. Her tears added lustre to her blue eyes, and as he looked down on her he could see her beautiful breasts rising and falling with every sigh. The effect was intoxicating: he wanted to put his arm around her and comfort her, to give her his love and support; he wanted to whisper in her ear that everything would be all right and that her friend would be happy. However, the rules of society would not permit him to do so, so he studied his feet, looked at the ceiling and played with his pocket watch, turning it in his hand as he distracted himself with thoughts about Iona and Blair making their way through France.

When the bride and groom had completed the register the wedding party returned to the house, where Mrs Dredge had laid out a wedding breakfast of hot buttered toast, tongue, and ham and eggs, all of which was served with negus, a hot spiced wine, drinking chocolate and wedding cake. Greenwood was already upstairs and enjoying the Margoose when Sinclair found him. "Where were you? I didn't see you at the church."

"I took a leaf out of your book and stood at the back," said Greenwood with a huge smile on his face.

"Aye, well, I couldn't get away with that this time. So how is my rich friend these days?"

"Still rich, Jamie. I haven't spent or gambled away my little stash, you'll be glad to hear."

"Except for the clothes, Frank: you look braw and bonnie in those new breeks."

"Thank you. I've always liked good clothes. I feel less dilapidated with some new threads on my back, and warmer too; I really missed that greatcoat I lost on the *Sherwell*."

"I know what you mean. I bought myself a new coat at Christmas and another pair of boots. Have you decided what you'll do with the money?"

"Yes. I'm going to buy a farm or take one of the tenancies on my father's estate, but before I do that I thought I might pay Miss Leadam a visit in Yorkshire."

"I'm sure the Leadams will be pleased to see you. You did them a great service at Christmas. I've heard Mr Leadam is making a slow recovery, and is no longer in danger."

"I can't go immediately, " said Greenwood, taking another gulp of wine. "Lord Wroxeter has asked me to do a special job for him, so I'll be engaged until the middle of April; then I'm free to do as I please. Here, have a glass of Margoose," he said, handing Sinclair a large glass of red wine.

"It's a bit early for me. I still have patients to see and hospital rounds to do."

"Oh, one won't hurt, Jamie: it's to toast the bride and groom. Come on, old man, get it down you and be happy for the lucky couple."

From behind them they heard Dr Martin say, "Hear, hear, gentlemen. Might I have one of those?"

"Of course, sir, said Greenwood, pouring another glass."

"Good to see you again, Sinclair," said the doctor. "You know Mrs Peacock, don't you?"

"Yes, we've met before," said Sinclair, remembering the woman from the Navy Ball.

"Mrs Peacock wanted me to say how grateful she is for what you did for Mrs Husselbee; she was her friend."

"I was happy to do what I could for the unfortunate woman, Dr Martin."

"You're a compassionate man, Dr Sinclair, and it's greatly appreciated. I'm sure Mrs Peacock will recommend your services to her many friends, but I hope not too many – as most of them are my clients."

The two men smiled.

"I have no desire to rob you of your patients, sir. I know you respected Mrs Husselbee's wishes regarding examination. You're an excellent physician, sir."

"Thank you, Dr Sinclair. I'm not ready to admit defeat just yet. I have a few more years in me before I retire. Now where's my daughter? Her mother's plans have happily gone awry to the advantage of Miss Collingwood for now, but I suspect my wife and her friend will not want to make the same mistake again," said Dr Martin with an obvious wink. "

"What was that about?" asked Greenwood.

"I think he was alluding to Mrs Martin's plans to marry Charlotte to Mr Masterson."

"Why would he tell you that?" his friend asked, watching Sinclair's face flush. "Oh, I get it. He's telling you to get a move on if you want her."

"Frank, not so loud, please," said Sinclair.

Greenwood chuckled, "Well, do you?"

"Yes," Sinclair whispered.

"Goodness, Jamie, you're full of surprises. I thought you didn't like her."

"Well, I know her better now. Don't you know that opposites attract?"

"Like magnets, you mean. Is that what you like about her? I suppose you're hoping that temper of hers is an indication of a passionate nature."

"Frank, can we change the subject?"

"Of course; but we should lay a bet to see which of us reaches the finishing post first. Will it be you with Mrs L or me with her niece?" Greenwood chortled.

"I'm not in a race, Frank," snapped Sinclair. "I shall take as much time as I need."

"Absolutely, old chap: taming a tigress takes time," Greenwood tittered as he helped himself to another glass of wine.

When it was time to say goodbye to the newly weds the guests pelted them with old shoes for good luck and sent them on their way in their hired carriage. Exhausted Charlotte collapsed into her favourite chair in the parlour and cried. Thinking she was upset about losing her friend, Sinclair decided to close the parlour door and leave her to her tears while he got on with the business of the day. He left the notice in the window saying the apothecary shop was closed, and took William and John off to Mr Hunter's museum with instructions to select one specimen from the collection, draw it and label it, then meet him in the dissecting room at St Thomas' at four o'clock as he had procured a hand for them to dissect. Then he collected his bag and went off to visit his patients and do his hospital rounds.

He returned at six, and found Charlotte making a batch of laudanum and chatting to her friend Fanny Naylor about the events of the day. Sinclair decided she looked more cheerful, and commended himself on having done the right thing by leaving her alone. He put his head around the scullery door and asked Mrs Dredge for a cup of tea.

"If you think you deserve one after what you've been up to," the old woman said with a scowl.

"What do you mean, Mrs Dredge?" he enquired casually, determined not to show his heart was in his mouth.

"The mistress has seen those sheets you've been hiding in your room."

"What sheets would those be, Mrs Dredge?"

"Don't come the innocent with me Dr Sinclair. You know exactly which sheets I'm talking about – the sheets off your bed," she said, folding her arms across her chest. "She must be a right little hussy to get in your bed with her husband sleeping down below. I thought you had more sense," the old woman sighed, putting the hot water into the teapot. "But you're a man ain't you, and men have very little sense when it comes to that sort of thing.

361

Reason and passion always point in opposite directions, but somehow passion always wins out, don't it?"

"Aye, it would appear so, Mrs Dredge," he confessed red faced, knowing there was no pulling the wool over her eyes.

"The mistress is very angry with you, but I've talked her out of turning you out on your ear. You're too useful to be just let go."

"I'm in your debt, Mrs Dredge," he said, taking his tea.

"If you ever hurt her like that again I'll shove you out of the door myself. Do you understand?"

"I do, and I'll apologise to Mrs Leadam after supper this evening."

Sinclair took the tea and went directly to the surgery, where he sat down with his head in his hands. That's why Charlotte was so upset. It wasn't about Connie getting married; well, not entirely. She knew his secret and now he had lost her. He was back to where he started; in Charlotte Leadam's bad books. But this time the slight was real, not an accident or imagined. He had profoundly hurt her, and she would probably never trust him again.

After supper, he spoke to her in the parlour. With his dinner sitting like a piece of lead in his chest, Sinclair opened the parlour door. Charlotte was sitting in her usual chair, tapping her hands on the arms in unrestrained irritation. He hesitated, then walked over to her and sat on the green velvet chaise. Without looking at her, he mumbled, "I've come to apologise, Mrs Leadam."

"Thank you, Dr Sinclair," she said, her voice cracking with emotion; but still he did not look up.

"Mrs Leadam," he continued, "you've treated me with nothing but kindness and generosity since I arrived. I know that

I've abused your kindness most vilely, and for that I'm truly sorry."

Charlotte said nothing for what seemed like an eternity. The only sound in the room was the ticking of the clock, marking out their torment. Sinclair sat looking at the floor until he could stand the silence no longer. He raised his eyes to see her angry face before him. Having gained his attention, she said, "You haven't hurt me, Dr Sinclair; our arrangement is one of business, not sentiment."

He knew Charlotte was lying; her crying was testimony to her feelings for him. Knowing she returned his feelings made him all the more miserable. For a few wonderful nights of pleasure, he had forfeited everything they might have had together. He had made a terrible mistake, he had wronged her, and it was time to take whatever punishment Charlotte Leadam was handing out.

"I'm disappointed in your moral conduct. Your apprentices need strong moral guidance. I know you don't like the Church, but as the son of a clergyman you cannot claim ignorance of either morality or the law."

"You're absolutely right," Sinclair agreed, still averting his eyes from her gaze.

Charlotte continued in the same high-minded vein. "I have had to ask myself if you're the right person to be in charge of the education of minors."

"I understand your position completely, Mrs Leadam."

"But I've decided you should stay, for now at least. You're doing a good job with the boys, and they're happy, and the business here is going well."

"Thank you, madam; I'm in your debt. Once again, I'm very grateful for your generosity. I understand I don't deserve it."

363

"Very well," she replied. "We'll say no more on the subject. Goodnight, Dr Sinclair."

* * *

John and William were immediately aware of the chill wind blowing through the house. Within a matter of days Charlotte and Sinclair had organised their lives to ensure there was as little contact between them as possible. Communication was formal and mealtimes were brisk. Mrs Leadam no longer poured the doctor's tea or buttered his toast in the morning, and Sinclair stopped coming back to Tooley Street for lunch, choosing instead to take his meals at an inn or coffee house. Sometimes he stayed out all day, and when he was at home he retired to his rooms as soon as supper was over.

On Wednesdays Sinclair took his apprentices to Mr Hunter's Museum and afterwards to the dissecting room at the hospital, where he provided his students with an organ or limb he had acquired from the mortuary for them to practise on. He began to take both John and William with him to hospital committee meetings on Fridays, meaning they did not get home until after nine o'clock, and on Saturdays he met Bowman in town. On Sundays he rose late, skipped breakfast and did not attend church. There was no Sunday lunch at Tooley Street any more. Charlotte always made sure she had somewhere to go, be it her mother's, her sister's or Connie's, leaving Sinclair and William to fend for themselves in the Red Lion.

At the end of morning surgery one day towards the end of March, Charlotte suddenly announced she would be taking John to Yorkshire for three weeks at the end of April, to attend her niece's wedding in Beverley.

"Please send Miss Leadam my congratulations. I presume she's marrying the tannery man?"

"She is, Dr Sinclair, and her parents are very happy," said Charlotte with icy pride.

"I'm glad things have worked out for them," Sinclair lied, thinking of Greenwood.

Charlotte's news was a relief and a blow at the same time. Sinclair was relieved the source of his pain and vexation would be away for three weeks, but at the same time he knew he would have to tell his friend that Lucy Leadam was engaged to Mr Chapman. When Charlotte had gone he sat alone in the surgery, thinking that everything that could go wrong had, feeling thoroughly despondent.

Breaking the news to Greenwood was not easy. His friend's distress initiated a confession of his own misery.

"You did what?" howled Greenwood in disbelief.

"I slept with Iona. She was in my bed; she was naked, well almost, she only had her nightdress on; and she was touching me, you know, touching me where it's very difficult not to say yes."

"You mean you didn't want to say no."

"You're right; I have needs. I'm not a saint!"

"No, you're not, my friend. And Mrs Leadam found out?"

"Aye, Frank, and now she looks through me, she doesn't speak to me unless she has to, and she excludes me from everything. I'm persona non grata."

"I don't blame her. So much for your high ideals, Sinclair; so much for your claims to want to control your passion with your reason. Where was your reason when you needed it? You always said you should be careful what or whom you desired."

"Well, I proved myself right. I made a bad choice; I chose passion when my reason told me I was jeopardising my future happiness. That's the thing about the pursuit of happiness; if you make the wrong choices happiness turns into misery. I don't believe in sin, original or otherwise; I believe in reason. But I'm subject to failures in it like any man. I was weak; I gave in to carnal desire, lust, whatever you want to call it, when I should have listened to my better self."

"So now you've ruined your chances with Mrs Leadam?"

"Aye, Frank."

"Well, that's both of us done for," bleated Greenwood, throwing his arms in the air with exasperation. "We're bloody useless when it comes to women."

"I know, and I've never felt so wretched in all my life."

"I feel pretty wretched too," said Greenwood. "I should have gone to Yorkshire and not spent a month chasing a gang of petty pilferers in Chatham. If I'd gone to Yorkshire I could be engaged to Miss Leadam now," he wailed. "I could be sitting next to her and contemplating marital bliss instead of sitting here with you, Sinclair!"

"Steady on, old chap; try to stay calm."

"You're telling me to stay calm! Mrs Leadam isn't getting married to some stinking hide merchant in a few weeks' time. You have a chance to get her back. I'm lost, completely lost, Jamie. I need a drink. In fact, I need to get very, very drunk."

"Good idea. I'll join you if I may," said Sinclair. "Where's the wine?"

* * *

The farrier slipped a wrought-iron leg brace onto Robert's battered leg and fastened the thick leather straps to hold it in place.

"Try to put some weight on the leg, Mr Leadam," said his doctor as Mariah stepped forward to help her husband off the bed. Robert put both feet on the floor and stood unaided for the first time in three months. With his wife holding his right hand and his doctor holding what was left of his left arm, Robert shuffled towards the edge of the room. He looked out of the window onto the bare brown fields through his good eye. "Tell Mr Swailes and Tom Pick to get ploughing. There's seed corn in the barn."

"Now Robert, there's no need to worry about that. Lucy and Mr Chapman have everything in hand."

"What does a hide merchant know about farming, woman?" Robert barked. "I'm crippled not dead! It's my farm and I'll give the orders around here, do you understand?"

"Of course, my love," she soothed, taken aback by his burst of temper and his determination to take back the reins. "But our Lucy does, so don't fret. Your job is to get well; we can manage everything else. You do want to walk Lucy down the aisle, don't you?"

"Aye, I do. She's my daughter and I want her married right."

* * *

In Beverley Lucy was viewing the home Mr Chapman had acquired for her. It was a large and elegant town house close to the North Bar Gate. It was three storeys high with an attic and a cellar, with Doric columns and a pedimented porch, and was one of the newest and most fashionable abodes in town. Her fiancé had given her a budget of five hundred pounds in the form of letters of credit at various suppliers in the town to decorate and furnish it as she saw fit, but as she walked around the empty space she found herself totally intimidated by the task. How, she wondered, was she supposed to turn these cavernous rooms into a home?

It seemed unfair that Mr Chapman had left the task to her while he went off to London. Surely if she were to create a home she needed to know his tastes, and what he thought comfortable.

The spring sunshine broke through the clouds, flooding the parlour with light. Lucy watched the dust particles dancing in the air as she made up her mind. A combination of neatness and gentility was what she required; simple decoration without too much in the way of ostentation; cool colours for the south-facing rooms and warm for those facing north, just like the rooms at Panton Hall.

Thinking of Panton Hall made Lucy think of Frank again. What sort of home would they have made together, she wondered. That would have been easy, because it would have been a farmhouse. They would have horses and chickens and blond curly haired children who splashed in puddles and threw sticks for the dog. They would ride with the hunt every winter, have rosy cheeks and shiny skin, and they would work hard and fall into bed happy and contented at the end of the day. But that life was not to be. Soon she would be Mrs Lucy Chapman, and she would live in town, receiving and entertaining her husband's business associates and friends in the elegant home he had provided for her. She would bear neat well-behaved children who went to school and learned how to make money like their father; and when her husband was away on business in London, which as far as she could see was most of the time, she would visit her parents in their shop.

* * *

Charlotte and John left for Yorkshire at the end of April, leaving Sinclair and William to run the apothecary shop and surgery. Although the house seemed unusually quiet without them, Sinclair felt he could relax for the first time in months.

The first week passed without incident, and on Saturday morning they closed the shop and joined Bowman and Greenwood in town. On Sunday they slept late, then skipped church and went to the Red Lion for lunch, where they ate beef and oyster pie and drank tankards of white frothy ale. In the evening, when they had finished their hospital rounds, Sinclair lit his pipe and poured himself a glass of red wine, settling himself by the fire in the parlour with his favourite book. He opened his copy of 'Candide' and started to read. He chose the passage where Candide asks his companion Martin, a man who is as pessimistic as Dr Pangloss is optimistic, if he has ever been to Paris. Martin says he has, and describes his previous encounters with the French, and his disgust at what he calls their lack of manners. This made Sinclair laugh, and he thought of Iona and Blair struggling with the mortifying indifference of French innkeepers and the dirt and gloom of their inns. He read the part where Candide asks Martin why the world was made, a question to which Martin replies, "to make us mad", and Sinclair as usual found himself laughing. The world was truly designed to drive men insane, he thought. Idiots excelled and clever men like him failed at every turn. Then Candide asks Martin if he believes that men have always done evil things. His answer this time is a cryptic one, concerning hawks eating pigeons. Martin's opinion is that if nature's beasts do not change, then men do not either; but Candide disagrees, claiming that men have free will and can choose what they do. Ah, the problem of free will, Sinclair thought as he took a sip of wine. Will, or his lack of it, was what had brought him to this unhappy state, sitting the parlour in Tooley Street alone and miserable. He was ruminating on the thought, and wondering if he was innately wicked as his father often suggested or just human and subject to failings like any other man, when William knocked on the parlour door.

"Dr Sinclair, there's a woman outside saying that she needs a surgeon."

"Oh no, doesn't she know it's Sunday?" moaned Sinclair. "What does she want?"

"She wants you to attend a woman in labour in Harp Lane."

"In Harp Lane; that's near the Tower. Couldn't she have found someone nearer, for goodness' sake?"

"She says you've been recommended."

The doctor looked at the clock: it was past nine. "Tell her I'll be with her in a few minutes. I'll get my boots on and collect my things."

Sinclair followed the woman along Tooley Street, past St Olave's Church, the old grammar school, the Red Lion and onto London Bridge, by the light of an almost full moon. The City and the river were bathed intermittently in its bright, milky light, then plunged into darkness as black clouds scudded across its face. The woman he was following was wearing a long red cloak and what looked like a dark veil over her head. The woman did not speak and moved quickly, almost running at times, but Sinclair was never far behind her. He followed her as she turned right at St Magnus's Church into the wide thoroughfare of Thames Street, with its numerous narrow alleys and wharfs leading down to the river past Billingsgate, then she turned left into Harp Lane where the Customs House stood on the corner, and to a narrow three-storey house opposite the Bakers' Hall. Finally, the woman knocked on a door, and it was opened almost instantly.

"Come, doctor, you're needed," said a grey-bearded man with a husky foreign accent. The man was wearing a skullcap and a long black coat. Sinclair could only assume that he had been brought to the house of a Jewish family, which was unusual as there were many well-qualified Jewish doctors in the City they could have called on.

"Where is the patient?" he demanded as he crossed into the brightly lit hall.

"I will show you," said the grey-bearded man, and he led him up the stairs to a bedroom at the back of the house. A young and beautiful woman was lying on the bed, her ropes of jet-black curls spreading over the pillows as she tossed and turned with every painful contraction.

"How long has your daughter been in labour, sir?"

The woman who had fetched him came forward. Looking at her properly for the first time, he realised the family resemblance with the woman on the bed was striking.

"Is this your daughter's first child?" asked Sinclair as he took off his hat and coat.

"Sim. It's Rosa's first."

"And how long has she been like this?"

"Oito horas, senhor," she replied, soothing her daughter's head.

"I need to have a look at you, Rosa; I'm going to see what's happening with the baby."

The girl turned to her mother with frantic eyes, but her mother soothed her. "Tudo bem que ele vai ajudá-lo. Take my hand, my love."

The girl did as her mother said, and Sinclair felt for the child's head. Then he listened to its heart; it was strong and steady. "This baby is ready to be born; we won't need the forceps," he said. With his patient well supported on pillows he encouraged the girl to push.

"I can't, I can't do it," she screamed between the pains.

"Aye, you can. Come on, the next one's coming now – push."

The girl gritted her teeth and pushed with all the strength she had left.

"Good girl. Now pant."

Rosa looked at him, not understanding what he was saying, so he gave her a demonstration, and she started panting until the next contraction came and she pushed again.

"That's it and again," Sinclair encouraged; and little by little the child's head began to appear. "Well done. Now I want little pushes, not big pushes; the baby's nearly here."

The girl gave out a searing scream as her child emerged into the world.

"You have a bonnie wee son," Sinclair beamed. "Well done, Rosa."

He wrapped the child in a towel and handed him to his exhausted mother. When he was sure both mother and baby were well enough to be left, he asked whom he should make his bill out to.

The grey-bearded man said, "To my son-in-law. He's away on business. His name is Mr Chapman, Mr Marcus Chapman."

The name sent a cold shiver down Sinclair's spine. Could he be the same Marcus Chapman who was about to marry Miss Lucy Leadam in Beverley? Sinclair collected his thoughts and wrote out the bill.

Outside the moonlight had disappeared and it was pouring with rain. He walked slowly. It was past midnight, and the streets were empty save for rats and stray dogs huddling in the doorways of the rich merchants' houses and shops along the street. As he kicked his way through the puddles his mind was racing as he wondered what he should do. Should he tell Frank? Should he write to Charlotte? What if by some strange chance there were two Marcus Chapmans, and the Mr Chapman in Yorkshire was a completely different Mr Chapman to the one living in Harp Lane; and what if the woman who had just given birth was his mistress and not his wife? Before he did anything he had to find out more, and he would do that when he returned to collect his fee.

After Sinclair and William had dealt with the Monday morning rush at the surgery they breakfasted upstairs as usual. Sinclair was tired, but he knew he would have to move fast if he was to prevent what he thought might be about to happen in Yorkshire.

"William," he said, "when you've finished at the hospital would you do something for me?"

"Of course, sir. What do you want me to do?"

"I want you to go down to the wharfs, Chamberlain's Wharf, Toppings Wharf and Coxes Wharf, and the Stone Yard as well, and see if you can find Mr Chapman's warehouse. If you find it don't do anything, just come back and tell me; I want to speak to him."

William looked at him suspiciously. "Why?"

"Because I need to check something; I'll tell you all about it when I know more. In the meantime you must trust me."

Intrigued, William agreed, and took himself off to the hospital to change Mr Ellesmere's patients' dressings. Then he went down to the wharfs and started to look around for Mr Chapman's hide warehouse. He eventually found it on Toppings Wharf, close to St Olave's Church and the dye works, busy with men unloading skins from a boat that had just arrived from

Argentina. He asked a man who looked like the foreman if Mr Chapman was in his office, and found out that he was on his way up to Hull on one of the company's ships. At lunchtime, he reported his findings to an appreciative Sinclair, who immediately took off without saying a word, leaving William to look after the shop.

Sinclair went directly to Harp Lane to collect his fee and to find out what he could about the woman who was calling herself Mrs Chapman.

"I'm sorry, but I don't know your name," he said as he followed the woman in red up the stairs.

"I am Senhora Da Silva," the woman replied, showing Sinclair into the well-furnished and comfortable bedroom.

"Good afternoon, Mrs Chapman. How are you today?" he asked Rosa, who was resting in bed with her baby in her arms.

"I am well, doctor," the girl replied in a thick Portuguese accent.

"And your son?"

"He is well, thank you," she said, with a smile that lit up the room.

"And your husband, Mrs Chapman?"

"He is in Yorkshire: he has a business there."

"He will be very sorry that he has missed the birth of his son," said Sinclair.

"Sim. He will be glad he has a boy."

Sinclair examined his patients. The girl seemed well: there was no excessive bleeding and no fever, and the baby was a good weight and obviously content. Sinclair cradled the child in his arms, and asked the girl as casually as he could how long she had been married.

Her face flushed. "Only a few months, sir. I was Mr Chapman's maid, but now I am his wife," she replied proudly.

"Well, love isn't a crime, is it?" Sinclair replied, with a smile. The girl smiled back at him with her beautiful mouth and shining ebony eyes. "We had a beautiful wedding," she said, looking tired but happy.

"Your husband is a generous man, Mrs Chapman."

"He is, senhor."

"Where did you get married?"

"At the synagogue in Duke's Street. My mother and father were very proud; it was a great day for our family. My father is a good man but we are very poor. Before I married, we were nothing in our community, but now I am a lady and my parents can hold their heads up high. Our only sadness is that my husband's parents cannot share our joy; they are dead, and my husband has no relations in London."

"But you will write to your husband to let him know he's become a father?"

"I cannot," the girl blushed again. "I do not know your English writing and my husband does not know Portuguese."

How convenient, thought Sinclair as he packed his bag. He collected his fee and made his exit, feeling sure that the Marcus Chapman of Harp Lane was the self-same man as the Marcus Chapman who was about to marry Lucy Leadam in Beverley. He decided he would go to the synagogue in Duke's Street and ask to see the marriage registers, but that would have to wait until tomorrow; he had to get back to the hospital and to evening surgery.

He arrived at St Thomas' at four o'clock and made his way to the Cutting Ward. Mr Ellesmere had two patients there. The first was a young man with a hydrocele, an accumulation of fluid in the scrotum, which had become so large and uncomfortable that he was unable to work. Mr Ellesmere had drained the fluid successfully but the skin around the incision was hot and swollen. Before he left for a lecture in Birmingham he had, as usual, ordered the wound be dressed with a milk and bread poultice, on the assumption the milk would provide a cooling balm to the heat of the wound. Sinclair examined the patient, and finding no fever he removed the poultice. "Let's see how you get on without this soggy bandage, shall we?" he said, knowing the man would stand a better chance of recovery with a dry dressing or no dressing at all. "If that cut heals up tonight you could be going home in a couple of days."

"But the surgeon insisted on the dressing," protested the patient.

"Aye, well, I'm a surgeon too. You leave Mr Ellesmere to me and get some rest," soothed Sinclair, hoping he could save the man's life. "I'll be back tomorrow to see how you're getting on." He had no intention of mentioning the removal of the poultice, as Ellesmere was likely to dismiss him if he did. With Ellesmere away there was a chance the man would live.

While he was at the hospital the ward sister introduced him to a new colleague, Dr Shaw, a house surgeon and an Edinburgh man like himself.

"Good day to you, sir," said Sinclair, shaking the new recruit firmly by the hand. "I take it you're from Fife with that accent."

"Aye, I am, Dunfermline in fact. And good day to you too, Dr Sinclair."

"I'm sorry, but I must be on my way. We can talk while we walk if you like."

"Aye, thank you," said the young man following at Sinclair's heels as he made his way along the corridors and out into the quadrangle. "London's big, isn't it? I thought Edinburgh was enormous but London is vast. Have you been here long?"

"About a year now. Before that I was at St George's."

"With Mr Hunter and McNeal?" asked the young man admiringly. "My goodness, I'm envious of you."

"Aye, it was good experience," replied Sinclair, feeling he had given more than he had received from the pair of them. As they passed St Thomas's Church and turned left into St Thomas's Street, he added, "Do call me Jamie."

"My name's Davy. I didn't get in at St George's. I had no introduction or connections there, so I tried at St Thomas' and Mr Fordyce said he would take me on."

"Well I'm sure you'll get on well with Mr Fordyce. Hunter attracts a lot of students, which means you don't get much individual attention from him, but his lectures are very good. Mr Fordyce is a very good teacher and will be able to spend more time with you, as he has fewer outside commitments."

"So you think I'm better off here?"

"Aye I do, Davy."

"You don't happen to know of any accommodation around here, do you? I'm staying at the White Horse in the Borough, and it isn't very good."

"I don't know about accommodation, but I can offer you supper if you like," said Sinclair, feeling much more able to offer hospitality with Charlotte away.

"I would like that very much, Jamie. That is very kind of you indeed."

"Come to the apothecary shop in Tooley Street at seven o'clock; we have supper when we've finished our evening surgery."

22
Yorkshire Weddings

"I can't walk down the aisle sounding like a door grating on its 'inges, Mariah," moaned Robert Leadam, dragging his iron brace over the flagstones in the parlour.

"'Ave you got any ideas about what we can do with your uncle, John?" said his aunt, looking up from her sewing. "He never stops whinging these days."

"That's probably a sure sign he's getting better, Aunt," replied John, anxious not to get embroiled in their bickering. "You could try wrapping the bottom of the brace in cloth or leather."

"Now why didn't you think of that, Mother?" boomed Robert from the far side of the room.

"Because I can't think of everything. I've got a wedding to get ready for if you haven't forgotten."

"There's no chance of that, is there? I'd be a sight more content if that Chapman fella would show his face. We've seen neither hide nor hair of him for over a month. What sort of fiancé leaves his betrothed as soon as he's proposed? He's left Lucy to do everything."

"You mean he's left me to do everything; but I don't mind: he's a busy man. Never fear, me and Lucy's doing fine with Charlotte's help. Lucy's got nearly everything she needs for that lovely house in the North Bar and Mrs Arkwright's mekking dresses for Margie and Charlotte. Charlotte will be Matron of Honour and Margie the bridesmaid."

"Oh, aye, if you say so," Robert said, bending down and pulling at the heavy frame in frustration. "Tek my advice, John, if you ever get married elope to Gretna Green and avoid all this fuss and nonsense."

They had been in Yorkshire for nearly a week, and his aunt and uncle had bickered non-stop ever since they had arrived. John had visited his father's grave with his mother. The headstone Robert had paid for was made of the same creamy white limestone as the weathered headstone of his grandparents, Robert and Elizabeth Leadam, whom he had never met. The inscription gave his father's date of birth and the day he died; it was simple, beautiful and final. As he looked at it, John felt his life had changed so much in the sixteen months since his father had died that he hardly seemed to be the same person. He still missed his father, and part of him was still angry with him for dying and leaving them in such terrible trouble; but he was no longer sad all the time and neither was his mother. Now she was angry; she was angry with Dr Sinclair, and he did not know why. John thought his cousin Lucy might know, but she was too busy with the wedding arrangements to talk to him.

Everyone seemed happy about the wedding, but John sensed that Lucy was more nervous about it than she was letting on. Lucy had changed. In London, his cousin had been cheerful, curious, and enthusiastic, but now she was solemn, dutiful and resolute. John put this down to her father's accident and the fact that Lucy was about to take the most important step of her life, but he was sad that she wasn't happier.

Each day John helped his uncle down the stairs and supported him as he walked around the courtyard in front of the house. Robert tired easily and soon gave up with the walking, but as soon as Mariah was out of earshot he talked about his boys, saying he was sure they were alive. John listened to the same story every day, but said nothing. His mother had told him his uncle was confused and that the boys were dead.

With nothing else to do, most of the time John found himself bored and restless. He wanted to learn to ride, but everyone was too busy to teach him. His mother spent most of her time with Lucy getting her house ready in Beverley, and his aunt was busy with making and ordering food and flowers and fiddlers and barrels of beer. John missed the apothecary shop, he missed William, he missed his trips to Mr Hunter's museum and he missed going to the hospital committees with Sinclair each Friday night. In fact, he couldn't wait for the whole affair to be over so he could go back to London.

* * *

Garraway's coffee house was crowded as usual when Greenwood and Bowman arrived on Saturday morning. Sinclair was waiting at a table by the window with William by his side.

"Ah, gentlemen, I need your assistance," he said, greeting his friends.

"This sounds ominous. What do you want to rope us into this time?" chuckled Bowman, taking off his hat and wiping his face with his handkerchief in mock exertion.

"What is it you're after?" Greenwood demanded, hoping for some sort of adventure to brighten his otherwise dull days. When everyone was comfortable, Sinclair told them his news.

"So you've checked the marriage register at the synagogue?" said Bowman.

"Aye, his name's there all right. He married Rosa Da Silva on the sixth of November last year."

"You mean he was already married to a woman who was pregnant with his child when he called on Miss Lucy?" said Greenwood incredulously.

"Aye, Frank."

"The blackguard! I want to kill him!" Greenwood made fists with his hands and turned a dark shade of puce.

"Calm down, Frank: I don't think that would be very wise," interjected Bowman. "Jamie, you said that the wedding is due to take place next week?"

"Aye. As far as I know it's on Saturday morning."

"Well, you must send a message to Charlotte."

"I'm not sure a letter will be enough, especially if it's from me."

"Oh yes. Frank told me you were in the widow's bad books." Sinclair shot Greenwood a look of consternation.

"You didn't say it was a secret," Greenwood protested.

"He told me everything," said Bowman with a disapproving look. "But I think you're right: we need to prove this man is a scoundrel and planning to enter into a bigamous marriage, and for that we need more than a letter."

"Oh God," groaned Sinclair, with his head in his hands, while William looked on perplexed, still not knowing what terrible thing Sinclair had done to upset Mrs Leadam.

"Is the wife fit to travel?"

"Hardly, Henry: she's just given birth!"

"You'll just have to take the rabbi who married them," Bowman replied, draining his cup. "Of course you'll have to pay him; I can't see anyone volunteering to go to Yorkshire for nothing, especially if it involves working on the Sabbath."

"I'll pay," said Greenwood, "and I want to be there when this bastard gets what's coming to him.

"The Sabbath ends at sunset, so we can call on the rabbi this evening," said Sinclair.

"Does that 'we' mean you're coming with us, Bowman?" demanded Frank.

"Oh yes, I wouldn't miss it for the world. This is so much more interesting than contracts and wills!"

* * *

It was Wednesday when Greenwood set out for Yorkshire with Rabbi Moses Mendoza in his father's coach. Mendoza cut a slight figure: he was small and wiry with concave cheeks, a long grey beard and large brown eyes that stared out from under his oversized cocked hat. Like Frank, he was dressed for the season, but his costume was black like his hat.

The early morning rain cleared to sunshine as they climbed Highgate Hill, and soon they were making good progress towards their first stop at Eaton Socon. They changed their horses there and carried on up the Great North Road. The weather changed again: the wind got up and soon the warm spring sunshine was obscured by tall and dense black clouds that pelted them intermittently with heavy squalls of hail and sleet. Cold, wet and tired, they stopped at the pretty village of Stilton in Cambridgeshire for the night, taking rooms at the Bell Inn and drying themselves out ready for the next day's travel.

They began early. Greenwood cracked the whip and pressed the horses to go faster. They cantered along the turnpike, passing the milestones for Grantham at speed until there was a sickening crack. Greenwood pulled up the reins and slammed on the brake.

"What was that?" demanded the rabbi.

A harassed-looking Greenwood got out and looked at the wheel on the driver's side.

"Damn it, we've lost a spoke. We'll have to slow down until we get to Grantham. This is all we bloody well need," he cursed.

"I would ask you not to blaspheme, sir. Please do not take the Lord's name in vain," said the weary looking Mendoza, who was clearly not enjoying his sojourn into the country.

Hours later they limped into Grantham, and it was mid-afternoon by the time they were on their way again. Frank pressed on, only stopping to change the horses at Ekersley; then much to the rabbi's chagrin he continued to Doncaster, arriving well after dark. The little man in black was becoming a thorn in Frank's side, complaining of being cold or sick or moaning about the bumps in the road; but Frank ignored him, focusing on his vital quest.

They took rooms at the Old Angel Inn, and Greenwood bought supper. As on the previous evening, the rabbi refused to eat anything but bread, much to Frank's annoyance, saying that the Talmud viewed all non-Jews as potential idolaters and therefore it was impossible for him to eat anything prepared by them. Anything, that is, except bread and hot mulled wine, which he drank liberally. When the two men had had their fill, Greenwood put his irritation aside and asked the rabbi what would happen to Marcus Chapman and his wife after he was exposed as a bigamist and adulterer. To his surprise the rabbi started to speak a language Frank understood.

"When a man and woman marry it is our belief they become a single soul," explained Mendoza. "Indeed, in our tradition a man who is not married is considered to be incomplete."

This was something Greenwood understood. There was nothing he wanted more than a wife who loved him and a family to call his own. The Talmud, the rabbi told him, stated that a man should love his wife as much as he loved himself, and that he should honour her more than he honoured himself. This Mr Chapman clearly had not done, as he was planning to dishonour his wife and himself by seeking a second marriage. God, the rabbi said, would count Rosa's tears and would not blame her, but Mr Chapman would be cast out to be with the gentiles.

"Not much of a punishment," said Greenwood, "as he already is one."

"I leave your English law to punish him," smiled the thin little man. "I have in my satchel a document we call a ketubah. It sets out the financial terms of the marriage. Rosa was poor before she married, but nevertheless her father was wise and a sum has been set aside and paid into a bank account in the event of a divorce or in the case of Mr Chapman's death. When all of this is over, she may call on the money if the situation cannot be reconciled between them."

"So there's already a provision for divorce. Lord, we Christians don't do it like that, Mr Mendoza! I'm not sure I'd like to start my married life like that. I'm definitely a 'till death us do part' sort of a man."

"That is very commendable, Mr Greenwood. Divorce is not a desirable outcome to any marriage. I believe Mr Chapman's soul will be condemned to the wilderness for what he has done. Of course, should they divorce the child must remain with his father; that is the law in England."

"Well, I hope the constable slaps him in gaol and throws away the key," said Greenwood, "and his wife should get to keep the child. She's done nothing wrong."

The rabbi nodded his agreement. "Chapman is unlikely to be prosecuted, but I hope we get to Walkington before the nuptials are complete. It will spare Miss Leadam much distress and the costs of a court case." Greenwood could only agree with him. The thought of Chapman bedding Lucy in these circumstances made him feel sick to the core.

They left Doncaster at first light on the Friday morning with fresh horses and headed towards Thorne, where they ate lunch and changed horses again. They crossed the mighty Ouse by the bridge at Booth Ferry and headed east across the river's great flood plain towards Howden and the Beverley Road. The easterly wind from the day before had been replaced by one that was blowing from the west. The air was warm and the sun was dazzling as they continued eastwards under the wide open sky. The little covered coach skipped along the turnpike gravel, with a patchwork of flat, brown and green fields on either side of them for mile after mile. Eventually the sun disappeared behind them as they drove further and further east, bumping along hour after grinding hour through Gilberdyke and Newport where they changed horses again, then on into North Cave and High Hunsley, and finally into Walkington, where they took rooms at the Fawsitt Arms close to All Hallows' Church, where the wedding was due to take place in the morning.

It was late when they arrived and both men were exhausted. Although Greenwood was relieved that they had made it in time, he was apprehensive about what he had to do in the morning. As he lay in his bed that night he wondered for the first time whether Lucy actually loved this Marcus Chapman. Although he loved Lucy, he had no idea how she felt about him. Indeed, his courting of her had been so brief and disastrous he was sure he would have to start all over again in the hope of making a better impression. Would she hate him for barging into her wedding and ruining her dreams? Whatever happened, thought Frank, Chapman was the liar and the cheat, and it was better to stop him ruining Lucy's life forever, even if she hated him for it.

In the morning they watched the wedding guests start to assemble outside the church from Greenwood's window. Just before nine a pony cart with Lucy and her parents on board arrived, with John and Charlotte Leadam and another woman walking behind them. Greenwood watched John help Lucy and her father down the steps. Lucy was wearing the dress she had worn to the ball at the Barber Surgeons' Hall, and she looked just as beautiful as he remembered.

"Come, Mr Greenwood," said the rabbi. "We must do what we have come here to do."

Greenwood breathed a reluctant sigh, picked up his coat and hat, and headed for the door. They crossed the street and walked up the lane to the church. The sound of organ music filled the air,

386

and Frank knew that Lucy and her father were already walking up the aisle. While the organist was still playing, Frank and the rabbi opened the door quietly and took their place at the back. The church was drenched in early morning sunshine streaming in through the great east window, and was decorated with spring flowers, daffodils and ivy and bunches of rosemary, all tied up with pale pink ribbons. The front pews were full. Mariah was there in her grey hat and green dress, sitting next to what he assumed were her brother and his wife and their sons, with a space for Robert to sit down when he had played his part. On the groom's side he could see the finely dressed Mr and Mrs Chapman and their family and friends. It looked as if half of Beverley was on the Chapman side.

When the music stopped the vicar began to read the beginning of the marriage service. "I require and charge you both, as ye will answer at the dreadful day of judgement when the secrets of all hearts shall be disclosed, that if either of you know any impediment why ye may not be lawfully joined together in Matrimony, ye do now confess it. For be ye well assured, that so many as are coupled together otherwise than God's Word doth allow are not joined together by God; neither is their Matrimony lawful. If any man do allege and declare any impediment, speak now or forever hold your peace."

With his heart thumping in his chest, Greenwood stepped forward. "I object, sir!" he declared as loudly as he could without shouting. "I know of a lawful impediment."

Charlotte turned, recognising Frank's voice. "He's married. Marcus Chapman has a wife in London." Chapman turned to see his accuser as Mariah screamed. Robert wobbled, but Lucy held him tight. There were gasps of disbelief, then a low rumble of disapproval spread through the congregation.

The rabbi stepped forward: by now everyone's attention was on them. "I confirm what Mr Greenwood has said. I married this man to Miss Rosa Da Silva," the rabbi said, pointing to Chapman. He lives at 22 Harp Lane in the City of London and he was married at the Jewish Synagogue in Duke Street on the sixth of November last. I have the marriage agreement signed by Mr Chapman here in my satchel."

"Don't be ridiculous, you stupid little man. That doesn't count," seethed Chapman. "Who do you think you are making such accusations?"

"These men, whoever they are, are right," said the vicar, looking at Frank and the rabbi.

There were more gasps of disbelief from the congregation. They were astounded at the man's arrogance. Marcus Chapman, one of the most respected men in Beverley, was not only attempting to dupe Miss Leadam into a bigamous marriage; he had married a Jewess and a foreigner. Sensing his game was up, Chapman began to glance around, looking for a way out. A second later he made for the south aisle, but Frank cut him off, caught him and grabbed him by his velvet lapels, then gazed into his cold deceitful eyes and headbutted him with a sickening thud. "That's for your wife, you scoundrel," he bellowed. While Chapman was reeling from his blow, Frank sank a punch into his rival's stomach. "And that's for your son, you cheating bastard." Chapman was bent double, but Frank wasn't finished with him. He placed his hands squarely on Chapman's shoulders, looked him in the eye, lifted his knee and sank it firmly into Chapman's balls. "And that's for Miss Leadam!" Chapman fell to the ground writhing in agony. Greenwood stood over him like a victorious prize-fighter, watching his opponent's face contort in agony.

"Fetch the constable and get this man locked up," he commanded, rubbing his right hand. "There will be no wedding today."

With the job done, Greenwood sank into the nearest pew while Lucy's cousins manhandled Chapman out of the church, followed by his embarrassed relatives. Frank felt a hand on his shoulder; it was John Leadam. "Uncle Robert wants to speak to you," he said. "You were amazing."

Greenwood stood up and walked slowly up the aisle, to where the vicar and the rabbi were speaking to Lucy and her father in front of the pulpit. As he walked he was joined by Charlotte, who put her arm around him and kissed him on the cheek. He stood next to the brass lectern opposite the wedding party and gazed at Lucy's tearstained face: she looked distraught, but she beckoned him over. Robert shook his hand firmly, then Lucy startled him by throwing her arms around him, burying her face in his chest. She was crying and her body was trembling. He hesitantly put his arms around her to comfort her. "Thank you, Frank, thank you so much," she wept.

He held her tight, not wanting to let her go, breathing in her perfume and feeling enormously satisfied with himself. Then she looked into his handsome face. "Take me home, Frank. I want you to take me home."

23
Robert's Boys

Back at the farm John helped his mother and Tilly hand out glasses of beer and sherry and plates of ham and cheese to members of Lucy's extended family. Most of the wedding breakfast lay untouched; no one felt like eating.

Standing next to the inglenook in the parlour, Lucy's Uncle Toby and her cousins were flexing their riding crops, telling anyone who would listen that if they had their way Chapman would be horse-whipped and put in the stocks for a week. On the other side of the room, Mariah was weeping while her sister-in-law tried to assure her that the family's honour, what was left of it, was not entirely lost.

Outside, Lucy walked with Greenwood in the kitchen garden. She put her arm in his as they walked between the banked rows of earth where the potatoes and cabbages would grow later in the year. The spring sunshine was bright and warm, catching the golden faces of the wild daffodils poking their heads out from under the garden's boundary hedge. As they walked, Greenwood explained how Sinclair had found out about Chapman's wife, and how he and Henry Bowman had persuaded the rabbi to accompany him to Yorkshire with the proof of the marriage. Frank looked into Lucy's beautiful blue eyes. "Did you love him? Did I ruin everything for you?"

She gazed back at him. "I was going to try. I needed to make a good match and Mr Chapman seemed perfect in so many ways. Many women in these parts would have been right jealous of me if I'd been Mrs Marcus Chapman. I had nothing to complain about."

"But you didn't love him?"

"No, I didn't. Oh, hold me again, like you did in the church."

Greenwood slid his arms around her waist and held her tight. "Like this?" he whispered.

"Aye, that's perfect," she said, feeling the warmth of his body against hers and breathing in his scent. She rested her head on his chest and whispered, "It's you I love."

"Oh, Lucy, I love you too," he said, gently stroking her back.

"I know you do. You proved that to me at Christmas. I'd never have said yes to Mr Chapman if I thought for one minute you were going to come back for me; honest I wouldn't, Frank."

"I'm sorry, that was my mistake. At Christmas I didn't have any money and I couldn't make you an offer of marriage as I wanted to. Then when I came into funds I left you to do a stupid job for my father's friend. I've been such a fool, Lucy. Will you forgive me?"

"Surely, my love," she smiled. "But you'll have to promise to marry me and give me lots of children," she giggled. He bent his head and kissed her gently on the mouth sending a wave of exquisite pleasure coursing through her body. "Do that again," she commanded, and he was happy to oblige.

"I'll speak to your father and ask for your hand," he said breathlessly, brushing his lips against hers for the third time.

"Oh, Frank, that's so nice," Lucy said, feeling she was floating on air. "I love you so much." Then she pulled on his waist so that they spun around in a circle. "You'd better be snappy with that proposal because I'm very much in the mood to be married to you." Then she ran off towards the stables, and he followed her.

* * *

Early on Monday morning Frank and John took the pony cart into Beverley to retrieve Lucy's things from the house by the North Bar Gate. Frank was now Lucy's fiancé, and he had already asked the vicar at All Hallows' to request a special licence from the Archbishop in York so that they could be married on the following Saturday; a request the vicar was more than happy to fulfil for the son of a baronet and a Member of Parliament.

As they were bumping along the lane heading towards town, John asked Greenwood if he thought Mr Chapman could have lied about other things besides having a wife in London.

"Like what?"

"Well, Uncle Robert keeps talking about his boys: Robert and Edmund. He swears they were alive before he went back into the burning building to save their mother, but Mr Chapman said they were dead."

Greenwood tapped the reluctant ponies with the tip of his whip. "Your uncle was very badly injured in that fire; he could just be confused."

"I know, but we only have Mr Chapman's word for it, and if the matter could be settled one way or the other I'm sure my uncle would find some peace."

"I suppose it won't do any harm to ask," said Greenwood.

When they had collected Lucy's possessions, they drove to the house of Mr Chapman's parents. The Chapmans had left town but their housekeeper took the key and provided them with the information they needed; that there were two workhouses in Beverley: one at Minster Moor Gate and another in the West End.

They made for the old workhouse first, at Minster Moor Gate, and parked the pony cart in the wide street outside its massive and austere limestone walls. It reminded John of a prison. Frank rang the bell on the postern gate and asked to see the governor. They were shown into a plain room with lime-washed walls and flags on the floor. At one end of the room there was a large desk upon which sat a black leather-bound ledger. There were no seats, so they stood. The governor was as austere as the room, dressed in black from head to foot and wearing a coarse horsehair wig. John thought he had the air of a man who enjoyed the power he had over others. The governor scrutinised them with his glassy grey eyes and demanded to know their business.

Greenwood cleared his throat. "I'm looking for two boys: Robert and Edmund Featherstone. Are they here, sir?"

"And what business is it of yours if they are?" retorted the surly man.

"I'm here on behalf of their father, who wishes to be reunited with them. If they were brought here it would have been just before Christmas, when their mother was killed in a fire at the

North Bar tenements. Their father was seriously injured in the blaze and has since been incapacitated, but he's now in a position to care for his children again."

"Well, that's to be commended," said the officious man, rubbing his skinny blue-veined hands. "No child who has a father to support him should be a burden to the parish." He opened the huge ledger and ran his bony finger down the long list of names written in fine copperplate script. "You say the boys were admitted around Christmas-time?"

"Yes, that's right, sir."

The man in black looked up from his deliberations and scanned them again. "We have two boys admitted around that date, but they are not listed as Featherstone. How old are they?"

Greenwood looked at John, who shrugged his shoulders. "About five and three, I think."

"I believe two boys of that age were brought here after the fire, but their name is Metcalf."

An order was issued to the matron to fetch the boys, while the governor explained that he was willing to discharge the children for a fee to cover expenses if they were the children they were looking for.

Presently two boys with hollow cheeks and dull violet eyes were presented, wearing workhouse uniforms: pale linen trousers and blue coats, marked with the workhouse badge. They had wooden clogs on their feet and each had a blue felt cap on top of his closely cropped hair. The boys stood silently, looking at the floor. John stepped forward, bending down to make himself less frightening, and asked them their names. The older boy took off his hat, looked at him with his huge, sad eyes, and whispered something that none of them could hear.

"Speak up, boy," bellowed the governor, making the younger child cry. "I won't have whispering when you're asked a question by a gentleman."

The boy twisted his hat in his hands, and received a clip around the ear from the matron. John put his hand up to dissuade the woman from punishing the child again. The boy was clearly terrified but whispered his name again, this time a little louder.

"So, your name's Robert Featherstone; that's very good. I'm John. What's your brother's name?"

"Edmund," the boy replied.

The matron clipped the older boy round the head again. "Manners, boy; you say sir when you answer a gentleman."

"There's no need for that, madam," said Greenwood. "The children are a credit to you and the governor." The woman's face creased with an obsequious smile.

Greenwood turned to John. "I think we've found them."

After paying the governor his fee, Greenwood picked up the younger child and slung him round his waist, while John took Robert by the hand and led him out of the workhouse into the bright morning sunshine.

"Now let's go and see your father, shall we?" said Greenwood, as he lifted the children onto the pony cart.

"Will Mother be there?" asked Robert as he settled in his seat.

John climbed up next to the child and put Edmund on his knee. "Your mother's dead," he said, knowing that lying would be a mistake.

The child looked up at him. "Does that mean she's not coming back?"

John stroked the boy's head, thinking of his father. "Yes, Robert, she's not coming back. Your mother's gone."

"Oh," replied the boy, looking dismayed. Then he looked up. "Can we 'ave a cuppa tea when we see Dad?"

"I'm sure that can be arranged," smiled John, and the two boys sank back into silence. Greenwood drove the pony cart along the streets and out of town, feeling pleased with himself for the second time in less than a week.

As they were nearing the farm John said, "What is Aunt Mariah going to say when we turn up with these two?"

"Oh Lord, I hadn't thought about that," said Frank. He gave the ponies a gentle tap with the whip. "Well, whatever she thinks she'll have to do what your uncle says: a wife is duty bound to obey her husband."

* * *

In the stables, with Buckeye breathing down their necks, Frank was talking to Lucy between kisses. "I'm a farmer's daughter Frank," said Lucy. "My heart was in pieces at the thought of living in the town. I love this place with all my heart and I'm so glad we'll be staying here."

"If your father is agreeable, I'm willing to invest in the farm. We could introduce Lord Townshend's crop rotation system, and buy some of those long-legged Arabians."

"Arabians!" Lucy gasped.

"Yes. I believe they're not at all hardy so we'll need a new stable," chuckled Frank, knowing that Lucy would love his idea. "I'm sure we can get a thousand a year out of this farm with a few changes."

"A thousand pounds! I'm sure Dad makes no more than three hundred."

396

"Now that I'm to be your wife, will you tell me how much you have?"

"Nearly five thousand pounds."

"Five thousand! How did you get that much money?"

"I had a quarter-ticket on the first prize in the National Lottery. Do you know how much the ticket cost me?"

"I have no idea," Lucy said in amazement. Five thousand pounds was more than her father had won in a lifetime of gambling.

"Three pounds, five shillings and sixpence!" he chuckled. "But don't be afraid, my love: gambling isn't my habit. I swear I'll never do it again, save a few bob on a horse every now and again. A man can't own horses without having the occasional flutter. But rest assured I intend to be very sensible. I have spent a few hundred on this and that, but the rest is safely locked up in the bank."

She kissed him again, this time parting her lips to allow his tongue to caress her as he cradled her face in his hands. "I'm such a lucky girl," she gasped as they parted. "Frank, I feel so happy that I'm quite scared."

"Scared of what?" demanded Frank, completely perplexed by the idea of being scared of happiness.

"I'm scared this dream will end, and that I'll wake up and you'll be gone."

"I'm not going anywhere without you. You've got me for life," Greenwood said, hugging her tight. "I've been close to death and stared it down. I was despondent even though I'd survived the 'Sherwell', thinking my life would amount to nothing. Now I have you, my love, I'm never going to let you go. I want a house full of children. I want us to raise the best horses in Yorkshire and to be happy for the rest of our lives."

"I think you're just too perfect, Mr Greenwood," Lucy said, pecking his cheek with another kiss, "but I'm sure summut will come along to knock your halo off sooner or later. You're a man, after all."

* * *

To say that Mariah was tired was an understatement; she had experienced every emotion except grief in less than a week. Having cried all day Saturday and most of Sunday, she stopped briefly to congratulate Frank and Lucy on their engagement; then started all over again with the relief of it all.

Mariah had always liked Frank Greenwood, and now that he had five thousand pounds to his name she liked him all the more; but her heart sank at the thought of spending the rest of her life on the farm. So when Frank and John arrived with Robert's bastards in tow her heart sank again, feeling that her humiliation was complete. She had lost her husband to Rosie Featherstone's charms, had her family's good name besmirched in the magistrates' court; she had been wrong about the character of Marcus Chapman; and now it seemed that her husband and family expected her to take on the care of his bastards. It was all too much for her, and by Tuesday Mariah had taken to her bed with a migraine and her bottle of hartshorn.

In the days that passed between Lucy's failed wedding to Marcus Chapman and her marriage to Frank Greenwood, Charlotte could not help wondering about Sinclair. Once again he had saved her family from calamity. The grateful part of her wanted to love him for it but the other part of her, the part that still felt betrayed and humiliated, wanted to make James Sinclair suffer. Looking at Frank and Lucy and their happiness, she could not stop a spike of jealousy rising in heart. She wanted to feel like they did. She wanted Jamie Sinclair to look at her the way Frank looked at Lucy, but more than that she wanted to be in the rapture of his embrace.

Charlotte hated the feelings Sinclair aroused in her. Why was it, she wondered, she had so little control over whom she loved? She had loved Christopher Leadam without understanding why and she had tried hard to be sensible about Sinclair, but she had failed. She had fallen for his good looks, his seductive smiles and cheeky sense of humour, but he had done the very thing she knew he would: he had taken up with a younger woman, and what was worse with another man's wife, and he had done it under her very own roof! How could she not hate him for such deceit and betrayal?

In bed that night she imagined going back to London to find Sinclair gone, and the thought frightened her. Without Sinclair, she would be alone in the world again, with a shop she could not run and with apprentices she could not train. Without Sinclair, she would be at the mercy of her mother and Mrs Peacock, and they would pressure her to marry the womanising libertine, Mr Masterson; and she did not want to do that.

* * *

Charlotte and John returned to Tooley Street in the middle of May to find Sinclair spending more time with Davy Shaw in the inns of the Borough High Street than at home.

Davy Shaw was the son of an apothecary who had trained in medicine under Sinclair's old professor, Alexander McNeal. They spent their evenings discussing Robert Burns's poetry, Mr Fordyce's lectures, the poor state of Mr Ellesmere's surgery and the politics of the Union, finding they were both of the same Whiggish persuasion. On Saturdays, Sinclair spent the day with Bowman, and on Sundays he skipped church, then took William to the Red Lion while Charlotte and John visited their family and friends. As the weeks of his estrangement from Charlotte went by, Sinclair felt his world becoming smaller. He was lonely, and what was worse he felt that the life he had made for himself after the 'Sherwell' was gradually and painfully being sliced away from him. He had lost Iona, he had lost Charlotte and now he had lost Greenwood. The comfortable world he had walked into in Tooley Street was disappearing bit by bit.

Charlotte was concerned about his drinking. She had no idea how much he was putting away each night, but she was sure it was too much. When she spoke to him he was grouchy and taciturn, although while he was coping with his work she didn't feel she could bring the subject up.

Spring turned into summer and the temperature in London soared. Sinclair spent most of his evenings in the courtyard of the White Horse or Talbot Inn drinking ale and brandy with Davy Shaw. He knew Charlotte hated his drinking, but the alcohol soothed his pain, and as far as he was concerned she would have to put up with it or throw him out.

One particularly hot Friday evening towards the end of July the sky cracked with thunder as he staggered home. The heavens opened, soaking his summer coat through to his shirt. As the white flashes of lightning crackled across the blue-black of the sky a searing terror erupted from the pit of his stomach. Confused, he started to run, to get away from the danger all around him, but his legs gave way and he tripped. Sinclair felt the thud of his head cracking against the pavement, he vomited, and blood started to mix with the rain running down his face.

Somehow he heaved himself upright and staggered back to Tooley Street. He put the key in the lock and pushed the door open. In the half-light he started to climb the uneven stairs and the room started to spin. He felt his stomach retch as he vomited again, then he collapsed, banging his head on the wall. In his mind, he was on the 'Sherwell' again. As he gasped for air he felt as if his lungs would burst. He cried out for help, then everything went black.

When he awoke his head was aching. He had no idea of the time, but the street was busy so he guessed he had missed his morning surgery. He was confused: he knew he had been drinking, but he couldn't remember how he had got to his bed. Someone had taken his clothes off and bandaged his head. He hoped it was one of the boys. His arms and legs hurt when he moved them. He was reaching under the bed for the piss pot when Charlotte knocked on the door and let herself in. "Ah, Dr Sinclair: you're awake at last."

He looked at her beautiful body framed in the doorway. She was dressed in a blue summer frock with her auburn hair in a thick plait. She looked radiant, but his heart sank; this was it, he thought. She was going to give him his marching orders, and his misery and punishment would be complete. He hauled himself up and tugged at the sheet to cover his nakedness. Charlotte walked in without invitation and sat on his bed, then started to unwind the bandage on his head. "I just want to have a look at this wound to make sure it's healing," she said. "There was a lot of blood, but then there usually is with head wounds, isn't there?"

"Aye," Sinclair mumbled, still holding the sheet against his chest.

Charlotte uncoiled the bandage and gently removed the linen wadding. "Oh, that looks all right. William gave you a couple of

401

stitches and they seem to be doing the trick." She smiled and asked if he would like some tea.

"Aye, I would, thank you," Sinclair replied, not knowing what would happen next.

"Get yourself dressed and come downstairs, and I'll get Elsie to make a fresh pot," Charlotte said, and left him to dress.

He raised his aching body out of the bed and checked the bruises on his arms and legs: they were all fall marks, bruises on his knees and the outside of his arms. There were no bruises on his face or chest so he had not been fighting, which was a relief. He washed and shaved slowly, resigned to his fate. The part of him that wanted Charlotte to punish him for his stupidity was getting what it wanted, and in a way he was relieved. The torture of living in the same house and not being with the woman he loved was going to end. He would no longer have to live with the agony of rejection, or with knowing she was being courted by other men.

He knew he deserved what she was about to do to him, but as he walked down the stairs to the dining room he realised she was going to do it in the cruellest possible way – with kindness.

24
A Long Hot Summer

Bruised and raw Sinclair opened the dining room door, feeling like a condemned man walking onto the scaffold. Charlotte was sitting at the table waiting for him. He sat down opposite her so that she was framed by the window. Her face was in shadow, but the strong summer sunlight caught her hair, giving it the burning glow of seraphim. She poured a cup of tea and added milk and sugar, then stood up, walked around the table and sat next to him. She stirred the tea slowly, and presented it to him without saying a word. He took it and mumbled a thank you, lowering his head, unable to look at her.

Charlotte put her hand on his. "I want to talk to you, Dr Sinclair."

He turned towards her and said what he had been rehearsing since she left his room. "I know my behaviour's been unacceptable, Mrs Leadam. I don't wish to cause you further trouble or embarrassment, so I'll leave today."

She squeezed his hand. "We don't want you to leave us. We just want the old Dr Sinclair back."

He closed his eyes, feeling the blood in his temples thumping against his worn out brain. "The trouble is that this is the old Dr Sinclair. This is the real me; the man who ruins everything; the man who drinks too much; the man who can't be trusted." He felt her hand on his face: she was stroking it and it felt so good, so utterly undeserved. His tears began to flow freely.

"You're too hard on yourself, Jamie Sinclair. You're a good man, a good doctor, and you've been a great help to me and my family. You were happy here before…," she paused, unable to say Iona's name, "before that woman came here and ruined everything."

"You mean Iona?" Sinclair said, wiping his face.

"Yes. Do you love her? Did she turn you down for your nephew?"

"Do you think that's why I drink?"

"I don't know. I thought I should ask. You slept with her." Charlotte took her hand away.

He wanted her hand back, so he took it in his. "It's complicated," he said. "I used to love her, or I thought I did, but that's not why I'm unhappy."

Charlotte looked at him and began to prattle on about being a selfish woman, apologising for not thanking him for looking after her when she was ill or for saving her niece from the clutches of Mr Chapman. He listened as she manoeuvred around the truth of their relationship, determined to protect her feelings and her pride. The pain in his head was still thumping, but for once he felt strangely calm. The calamity he had been dreading for months was finally happening, and he knew it was time to be honest with her.

"Shush," he said softly, squeezing her hand. "None of that is important." Then he ran his hand down the side of her face, letting his fingers skim over her hair, "I knew we had feelings for each other when I slept with Iona. I was stupid and I hurt you, which is the last thing I wanted to do. I was weak; I didn't understand what I was jeopardising when I gave into my lust. Charlotte, you're a beautiful woman, but it's not your beauty I've come to love; it's the way you make me feel. You make me good. You make my life worthwhile. When you turned me out of your life, when you no longer looked at me, when you refused to speak to me, when you didn't want me in your company, I was bereft. As the weeks of estrangement went on my discomfort became an actual physical pain. I know I've done you wrong and you have every right to punish me. That is why I drink."

Charlotte's body shrank as the bluster holding her up dissolved. Tears pricked in the corners of her eyes, and her lips trembled as the pain caged in her chest began its slow escape.

He brushed his hand against her face again. "I know I should've sent Iona away but I'm a man Charlotte, not a saint. I succumbed to the temptations of the flesh. All this pain is my fault and I don't blame you for hating me. You have every right to want me out of your life."

"But I don't," she cried. "I don't want you to leave. I want us to be like we used to be, before you ruined everything. "

Sinclair stroked her face and looked into her eyes. "We can't, my love; we can't pretend none of this happened, and we can't pretend that we don't love each other." He put his arms around her and she buried her head in his chest. "I'm so sorry I hurt you, Charlotte," he said, rubbing her back as she sobbed. "We can't go on like this. I can't live a lie any more. I can't pretend that I don't love you or that my heart's not broken, even if it's a self inflicted wound."

"I couldn't help it; I was so very angry with you," she mumbled into his jacket. "I was so angry with Iona for taking you away." She raised her head, her face wet with tears. "I've punished you cruelly, Jamie. I've driven you to this sorry state. I'm as guilty as you are for our unhappiness."

"No, the blame's mine," Sinclair said, kissing her hair, brushing his lips over the soft silky strands and breathing her scent deep into his body. The throbbing in his head was no longer relevant; he was in her thrall. "Tell me what to do, Charlotte. Show me how to behave," he said, burying his face in her hair. With each breath he wanted her more. He wanted to become part of her, to disappear, to be consumed by her love. He cupped her face in his hands and kissed her softly on each cheek. "We must forgive each other; we've both been cruel in our own way."

"Do you truly love me, Jamie?" she sighed.

"With the entirety of my soul," he whispered, brushing his lips across hers.

She kissed him. "Will you forgive me for all the pain I have caused you?"

"Aye, if you will forgive me."

"I do. I forgive you."

"Now, can I kiss you, please?" he said.

"I thought you already had," Charlotte smiled, with tears still welling in her eyes.

"Not properly I haven't," he said, standing up and pulling her into his embrace. With her body next to his, he fixed his lips firmly on hers, and they kissed for a minute or maybe two, tasting and exploring each other, oblivious to the world around them; overwhelmed by the powerful mixture of relief and desire flooding through their bodies. The relief was like gulping in the sweet air of the cave on the night of the wreck, and he felt that life and happiness were possible again. "Mrs Leadam, please tell me to stop this and go back to work, because if we carry on I don't think I can be responsible for my actions."

Charlotte leaned back in his embrace and affectionately ran her fingers through his hair. "Dr Sinclair, I insist that you go back to work. We have a business to attend to and there are patients to be seen."

He smiled back at her. "You're a very bossy woman, Charlotte Leadam."

"I thought that was one of the things you liked about me," she laughed. He pulled her back into his embrace. "Aye, but it's not the only thing," he said, giving her breast a gentle squeeze.

* * *

The July storms ran into a sweltering August. It was an uncomfortable time for everyone. The slow-moving city air was stale and tainted by the reek of rotting riverweed and mud at low tide, together with pungent odours from nearby breweries and the paint factory. At night the foul odours wafted into the house and into their bedroom on the gentle night breeze that ran along the river, making them long for the autumn chill.

In the City, scarlet fever cases were reaching epidemic levels, and Sinclair was being called out to treat the children of the borough's wealthy families. The problem was that the disease spread like wildfire in the hot, close conditions. Every day there

407

were funeral parades at St Olave's and St John's, with parents carrying their children's coffins. It depressed them both. The nights were too humid and sticky for clothes, which suited Charlotte and Sinclair well. They had been sharing a bed for a month and he was familiar with every soft velvety fold of her skin. He rolled on top of her and stroked her hair, the part of her he had first admired, and kissed her again softly on the mouth. She pushed him away. "I'm too hot," she complained, "and it's not the right time."

"Not the right time?" he queried.

"Well, you're the doctor, for goodness' sake; you know how women work," she snapped.

"Oh, that sort of time," he said, wrapping his arms around her to reassure her; but he could tell something else was bothering her. "What is it? What's wrong?"

"There's nothing wrong, except that we're living in sin."

"Well, you said we should wait a while so that John could get used to the idea of us being reconciled."

"I know. I still think we should give him time. I want him to be happy when we tell him, not concerned that I've made a poor choice."

"So what's the problem?"

"Connie's pregnant," Charlotte said flatly.

"That's wonderful news," Sinclair said, rolling back to his side of the bed.

"I know it is, but I hate her for it."

"Is that because you can't..."

"Because I can't get pregnant? Oh God, you can't even say it," she wailed slapping him across his bare chest. "Of course it is. Don't you know how hard it is for me? I'm surrounded by other people's babies all the time in this job. Mrs Prentice next door just pops them out like peas from a pod, and now my best friend is having a baby too."

Sinclair stroked her flushed cheeks. "It's not important to me. I knew from the start that you couldn't give me children."

"But it is to me. I thought I was over it, over wanting or needing children, but now I find you've stirred up such feelings in me that every time we make love I want a miracle. I can't help it, Jamie, I want a child; my body aches for it. It may be of no consequence to you but it is to me."

"Oh my love, my poor wee hen," he said, stroking her hair and kissing her face. "I love you just as you are. We have enough; you have John and I have my apprentices. Besides, I'm glad I won't have to suffer the uncertainties of childbirth with you. Now I have you I don't want to lose you. We'll be very happy together without children, I promise. I'll see the vicar as soon as you tell John we're to be man and wife."

* * *

The summer months brought Greenwood weeks of back-breaking toil. When he had decided to become a farmer he had simply no idea how hard the job would be. He spent his days cutting and storing hay, hoeing rows of turnips and beans, farrowing sows and keeping a watchful eye on his fields of ripening wheat and barley. The horses required a good deal of his attention too. He worked with his father-in-law and his wife to sell off their old stock at the Beverley Fair and bought five high-class broodmares to put to his Arabian stud, a tall and handsome chestnut they called the Persian Prince which they had acquired from Colonel Croft in Bedale.

Lucy spent her days working with little Robert in the kitchen garden, planting lettuces, radishes and spring onions. They put in rows of potatoes, carrots, parsnips and cabbages for the autumn and covered the fruit bushes with nets to keep the birds away. In the dairy, she and Tilly made cheeses and salted sides of bacon ready for the winter, and she hung legs of gammon in the chimney to be smoked by the fire.

Her father was content to advise from his chair most days, but occasionally he got up and limped around the farm supported by Mariah or Lucy, trying to keep an eye on his young son-in-law's efforts; but mostly he sat and played snobs or marbles with Robert and Edmund in the courtyard.

Mariah had to admit that once the boys were out of their workhouse clothes they looked lovely. Playing together in the sunshine, they looked like a pair of golden-skinned angels with their blond curly hair. Of course, they could soon turn into little demons if she left them unattended. One day little Robert tied a ribbon to Pincer's tail, making the poor dog bark until it was hoarse and driving the animal half-crazy as he ran around in circles trying to bite the damn thing off; and Edmund was in the habit of helping himself to any food left in the kitchen no matter whose it was, even the dog's!

Despite his injuries, Robert was the happiest Mariah had seen him for years. He clearly loved having his boys around him. He was teaching young Robert to read, so he could go to the grammar school when he was seven, and Lucy was teaching him to ride. The farm was a happy place again, and Mariah was resigned to caring for her husband and his boys. With the son of a Member of Parliament for a son-in-law and a successful horse business, she could hold her head up high in Beverley society;

410

and she had the sympathy of the town when it came to Marcus Chapman.

As sultry August headed towards September, Greenwood spent long days in the fields, bringing his harvest in. He rubbed the grains between his fingers: they were fat and he knew the harvest would be good. He had never worked so hard or been so happy. The dreams of Susan Morris and the *Sherwell* were gone from his mind. When he dreamt now he dreamt of building a new house for Lucy or of one of his horses winning a race at Beverley or York; and when the harvest was in Lucy made his happiness complete by telling him she was with child.

* * *

At the beginning of October, a letter from France arrived in Edinburgh via the offices of the 'European Magazine'. Morag was having breakfast with her husband and daughters when the maid brought it in. She ripped off the seal and started to read watched by her family, who were all eager for news of Blair and Iona's adventures.

"So what have they been up to?" asked Andrew, taking his cup of tea and buttering a piece of toast. Morag put the letter down and looked at her husband: the colour had drained from her face.

"Mother, what's wrong," demanded her daughters.

"It's Blair: he's been injured. A man stabbed him in the street in Paris. Iona's looking after him."

"Stabbed! My God, is he all right?" her husband demanded.

"Iona says he's very ill. Here, read what she says for yourself." Andrew took the letter and read it aloud. The girls gasped with horror as he revealed the details of the attack. Blair

411

had been walking through Les Halles when he challenged a pickpocket who was trying to rob him. The pickpocket stabbed him and left him for dead.

"What are we going to do? We can't leave Iona to cope alone," said Morag.

Andrew looked at his wife. "He could be dead already. This letter has taken a fortnight to get here."

"No, don't think like that, my love," Morag said, terrified that he might be right.

"We must get them back. We must get them home."

"How are we going to do that? We're not young, and we can't just drop everything and go to a country we know nothing about."

"I know France; I've been to Paris before," countered her husband. "I could take a ship from Leith and find them."

"Papa, I'll come with you," said Ailsa. "I can speak French."

The thought of her elderly husband and daughter taking off for France alarmed Morag more than she could admit. Andrew was an impractical academic. His skill was in writing and arguing; he was a man of the classroom, not the real world, and her enthusiastic daughter was the same: she was young and bookish like all the Rankins. A flicker of an idea sparked in Morag's mind. "I have a better idea. We should ask my brother to go to Paris for us. Jamie's in London, he's a doctor so he could care for Blair and Iona, he's been to Paris more recently than any of us, and he speaks the language. What's more, he has no family or commitments to tie him down. It would only take him a week or so if he travelled from Dover."

"Morag, you're a genius," her husband declared. "Will you write to him today and ask him to leave immediately?"

"I shall do better than that. I shall go to London and ask him myself. I don't want to leave a matter of such importance to the vagaries of the postal system, or to his inclinations for that matter. If I ask him in person he's sure to do it."

* * *

Five days later Morag and Ailsa arrived in Holborn.

"What if Uncle James isn't there?" said Ailsa as they were crossing London Bridge in their hired cab.

"We'll stay at an inn, or with Sir Donald; there's no need to worry," replied Morag, determined to see their mission through. The cab pulled up outside the shop with the golden pestle and mortar sign hanging over the door, and the women got out. It was dark and cold but they could see lights on in the upstairs windows, so they were hopeful of success. Morag gave the knocker a firm rap and a young man's head appeared out of the upstairs window.

"Do you need the surgeon, madam?"

"Aye. I've come to see Dr James Sinclair. Please tell him his sister is here from Edinburgh."

The young man disappeared, and some minutes later opened the door for them. "Hello, Mrs Rankin. My name is John Leadam. May I take your bags? My mother and Dr Sinclair are waiting for you upstairs."

In their cosy parlour Sinclair threw his arms around his sister and then his niece. "My God, what are you two doing here? Why didn't you write to let me know you were coming?"

Charlotte shook their hands warmly and invited them to sit while she organised refreshments. While she was out of the room Morag started to tell Sinclair what had happened. "Oh, that's

413

terrible. What on earth was he doing in Les Halles? It's a pit of a place."

"I know: that's what Andrew said. The thing is, we need to get them home."

"So are you planning on going there yourselves?" Sinclair enquired as Charlotte arrived with a tray of tea and bread and butter.

"We were hoping to persuade you to go for us," his sister said, taking the dish of tea Charlotte offered her.

"Me?" he said with incredulity. "Why? Surely Iona and Blair have family of their own who could help them. Blair has a brother and Iona has three."

"Jamie, you know that Charles is as useless as Andrew when it comes to practical things, and Iona's brothers have wives and families: they can't just drop everything and go to Europe."

"But I can, is that it? Is that what you're thinking?"

"Jamie, you're not married, you have no children and you speak French. And you're a doctor as well. You're the ideal person to help them."

"Uncle James, please say yes," pleaded Ailsa.

"I'm sorry to disappoint you, but I have commitments here. I'm not a free agent, am I, Mrs Leadam?"

Charlotte nodded her agreement, unsure where the conversation would end.

"I have patients to care for, a business to tend to and apprentices to teach. I'm sorry, Morag, I can't just drop everything because Blair's been hurt. They decided to go to Europe and they have to take responsibility for what happens to them; they're not children."

"But Iona's pregnant; she's going to have a baby very soon."

414

"What's that got to do with me, for God's sake?" Sinclair retorted, feeling a powerful shot of guilt coursing through his veins.

"Jamie, please don't take the Lord's name in vain," said his sister.

"I will if I want to: I'm not in Edinburgh now. Besides, couldn't Alexander McNeal write to one of his professor friends in Paris and get him to look after Blair and Iona? Do either of you have any idea how far away Paris is, or how long it'll take to get there?"

Charlotte looked at Sinclair; she could see he was tired and angry. The news of Iona's pregnancy had hit her with the same surprise as it had him. Feeling nothing useful was going to be decided that night, she said. "Do you have rooms for the night, Mrs Rankin?"

"No, we don't. We came here as soon as we arrived. Is there somewhere nearby we could stay?"

"My goodness, surely you don't think I would send Dr Sinclair's family to stay at an inn? You'll stay here. I have a room you're welcome to. It's a bit chilly as I didn't know you were coming, but I can give you a bed-warmer."

"That is very generous of you, Mrs Leadam. Ailsa and I are very happy to accept your offer. I have to admit we're fair done in with all the travelling."

Sinclair went off to his attic room as usual, put on his nightshirt and waited for the house to be still before he slipped into Charlotte's bedroom. When he opened the door he found her still getting undressed. "Here, let me help you," he said, slipping the fastening loops of her corset, then putting his arms around her waist and nuzzling her neck.

"It's all right; I can do it," she said, with a little irritation.

"I know, but I like doing it," he whispered. "I used to daydream about taking your clothes off." And he buried his head in her neck again.

As her corset fell to the floor she turned and kissed him. "You're an incorrigible rascal, Jamie Sinclair," she said, coaxing a smile from his tired face.

"I know. Come on, let's get the rest of this stuff off you and get into bed."

After they had made love, Charlotte broached the subject of Iona's baby. "Do you think it's yours?" she said softly. Iona's name tasted sour in her mouth, and the thought she was carrying Jamie's child made her sick with envy.

There was a long pause, "It's possible," he said, knowing how much the conversation was hurting her.

"How would you feel if it is?" said Charlotte, feeling as though her heart was about to break.

"I don't know, my love," he said, rolling on top of her and kissing her face. "I suppose I'd be curious to know what the child was like. But it wouldn't be my child: when this child is born, whoever the father is, it'll be Blair and Iona's."

"But could it be Blair's?" said Charlotte.

"It's unlikely, I have to admit."

"So he was in this Les Halles place picking up a boy, just like men do in Covent Garden?"

"Aye, I suppose it's possible, much as it pains me to say it."

"Jamie," said Charlotte, with an ache in her throat, "you can't leave Iona to cope with a sick husband and a baby on her own in a foreign country. If there's any chance the child is yours you must help them. As much as I hate her I wouldn't want her to be on her own at such a time."

"But I don't want to leave you, Charlotte. Who will run the business if I go to Paris?"

"We'll manage somehow. If you don't help them you risk losing all of them, and you'd regret that. You'd never forgive yourself if you didn't do what was in your power to help."

"Aye, you're right, my love. You're always right. The trouble is I'm not sure I can."

"What do you mean? Of course you can."

"I mean, I don't know if I can get on a boat again. When I think about water or the sea, I'm petrified with fear just like Frank. When I did this," he said, pointing at the scar on his forehead, "it all came back to me. I don't know if it was the drink, the knock on the head or the thunderstorm, but I felt I was under the waves again and fighting for my life. I thought I was going to die so many times on the 'Sherwell' that the fear is imprinted on my brain, and I can't remove it."

25
The Night Journey

John and William ate a hasty breakfast and made their excuses, leaving the adults to their conversation. While they were waiting for Sinclair, William took the opportunity to watch Mr Prentice and Alice as they took their daily walk to his drawing school in the Strand.

"Will you stop gawping out of the window and help me over here?" John complained.

"In a minute they're nearly out of sight. Oh God, she's lovely. If her father painted a picture of her I'm sure he'd sell a thousand."

"And you'd be first in the queue with your two shillings and sixpence for a print, I suppose," John smiled.

"Quite true, my friend. I'd like a picture of her to drool over whenever I wanted instead of having to watch her from a distance." William reluctantly stepped away from his vantage point. "What do you think is going on upstairs?"

"Mrs Rankin wants Dr Sinclair to go to Paris to fetch Iona and Blair back home."

"What, back here? I'm not sure that's a good idea. I'm sure it was them that turned your mother against Sinclair, and that was awful. Have you noticed they're getting on much better now?"

"You mean have I noticed that my mother pours Sinclair's tea in the morning and that he looks at her like a lovesick pup? Just like Frank Greenwood looks at my cousin Lucy?" said John.

"And that he comes home for lunch again and doesn't go out drinking any more."

"And that I'm not being dragged off to visit all my relatives every Sunday. Yes, I've noticed, and it's a blessed relief because Grandmamma and Aunt Em are hardly speaking to Mother now. Apparently she's turned down what they call a very attractive offer of marriage from a banker called Masterson. I think they're in love, William."

"Who? Your mother and Sinclair?" William replied nonchalantly, filling a vial with laudanum, not sure John really wanted his mother to be in love with anyone except his father.

"Yes. Don't you think the way they're behaving is very strange? Everything seemed normal, then Iona and Blair Rankin came to stay and suddenly Mother and Sinclair couldn't stand the sight of one another. Since Sinclair came home with a cracked head they've been the best of friends, and neither of them can stop smiling at the other."

"Well, I suppose anything's possible. Your mother's a very attractive woman and Sinclair is…"

"Sinclair is what?" demanded John.

419

"He's attractive too. Perhaps he was a bit too attractive to Iona and your mother got jealous."

"I think it must have been more than that," John said, thinking about his uncle's antics. "I'm sure what's being discussed upstairs has something to do with it."

About an hour later, Sinclair appeared in the shop ready to do his morning rounds. "Is my bag ready, John?"

"Yes, sir."

"Good. William, get your coat and come with me," Sinclair commanded. "John, you stay in the shop. I'm going to France in a few days, gentlemen. But I have to put some arrangements in place to ensure the shop and the surgery stay open while I'm away. I have a colleague at St Thomas', Dr Shaw, an Edinburgh man like me. I'll ask him to cover for me, as Mr Hoares has too much to do in looking after his wife at the moment; she's very ill. I hope Dr Shaw will be able to join us for supper this evening, so that you and your mother can meet him."

* * *

The next few days were hectic as Sinclair made his travel arrangements. Mrs Leadam and Elsie washed and pressed the doctor's clothes, sewing ten gold sovereigns into the lining of his greatcoat and ten into the lining of his waistcoat and frock coat in case of emergencies, while John made up a bag of medical supplies and equipment from a list compiled by his mother, including medicines, forceps, scalpels and bandages.

When everything was ready, they followed Sinclair down to the Talbot Inn in the Borough High Street, where he took the night coach to Dover – all except John, who pleaded illness and took himself off to an early bed. When his bags were on board

Sinclair said his goodbyes, kissing his sister and his niece on the cheek, shaking William's hand and kissing Charlotte for the first time in public. "I'll be back as soon as I can, my love, and I'll write to you to let you know how things stand when I get there. If Blair and Iona are fit enough to travel, I'll be back in less than a month, but if they're not it'll take longer."

"I know," said Charlotte taking her last chance to embrace him. "Please stay safe."

The ground was hard with frost as Sinclair walked up Shooter's Hill in the moonlight. Behind him were the poor unfortunate souls riding post that night. He was glad he was not one of them, and that he would be getting inside the coach when they got to the top of the hill. Walking behind him, John kept his distance, pulling his hat down over his face so that Sinclair would not recognise him if he turned around. At the top of the hill John watched the doctor get back in the coach, then climbed on top, and the Dover coach trundled on into the night.

Hours later, as the red light of dawn crept across the eastern sky, John saw the Channel for the first time. It was a glorious sight: the sea was still and black in the frosty morning air. Lying off the beach was a small fleet of ships at anchor: two East Indiamen, a cutter and two packet boats. The coach driver eased in the brake as they started their descent down the great chalk escarpment and into the town. Down they went along the narrow Dover streets and on to the shingle beach, where a posse of ragged men and boys were waiting to ferry them and their luggage to the waiting packet boats. The men carried the trunks and portmanteau, while the boys made off with the hat and wig boxes, demanding sixpence for the privilege.

When the luggage was aboard, the eight passengers from the coach were embarked at a guinea a head. Sinclair was the first to take his place. He sat on the cold damp seat in the middle of the boat, took out his pocket watch and checked the hour. Rolling it in his hand, he felt its warmth; they had survived the 'Sherwell' together and now he hoped its charm would work again to protect him as he crossed the treacherous sea. The calm suited his nerves, but he knew they would be going nowhere until the wind picked up. John sat at the back of the boat with his hat down and his collar up, watching Sinclair and feeling excited and apprehensive. He did not want to be discovered yet; not while they were in England and Sinclair could still send him home.

He knew his mother would be reading the letter he had left for her, and that she would be worried and angry, but it was a price worth paying to make sure Sinclair came back to Tooley Street.

When everyone and everything was on board the rowing boat, the men pushed it off the beach and the sailors started to row out to the waiting packet boat. The passengers scrambled up a rope ladder onto the wretched hovel of a ship that was to take them to Calais. The cabins were nothing more than filthy little boxes with soiled, coffin-like cots for beds. Sinclair looked at his, took out the vial of brandy and laudanum he had made to calm his nerves and drank it in one gulp. The taste was so bitter it made him gag, but within minutes he could feel its effects. Feeling woozy and sick, he laid himself on the floor using his bag as a pillow, and was soon unconscious to the world.

Sinclair was woken from his drug-induced sleep by a knock on the door. Feeling stiff and groggy, he opened his eyes reluctantly; he had no idea how long he had been asleep. Remembering he was on his way to France, he looked around the squalid cabin with dismay. The boat was rolling underneath him, sending spikes of fear into his heart. There was a second knock;

he scrambled to his feet and opened the door. In front of him was a tall young man dressed in an oversized greatcoat and hat. The young man looked familiar. Sinclair blinked and ran his fingers through his thick, dishevelled hair, "John! What are you doing here?"

"Good afternoon, Dr Sinclair. We're lying just off Calais, but the wind is blowing off shore so we can't enter the harbour. We'll have to be rowed ashore."

Sinclair rubbed his aching head and repeated, "John, what are you doing here? Your mother will be beside herself with worry."

"I left her a note. She knows where I am, and that if I'm with you I'll be safe."

"Oh, for Christ's sake, John! You'll have to go back. I can't take you with me." Sinclair shook his head with disbelief and annoyance.

"The master says a boat is coming to fetch us and take us ashore."

"Well, you won't be on it. I'm sending you back to London," Sinclair barked.

"You're not my father; you can't tell me what to do."

"You're right, I'm not, but I'm your mother's friend, and I know how worried she'll be until you're back home."

"I'm not a child. My father, who was a far better man than you will ever be, told me to look after my mother, and that's what I'm doing."

"What on earth do you mean?"

"My mother loves you. I don't understand why but she does. She needs you, so I'm going to make sure you go back to her."

"John, of course I'm going to go back to your mother. I love her, and I want to marry her."

"Good, I'm glad to hear it; but I'm still coming with you. The Leadams don't trust Scots and I don't trust you and Iona Rankin. She caused so much trouble when she stayed with us. I'm not a fool. I know you and Mother fell out after she left, and the only reason two people fall out like that is when one finds out the other's been cheating. I'm pretty sure it wasn't my mother who was doing the cheating!"

Sinclair stood silently, absorbing the boy's anger.

"I'm pretty sure you fell out when Mother found out you'd been sleeping with Iona! Don't you know you made our lives hell for months?" the boy shouted.

Sinclair looked at him. "You're right; you're no child and you're no fool, John Leadam. I'm sorry for what I did and your mother has forgiven me." Sinclair felt ashamed that he had caused so much trouble, but decided not to dwell on it as there was nothing he could do to make it right. He picked up his bag and followed John out onto the open deck. His legs felt weak and his chest felt tight. Blood pounded in his temples and his heart raced as the fear of the sea gripped him again. They watched as a couple of rickety old rowing boats pulled alongside, and the crew started to secure them with ropes. Sinclair swayed and stumbled as the packet boat rolled on the swell. John caught him, and whispered, "I'm pretty sure Iona's having your baby."

"Well, you really don't miss much, do you? Perhaps you'll be useful after all," Sinclair muttered, resigning himself to the fact there was no getting rid of the boy.

Before they were allowed to quit the ship, they were obliged to tip the cabin boy for his attendance, although neither of them had seen him the entire journey. When they had paid their dues, they clambered down the rope ladder into the rowing boat and set off towards the Customs House. They arrived cold and damp. In

424

the Customs House, a bad-tempered officer with dirty fingernails and a row of brown broken teeth demanded another guinea for rummaging through their bags, and charged Sinclair the best part of a further guinea to import his medical supplies. Finally they were permitted to walk to the town to find lodgings for the night.

By the time it was dark they were ensconced in a dismal auberge eating plates of stale bread, hard cheese and drinking thin red wine like Frenchmen, all the good Bordeaux and Burgundy being in the English warehouses along the quay.

Rising early from their cold and uncomfortable beds the next morning, they set off to the other side of town with their luggage, hoping to hire a berline, a small carriage with two inside seats. Sinclair scanned the four available at the livery stable: two were obviously dilapidated. "John, do you know anything about coaches or horses?" asked Sinclair, looking underneath the smartest of the other two.

"No, sir."

"Neither do I. We'll just have to do our best and trust to luck. I reckon this one's all right," said Sinclair, pacing around and trying to give the impression he knew what he was looking at.

"I can't see anything obviously wrong with it, sir," agreed John, following behind him and bending to scratch the bites on his legs.

"I'll see what I can get it for. Wait here while I go and haggle with that devil over there," said Sinclair, heading in the direction of the lean, sinewy man smoking a pipe who had been watching them suspiciously. Half an hour later he came back having hired the berline and four horses with a postilion and a driver called Joseph. Four bay-coloured horses were hitched to the traces and a tall, bronzed man in an enormous black hat and a heavy grey coat appeared to take charge of the vehicle. Their driver was followed by a much younger man wearing a battered cocked hat, who threw their luggage into the carriage, then invited them to board before taking his position on the back of the nearside horse. Sinclair instructed the driver to drive to Paris on the post road via Boulogne, Abbeville and Beauvais, and then jumped inside.

For the next three days they rose early, skipped breakfast and stopped at an auberge en route at around ten to take refreshment, change the horses and pick up some bread, cheese and wine for lunch. This they ate at about three o'clock when they changed the horses again.

Sinclair pulled out a much-worn copy of his favourite book and started to read. "John, will you please stop doing that?" he demanded, irritated by the boy's constant scratching.

"I can't help it. I've never had so many bites. This country is filthy and so are its people. I've been to Yorkshire twice and never been bitten like this. And the food's awful too."

"Well, you insisted on coming. You've only got yourself to blame," beamed Sinclair, with his pipe between his teeth.

"I can't understand why you wanted to come here. Everything is so decrepit I can't believe that they have anything to teach us."

"Surprisingly they do. The French approach to medical training is in many ways superior to your chaotic English system; well, in Paris at least. Of course there are quacks and charlatans everywhere, but there's a considerable effort to ensure that those who call themselves surgeons have some minimum level of skill and qualification in France. In fact the Scottish system, particularly that in Edinburgh, is based on the programme of study at the Paris College of Surgery where true experts, not men like our Mr Ellesmere or Mr Lucas at Guy's, teach under the direction of the King's premier surgeon. When I was at the

College there were many experts, and they all gave lectures in a vast semicircular amphitheatre with seating for over a hundred students. It's lit by an oculus in the roof that lets in daylight, brilliant for demonstrations – unlike the dark and cramped theatres we have in London. In France there's much greater emphasis on instruction and teaching than in England. When I was in Paris I attended lectures and demonstrations on bone-setting, conditions of the eye, dentistry, conditions of the feet and cutting for stone. All French surgeons are trained in hospitals, unlike in England, and they have to complete a programme of practical training in pathological anatomy, dissection and clinical medicine. Their knowledge and skill in childbirth is second to none. I learned a great deal from studying their surgeon-accoucheurs."

"I'm surprised," said John. "In every town and village we pass through there are vagrants on the road and groups of young men looking for work. In the woods and along the roadside there are women and children foraging for food. It looks as if they're gathering weeds and snails. From what I've seen so far I am not impressed."

"I agree: things look pretty bad."

When they stopped for lunch, John decided to ask their driver, Joseph, about the cause of the malaise.

"It's because of you British," he replied sourly. "The men who weave are without work. This new Commercial Treaty will be the death of us. We cannot compete with your English factories. And now there is no food. In the summer, it did not rain, then the Lord sent us hail the size of men's fists that destroyed what crops had survived the drought. This harvest is the worst in living memory. The bread you are eating is most probably made of English corn, and the oats we feed the horses

427

are English too. There is nothing here, but the landlord must still have his rent. The King has been merciful and has suspended the collection of taxes, but the country is bankrupt. Someone has to pay for fighting you British in America and Canada. The trouble is the nobles do not want it to be them; they think we little people should foot the bill. France is in crisis, Monsieur."

"So, has there been trouble in Paris?" asked Sinclair.

"Oui, monsieur. There were riots in the summer, and in my opinion matters will only get worse. Food is already short in the city and prices are rising, from what we are hearing."

"Well we don't want to get caught up in that," said John. "I remember the riots in London. We had to shelter under the stairs with Mrs Dredge while my father guarded the front door with the poker and the fire damper. Hundreds of mad men ran around Tooley Street smashing windows and looting the shops. They broke into the old Clink prison and set fire to it. It was terrifying. We lost our shop window, but there was nothing the mob wanted from our shop so they passed us by on their way to release the prisoners from Newgate and the Fleet."

"Aye, we should make haste. Cities can be ugly places when times are hard," agreed Sinclair.

They spent a second uncomfortable night in Abbeville, the centre of the woollen trade. The town was as dilapidated as their auberge. Everywhere there were crowds of men without work, and many were begging for food. Sinclair and John shared a room, both refusing to get into the grubby bed and choosing instead to sleep in their coats. The next day they rose bad tempered and still scratching. They cursed French hospitality as they climbed into the berline and pressed on to the ancient town of Beauvais. The road was good but the weather was cold. In Beauvais they had their first decent dinner: delicious vegetable soup followed by roast chicken and baked pears. With full stomachs and comfortable beds for the first time in days, their tempers mellowed and they slept soundly.

After five days on the road, they found themselves in a queue of traffic outside one of Paris's city gates on the Rue Saint Denys. They waited patiently as each carriage in the line was searched by two musket-wielding soldiers from the city garrison. When it came to their turn to be searched the soldiers insisted they get out of the coach, one checking the carriage while the other rummaged through their bags, demanding to know their business in Paris.

"My goodness," John breathed with relief as they got back in. "Imagine if that happened in London."

"The queues would be very long," laughed Sinclair. Then on a more serious note he added, "It's not until you go abroad you see the true value of our liberty. Despite the corruption of the money men we should count ourselves the luckiest men in the world to live in Britain."

26
An Inquisition in Wimpole Street

"So he's abandoned you and gone in search of his lover," crowed Mrs Martin over the supper table. "I always knew he was a bad sort. Mr Husselbee is still one of his patients, is he not? He should have been your father's patient, but bad attracts bad as good attracts virtue, so perhaps it isn't surprising the two should end up in cahoots. Just think about poor Isabella…"

"Eliza, you're talking about things you don't understand, my dear," rebuked her husband. "Now be still and give us some soup."

Mrs Martin proceeded to dish up the soup but continued in the same venomous vein. "So where are his relatives?"

"They're staying with Sir Donald McNeal at his house near Hyde Park," replied Charlotte.

"How very sensible of them. Who in their right mind would stay in Southwark when they can stay at Hyde Park?" her mother opined. "I'm sure his relatives are very respectable, but he's gone off to France to chase a flibbertigibbet. The man is a scoundrel and you're uncommonly careless, Charlotte. First you lose your husband, then you turn down a perfectly good marriage prospect, now your so-called business partner has run off to France in pursuit of a married woman – and he's taken your son with him to boot! I ask you, is that not a sorry state of affairs?"

"Mother, that's cruel and unjust," said Emma, feeling she had gone too far.

"I agree," said Dr Martin. "Eliza, I know you're disappointed Charlotte rejected Mr Masterson, but you have no business making our daughter more miserable concerning John's stupid escapade to France than she already is. We're all worried about them both."

"Thank you, Papa; and Mother, what makes you think Dr Sinclair is chasing a flibbertigibbet? He's gone to France to help his family."

"Ask Emma," her mother retorted, with a patronising scowl.

Emma's face flushed pink, then scarlet, "It was just something Henry said. He told me what that nice Mr Greenwood told him. That Dr Sinclair slept with his niece when she was staying with you."

"I told you not to breathe a word of that, Emma," her husband mumbled through gritted teeth. "My God; I swear I shall never tell you anything again!"

"Oh, of course you will, Henry," his wife chirped. "You know you tell me everything eventually. We don't like secrets in this family. Mother and I discuss everything, that's what mothers are for. And Mother is only calling that woman a flibbertigibbet to be polite."

Bowman bent his head, unable to look at Charlotte or her father. His stupid wife had gone too far this time; she had accused their friend of incest, and now Eliza had the bit between her teeth.

"With his niece!" she boomed, with all the moral indignation she could muster. "I didn't know she was his niece. Good God, the man is depraved! I knew having an unmarried man under your roof would lead to trouble, Charlotte, but no one would listen to me. An unmarried man can't be trusted with women from any station or rank. Their desire is to seduce all females they come into contact with. But I did not think Mr Walpole's tragedy would be enacted under my own daughter's roof!"

Charlotte stood up, red faced. "Mother, please don't exaggerate. There is no similarity with Mr Walpole's play and what happened in my house. This is not a case of a young man sleeping with his sister knowingly or unknowingly. I see I have no option but to tell you everything. Iona Rankin is not Dr Sinclair's niece; she's the wife of his step-nephew. There is no blood relationship to either party and so there can't be incest!"

"But there was adultery," said her father. "I'm disappointed. I thought the man was better than that."

"That is true, but he's still a very good man, Papa, and he has apologised to me for it." Charlotte sat down again, feeling she had clarified the situation, at least to her own satisfaction.

"Well, if he hasn't committed incest he's an adulterer, as your father says. Is that not an abomination? Especially as I believe the couple were newly wed. Surely that's the time when relations between a man and woman are at their most, shall we say, exciting. Surely Dr Sinclair should be apologising to her

432

cuckold of a husband and not to you," said her mother, fishing for more information.

Charlotte knew that she had said the wrong thing, and that the cat would have to be brought well and truly out of the bag and displayed for all to see. "I can see you won't be satisfied until you know absolutely everything," she sighed.

"Of course we won't," replied her mother indignantly. "I want to know everything and so does everyone else. Come on, we're waiting."

Charlotte reluctantly explained what had happened, without mentioning that she and Sinclair were now lovers and intended to marry. She knew her family would object to the match, especially after what she had told them, but she decided she would deal with that when Sinclair returned.

"So the works of the flesh are made manifest," spluttered Bowman. "Iona Rankin's child is most likely Sinclair's."

"Yes," replied Charlotte.

"Well, this is a rum do and no mistake," said her brother-in-law, helping himself to the mutton and leeks. "All I can say is it takes all sorts to make a world, and I suppose if they are happy with the situation who are we to criticise?"

"Well, I think they're all thoroughly immoral, Henry," said Emma. "Dr Sinclair and that woman are adulterers and her husband is a sodomite!"

"Hear, hear," agreed her mother.

Henry turned to his wife. "You've never liked Sinclair, Emma, and neither have you, Eliza. I know he's done wrong but he's a man with a good heart. Sinclair is my friend and he's acting honourably; he's helping his family and he's helped Charlotte's family too. If it weren't for him, Miss Lucy Leadam would now be in the clutches of a vile bigamist, and now he's gone to the aid of two people who are in desperate trouble in a foreign land. I won't have you criticise him so. He may not be perfect, but he's an excellent surgeon, a good man and a good friend."

I can't condone what he's done," added Dr Martin. "Nevertheless we would all benefit from having a friend like Dr Sinclair. Eliza, let me tell you he treated your friend Mrs Husselbee with a combination of skill and kindness I envy, and he never once criticised me for my failure to diagnose her cancer."

"And he didn't take John with him. John ran away to be with him," said Charlotte, bursting into tears.

"There, there," said her father, handing her a handkerchief. "My grandson has developed a great sense of responsibility, especially since his father died. I'm sure he is trying to protect you in some way, my dear."

"I just pray they can all be brought home safely," wept Charlotte.

"That is very Christian of you," said her mother. "I'm not sure I can be quite so charitable."

"I know you can't: you make tyranny into an art. But I forgive you because you're my mother, and I will forgive John too when he comes home because he's my son and I love him."

* * *

The house in Rue Grenelle-Saint-Germain was much larger than Sinclair had imagined, with two large rooms and a kitchen on the ground floor either side of a large double gate that gave access into a courtyard. There were three rooms above. The street was typically Parisian, narrow and lined with uniform three-storey stone town-houses on either side, but there were larger houses between the mansion blocks: the house that Iona and Blair had taken was the smallest of these.

As their coach pulled up to the double gates, Sinclair pointed to a black ribbon hanging from the doorknocker. "I fear we're too late," he said, bracing himself for the ordeal to come. John felt the same. Knife wounds were tricky: they were so easily infected with strands of cloth from the victim's clothes, and once an infection had taken hold there was very little a doctor could do except wait for nature to take its course. If the wound was small and the victim strong a man could survive, but otherwise death was almost certain.

Sinclair knocked on the door; "Bonjour. Je m'appelle Dr Sinclair, et je suis ici pour voir Monsieur et Madame Rankin."

The maid replied flatly, "Vous êtes trop tard. Monsieur Rankin est mort."

"Vous avez mes condoléances. Je voudrais voir Madame Rankin, s'il vous plaît."

"Elle se repose dans sa chambre. Elle est très fatiguée qu'elle ne peut pas être perturbé aujourd'hui."

John watched from the pavement, while Sinclair explained to the woman that he had travelled all the way from London and that he was Mrs Rankin's physician; but the maid replied that her mistress already had a French doctor who had given strict instructions her mistress was not to be disturbed. Finally, Sinclair lost patience, pushed the woman aside with an 'excusez-moi' and went into the house. John decided to follow him while the maid was recovering from the shock. Ahead of him, Sinclair was making his way up the stairs, calling out for Iona. John watched as he flung open the first and second chamber doors, to find the rooms empty, but in the third he found Iona in bed propped up on a pile of pillows. John realised how big her belly was as she struggled to sit up.

"Jamie," she cried. "Oh, Jamie, thank God you're here."

Sinclair helped her off the bed and held her in his arms. "I'm so sorry we got here too late."

Iona held him tight. "There was nothing you could have done to save him. The wound was too deep. It became infected after only a few days, but he fought so hard, Jamie. He didn't want to die; he was so brave."

"I'm so sorry, my love. John Leadam is here with me. We've come to look after you and take you home."

Iona looked at John standing in the doorway, and said hello. Sinclair kissed her affectionately on the forehead, noticing she was rather too warm to be well. She pulled away from him. "I'm a bit under the weather. I picked up a chill and I can't shake it off. My throat's been sore for days and it seems to be getting worse. I ache all over. My very nice French doctor, Monsieur de Bois, says that I must rest because I'm pregnant and in shock."

Sinclair put his hand on her forehead and felt its heat. "I think Monsieur de Bois is right. You should go back to bed. Is there room for our carriage in the yard?"

"A carriage? You've brought a carriage?"

"Yes, and we intend to take you and your baby home in it. I have strict instructions from Morag and Andrew to look after you and take you home."

"Oh dearest Morag, how I miss her. I wish she were here, Jamie. Will you write to them and tell them what's happened? I haven't had the heart or the energy." Iona settled herself back in bed. "Please make yourselves at home. My maid Allete is a bit of a tartar, but if you smile at her she'll do anything you ask. She's

436

very upset that Blair died: she loved his red hair and his Scots accent. I expect she'll love yours too."

They left Iona to rest and took a bedroom each. Downstairs there were piles of papers, letters and pieces of manuscript lying around on tables and chairs. Iona and Blair had been busy. John made up a batch of tea using Peruvian bark and spoon-fed Iona while Sinclair organised the household, insisting fires be lit in their rooms and instructing the maid to prepare supper for them and their driver and postilion.

At six o'clock Sinclair took a tray of soup and bread to Iona and tried to get her to eat, but she complained that she was too unwell and had no appetite. The doctor opened his medical bag, took out a spatula and called for John to bring a candle. Sitting on the edge of her bed he said, "Open wide, Iona, I want to see what's going on in that throat of yours." Slowly, she opened her mouth and he slipped the spatula onto her tongue while John held the light. "John, what do you think?"

"I think it's cynanche maligna," John replied, reluctantly hoping Iona wouldn't know what he had said or its possible consequences.

"I agree. Now let's have a look at this wee bairn, shall we?" said Sinclair, turning down the bed covers. John could see that Iona was exhausted. Lying on the bed, she raised her tired eyes and looked at Sinclair with such an affectionate gaze it melted John's angry heart: she clearly had a very strong attachment to him. Much to his surprise John found himself thinking that Iona was not the cold and wicked person he thought she was, and watching Sinclair put his head on Iona's belly and listen to his child's heart for the first time filled him with emotion.

"Aye, it all sounds as it should in there. Now let's have a look at the wee bairn's position." Sinclair felt the hard ball of her

437

belly through her white cotton nightdress. "Do you mind if John has a feel, Iona? He's got to learn." She nodded her consent and John followed Sinclair's instructions. "So what do you think?"

"The head seems to be pointing down, sir."

"So it does," the doctor agreed, rolling down his sleeves and covering Iona again. "So not long to go now," he smiled. "All we have to do is get you well enough to travel, and you'll be home to have your baby."

Outside in the corridor, Sinclair threw his head back against the wall in despair.

"What's wrong?" John asked, feeling confused. "You sounded so optimistic in there."

"I was lying. Sometimes we doctors have to lie. It's bad, that throat: you saw it yourself. You know what can happen when a person has a throat like that. We must keep a careful watch on her. If the bark doesn't quell the fever and the agitation in her blood I'll have to bleed her for the sake of the child; and if her throat closes I have only two options. Neither of them is good. I can let them die peacefully of suffocation or I can lance the boils – which might just save them or might make matters worse. If Iona doesn't react well to the lancing she and the baby will die a horrible death, as the poison enters her blood and spreads through her body, killing them both."

John put his arm on Sinclair's shoulder. "Let's hope it doesn't come to that. I'm sure you can save them."

"Thank you for your confidence. Let's get some more of that bark solution into her and see what happens. We can take it in turns to nurse her. I'll get a bowl of water and some towels."

As the hours passed, Iona slipped in and out of sleep. Despite their ministrations her body grew hotter, her breathing became shallower and her pulse raced. At midnight, Sinclair decided he had no option but to bleed her. He pierced a vein in the middle of Iona's left arm with his lancet, then watched as the bright pulses of liquid filled the earthenware bowl from the kitchen. "Let's hope that does the trick," he said pressing the wound shut and bandaging her arm.

For the first time since he was a boy Sinclair felt the need to pray. The sensation was strong and uncomfortable. Even on the *Sherwell* as he faced death he had not wanted to do so, feeling that it was pointless folly. He had not sought divine intervention as the black waters of the ocean dragged him under and held him until his lungs felt as if they would burst. Then, he had been open to the experience, wondering what death would be like as his own life did not matter; at least not to him. But now, as he looked at Iona lying in bed wet with sweat and burning with fever, he felt helpless and afraid. When he thought about what might happen he felt that a hole was opening in his soul and that his heart was going to break. It was all so confusing. He loved her, he loved his child, and right now he could think of nothing else but begging God, whomever he was, to save them. What sort of deal could he offer, he wondered? What bargain could he strike with this God who gave out life only to take it back whenever he felt like it, sweeping away the righteous and the wicked with no obvious concern for either? Promising to go to church on Sundays hardly seemed enough for a life; for two lives even. If he was going to strike a bargain, it had to be something else, something that was a real sacrifice for him, something he really did not want to do. Then it dawned on him: it was Charlotte. He should promise to give her up so that he could do the right thing by Iona. Surely sacrificing his love for Charlotte and their life together in Tooley Street would be enough. Then he looked at John, who was patiently bathing Iona's forehead, and he knew that this God was

439

not a bargain-maker: no amount of praying had saved Christopher Leadam. Who lived and who died were of no consequence to this God, if he existed at all. Sinclair decided that he would not demean himself, or Charlotte for that matter, by offering her up in such a pointless bargain. Whatever he promised it would make no difference. If Iona lived he would have to come to some accommodation with her concerning the welfare of his child, and if she did not he would have to bear the pain of her loss. But before he did that he resolved to do his very best to save them.

Sinclair took out his pocket watch and checked the hour. It was two o'clock. Iona seemed cooler and calmer, so he told John to go to bed. Sitting next to her in the quiet, he held Iona's hand. "Do you remember when we danced at the Assembly Rooms? Your dress was this colour," he said, showing her his watch. She opened her eyes briefly and nodded.

"It was fun," she whispered.

"Aye, it was," he said. "I got so blooted afterwards because I knew you could never be mine. Your father would never have let me marry you. The only way we'd have been married is if we'd eloped to Gretna Green."

Iona smiled. "Save our child, Jamie."

"I'm planning on saving you both." He hoped that perhaps the worst was over. "Go to sleep and I'll have a wee rest here in the chair. You'll feel better in the morning."

The Matins bells clanged as Allete entered the room with a cup of hot coffee. "Comment est Madame aujourd'hui?" she asked as she put the cup on the table.

Sinclair pulled himself up from his chair and put his hand on Iona's forehead. "Oh no!" he cried, feeling her cool clammy skin. He leaned over her, putting his cheek to her cold blue lips: she was still breathing. "Oh Dieu, merci," he said. "Allete, réveiller Monsieur Leadam; vite, allez vite!"

John came running in half-dressed, demanding to know what was wrong.

"Help me get her up: she's having trouble breathing."

Between them they lifted Iona while Allete rearranged the pillows.

John looked at Iona's ashen face and then at Sinclair's. "What's happened?" he demanded, registering the same change in Iona he had witnessed in his father's final hours. Her body was giving up its fight for life.

"She seemed to be improving last night; the fever was abating. I fell asleep and …" Sinclair fell onto his knees and thumped his chest, knowing he had failed.

John took Sinclair's hand. "I think we should pray, sir," he said, kneeling by his side.

"I don't want to," Sinclair cried.

"You've done your best, sir. You did everything you could; she will be at peace soon."

"No," Sinclair moaned, from the bottom of his breaking heart. He sank his fist into the bed with weariness and frustration. "Why them? I'm the sinner. I'm the one who doesn't believe. Take me, not them!" he shouted up at the ceiling. Then he roared, "God! Am I so bad? Am I so bad you must take away everyone I love?"

John put Sinclair's hand in Iona's. "Say something to her. Tell her that everything is going to be all right."

Sinclair held Iona's hand and kissed it. "I love you. I love our child. Always remember that, Iona. Remember that Blair loved you in his own way, and so does Morag and Andrew and Ailsa and Fiona and Rhona and Charles and your father and your

441

brothers too. Everyone loves you." He sat with her hand in his until he felt no pulse, then stood up and brushed her hair with his hand, letting his fingers sweep across her cheek. "I think she's gone." And he walked over to the window.

Allete was wailing in the corner of the room. John stood up and put his head to Iona's chest. There was no sound from her lungs or heart, but there was something else, something faint but fast. "The child, sir," said John. "It's still alive."

Sinclair sank to his knees with his head in his hands. "Oh no, oh God. What am I to do?"

"Aesculapius," replied John.

Sinclair looked at him dumbfounded. "What?"

"Aesculapius, you know on the roof at Guy's. He was the son of Apollo. When Apollo killed his wife, he cut him out of his wife's womb. Come on, we haven't got much time." John picked up Sinclair's medical bag and put it on the bed.

Sinclair walked slowly over to the bed and looked at Iona, her pale face at peace. As he looked at her, the last words she had said to him started to reverberate in his head. She wanted him to save their child. He pulled the covers back, exposing her body. "Let's turn her round so that she's lying across the bed: it'll make the operation easier."

Allete looked on in horror as they moved her mistress's body to where they wanted it. Sinclair draped the top sheet around Iona's legs for modesty, then pulled her nightdress up. "Bring me those cloths; this is going to be messy," he said, hunting for the right blade in his bag. Allete gave a small scream as he placed the point of his blade on Iona's skin; then he hesitated. "I can't do it! I can't cut her."

"Yes you can," John retorted. "Do it now, and save the child."

Sinclair took a deep breath, then cut a vertical slice through the skin of Iona's abdomen. She did not move. The next slice of the blade exposed the bright red wall of her uterus. "John, you're going to have to help me. When I cut into the womb there'll be a lot of water and blood, and you'll have to help me keep it open so I can grab hold of the child."

"I'm ready," said John, rolling his sleeves up.

Sinclair made the next incision, covering them both in steaming amniotic fluid. He plunged his hands into Iona's body and pulled the child out feet first. John took it from him and cut the cord, then he wrapped the child in a towel and put it over his shoulder. The baby made no sound, but John continued to stroke and pat its tiny body, trying to cajole it into life. Its eyes were open but it wasn't breathing. Sinclair pushed his finger into its mouth and they heard the first whimper; then the child sucked in its first breath and gave out a loud cry. Allete clapped, and John handed Sinclair the little bundle with a wide smile. "You have a daughter, Dr Sinclair!"

Allete put her arms around them both, and Sinclair looked up at John with tears in his eyes. "Thank you, John," he said, looking into his daughter's small red face. She gazed at her father quizzically. He smiled back and kissed her forehead. "I shall call you Margaret after my mother and Iona after yours. Welcome to the world, my wee darling girl."

* * *

Preparations for their journey home took longer than expected. Two days after her death they laid Iona to rest next to Blair in the cemetery at St Paul's on Rue Saint Antoine. The priest obtained the permission of the Bishop to perform a simple burial service with a mass for his Protestant clients, who were made to pay handsomely for the privilege, as Protestantism was still illegal in France. Then there was the issue of the 'droit d'aubaine' to sort out. A well-dressed official from the Intendent's office arrived with a group of men to impound everything in the house as soon as they returned from the funeral, claiming their right to seize all the effects of deceased foreigners. As Sinclair was protesting that everything was to be returned to Edinburgh, the smooth and gracious official said, "Pourquoi avez-vous pas me dire que vous étiez écossais. Les Ecossais sont exempt parce que de l'ancienne alliance." Sinclair was amazed but grateful that the Auld Alliance between France and Scotland was still recognised, as Scotland no longer existed as a country in its own right; and as soon as he was able he showed the official to the door. He was keen to be on his way: the atmosphere in Paris was poisonous. Everywhere the conversation was of the crisis and the hope of reform, but there was a dark undercurrent of violence and threat, coupled with the overwhelming feeling that some sort of catastrophe was looming, and he didn't want to be around when it started.

That evening Sinclair wrote two letters, one to his sister and one to Charlotte, neither of which was entirely truthful. The letter to his sister was the saddest letter he had ever had to write; he knew her heart would be broken when she read it, but there was nothing he could do to prevent that. In his letter to Charlotte, he assured her that John was well and that he would be home as soon as he could, but that it would take him some time to wind up the Rankins' affairs in Paris before he could leave. In the meantime, he suggested Charlotte should try to persuade Morag and Ailsa to go home to Edinburgh, as there was no point in remaining in

London. He took the letters to the post office and paid the fees, hoping they would arrive in London within the week.

The main obstacle to their departure was the need to secure the services of a wet nurse for Margaret. Allete had found them a local wet nurse within a couple of hours of the child's birth, but the woman was married with a husband and two children of her own so she could not travel with them to England. Without a wet nurse their journey would be impossible, so Sinclair asked Allete if there were any hospitals where unmarried women went to have their babies. She pointed them in the direction of L'Hôpital des Enfants-Trouvés at Notre Dame, but said she could probably find them someone herself if she had a little more time. So they packed up the Rankins' papers and effects, and waited.

Three days later Allete appeared with a young girl.

"This is Esmé," she said. "Her baby died yesterday. She's very thin; but will she do?"

The girl curtsied, keeping her eyes fixed to the floor. She was wearing a thin cotton dress and white cap with an apron; her legs were bare and she had wooden clogs on her feet. The girl looked no more than sixteen, in Sinclair's estimation.

He offered his condolences, and asked if she was willing to be a wet nurse for his daughter. The girl said that she was, and asked how much she would be paid. Sinclair explained she would have to accompany them to London.

"I have no family here, sir," the girl explained. "I am from Bordeaux. I am an orphan."

"She was in the service of the Duc de Ventadore. The silly girl got herself knocked up by one of the grooms, so they threw her out, monsieur le docteur," Allete explained scornfully; and the girl silently blushed.

"Esmé, do you want to come to England with us?" asked Sinclair.

"Oui, monsieur," the girl replied.

"Very well, but I will have to examine you first." He sent the girl upstairs with Allete to undress. Turning to John, he said, "If she comes with us she's going to need a good wash and some different clothes; she'll freeze in that dress. Would you unpack a few of Iona's things for her? I don't think I can do it. I can't touch her clothes. It's too painful."

"Of course. Do you think you'll be all right when she wears them? I understand how you feel. I've been wearing my father's hat and coat. I chose them because they're newer and warmer than my own, and so you wouldn't recognise me, but I don't want my mother to see me in them; I'm sure it'll upset her."

"That's very considerate of you, John; you're a good son to your mother. She should be proud of you. From what I've seen of you on this trip I know you will make a good surgeon. Your mother will think so too. If your father were here he would be proud of you. Thank you for asking about the clothes, but I'm sure I'll be all right when she's got them on." Sinclair put his hand on John's shoulder and gave it an affectionate squeeze. "I'll go and see how much milk this girl's got, and make sure she's free of all the usual complaints before we commit ourselves."

When he was satisfied that the girl was still lactating and that she was free from infection, Sinclair asked Allete to bring a bowl of water and some soap for her to wash. Esmé was shorter than Iona by several inches, her face was pinched from lack of food, and her hair was a dull mousey blonde. All the clothes were too big: the bodices were loose and the skirts and petticoats needed Allete's attention before the girl could wear them. Iona's shoes were too big but only slightly, and would do.

446

That evening they introduced Margaret to her new nurse. The child was reluctant to take to the new breast at first, but as her appetite sharpened she latched onto Esmé's milky nipple and was comfortably settled before they went to bed. The following day they packed up their things, said goodbye to Allete and set off for Calais.

Five days later, they were making their way along the last twenty-four miles over the paved coastal road between Boulogne and the closest port to England. The weather was colder than it had been when they set out, with the frost barely lifting off the fields by noon and freezing again as the sun sank in the afternoon. The sea was calm but to Sinclair it still felt threatening and dangerous; he would never trust it again, no matter how calm it appeared.

John noticed Sinclair looking at the sea. "Why did you want to go to India, sir?"

"Oh, that's a long story. Let's just say I was a different man then. I thought being rich would make me happy. It's a strange thing to say but I think being shipwrecked was the best thing that ever happened to me. It saved me from a lifetime of loneliness and hypocrisy thousands of miles away in a foreign land."

"How come?"

"Your mother gave me the chance to work with her in the apothecary shop, and I found that I liked it. It's hard work, but I've realised I don't need a lofty position in a hospital or in the East India Company to feel useful. I like the midwifery: there are few things more joyous than helping a reluctant child into the world," said Sinclair, looking at Margaret nestling snugly in Esmé's arms. "Or saving a mother when I'm able. A mother is the heart of a family, and I know the pain of living without one. I can't remember my own mother, but I remember what it was like

447

to live without her. You see, I don't get on with my father. My father's a good man but not a kind one. I went to India to get away from the cruel things he says to me and about me."

"I remember what Sir Donald said at Grandmamma's party," said John sympathetically. "Grandmamma can be cruel too."

"I know, but your mother is a better person than me: she forgives your grandmamma. I'm afraid I haven't found it in myself to do the same for my father, much as my sister Morag wishes it."

"I expect Mother will be having a hard time of it," said John, gazing out to sea. "Grandmamma will be taking every opportunity to make her do what she wishes."

"Your mother has a good ally in your grandfather, so don't worry too much. He'll look after her; and she's quite capable of standing up for herself."

The boy nodded, knowing that Sinclair was right. He loved and admired his mother, and he was anxious to get back to London to relieve her of the burden of worry he had placed upon her.

"And I like teaching," said Sinclair to lighten the atmosphere. "I wasn't at all sure about having apprentices like you and William. I thought that a man should keep his knowledge for himself and exploit it to make a living, but I find that sharing what I've learned with others is a great joy to me. I'm grateful to you and your mother for allowing me to discover that. I was lonely and unhappy when I set out for India, but thanks to you and your mother I'm now a happy man."

The next day they boarded the Dover packet boat from Calais' pier, which was a great relief to Sinclair who had no desire to get into a rowing boat ever again. He insisted on carrying Margaret onto the boat himself, leaving John to help

Esmé with the luggage. When they were aboard they sat on the floor of their cabin. Sinclair cradled Margaret tightly in his arms while Esmé slept or stared vacantly into space; she had said very little since they left Paris. Margaret was small, at least a month early, but John could already see that she looked like her father; she had his eyes and his nose. Her eyes were slate blue, but he knew that they would become either hazel-green or blue with time, and the mat of thick black hair on her head would eventually be replaced by hair of a lighter redder shade, more akin to that of her parents.

The boat took the best part of a day to cross to England in the calm and windless conditions. Halfway across, John went on deck to take the air and admire the view. The white cliffs of Dover were sparkling in the late afternoon sunshine, the freezing air barely moving as the boat slowly cut through the shallow blue-green waves. The thought of being in England again filled him with relief. As far as John was concerned, France had nothing to recommend it. It might have been a great country once, but it had been brought low by the folly of its elites. Now that there was so little food he was sure there would be trouble in Paris; it was just a matter of when and how bad it would be.

The sun had set when they arrived at Granville dock in Dover. The gang plank was lowered and Sinclair was the first off, with Margaret in his arms. The doctor hired a barrow and a boy to carry their luggage, then headed towards the Customs House, where a scarlet-coated officer rummaged through their bags and the Rankins' trunks for a good half an hour. Satisfied they had no contraband, the officer allowed them to leave for the town, to find their accommodation for the night.

At six the next morning they were on their way to London on the London Flyer. Like all the men on board John and Sinclair

449

had to walk up the steep escarpment out of the town, but unlike the walk up Shooter's Hill on their outward journey they did it happily, walking arm in arm and enjoying the view and each other's company.

They arrived at the Talbot Inn in Southwark just before seven o'clock that evening. The Borough High Street was busy as usual. As they were unloading their bags and trunks Sinclair said, "I'm not sure who'll be at the house when we get back. I don't want my sister to see Margaret."

"Why not?"

"I haven't told her she survived. Margaret's my child, John, and I won't let my sister take her back to Edinburgh. Do you understand?"

"Yes, sir. Does Mother know?"

"Not yet," Sinclair confessed. "I'll tell her this evening. I think we should ask Esmé to stay here at the inn with the baby until I've explained everything to her."

"If you say so."

"It won't take long if your mother's persuaded Morag and Ailsa to go back to Scotland."

They hired a cart and a small boy to pull it, and left Esmé in the inn nursing the baby. Twenty minutes later, they were throwing their bags onto the hall floor in Tooley Street. John shouted, "We're back," and the scullery door burst open. Charlotte ran out, threw her arms around her son and kissed him, then slapped him round the face and said, "Don't ever do that to me again!"

John smiled down at her, still smarting from her blow. "No, I won't," he said. "You have my word. I'm never going to France again. It's an awful place."

Then Charlotte threw her arms around Sinclair. "We're so glad to be back," he said, lifting her into his arms and kissing her.

"Is Morag here?" he asked tentatively.

"Your sister and niece took themselves off to Sir Donald's about a week after you left."

"Is she there now?"

"Yes. I tried to persuade her to go back to Edinburgh, but she decided that she wanted to stay in London."

Sinclair tapped John on the shoulder. "Could you go back to the inn and get those things we couldn't carry?"

Upstairs in the parlour Sinclair kissed Charlotte again. This time their kiss was passionate and slow as they savoured the heady mixture of comfort and excitement that their reunion aroused. "I've missed you so much, my love. I don't ever want to go away again."

"I've missed you too," Charlotte said between kisses. "I'm sorry things have turned out so badly for your family."

"I thought you hated Iona."

"I hate what she did to us, Jamie, but I'm sorry she and Blair are dead. They were so young, so bright and they had so much life to live; and the baby, you lost the baby. The whole thing's so tragic."

Sinclair sat Charlotte down on the green chaise. "Well, that's not quite true," he said, holding her hands in his.

"What do you mean? I don't understand what you're saying. How can it not be a tragedy?"

"Well, by some miracle John and I saved the child."

"You what?" Charlotte said. "I don't understand. I thought that you said Iona died before she could give birth."

"That's true, my love, she did."

Charlotte was bewildered. "What are you saying, James Sinclair? What happened?"

Sinclair explained what he and John had done.

"Why didn't you say that in your letter?" Charlotte demanded, looking at him with astonishment and incredulity. "Why did you lie to me?"

"Because I don't want Morag to know. The child is mine and I want to keep her. I don't want Morag to lay claim to her and take her back to Scotland."

"Do you think she would?" said Charlotte, taking in the enormity of what he was saying.

"Well, we haven't told her what happened when Blair and Iona were here, have we? And I don't think they have a clue about Blair's true nature."

"You mean they don't know he was a sodomite."

"We didn't mention it when I agreed to go to Paris, and I'm pretty sure my sister wouldn't have let her stepson marry Iona if she'd known he couldn't be a proper husband to her. Morag would be appalled if she knew what really happened."

"That's totally understandable; it was appalling," Charlotte said, wearily taking in the complexity of the situation. "Where's the child? What have you done with her?"

"She has a name. I've called her Margaret after my own mother and Iona after her own."

Charlotte swallowed deeply. She didn't know if she could face seeing Iona's child. Her feelings of envy and disgust were too raw. "I see," she said, as calmly as she could. "Where's Margaret now?"

"I've just sent John to fetch her, along with the wet nurse we hired in France. They should be here in a few minutes, and you can meet them.

"Oh," said Charlotte, not sure how to feel.

Sensing her confusion and her insecurity, Sinclair cupped her face in his hands and rubbed her nose affectionately with his, making her smile. Then he said softly, "I know you can't give me children, but that will never be a bar to my love for you." Charlotte started to cry; the emotion was too much to bear. Smoothing her tears away with his hands, he said, "I'd like to give you the child I have if you'll have her. She's an innocent in all this; Margaret has done nothing wrong. I know I'm asking a lot of you, but I'd like you to be her mother."

Charlotte looked into Sinclair's warm, hazel-green eyes. "You want to give me your child?" she stumbled, her voice cracking with emotion.

"Aye, Charlotte. I want to be your husband and I'd like you to take care of my child," he whispered, holding her close. "Do you think you could do that for me? Will you look after my child and love her as though she were your own, as I love John?"

Through trembling lips, she said, "I don't know; I don't know if I can. Your daughter's Iona's child. The thought of that woman with your child in her belly made me feel sick with envy. I don't know if I could love her."

Sinclair heard John arriving downstairs. "Wait here," he said. "I'll bring her up to you." When he came back, he laid his daughter in Charlotte's arms and waited for her reaction. Charlotte held the child close and gazed into her tiny face. Margaret gazed back in the same quizzical way she had looked at her father when she was born.

"She's so like you, Jamie; she has your eyes and your nose," Charlotte finally said. Sinclair could see tears pricking in the corners of her eyes as she kissed the child's forehead. "She's beautiful, so small and so perfect." Charlotte cradled the child in her arms, as she wrapped her tiny hand around her finger. "Oh, Jamie, she's such a sweetheart."

"I knew you'd love her when you saw her," Sinclair said. Then he crouched down and wrapped his arms around them both. "I love you, Charlotte Leadam," he said, kissing her softly on the cheek. "I want us to be a family: me, you, John and Margaret. I want you to be my wife, and I want us to be happy."

27

The Wedding Breakfast

The Rankins departed for Scotland a week after Sinclair and John had got back from France. Sinclair felt bad about taking Andrew's money for a trip that had turned out so disastrously. He also felt bad about depriving them of their much-anticipated granddaughter, but Margaret was his, he reasoned, and not theirs.

The Thames froze at the end of November and the Frost Fair began in December. Stalls and booths selling roast beef, hot chestnuts, gingerbread and beer appeared on the thick plate of ice and business was brisk. Sinclair took John and William skating every Sunday after church, while Charlotte sat by the fire cradling Margaret in her arms, looking into her slate-grey eyes, hoping they would be the same hazel-green as Sinclair's and not the pale blue of Iona's.

Although it was the coldest winter in years, in the parlour in Wimpole Street Eliza Martin's temper was keeping her warm. "How could she do this to me?" Mrs Martin shrieked at her husband, waving her daughter's wedding invitation in his face. "How could our daughter be thinking of marrying that man?"

Dr Martin looked up from his chair and put down the newspaper he was reading. "She loves him, Eliza. Don't you remember what that feels like, my dear? Don't you remember what it was like to be in love with me?"

"Oh fiddlesticks, Charles. This isn't the same. Charlotte has no right to treat us like this. And she's taken in his bastard," she railed, pacing round the room. "You must do something to stop her."

"Technically speaking, Henry assures me, the child's an orphan as both her legal parents are dead. Besides, what can I say, my dear? Our daughter is a grown woman with a mind of her own."

"What you must do is change it then. She listens to you. Our daughter cannot marry this adulterer."

"I seem to remember you and your friend Mrs Peacock were very keen on our daughter marrying Mr Masterson, a man with the habits of the proverbial tomcat from what I've heard. At least Sinclair's only guilty of one transgression, for which he's heartily sorry by all accounts. You should be careful. Your moral high ground has all the strength of sand, my dear, and we know what the good Lord says about that, don't we?"

"I won't accept this invitation, Charles. I cannot sanction their behaviour."

Dr Martin stood up, and walked towards his wife with his index finger raised. "You are my wife, Eliza, and you will do as I

456

say. I know you have the welfare of our children at heart, but on this occasion you're wrong."

* * *

On the last Saturday before Christmas, the sign in the apothecary shop window said closed and upstairs the parlour of 65 Tooley Street was full to bursting with assembled family and friends. As the last of their guests climbed the stairs, Sinclair took his wife's hand and led her up the stairs. He paused for a moment and took her in his arms again.

"Jamie, we have guests," his wife complained.

"I know, but I want just one more kiss," he said. "Once we're in the parlour I won't see you again until bedtime."

She smiled back and kissed him on the cheek. "I look forward to it."

"You're a wanton woman, Mrs Sinclair," he smiled, and pulled her into his embrace.

Charlotte giggled like a giddy schoolgirl and he kissed her again, feeling her body yield to his with immense satisfaction. He was happy at last, and he hoped they would be happy together forever.

Taking her by the hand, Sinclair led her towards the parlour door. "Come, madam, no more of this kissing: our guests are waiting." As they entered the room their friends and family cheered. Bowman offered the bride a glass of Madeira and gave her an affectionate peck on the cheek. Dr Martin handed his new son-in-law a glass of Margoose, offering his congratulations again.

"May I say how lovely you look, Charlotte?" her father said. "Doesn't our daughter look lovely, Mother?" Eliza forced a half-hearted smile and agreed with her husband for the sake of family peace, although she was anything but pleased with her daughter's marital and domestic arrangements – and her daughter knew it.

"Thank you, Papa," Charlotte replied as Sinclair nodded his agreement.

On the far side of the room, the fire was roaring, making the room warm and cosy. "Where's Margaret?" said Charlotte. "Where's Esmé?" The strange little French girl was hiding in the shadows, but Charlotte spotted her daughter in her sister's arms, Connie doting over her and nursing her growing baby bump.

"Isn't she's gorgeous?" said Connie to her husband. "I want one just like her."

Her husband smiled. "Well, I was rather hoping for a boy this time."

"I wouldn't mind one like this little angel myself," smiled Emma. "There are too many boys in this family. It's time we evened the score, isn't it, Margaret?"

Esmé watched her little charge from her position at the edge of the room, wishing Margaret was hers. In the weeks she had been feeding the child she had come to love her. Every time she put her to her breast, she thought of her lover Gaston and the child she had buried in Paris, wishing that by some miracle Margaret was theirs. Although Esmé was being better treated than ever before, she felt lonely and miserable. She didn't like Mrs Dredge and she didn't understand what people were saying to her; she longed to go back to the place and the people she knew.

"She's lovely," Emma cooed. "I'm sure my mother will come round eventually. How could she not love you, my little darling?" She handed her new niece to Charlotte, who took the child and cradled her in her arms. Charlotte already felt fiercely protective of her, and jealous of Esmé's closeness.

458

In the dining room, William and Henry junior were vying for the attention of Alice and Jessica, the eldest of the Prentice girls, flirting with them over plates of bread and butter and slices of pie. John, as usual, was being responsible, aided by Connie's stepdaughters, following their guests' rowdy younger siblings around the table making sure they took only what they could eat, and stopping them from pressing their grubby little fingers into everything they could touch, including the soft white sugar icing on the wedding cake.

In the kitchen, Mrs Dredge was lying on her bed listening to the party upstairs. She was tired but happy. Her heart was filled with a deep contentment; the house and the people she loved were happy once more. Queenie the cat jumped on the bed beside her; and Elsie closed her eyes, sighing contentedly. Soon she was in the loving arms of her Jack, and the years of separation melted away.

Historical Notes

The Tales of Tooley Street novels are inspired by the Leadam family. The Leadams were apothecary surgeons who lived and worked in Georgian London. They came from Walkington, East Yorkshire and were descended from John Leadam the younger, "of Walkington and Willerby, gentleman", born 1609, died 1752. His son Christopher Leadam, the fifth of ten children, attended Beverley Grammar School and was apprenticed as a surgeon in York when he was fourteen. He went to London, and practised as a surgeon there at 65 Tooley Street. He married Jane Martin in St James Piccadilly in 1778 and worked at Guy's Hospital where he and his partner, Mr William Hoares, were joint secretaries to the Hospital Committee. The real Christopher Leadam died in 1793, leaving his widow Jane and his fourteen-year-old son, John, to run his shop. He was buried in Walkington, not in London. His male descendants for three generations became surgeons and physicians.

The East Indiaman, 'Sherwell', is loosely modelled on the 'Halsewell', a ship that was wrecked on 6 January 1786 at the start of a voyage from London to Madras. She lost her masts in a violent storm in the English Channel, and was driven onto the rocks below a cliff on the Dorset coast. The story was a sensation at the time, mainly because of the drowning of the female passengers, the captain's daughters and his niece. The government of the day, influenced by the East India Company, sought to blame the disaster on the crew and promote its captain, a man called Richard Peirce, into a national hero.

The story of Sinclair is fiction; James Sinclair never existed. I created him to contrast the English and Scottish systems of medical training at the time. In Edinburgh medical education was dominated by the Munro family for three generations: Alexander Monro (1697–1767) was the founder of Edinburgh Medical School; his son Alexander Monro II (1733–1817) followed him as head of the Medical School, and inspired the character Alexander McNeal in this book; and his son Alexander Monro III (1773–1859), who had none of his ancestor's brilliance according to his most famous student, Charles Darwin, was the last to inherit the chair.

Finally, students of Edinburgh history will know that the Assembly Rooms opened on 11 January 1787 for the Caledonian Hunt Ball, but in this book I have taken the liberty of opening them in 1785.

Estranged from his family for his views on religion, Edinburgh surgeon James Sinclair is prepared to sacrifice all he holds dear for his ambition. As a man of the Enlightenment, Sinclair prides himself on his rationality; that is, until he finds himself in love with two very different women.

Set against the corruption of the East India Company and the nepotism of the late eighteenth-century medical profession, this story of love and friendship has a cast of characters who will imprint themselves onto your heart forever.

Julia Herdman
www.juliaherdman.com

The Fontaine Press

Printed in Great Britain
by Amazon